THE ORB OF THE PHOENIX

Andrew Maes

To Anastasia,

Even when I gave up on myself,

You didn't.

PROLOGUE

He was grateful for the times he could rest. He did not resent how far he had to travel, nor how urgently he must do so. He had learned to relish in the times that he could sit and relax without the need to be somewhere, to constantly be on the move and travel. It was the small things in his life that he truly learned to appreciate now that they were scarce. Nothing had changed in the past twenty-eight years, his duty had always been this demanding, he just learned how to adapt. How to take the time to find the peace that nature offered, how to ease the burdens and stress so he did not carry them around with him. His wife helped a great deal, always by his side no matter the situation. She was always there for him, his duties now hers as well, and sharing in the enjoyment of the small things together.

Unfortunately, this was no time for relishing.

He ran as fast as his legs would take him. The adrenaline pumping through his body helped him ignore the burning in his lungs. His muscles began to tire, but this was no time to take a rest. He had received word of a village being attacked by unknown assailants, the likes of which had not been seen before by the terrified messenger.

He pushed on, the smoke of the fire that burned the homes and people reaching his nostrils as he drew closer. The smoke was bitter, carrying with it the deaths of many lives. He needed to reach the village, and he needed to reach it now if he was to save anyone left.

He finally broke through the outskirts of the village, barging towards the center without hesitation, the flames that threatened to burn him doing little more than singe his clothing. He paid them no heed, focusing only on any living beings that still remained. The village was littered with the corpses of innocent lives, cut down by weapons and animalistic clawing before their bodies would be fed to the wild flames that enveloped the village further.

He had been too late. No one moved. No one was left. The houses would be void of any living beings, and no one had fled the village as he ran towards it. He stood amidst the flames that disintegrated the homes of many people into ash, and amidst the bodies that resembled his failure.

He never truly understood how eerily silent a burning village would be. No screams. No crying. No shouting.

Nothing save the crackling fire, happily feeding at the wood, uncontested.

He stood, wondering how he could have arrived so late that no one had survived, or even able to have fled the village. Whoever brought upon this attack was efficient, and well organized. The fire appeared to have started from various places to help its spread of destruction, gradually forming one large fire that now reigned over the remains. The fire should not have spread this quickly. It seemed whoever was behind this had an ulterior motive for the actions they made. He saw no looters, no scavengers stealing what remained in the houses of the dead who could no longer claim them.

He saw no one. The mysterious beings described by the messenger nowhere to be seen, as if they had vanished in preparation of his arrival, or simply had never existed.

He stood, his wife beside him, unable to do anything but watch the village slowly burn away. There was naught he could do now. The villagers were gone, seemingly slaughtered in an act of unnecessary violence.

"I'm glad that you came, Balkyeros," a voice called from behind him. They spun around, surprised to hear a voice amidst the death. A man stood behind them, his back turned, his posture indicated he was relaxed as he watched the flames rather than being horrified by their vicious taunts. His hands were clasped behind his back, and he stood with an air of purpose. It was as if he was transfixed by the fire, satisfied by the way they ate at the wood.

"This is your work? Who are you?"

"It is my doing, yes. It was all so I could meet you," the man did not turn around, continuing to stare into the flames as the village disappeared around them.

His wife raised her weapon, and he followed suit.

"No need for that. As you can see, there are no witnesses, nor can you cause any more destruction that the flames have not already done. You can show me," the man provoked, urging them to reveal the secret that was apparently already known.

His wife looked at him, nodding to him in encouragement. They had to keep his secret unless it was during dire cases.

And this was a dire case.

He sprouted his fiery wings, unfurling from thin air as they spread out in preparation. He readied himself to charge, preparing to unleash his anger and frustration as swiftly and fiercely as he could.

Yet the man remained unbothered.

"Before you do anything rash, perhaps we should have a quick conversation," the man turned around slowly, donning a smile as if he had already won.

CHAPTER ONE

"The world needs historians to find the things that get lost between the cracks of time. However, not all of history should be uncovered."

The suns' rays leaked through the shutters, landing on Davun's face causing him to wake. He rubbed his eyes to rid the sleep stuck in the crevices of his face. He rose out of bed to dress himself and prepare for his day. This is how most days began. The light would let him know when to wake for his day of work, and then he would nudge his brother awake and they would dress and set out for the kitchens. Most days began in the kitchens, usually preparing food for the cooks. Today was no different, as he walked over to Jethro's bed and dragged the sheet off to wake him. As usual, Jethro was reluctant to wake, preferring to sleep in, though who wouldn't? Davun sighed to himself. He was only five years older than Jethro, but he had understood the importance of waking on time many years ago. Averly had made sure of that.

Davun stared at his brother, dark brown hair a mess, one of his brown eyes peeking open to check to see if Davun was still standing by his bed.

He's ten, and still doesn't get how it works around here.

"Come on Jethro, please don't make me get the bucket again." Davun threatened, annoyed that his brother still had not gotten out of bed. The threat always worked though, Jethro immediately began to move, as slow as it may be, and began to dress himself in his labour clothes.

The brothers made their way to the kitchens and immediately began to peel the potatoes. They preferred to get the most tedious task out of the way first, and peeling vegetables was definitely on top of that list. The pair were usually the only ones in the kitchens in the morning, the cooks barely bothered helping with such low work. Occasionally they would have another kid, whose parents wanted to teach them some responsibility by sending them to work, or of their own volition to earn some money. Very rarely, there would be days that someone was put to work in the kitchen to pay off a debt.

This must have been one of those days, as there was an adult already in the kitchen when the brothers entered. He was an odd fellow, with his pale blond hair in multiple braids down the back and sides of his head. He stood straight-backed as he peeled potatoes and was whistling a cheery tune. He turned to the boys as they entered, and now they could see that his face had a few small scars. He wore a beard that had recently started growing back, and his bright green eyes spoke of warmth and kindness. The man was clearly from the North. Braided hair and bright green eyes were classic Northerner traits.

"Ah, why hello there laddies. You up early too, eh?" the stranger spoke with such an upbeat attitude as if it weren't in the early hours of the morning. He smelled slightly of ale, which told Davun all he needed to know.

Probably another drunken fool breaking something. Probably furniture, the Northern people like to dance on it.

"Indeed, sir. We work here, so it requires us getting up and early to make sure we do our jobs on time." Davun spoke with authority. He didn't care much for the stranger's age, he wanted to make sure that this man knew who was in charge here.

"I suppose that makes a bit of sense then. Didn't really take you lads for the kind to drink a copious amount of ale and then attempt to duel another man with a chair. You seem more like the kind of folk to use something small and sharp." The stranger chuckled to himself as he handed them both knives to help with the peeling. Davun reluctantly took the knife, he didn't want to show gratefulness in case this stranger took that as a weakness. Jethro didn't appear to care at all about what this man thought of him, he seemed to be going along with the strangers' upbeat attitude.

"Why did you try dueling with a chair?" Jethro spoke with genuine curiosity. Davun had also been wondering but refused to try and create a casual conversation with someone he didn't care much about.

The stranger smiled and laughed loudly. "At the time it seemed like a great idea. I couldn't just sit around as a man insulted my dancing, I had worked very hard on that dance! I couldn't persuade him to join me, but I also couldn't let him continue his negative attitude, it was impacting my performance. I figured a chair couldn't do that much harm, so I challenged him to a duel with the mighty seat! Both of the chairs ended up breaking and somehow, I'm the one at fault! I don't understand why, you don't just insult someone's work like that!" he narrated, clearly enjoying the memory of the previous night. Jethro became completely enveloped by the story and had stopped peeling, so Davun had to nudge him to remind him. "That wasn't very smart, Averly loves her furniture. She gets it all hand-made from the family in the city." Jethro explained to the man.

"Ah yes, I received the full lecture about it after my victory." The man almost sounded like a normal person, having very little cheeriness in his voice. Davun was relieved, he wasn't sure how long he could stand someone being so cheery in the morning. But the relief only lasted a moment as the man started up his upbeat tempo again and began whistling as he peeled away.

"So, what's a Northerner working in an inn in the south anyway?" the man spoke, interrupting his own tune. His question had been directed at Davun. Davun's bright green eyes and dark blonde hair often lead to people mistaking him for a Northerner. "I'm not a Northerner. One of our parents must have had some Northerner blood in them, but I was born here, and lived here my whole life in the South." Davun replied bitterly. For some reason, Davun became irritated whenever someone mistook him for a Northerner. Jethro nodded in agreeance.

"We're brothers, but people always think Davun's a Northerner and not me," Jethro explained further. The strange man eyed them both, as if comparing the two, but looked at them quizzically.

"Davun? That's a Northern name. I'd say one of your parents had more than just 'Northerner blood' in them. I'd say at least one of them was a full Northerner. And judging by the fact we are using the past tense, I'd say they're no longer with us. Sorry," the strange man sounded sincere, which startled Davun a bit. He wasn't sure if it was because the man showed an emotion other than utter cheeriness, or because a complete stranger seemed completely genuine about his loss.

"It doesn't matter," Davun shrugged. "It was a long time ago. Shortly after Jethro was born, and I don't even remember them. It's just been us. Always has been." Davun tried to sound less irritated about the subject but wasn't sure it worked. He hated thinking about their parents, much less talking about them. Thankfully, the conversation was interrupted when Averly barged in. She was the innkeeper here at Eraton. She had blonde hair and dark brown eyes. She was well-groomed as usual, she enjoyed looking well dressed all the time. Her pink dress was adorned with buttons – that may have no functionality, Davun could never tell – as well as golden threads embroidered into an intricate design towards the bottom. She also flaunted a shiny, golden necklace, which Davun was convinced she cleaned every morning and night. Averly enjoyed the finer things, everything in her inn was some kind of unique – and probably expensive – item, and somehow, she managed to treat all of them as her absolute most treasured possession. She was a hawk when it came to how others treated her stuff, and may the gods help anyone who dare ill-treat her property. Which is why it would be no surprise if this stranger were to work here for the next year as punishment for destroying her chairs.

"Hello boys" Averly directed her greeting towards the brothers, obviously making a point to ignore the strange man. The man shuddered and began looking around the room.

"Someone must have left a window open…" he spoke almost idly to himself. Jethro giggled, which earned him a sharp look from Averly.

"Boys, we will be hosting the mayor tonight, so when you're done peeling please grab out the good table spreads and make sure the fine silverware is clean and sparkling." Averly spoke with a smile on her face. She loved hosting the mayor because it meant she got to show off all of her finest possessions that she rarely ever had the opportunity to bring out. This brought Davun both relief and upset. Averly was even more controlling and critical leading up to the mayor's visit, but if all went well, she was in a pleasant mood for a few days afterwards. Obviously not as cheery as this stranger, but it was a period of peace for Davun and his brother. Davun gave a grin and nodded back, and Averly turned her attention to the stranger. "And you. Kalavud, was it?" Averly asked, not dropping her smile. The man simply returned the smile and raised his pointer finger.

"*Kalavud*, actually," the man corrected, pronouncing his name with Northern dialect. Northerner names generally pronounced many of their 'U' as 'oo'. It was a common mistake that Southerner's made, even Davun had to correct many people himself. The land of Teldario was split into two sections, the North and the South, having many cultural differences between them. There was some tension between the two sides, each thinking the other inferior, but it rarely led to hostile situations. Mostly, it was friendly rivalry.

"Of course it is. Now, I don't expect you to understand the importance of hosting the mayor, but I do expect you to listen to my every word very carefully. I won't accept anything less than absolute perfection today. I will not hear any complaints. Once the day is over, and assuming you manage to hold back your barbaric behavior, then you can consider your debt fulfilled."

"Of course, my dear lady. I always give my absolute best efforts in all that I do. Your mayor will be so pleased with how I've peeled these potatoes, he'll be asking for me personally!" Kalavud said with a graceful flourish and bow. Averly seemed unimpressed with his confidence, and simply left the room, reminding the boys to grab the good linen.

Davun and Jethro peeled potatoes for a short while longer but decided to take advantage of having another person in the kitchen and left the rest for Kalavud to deal with. They set off to do the other tasks Averly had given them.

Davun spent the day keeping an eye on Kalavud, to make sure he wasn't doing anything he wasn't supposed to, and to ensure that Averly's demands were being kept to her standards. The night went as planned. Averly became increasingly frustrated about everything being perfect, and of course, everything was with her around. Dinner came and went by without any issues, and the nightly routine of washing the dishes came as normal. Davun took his spot at the wash basin where he could stare out the window. He found letting his eyes wander outside helped the tedious task to go by.

Davun loved the night sky, especially on cloudless nights like tonight. He enjoyed seeing all the stars sparkle, and the moon had free reign to light up the lands with her white light. He could see the village, completely at peace. It brought him comfort, yet at the same time it also brought him sadness. As much as he loved staring out the window at night, it was always the same picture. Everything was as it always has been, and as far as Davun could tell, as it always will be. The same trees were always there, the same buildings were always there, and the mountain remained the same distance it always had been. The village had the same aroma wherever he walked. The village was all Davun knew. It was self-sufficient enough that trips to the city were rarely ever needed.

The most excitement he would get was with all the travelers that would pass in the inn. He loved hearing them talk of other places, even if he didn't want to speak to them directly. He found it difficult to really connect with other people. He wasn't sure if it was jealousy of them being able to travel, or because he didn't know whether or not they told the truth. Davun stood wondering if he should try and speak with Kalavud, to try and get details of what the North was like, from an actual Northerner - it wasn't common getting a Northern traveler after all- when something caught his attention. The same picture he saw every night, as it always had been, now had a new light. Far off into the distance, part way up the mountain, was a blinking light. It was tiny, but somehow very noticeable. Davun stared and pondered on the several possibilities of what could be causing such a light.

Hunters? In the mountains? No, that doesn't make any sense. Perhaps someone is trying to scale it to see what is at the top? It's known to be a dangerous climb, but some people are stupid enough to try. Why is it blinking though? Perhaps people are walking in front of a fire they set. Maybe it's more dancing from some Northerner's who got completely lost? No, surely that can't be i-

"Everything alright there, Davun?" Kalavud's calm voice cut into Davun's thoughts. Kalavud was standing directly behind him, though Davun had no idea for how long the strange man had been there.

"Everything is fine. Or as Averly would put it, perfectly fine. The night went as it should have, but washing dishes isn't exactly the most exciting of tasks." Davun responded quickly, feeling a little embarrassed that the new guy caught him slacking from his job. Kalavud looked at him for a moment, a mixture of concern, confusion, and doubt on his face. He took a glance out the window but didn't appear to find whatever had caught Davun's interest. Kalavud gave a slight nod, before the familiar smile reappeared along with the cheery attitude.

"Well lads, time I be off. The night went as it should have, which means my debt has been paid. Glad to have met the both of you," Kalavud spoke, before turning his attention towards Jethro "And worry not, little one. I'm sure things will change for the better soon enough. Just work on that smile of yours and you'll see the world in a completely different way." He ruffled Jethro's hair affectionately. Davun was a little shocked, clearly unaware of whatever Kalavud was talking about, or the fact that the two had spoken whilst he wasn't around. In truth, Davun felt a little betrayed. He always saw himself as the one who handled Jethro's issue, and he alone. It never occurred to him that perhaps Jethro sought wisdom from others. Davun became so lost in his thoughts that it took Kalavud clearing his throat to bring Davun's attention to the outstretched hand. He shook it, reluctantly. He wasn't sure if the bitterness was coming from not knowing the man, or because he felt left out. Kalavud gave a quick nod and set off out the door. It was strange. People had come in and out of the kitchens often, but Davun didn't really care much for talking to them. He had Jethro and that was good enough for him, or at least he thought it was. When Kalavud left, it left Davun surprised at the impact it had on him.

I probably just want answers from him, but I'll just have to get them from Jethro. I hope.

Jethro had returned to washing the dishes, a hint of a smile on his face. Davun considered immediately bringing it up but decided he didn't want to sour Jethro's mood. Clearly whatever Kalavud had said had a positive effect on him. Davun returned to the dishes as well, but this time he was too troubled to even glance at his favourite picture.

CHAPTER TWO

"There are many individuals, both royal and civil, who attempt to hide pieces of information to protect themselves. Then there are those who do it to protect others."

A week after Kalavud's departure, Davun and Jethro found themselves helping out the farmers. A couple times throughout the year, they would lend their hand to them as part of their job at the inn. They would assist in whatever way needed, and in return the farmers would give Averly a small part of their crops once grown. Davun didn't mind the work, he had grown accustomed to heavy labour, but Jethro always had issues trying to make it throughout the day. This time was different, however. Jethro appeared to be trying to push through it, even though Davun could clearly see he was tired. For some reason Jethro was determined to complete all the tasks, and whenever Davun suggested that he go home for the day, it earned him a snappy retort. It stung Davun each time, because Jethro never treated him like that before. He let it go, and put it down to child growth, it was bound to happen eventually. Davun may have been worried, but he couldn't deny he was proud of Jethro. Watching him really go beyond what he normally does, watching his determination to see the job through, brought a smile to Davun's face.

But what if it's because of Kalavud? Is he the reason Jethro has become like this?

Davun's thought made him sour. He did appreciate Jethro's new attitude, but he wanted to be the reason for it.

Am I no longer the person he looks up to? Davun froze. *Kalavud has probably seen lots of things and told Jethro about them. He's an honest man, albeit a bit too cheery. He's probably travelled to plenty of places. Jethro must..must want to be like him. I don't blame him.*

***

Davun vigorously attacked the ground with his hoe. He was venting his frustration hoping to distract himself from his thoughts. His actions didn't go unnoticed, as one of the farmer's scolded him for nearly breaking the tool.

After the day's work was done, the brothers travelled back home, at the inn. The farms were just outside the village, obviously to have enough land to grow their crops, so the walk home took a bit of time. It was dusk when the boys reached the skirts of the village. They had walked back without saying a word, each distracted with their own thoughts.

"Do you think there really is more out there, Davun?" Jethro asked curiously. Davun considered his question for a moment. Did he himself know the answer to that?

"Depends on what you mean by more. Yes, there are more people, more towns, more cities. More trees, more animals, more grass, more sky, mor-"

"Alright, I get it. I meant, is there more than we think there is? Are there places no one has been to yet? Are there really tall, or really small people? Is there anything out there for us?"

Davun was unsure how to respond. He had the same question, that he had been seeking an answer to through other people's stories in the inn.

"You too, then?" Davun smiled at his brother. "I've been wondering the same thing too, Jeth. I want there to be something out there for us. Something more than just working at the inn for the rest of our lives. But the truth is, I don't know. I wonder if I am too afraid to find out."

"Kalavud says there is, if we believe there is. He says if you believe there is something out there, then you keep on searching until you find it."

Davun considered the words. It was a motivating sentiment. He began feeling the energy he needed to actually leave. Go explore the world, go around meeting new people and stop being so...closed. All he knew was Jeth. He worked for Averly and knew what she was like, but they never really connected to form a close relationship. It would be nice to finally break free of his shell but, what may happen to Jeth when he does? Jeth was always his focus, his reasoning for doing anything. He had to look out for him, and what if going and exploring the world meant it may harm Jeth? He couldn't do that for his brother. Not for such selfish reasons.

But his brother also wants to see the world, that much is obvious. But Davun couldn't just take a ten-year-old out into the unknown. He knew the general direction of certain cities and towns, but he didn't have any experience.

That's when Davun realized what was happening. He was using Jethro as an excuse. He should just take Jethro with him, they've survived all this time together, and with careful preparation they should survive together out there. But how prepared is prepared? How long should they plan to travel for? Should they try find a map first? How much can they actually prepare for and carry for the multiple situations that may occur?

Davun cut off his line of thinking. It became pretty clear. If they were going to travel sometime soon, then they would need something to force them to leave. Or have someone to guide them for a while. Maybe if Kalavud came back sometime, they could leave with him for a while...

Then growling could be heard behind them. They'd been walking between the houses, and were close to home, when a Lakkerfel abruptly appeared behind him. At least, that's what

Davun believed it was. He had never seen it before but had heard about them through travelers. They were large dogs with tough hides that could resist even the sharpest of swords. Every time Davun had heard about them, it was related to battle. And this Lakkerfel definitely looked ready for battle.

It stood in an aggressive stance, ready to pounce. It had a few marks on its hide showing fighting experience, and it was missing one of its ears. It sniffed the air a few more times, approaching the brothers slowly. Davun took a step back, but realized his brother stood completely still. Shocked. The Lakkerfel must have smelled the fear, because it lunged straight for Jethro. The beasts' armoured head opened, and a series of razor-sharp teeth appeared, threatening to snap around Jethro's neck. Jethro was still too scared to move, he was just standing there, ready to accept his fate.

Davun couldn't allow it. He called out Jethro's name, and pushed him as hard as he could, causing the Lakkerfel to snap its jaw shut around his arm. Davun screamed in pain, being forced to his knees by the beast. He forced the courage to look at the wound. It was bleeding out of the sides of the beasts' mouth, still clamping shut and budging a muscle. Davun raised his arms to strike at the Lakkerfel's head, but suddenly the beast let go. It turned and ran, right out of the town without hesitation. Davun, still wincing in pain, turned to Jethro who was huddled with his head to his knees and arms over his head, as if preparing for an attack.

"Jeth. It's okay. It's gone now. It's okay, come here," Davun said softly, grabbing hold of Jethro's shoulder. Jethro slowly removed his arms, to peek out at the situation.

Damn. I scraped his cheek when I pushed him. And he's shaking so badly. Poor kid. That damned beast nearly scared him to death.

"I…I thought it knocked me down. I thought time had frozen or something because I was expecting it to bite but…it never came. I was so scared, Dav! I didn't know what t-" Jethro cut himself off, staring wide eyed at Davun's right arm. It was now covered in blood, as it seeped out of several puncture wounds. This brought it to Davun's attention, and realizing how much blood he was losing, he began to feel lightheaded. He swayed a little as he stood upright but managed to grip onto Jeth's shoulder to stop him from falling.

"Come on, Jeth. I'm gonna need you to help me get to Averly. She'll help. Do you reckon you can do that for me, Jeth?" Davun asked, as calmly as he could. He wasn't sure if Jethro heard the shakiness in his voice. But Jeth nodded, and clearly trying to hold back tears, lead Davun to the inn.

"I mean, she'll help us as long as I don't bleed on anything, right Jeth?" Davun tried to joke. He wasn't sure if it helped because he couldn't see Jethro's face, but it was all he could think of to do to help both himself and his brother.

Averly, confused and shocked, scrambled between performing what first aid she knew and making sure that Davun didn't bleed on anything. She eventually decided to wrap his arm in one of her less favourite cloths, before sitting him down in the kitchen and running off to get someone more suitable. Davun was feeling his head get lighter and lighter as the blood flow continued. He honestly wasn't sure what was going to happen. He'd never received a wound like this, and if the beast was rabid, his wound would most likely be infected. This could potentially be the end for him. And then Jethro would be alone. *No. I can't allow that. I won't die, it's not even that serious of a wound.* Davun glanced at the wound again and couldn't believe his own lie.

A moment later and Averly burst into the kitchen, followed by Loreli. She was the closest thing to the town's doctor as there was. She wasn't actually a doctor, but she had the most knowledge on medicine, so people always sought her out before travelling to the city. She was an elderly woman, though Davun wasn't too sure how old, asking would have been rude. Her hair was grey, and thick for her age. She was wearing her blue night robe, obviously having been disturbed from relaxing at home. She unwrapped the cloth Averly had attempted to cover the wound with and began prodding and squeezing Davun's arm. "How much pain are you in?" she spoke in a calm, yet commanding tone, whilst not taking her eyes off the wound as she began cleaning off the blood.

"Not much anymore. It's either settling down, or I'm a little numb and about to faint," Davun tried responding in a joking tone but was surprised to hear how wavy his voice was.

"You feeling light headed?"

"Yeah, I think it's been getting worse since it happened."

"Feeling sick?"

"No."

"Vision affected?"

"Things are a little blurry, I just assumed it had to do with being a little woozy."

"Most likely. You're probably feeling heavy too, but right now I need you to stay awake as best you can. You'll be able to rest soon but I need to dress the wound," Loreli finished cleaning up most of the blood, but the wound was still bleeding. She reached into a bag that she had brought with her and began sorting through several glass bottles. "It doesn't look infected, but I'm not wearing my glasses either. I was in a bit of a rush and forgot them at home. Here, read this for me please, Averly," Loreli handed a bottle with an odd green liquid within.

"Headaches, swelling, throbbing, bruis-" Averly began, but Loreli cut her off.

"That's not it, so it must be this one then" and pulled out another vial with a green liquid. She wrapped a soft cloth around the wound and poured the contents of the vial over the cloth, and it slowly absorbed the mysterious concoction. She then began rifling through her bag again, searching for something else.

"That cloth will hold the medicine, but I have a different fabric to wrap around that, so it stays clean and attached. Just give me a moment, ple-" she began, but Davun lurched forward.

He could no longer stay conscious. He didn't even feel hitting the cold, hard floor.

Davun woke suddenly. He was surprisingly hot and had been sweating. He managed to sit up, making sure not to use his wounded arm to support him. He was in his room. He glanced over to Jethro's bed, but it remained undisturbed. He walked over to the window, feeling a little weak in the knees. He opened the shutter, staring out into the night sky. *How long have I been out for? I feel so slow, like my body hasn't moved for days. Wait, could I have been out for days?* He checked his bandages. They appeared fresh, but perhaps Loreli had replaced them while he was asleep. He shuffled over to the door but flinched a little as it opened just before he reached it. Jethro entered holding a wet cloth, eyes red from crying. He stood still and was stunned for a moment as he stared at Davun. "Hey Jeth, how long have I been out for?" Davun decided to break the silence.

Jethro didn't answer but instead wrapped his arms around Davun tightly. "I thought something happened to you! You hit your head really hard, and you fell so suddenly!" Jeth spoke, managing to hold back tears. Davun became aware of the aching on the side of his head. He reached up to touch it and winced at the pain. *Yeah, definitely bruised. That must have played something into sleeping for so long.*

"Averly! Loreli! Davun is awake already!" Jethro called out, having let go of Davun. He remembered he had been holding a cloth and gave it to Davun indicating it was for his forehead. Davun was distracted though. *Awake already?* "Jeth, what do you mean? How long have I been out for?"

"Only about fifteen minutes. You gave us a scare. I didn't think you'd be up for a week. Loreli said you also got a fever, you started sweating and became really hot," Jeth explained to him. Davun was still processing the information when the two ladies rushed into the room. "Sit down young man, let me have a look at you," Loreli forced him to sit on the bed. She touched his forehead and inspected the bandages. Seeming satisfied with how her work was holding up, she rested her hand against his head. "Your temperature has gone back down, but clean off your face with the cloth, dear,". Davun accepted the suggestion, finally grabbing the cloth Jethro had brought to the room. He remained seated on the bed, fixated onto the floor as he tried to figure out the situation.

How could I have only been out for such a short amount of time? Maybe it's just the loss of blood that is making me feel like this. Perhaps I should sleep more.

" I appreciate the help, everyone, but I think I should get more rest now. I'm still not feeling quite right." Davun said as he handed the cloth to Loreli.

"Understandable, dear. With all that's happened tonight you really should get some rest. Just try and not wake up every fifteen minutes, okay dear?" Loreli chuckled, placing the wet cloth on Davun's bedside. The women promptly left the room, leaving Jeth alone with his brother. Jethro stood there, barely keeping his own eyes open, and tried to smile at his brother, but Davun could see the tiredness his brother was trying to resist.

"You should get some sleep too Jeth, you've been through a bit as well," Davun gestured over to the other side of the room, where Jethro's bed was.

"Yeah, I guess I should. Goodnight brother. Hope you're better in the morning," Jethro said whilst yawning. Davun smiled to himself.

He's a good kid. Maybe I could try just take him to the city, he'd like that. Davun continued pondering the idea, before he let himself slide into a dreamless sleep.

***

The next day, Davun set out on his scavenger hunt for supplies for his trip to the city. He decided he would tell Averly once he got all the supplies, but he was also keeping it from Jethro. He wanted to surprise his little brother with the good news once he was fully prepared, in case plans fell through and he only disappointed him instead.

He had to make certain he was prepared for anything on the trip. The idea of actually leaving filled him with adrenaline, but also fear. He was searching around for supplies for various events that may happen, so he could prepare for anything that would happen to Jethro.

He brought rope in case Jethro fell down somewhere. He brought enough rations to feed themselves for a week – even though the trip should only take three days – in case they somehow got lost for some unforeseen reason. He even bought a compass for such an emergency. He did realise he may be going a bit overboard with the preparations, but every time he thought about the trip a new scenario that put Jethro in danger would pop into his head. He had protected Jeth his entire life in the comfort of this little town. The townsfolk, especially Averly, looked out for them, but Davun always considered himself Jethro's guardian. He was about to take them both outside of their homes, their comfort zone, their only known place in the world, and he was not about to slack on protecting Jethro because of that. He was excited to see the world as well, but Jethro was his first priority.

* * *

Davun gathered all the supplies he thought they would need in the next few days. The wound still ached and throbbed, and he had felt lightheaded a couple of times. The process of finding the required items for their trip had become hindered by his fresh wound, finding it painful to perform mundane tasks. Jethro was constantly by his side, making it difficult for Davun to gather the supplies for the trip without letting Jethro catch on. His little brother was glued to his side, as if by guilt, constantly wishing to help in every task to ease Davun's burden of an arm. Though Davun did appreciate his little brothers' help, it did make gathering supplies difficult to complete covertly.

A few more days went by as Davun finished up his preparations. He had gotten all the supplies on his list, but he had been thinking of other possibilities he may have missed. Though Davun realized this was just a stalling tactic. He was still scared of leaving the village, but it was only going to be a short trip. He decided that it was time to face his fears and to tell Jethro of his plans, figuring it'll ease the tension on him. It was possible that Jethro had already figured out the secret, having grown oddly quiet in the past couple of days.

He also had yet to tell Averly of his plans, but he would be back in less than a week so he figured she would be alright with it.

Perhaps even pick up some stuff for her in return for letting them go.

He set out to find Jethro, who had excused himself from their kitchen work early from not feeling well. He not only wanted to check on his brother, but also hope he'd make him feel better by revealing the surprise. He was both nervous and excited it was affecting him physically. He finally reached their bedroom but stopped a moment before opening. He took a deep breath to calm his nerves and took a moment to work out his words. He then placed his hand on the door handle and swung the door open.

Davun froze in shock.

Instead of finding Jethro resting in bed, he found him halfway out the window, with a bag.

"J...Jethro? What are you doing?" Davun said in disbelief. He stared at his brothers' face, who was equally as shocked, and it appeared he was – or at least had been – crying.

"I...I was just...I'm sorry, Davun. I have to leave." Jethro choked on his words as he did his best to hold back tears. He still remained halfway out the window, uncertain of which way he should go. Davun also remained standing in the doorway, too stunned to make a move as processed the situation. "Where are you going?" Davun asked. He felt he had to use all his effort to squeeze the words out of his throat.

"I..I have to leave"

"What? Where? Why?"

"I thought it was easier if you didn't know. I was...scared. I couldn't tell you. I have to leave, Dav. I'm not destined to stay here in this village for my life. I need to go and see the world, just like Kalavud does."

That was it. Kalavud must have said something to him. He must have persuaded Jethro to make this decision. To leave everything he knew behind and just...go. Davun became angry.

"What did he say to you, Jethro? What did he tell you to do?"

"Nothing! He just told me all the stories about his travels, and what he's seen, and...I want to see them too, Dav. And that will never happen if I stay here."

"Jeth…look. This is not how you do things. You don't just pack what you have and leave, without telling anyone anything. How're we supposed to know you left to travel, and that something didn't happen to you? It's not a safe place out there, Jeth. Just like that Lakkerfel that bit me. What if you came across that thing again?"

"I brought protection!" Jethro exclaimed as he stepped back inside the room and began sifting through his bag. He pulled out a cloth and slowly unfolded it, revealing a kitchen knife.

"Jethro, you have no idea how to use it to defend yourself, let alone how to use it against a rabid Lakkerfel," Davun sighed, and opened his arms. "Come here, Jeth". Jethro slowly walked into Davun's embrace, knees wobbling as he did so. Davun subtly took the wrapped knife from his brother.

"Jeth. I really wished you decided to tell me about this. If I knew you were resorting to running away, I would have told you earlier" Davun spoke as calmly as he could, not wanting Jethro to misinterpret his words. Jehtro looked up at his brother, with a confused and curious look. "Tell me what?"

"We're heading to the city, Jeth. You and me. We're going to go for a few days, I have all the supplies already. I was planning on telling you tonight, but…well, you know." Davun smiled, trying to lighten the situation. Jethro's eyes widened and a smile appeared on his face. It was short-lived as his expression changed to grim. "I knew it was the wrong thing to do. I knew I should have at least tried to talk to you, but…I was afraid you'd say no. I didn't think you would want to come with me, so I thou-"

"Jeth?"

"Yes?"

"Shut up, will you?" Davun laughed and embraced his brother once more. Jethro returned the affection and smiled to himself, sighing with relief having gotten rid of the weight off his chest.

CHAPTER THREE

"Through my travels and journeys, I have discovered a multitude of lost civilizations, members of royal bloodlines, and artifacts. I have found cultural differences between our people now, and our people of a thousand years ago. Neither seemed aware of the truth."

The boys had set off from their village early in the morning, and immediately made way for the main road that lead towards the city. Averly didn't respond well to the news, at first. She was livid with the boys missing work for a week, but quickly changed her attitude once Davun promised he'd pick up the most recent tablecloth from Cravo Delroy, her favourite linen worker who owned one of the largest linen shops in the city, on her behalf. She normally had to wait for Cravo to send a courier once she sent a messenger with her order, which normally took a month or so, so the idea of having one within the week appeased to her.

They were both excited for their journey. They constantly talked as an outlet for their excitement, theorizing on what the city will be like once they arrived, and making plans of what they should do whilst on their stay there. There was so much about the city they'd heard and wanted to see every bit of it, from the amazingly hot smith forges, to the run-down dirty slums, to the beautiful variety of colours in the royal gardens. The boys imagined the city as a mystical place that was like walking through a portal to a different world at every turn. It held so much mystery that it both scared and enthused the brothers. They continued walking and chatting away, until they came across a horse and wagon, seemingly abandoned on the side of the road. The boys paused a moment, to take a look around, but both shared the same puzzling expression. "Where do you think the owner is?" Jethro broke the silence, as he ventured toward the vehicle.

"I don't know Jeth but be careful. They may have just gone behind a bush to the toilet," Davun said, as he scanned the nearby surroundings. "Or worse, someone may have gotten to them, possibly some."

"THIEVES! GET AWAY FROM MY STUFF YOU HOODLUMS! YOU CAN'T HAVE MY SUPPLIES! I NEED THEM TO FEED MY FAMILY, YOU CRETINS!" an angry voice came out of nowhere, causing the boys to jump in fright. The ranting man appeared from behind a bush, and was stamping his way towards the wagon, shaking his fist at the brothers. "YOU CAN'T HAVE MY STUFF EVEN IF YOU KILL ME! I'LL TAKE YOU DOWN WITH ME IF I HAVE TO!" the screaming continued as the man rounded the wagon to pull Jethro away from his property. Davun had already sprung forward and stepped in front of his brother as he staggered backwards from the jerked movement. Davun stood his ground, not backing down as the man attempted to intimidate him but yelling at him, inches from his face. Davun placed one hand on his brother, to protect him, and quickly moved the other into his pocket, grabbing the handle of the knife wrapped in cloth he had taken from Jethro the night before.

"I'm sorry sir! I-I didn't know anyone was here, I was just looking I swear!" Jethro pleaded, but the words were drowned by the man's continued threats. Davun pulled his fist back further to get more of a swing at the man's face, ready to release at any moment.

"Alright, alright, let's calm down now Hank. As much as you may want to beat up a couple of kids, I don't think it's necessary right now. They're not the – hey, I know you guys!" a second man rushed from the bushes to calm the first man. Davun stood in disbelief at the face with that familiar smile staring right back at him.

It was Kalavud.

"They aren't bandits, Hank. They're just a couple of nice kids from a small, nearby village," Kalavud reassured the other man, who seemed to have lightened up a little.

"But you told me there was bandits coming this way?"

"I know, I know. But these lads aren't those bandits. Wrong place at the wrong time, I'm afraid. The bandits still may be nearby however…" Kalavud responded, looking down the road. Turning back, Davun couldn't see anything, but wasn't sure if Kalavud was actually looking at something or just checking. The other man – Hank – decided not to waste any time and hopped up onto the drivers' seat of the wagon. "Well, no point hanging around and waiting for them. I reckon ol' Francine here will outrun them just fine," he called while patting his horse, not bothering to turn around when he spoke. "You boys headed to the city?" this time he spoke to Davun and Jethro, with the reigns in hands ready to set off.

"Yes, we are. We've never been before, so we're excited to see what it's like," Davun responded, however he still kept a hand on Jethro to make sure he was calm.

"Bah, you're not missing much. Too many people, too much noise. But it provides the best business for my stock, so I'm forced to make a trip when my storage gets full. Well, hop aboard then lads. I don't want to leave you alone while there's bandits about," the man scooted over on his seat to make room. Jethro smiled, but Davun remained on edge. They had just met the man, how could they trust him? Before he could respond, Kalavud spoke up.

"That's right. You lads have never left the village, have you? Well glad to see you venturing out there! There is so much to see, I'm sure you'll love every bit of it. No need to take them, Hank. I wish to show them one of my favourite spots in the area, then I'll escort them to the city," he spoke, not dropping his smile for even a moment.

"Have it your way, Northerner. Just don't let them boys out of your sight and be careful of those bandits! Don't hang around too long or they'll catch up," Hank said as he gave his horse the command to walk. It let out a whinny in response and obeyed its master. As Davun watched the wagon slowly move off down the road, he pondered on if this was the right course for them.

"Your friend isn't coming with us?" Jethro asked, puzzled that the man had abruptly left Kalavud.

"No, Hank wouldn't want to come with us. I only met him shortly before you guys came, but I get the feeling that he doesn't like sightseeing much."

Davun wondered how Kalavud managed to convince Hank to hide in some bushes if they had only just met but understood the reasoning if there really were bandits about.

"Well, lads. Shall we head off then? It's only a short walk, not too far." Kalavud began to walk off of the path, into the brush that he had been hiding in. Jethro didn't hesitate and began following. Davun, however, did hesitate. He watched Kalavud for a moment and eyed off his weapons.

Two swords, a bow, possibly a couple of daggers on his belt. A bit more armed than we last saw him. I don't like this.

He quickly caught up to Jethro, and purposefully put himself between Kalavud and his brother.

"Surprising to find you lads out here. Thought you may have been a couple of bandits, so Hank and I left the wagon as bait, and waited nearby to scare you off. Glad it was only you two though!" Kalavud started the conversation once the brothers caught up.

"We're surprised to see you too, Kal! I didn't even think that we might see you on our trip to the city. It's good to see you again!" Jethro spoke with a huge smile on his face, rather similar to Kalavud's.

"I'm happy to see you too, Jeth! What made you lads decide to finally leave the village and go adventuring?"

"You did, Kal. I wanted to see if you were lying back when you told me all those stories about what you've seen."

Davun swore that Kalavud looked at him through the corner of his eyes when Jethro had mentioned the reason. However, Kalavud didn't turn his head, or give any other indication of doing so.

"Well, I'm glad to have inspired such a positive attitude adventurer like yourself! I may have misled you slightly though, lad," Kalavud spoke, putting Davun on edge. Not only was he worried about what he had mislead Jethro with, but there was a slight tone in his voice that stabbed at Davun. It wasn't quite the usual upbeat tone he always spoke with.

"See, the world is a beautiful place, with many dazzling sights to see. But it's not as safe as I may have led you to believe. Where we are going is safe enough, but it's still best to keep alert. Beasts, bandits, brigands, boars-"

"Boars are beasts though?"

"Yes, but I wanted another 'B' word and was struggling to think of another one in time. Always keep your senses open to anything and everything. It's always best to know that something is there, even if you don't know what it is."

Something about this conversation was making Davun feel uncomfortable. His hand drifted near his pocket that concealed the basic kitchen knife.

Always keep on alert. Just like he said.

***

Jethro and Kalavud chatted away while they walked. Even Davun couldn't resist asking questions now and again. Kalavud told them about the plants and critters that they passed. He had a lot of knowledge to share, and the boys were eager to learn. It hadn't occurred to Davun that his hand no longer drifted near the knife, as he indulged on the information Kalavud was sharing. The experience was new to the boys, and they had many questions as they experienced things for the first time. They were in the outskirts of the nearby forest, but the aroma it produced was intoxicating for the boys. Every breath through their nose brought on a new smell and new questions.

Kalavud insisted on allowing them a short rest, assuming the brothers were not accustomed to long journeys, but working in the fields regularly built up the boy's stamina and were trying to politely decline the suggestion. In the end, Kalavud won, and he had the boys rest against a tree to rest their feet – lest they get weary of course. He told them further of the nearby plants and their vast number of properties if used in particular ways. The purple dyriads could wake a bear in hibernation, if crushed of its essence and boiled with a slight bit of vinegar to disturb the essence into producing a foul-smelling toxin that was then bottled, to use at the necessary time. Apparently, a royal alchemist discovered it when researching a method to keep the king's army awake for a longer period of time so that they may march during the night to surprise their enemy. The Alchemist was rewarded handsomely, for his research led their army to victory. However, prolonged use of the toxin had a debilitating effect on the soldiers, and many of their minds became muddled, and had to be retired due to being unfit to serve the army. The method was quickly prohibited in most kingdoms.

They drank from their wineskins and had a small meal of bread and cheese, and then continued on their journey to Kalavud's mysterious destination. He insisted it would not be too much longer, and it was well worth the detour. It occurred to Davun that they were travelling towards the mountain that he would ritualistically stare at through the kitchen window, and he suddenly felt elated. He still had the feeling of worry about going so far from the main path, but he was also happy that they had. Being so close to the mountain brought something up in Davun and his curiosity doubled, almost taking the lead away from Kalavud as a surge of adrenaline rushed through him. Though after a moment, he realized he left his position of being between Kalavud and Jethro as much as he could without raising suspicion, so he drifted back a bit to his original position, but his eagerness didn't falter. They stopped still on multiple occasions as wildlife would wonder closer, partially curious about them, and partially looking for food. At one stage, a deer wondered within reach, possibly smelling the food from their bags, but as Jethro reached up to try and touch it, it became skittish and ran off. Kalavud laughed, while Jethro felt a little disappointed at not being able to stroke its soft fur.

Not much farther through the brush, Kalavud suddenly stopped, holding up a hand to let the brothers know to halt.

"Do you hear that?" Kalavud asked softly. Davun and Jethro turned their heads in an attempt to hear what Kalavud was hearing but failed to hear anything other than the chirping of birds and light wind brushing the shrubbery, which had seemed no different from most of their journey thus far.

"No. What is it? Danger?" Davun asked, surprising himself by the lack of fear in his own voice. Davun had never left the village, and the idea of wondering out to the unknown scared him, but now that it was actually happening, his instincts of making sure nothing harmed Jethro appeared to override his fear. Kalavud remained silent. The lack of response only put Davun further on edge.

"That's the sound I'm after. It means we're there" Kalavud responded, as if the brothers could hear the same thing. Without waiting for a response, Kalavud moved on. Jethro didn't hesitate in following.

"Hear what? I can't hear anything other than what we've been hearing to the last hour or so," Davun responded irritably. His body felt tense, and he became aware that he had taken on some kind of fighting stance. Whether or not his reaction was to attack the possible threat, or defend himself from an attack, he wasn't sure. He loosened up, trying to shake off the feeling that he may have actually wanted it to be a threat.

Why do I feel like this? Did I really want there to be a threat? I should be relieved that it wasn't, but for some reason I don't. It must be weariness getting to me. Jethro must be feeling the same.

As the thought crossed his mind, he glanced at his younger brother, who had a huge smile on his face as he was attempting to keep up with Kalavud.

Right?

He pushed the thought out of his mind and focused on walking ahead. If they were within ear shot, that means they were close. After not much walking, Kalavud disappeared behind some tall bushes that were growing puripans, a bright green flower that they had also learnt about earlier.

"Over here, lads!" Kalavud called out from behind the plants. The brothers rushed through the bushes, hearts pumping in anticipation, and finally set their eyes upon – the Ordale river. The same river that runs near their village. Hardly the exciting sight the boys had wanted to see. The Ordale river ran near their village, and they made frequent trips to it whenever they were sent by the farmers or Avery. "Not really what we had expected to see, to be quite honest Kalavud. We've seen this river before," Davun explained dissapointedly. He could also see that Jethro felt the same thing just by looking at his face. He gave his brother a pat on the back.

"Lads, do you think I listened to you so little during my visit to Eraton? I'm a little hurt," Kalavud responded, trying to seem offended but couldn't drop his smile. Kalavud pointed up the river, the brothers traced his finger and their eyes lit up.

They were staring at a waterfall in the distance, where the river began. It was falling from a mountain cliff, and even from this distance it was a sight to behold.

"Are we going to see the waterfall?" Jethro blurted out in excitement. Kalavud laughed and nodded in reply.

"Let's not waste any more time staring at it from here, let's go have a closer look." Kalavud gestured forward, and Jethro immediately took the lead. It didn't take too long to reach the bottom of the waterfall. The water splashed on several jutted rocks on its way down and created a soothing noise that immediately calmed Davun of any remaining nerves he had. He was completely lost in the sight and sound, lost in his own thoughts.

This whole time…

"Don't venture too closely, Jethro," Kalavud's warning cut through Davun's thoughts. Jethro had ventured to the edge of the bank to get a closer look at the bottom of the waterfall. Watching the splashing of water on the rocks which continued falling into the water fascinated him.

"Jeth, come back a bit please. I don't think I know how to swim to be able to get you out," Davun said half-jokingly. Jethro stood a moment longer before stepping back to join the others.

"So, I know how fascinating falling water can be, but what say we venture a little further? I know a steep slope that we may climb to get a little bit of height," Kalavud suggested. Davun's instinct was to immediately say yes, but he hesitated.

"How steep is it?" he asked Kalavud, who had already begun walking. Kalavud stopped and turned. He looked at Davun quizzically then looked down to Jethro, and realization hit his face.

"Not too steep. Nothing dangerous as long as we take care with our footing. Even if one were to slip – and the gods forbid that they do – they won't suffer much other than a few scrapes." Kalavud spoke and gave a reassuring smile. Davun nodded, easily persuaded to take the trek he desperately wanted to go on. He let Kalavud lead, and stood behind Jethro, to catch him in case he did slip.

The loose gravel proved the most difficult part of climbing the slope. It wasn't as steep as the boys had thought but didn't expect the difficulty of navigating the gravel. They pushed through only slipping a few times, but not completely losing their balance and sliding. Kalavud appeared unaffected by the difficult terrain and graced up the slope with ease. Davun wouldn't admit it to him, but he was a little jealous of how Kalavud made it look so easy. Kalavud reached the top of the ramp, and stood near the edge of the cliff, hands on his hips and smiling. He didn't turn as the brothers joined him. They didn't bother asking him what he was staring at, as their attention was also grasped by the view. The beautiful landscape that was Teldario.

Breathtaking. It's so green. Full of life. And places unseen. So much I haven't seen... Davun began feeling faint.

Kalavud chuckled. "Not used to heights, are we?

Understandable. You've been in the village your entire life and we are quite the ways up. Speaking of which...Look right over..." Kalavud scanned the landscape, before pointing, "There. That is your village. Your home."

Jethro gasped in excitement. "But it looks so small. I thought our village pretty big. I bet I could see Averly's –"

Davun fell forward. The last thing he saw was the blur of the horizon before everything went black.

CHAPTER FOUR

"I do not know if I am the first historian. If any preceded me in this discovery, they decided to leave it as it was. This seems like the wise decision."

The first thing he saw when he awoke was the bright blue sky. *Am I still falling? No. No wind. I'm on the ground.*
Am I dead?
No.

"Good to see you awake, lad. Sorry about that, I should have expected something of the sort when I saw you swaying." Kalavud's voice broke Davun's focus on the sky. He turned his head towards the sound and saw Kalavud smiling at him. Davun was lying on a blanket that had been laid out for him, another blanket on top, and an unfolded bedroll as a pillow. Kalavud was sitting just next to him and offered him water as he sat Davun upright. Davun gladly took a drink and glanced around. They were still part way up the mountain but had moved further along it seemed as he didn't recognize the surroundings.

"Where is Jethro?" Davun questioned, realizing his little brother was not in sight.

"Ah. Well, here's the thing, I –" Kalavud begun explaining, however was interrupted by Jethro turning the corner.

"Dav!" Jeth burst out in excitement. He ran to his brother and embraced him. "It was scary, Dav. You almost fell off the cliff! Kalavud managed to grab you right before you fell."

The realization of the situation struck Davun, but he was unsure on how to feel about his close brush with death. Or how he felt about Kalavud saving him.

"This was a mistake. I think we need to go back home," Davun spoke, panic beginning to settle in.

"Please, do not leave just yet," a voice spoke from the corner Jethro came from, causing Davun to jump slightly as he spun around. The voice didn't belong to any of them. It was a deeper voice. His words were clear and authoritative. Davun stared as a man walked around. He was average height, long dark brown hair that was neatly combed back, and a neatly kept full beard. He looked like he was into his early thirties and his clothes were basic. A white drab shirt accompanied by dark brown pants. His sandals looked like they were from the North, but the most noticeable piece was his robe. It was a bright red, with golden lining and as he rounded the boys Davun also noticed some sort of golden pattern on the back. He walked with a sword sheathed on his belt, the sight of it causing Davun to be on edge.

"Forgive me lads, but I had an ulterior motive for our little side journey. I'd like you lads to meet Arkarnyrus. The real reason we made this journey."

"You may just call me by Arkarn. I also apologise for Kalavud's misdirection. That fault lays with me. I thought it best so that I may meet with you. I figured meeting an unknown man away from the main path was a bit of a hard story to sell to a couple of youths."

"I still think you should have at least let me try, Arkarn."

"I'm sure you would have been able to pull it off, but I much prefer to take the path with the higher chance of success."
"Well that just hurts, Arkarn," Kalavud mocked offence. Arkarn chuckled. Davun's throughts were still scrambling, but it didn't stop him from trying to get answers.

"So, who exactly are you? And why did you have Kalavud bring us?"

"The first is a difficult question to answer. The second will take time. I will do my best to explain it, but I do not know if you will believe me until you see it for yourself."

"See what exactly?"

"The unseen threat to this world. Kingdoms pretend it does not exist, figuring it is best to ignore it until it goes away, or hoping another kingdom will deal with it. The truth is that it is very real and remaining unseen is exactly what it wants. Kingdoms will not move against a threat it has not personally seen and will not seek the threat believed to be long dead. The enemy already has its plan set in motion, and we must do anything we can to stop it. That involves you both, Davun and Jethro. There are things you are unaware of that you are the key to, and I apologise for you having to be a part of this. The honest truth is that you, Davun, are the only one who can stop them from gaining the power they seek."

This was all too much to take in. Davun's head was spinning with each word Arkarn spoke, and none of it was making any sense. How could this mysterious figure, who had Kalavud deceive them and lead them away from their trip, spouted a bunch of nonsense, possibly have them believe this wild story during their first meeting?

The biggest issue was that something inside Davun was telling him to trust Arkarn. It was baffling him.

Why do I kind of believe this man? He shows up out of nowhere – while I was unconscious – tells me I am some kind of chosen one, who has to stop an enemy I didn't even know existed? It's completely made up and in no way does it make any sense. So why do I still feel like I should trust him?

Davun and Jethro were quiet. They were both staring blankly at the ground, lost in their thoughts. Arkarn could tell he had told them too much too fast. He sighed to himself and placed his face in hand.

"I see you aren't as well versed with children as you thought yourself, Arkarn," Kalavud teased, trying to lighten the mood. He saw the brothers faces sink as Arkarn finished his explanation and felt a little guilty for not having stopped Arkarn from giving so much information at once. The brothers were still young and not prepared for such a burdening task.

Davun shook his head and turned to Arkarn. "Wait. Even if I believe you, you said that both of us play a role in this, so why did you finish it with I have to stop them? What about Jethro?"

"Jethro also has a key role in that he will help you to succeed. You need to be the one to stop them, Davun. It has to be you. I believe that if we left Jethro behind it would only cause you worry and loss of focus. Having him along means we can guarantee his protection, and he will assist you in your mission. You will need someone you can talk to and who can help you. Your willpower might be tested, and I know that Jethro will be a great help to you. You will need your best friend" Arkarn explained softly. The words meant something to the brothers. Somehow Arkarn knew of their relationship, which shouldn't have surprised Davun considering how much Arkarn supposedly knew of them.

"This is all too much. There is no way that any of that is true. Even if it were, my brother and I have nothing to do with it. We're just a couple of young folks from a small town who have no experience in world saving. You have the wrong people. It was lovely meeting you and all, but my brother and I are going to continue our trip to the city, and then return home within the week. No time for any of this. So, if that's all to your story, we'll be off." Davun stood up to leave, grabbing his stuff as he did so, and set off where he believed they had come from while he was unconscious.

"Davun, wait," Jethro called out to him. Davun stopped in his tracks and turned to his brother.

"I think that we…we should trust him."

You too, Jeth?

Something inside him was almost thankful that Jethro stopped him. Each step he had taken felt like a mistake. That trusting vibe that Arkarn was emitting was still nagging at Davun.

"I understand it is hard. A lot of information to take in at once, but unfortunately time is not really on our side. Which is why, if you will give me what little time we may have, to take you somewhere that you can see for yourself. It is a bit of a travel, but that is something you boys wish to do, is it not? We will walk a couple days North, closer to the border of Vanguinar. We don't have much time to stop for pleasantries and sight-seeing I'm afraid, but along the way we will pass by many wonderful things. There is much in this world, and if you cannot - or will not - fulfill your role, then there won't be much to see after long."

If we go, at least then I will be at ease if this whole situation turns out to be nothing. I don't know why but I feel like I can't let this stranger down. What is it about him that makes him feel so...close?

Davun looked at his brother, who was staring at Arkarn. After a moment, Jethro turned to his brother and smiled.

He thinks it's best too. He's only ten and he wants to save the world. Those stories from Kalavud must have gotten to him.

"We'll go. But if this turns out to be some sort of trick, then...Well I guess depends on what kind of trick it is," Davun attempted his best to sound threatening. Arkarn burst out laughing. "Hahaha! Davun you don't have it in you to make those kind of threats," Arkarn managed to say through his laughter.

He doesn't know me at all, how does he know what kind of person I am? What exactly does he know about me? About us?

"But it is good that you have decided to come with us. It will make this experience easier. There is much for you to learn, and not much time to learn it. And not only learning, but some rigorous training. Just in case you want to follow up on your threats, Dav," Arkarn joked, making himself laugh again.

"It's Davun," Davun snapped. The only one who called him 'Dav' was Jethro. It felt weird coming from someone else, especially with someone he had just met and sold them a ridiculous story. Somehow.

Arkarn stopped laughing and cleared his throat. "I apologise, Davun. I'll make sure to show you more respect from now on. We should get started on our journey. Please gather your things and follow," he stood up and began making his way around the corner he had come from. Davun watched him walk, feeling a little guilty for snapping at him. *Why do I care if I insulted him? He's a stranger to me.*

Davun then grabbed his things, packed the blanket back into his bag, and set off with Jethro and Kalavud after Arkarn.

***

The first part of the walk was quiet. Davun was reflecting their decision to follow, while Jethro hung back a little bit with Kalavud, who was surprisingly non-talkative. They walked along the ridge of the mountain, and then down a different slope to the one they had climbed. They set off walking out of the forest that covered the side of the mountain base and walked off into the Alvarian plains. The boys were still excited to be travelling to new places, but that feeling was being oppressed by anxiety. They had no idea where they were going, or what was exactly being asked of them. All they had was an instinct in them to trust this strange man, and Kalavud, who didn't deserve the amount of trust either.

The plains had some wandering creatures that would keep their distance from the group which disappointed the boys. They wished to see all they could on their trip away from home, and this opportunity may even allow them to see different – if not more – than they had originally expected.

***

The group travelled for nearly two days, as Kalavud and Arkarn shared stories with great detail. Davun listened but kept on edge about the situation, though he found himself unintentionally losing himself in the stories and losing focus.

The boys saw a lot during their walking. Well, a lot to them at least. Davun suspected that in comparison to Arkarn and Kalavud, it was little. It still excited them none-the-less, to see creatures they had only heard about, and fauna that they never had. Jethro paid great detail to everything explained to him, constantly asking further questions, which admittedly bored Davun a little but at least it was keeping Jethro happy.

The boys managed to keep up with the pace set by Arkarn, walking through the Garvian woods. Davun was keeping an eye out for more creatures and critters, as he spotted something new every day. He was straining his eyes to see what would be hiding amongst the trees – hopefully a new type of bird – when he spotted something that was definitely new. He couldn't quite see what it was, but it was grey, possibly fur.

***

What is that? A bird with fur? Or is it just a large squirrel? It's got some kind of weird, dark circle...wait...did it just blink?

An arrow flew straight at Davun. It pierced into the side of his gut. The pain flared instantly throughout his whole body, but he was in too much shock to feel it. He stared down at the arrow sticking out of him. It felt like forever before anything seemed to happen, but when it did, it all happened at once. The pain in his stomach reached his senses. The wound on his arm struck him at the same time as the arrow pain. He began to faint. There was no resisting it this time. The last thing he saw and heard, was a large bald man, screaming as he charged towards him.

CHAPTER FIVE

"How many stories were just a cover up? How much has history been manipulated? What is the reason? How long can it last?"

Davun woke.

Ugh, not again. Was it the arm wound, or the arrow this time? Wait...I'm alive. What happened? Am I...?

He checked where the arrow hit. Fortunately, the arrow itself had been removed, and replaced with a patch of some kind. It was soaked in some kind of wet, thick, transparent substance. He felt around the wound, wincing from the pain of the bruise that had developed.

Yep. That hurt.

A man chuckled beside him.

"I wouldn't play with it if I were you. Feyra wouldn't appreciate you playing with her work. She's quite insistent about that," a deep voice spoke from next to him. It was a warm, kind voice, but it still made him jump. He turned and saw the same bald man he had before blacking out.

This man was sitting, but his frame gave away his large height and powerful frame. He was easily over six-foot tall, and apparently made of only muscles. He was holding a locket in his hand, that was strapped around his neck. His smile was welcoming, but eerily reminded him of Kalavud.

Who is this…where am I? Did I get kidnapped…?

Davun lay completely still, staring wide eyed at this mountain of a man who could easy snap him in half if he felt inclined. Davun really did not want to give him that inclination.

As if the large man could read his mind, he laughed loudly and rose to his full height. The man could have been mistaken for a building. He wore simple garb and appeared to have no weapons. He crouched down to Davun and extended a hand. Davun took a moment before grabbing it, and to his surprise the giant man's hands were completely soft. The man helped Davun gently to his feet.

"It may be best if you get a little moving done. Laying down for too long won't be of much help, as much as you may need rest. And now that you're properly standing, I can introduce myself. My name is Wayne. And you, I believe, are Davun. It is a pleasure to meet you," Wayne spoke with an upbeat attitude, extending his hand forward. Davun couldn't help himself from liking him, even though he was still tense about his situation, and he was still fixated on that smile. It was concerning how much it reminded him of-

"Davun, you're up!" as if fate itself knew, Kalavud appeared from nowhere. "I see Wayne is introducing himself. You may want to take that hand Dav, Wayne won't put it down unless you do. I once saw him follow around a poor merchant he was having a disagreement with until the guards were called on him! That poor merchant must have been scared as this brute followed him around town. I hope he's doing oka-"

"Kal, leave the stories for later, I'm sure Davun wants to see his little brother," Wayne interrupted, hand still extended. Davun took his hand and received a hearty shake.

Oh no. Davun thought to himself as he stared at the pair who stood there, just smiling. *It's worse than I thought.*

There are two of them.

Davun had been taken to some kind of encampment. Tents were pitched all over as people in mismatching armours walked about. Most carried weapons, but it all seemed rather disorganised. As he walked through with Wayne, many people greeted him and Davun could see the respect they held for him. He had been told that Wayne was one of the leaders that ran this place, along with a couple of others. He wondered if they all held such respect as Wayne did. Davun was taken to a decently sized tent near the centre of the camp. Inside, he found Jethro speaking with Arkarn and the two immediately stopped their conversation to greet him. Jethro went to hug Davun but stopped short, remembering the wound he had suffered. Davun felt a little sad and simply tussled his brother's hair.

"Glad you're okay Dav. Kalavud said the arrow might have been poisoned, but we rushed you here and a lady fixed you up. She said not to let the patch get wet for the rest of the day, or it'll wash out the…whatever it was she put on it," Jethro explained, eyes set on where Davun was wounded as he spoke.

"I feel better. I'm guessing whatever this goo is must be doing its job then. What happened anyway?"

"Ratlings," Arkarn responded with complete seriousness.

"Ratlings?"

Arkarn nodded. "They're Rattish humanoids, who will do anything for a slice of cheese. A species that prefers to remain hidden. They breed in surprising numbers, so there are usually a large group of them together. They're chaotic scavengers that only help themselves. Unless you can bribe them. There were six of them hidden amongst the trees. Fortunately, we had Kalavud, and thankfully Wayne came out to greet us. I'm sorry for what happened, Davun. I should have known they would be here."

Arkarn looked sombre. Davun could see he took what had happened personally.

"It's fine, Arkarn. None of us knew they were there. If they wanted food, I simply would have given it to them. It seems like the preferred method to being shot," Davun tried to laugh off the feeling, hoping to lift this burden off Arkarn. Arkarn's expression didn't change, however.

"It wasn't exactly a coincidence. They're part of the enemy we are up against. The ones hidden away."

They've been sighted around here before, but I thought we had driven them off for a while. It seems they're more eager than I thought. I must get to planning our next steps, please excuse me." Arkarn stood and walked to the flap of the tent, not making eye contact with anyone. Once he reached the opening, he paused. "And make sure you have Feyra look at that wound soon. She will want to make sure you haven't fiddled with it."

Davun just nodded. Arkarn walked away, leaving an awkward silence behind. Davun wasn't the only one feeling the tension, as the others all looked uncomfortable and confused.

"Well perhaps it is time we introduce you to Feyra then. Come with me," Kalavud broke the short silence. He beckoned Davun and Jethro to follow as he and Wayne ducked out of the tent.

***

As they approached the doctor's tent, Davun could hear a woman yelling.

"Honestly, you're just a whiner. This is barely a scratch and you want my expensive medicines for it? I don't think so. Letting it heal more naturally might teach you how to actually use a shield next time." The woman berated whoever she spoke to. At that moment, a man exited the tent, arm bandaged and in a sling. The man had only taken a step before a woman poked her head out.

"I don't want to see your arm again unless it's fallen off, otherwise I'll give you a proper reason to see a doctor," she threatened the man as he was hastily making his escape. The woman then turned her gaze on Davun, who immediately found that he couldn't move.

"You. In here. Now," she demanded, and her head disappeared back inside. Davun couldn't find the courage to step forward.

Kalavud chuckled. "Good luck to you. She gets in a bad mood after she thinks a patient has wasted her time."

"But that's every patient, Kal," Wayne responded

"You're right, Wayne, but he needs as much preparation as he can get. Davun, try not to talk unless she asks you a question."
"And try to not ask any questions yourself."

"Don't cry, she hates that."

"And whatever you do, always follow her directions," the two alternated, and ushered Davun inside.

There he saw a middle-aged woman, covering her hands with some kind of clear cream. She wore red shirt with black pants, and an apron covered with blood stains. She had shoulder length, grey hair that looked like it hadn't been brushed in a while. She stood as if she demanded respect, and she obviously received it.

"So," she spoke, not looking at him as she continued her preparations "First thing's first. Who let you stand up without speaking to me first?"

"Oh, uh…we found him walking around," Wayne spluttered out, elbowing Kalavud.

"Yes, that's right Feyra. Well, we better go. Gotta go debrief with the Captain," Kalavud quickly followed up, turning to leave.

"Shouldn't you have seen the captain when you arrived first thing yesterday?" Feyra asked sternly. The pair couldn't think of a response as they rushed out of the tent, eager to get out of her sight.

Davun turned back to Feyra, and he thought he saw amusement, but as she turned to him, he lost the ability to think. She was intimidating, and even someone like Wayne feared her. Jethro didn't appear to be as frightened, but he did remain silent.

"Right. Let's have a look at that wound of yours," Feyra gestured for him to lay down on a table that had been cushioned with thatch and leathers. Davun did as she ordered, lifting his shirt to reveal the patch. Feyra removed the cloth and began prodding around the wound. Davun winced at the pain, but she either didn't notice or didn't care because she kept poking.

"It's healing up nicely, though the medicine has worn off. Fortunately, it didn't go too deep, and it missed anything important. Just be glad that the Ratling couldn't aim very well. From what I hear, it caught you blind-sighted. I am a little surprised it didn't kill you. I'll apply another cloth with some avamoril," she explained as she grabbed a pot and scooped out a transparent goop with her hand. She lathered it onto his wound and massaged the area. It hurt at first, but the pain quickly faded the more she worked. "It might feel a little weird for a while. It will be numb for a few hours and try not to bump into anything. If you disturb the patch, then the pain may come back, and I won't be giving you more of the ointment."

Davun touched the area around the weird goop. "What is this stuff?"

"As I said, avamoril. If you rub it in it numbs the area of any feeling, including pain. The downside of course being that you don't feel anything at all and may not be able to control the applied area properly. Thankfully, it's just your side. Now, no more questions. Get up and go find your brother. He's been annoying me about your condition ever since you got here, and I'd rather not be disturbed while at work. Or at all, for that matter," she spoke dismissively, as if she didn't expect him to reply.

He decided not to delay and hopped off the table. He left the tent pressing his side to see how numb it really was.

Wow, that stuff really works. Where am I walking to? I don't remember-

"Hey! Laddy!" someone called out. Davun turned to see a man smiling and walking towards him. He had yellow eyes, and bright blond hair – a Northerner. "Hello there! My name is Evin. You were brought here by Arkarn, right? You must be the boy he went out to retrieve. It's an honour to finally meet you! Now we can finally finish this fight against th-"

Wayne appeared from nowhere, interrupting Evin and pulling Davun away. "There you are! Come on, we've been looking for you! Let's go get you boys something to eat, you must be starving." Wayne smiled and apologised to the peculiarly happy man, as he pushed Davun to walk.

"What was that about? Why does everyone know Arkarn set out to get me?" Davun was puzzled.

"Oh nothing, he's happy to have Arkarn back. He's a figurehead here, so when he has to leave for long periods of time it becomes a bit of a strain on moral," Kalavud explained, though Davun didn't notice him there.

"Weren't you two meant to be going to see the captain?" "Oh we already did yesterday. We were just waiting for you to leave Feyra. Didn't really want to be around if you had messed up her work. Not a sight you want to see," Kalavud seemed amused.

"Or hear" Wayne added. "Anyway, now that you've seen Feyra, we need take you somewhere to show you something."

"Show us what?"

"It's easier if we get there first."

***

Davun and his brother stood in an open field with Kalavud and Wayne, along with a wagon they brought along. It was covered with a blanket so they couldn't see, but it rattled with metal all the way over. They hadn't been told anything, and it seemed like dancing around the subject amused Kalavud and Wayne.

"Now, boys. It's time to let you in on something. Arkarn says it is critical that you two learn how to fight. He hasn't exactly explained why, but it's a useful skill to have regardless. I don't really expect either of you to get into a fight. Ideally, you'll be able to avoid it if possible, however it may very well be unavoidable. Now that you're here, things will certainly become more dangerous. For everyone. That's another thing you need to know now as well," Wayne crouched down to meet their gaze, his face intense, "No matter what happens to anyone here, they will not blame you, and you shouldn't blame yourself either."

"Wayne. Not now. They have to ease into it, you'll scare them if you don't," Kalavud stepped in, placing his hand on Wayne's shoulder. Wayne stared into Davun's eyes a moment longer, before standing to face Kalavud. "They have to know. Arkarn will only take his time with it, and I fear by the time he tells them it will be too late."

"Not now, Wayne. Leave it be. Please."

Wayne was visibly annoyed, but he took a deep breath and his cheery exterior returned. Davun was annoyed how they talked as if they couldn't hear. He wanted to know what they were talking about either behind his back, or before he got here. Everyone seems to know who he is before he even knew any of this even existed, and from what Wayne said, it's going to affect a lot of people. He remained distracted for a moment, before Wayne demanded his attention to begin teaching.

"Okay, it's time to start learning how to defend yourselves, should the need arise." Wayne moved over to the wagon, pulling off the cover to reveal weapons. There seemed to be a variety steel weapons, including a shield that caught Davun's attention. It appeared to be of an eagle, spread winged over a sword, sitting atop the sun. Wayne chuckled.

"I don't know how he knows, but he's always right about these things. Arkarn thought you'd take a liking to the shield, so he made sure I brought this one for you. He wants you both trained in unarmed combat, but he also wants you, Davun, to focus on how to properly use a shield. I can agree to that. I'd much prefer you know how to defend yourself rather than hurting someone else. Now, I'll teach you about a few of these weapons before we start you with basic exercises."

The boys learned the names of each of the weapons, and what they're generally used for. They got to hold and study each item, and as Arkarn predicted, Davun took a liking to the shield. It was the perfect size for him, and it just felt right as he held it. He was a little upset that he had to relinquish it, though Wayne promised that he would soon see it again. Wayne also had them run through some exercises to start building up their strength and stamina and was impressed to see how long the boys lasted. Though, they did have to stop frequently to make sure they hadn't messed up Feyra's work.

Nobody could be trained for that.

By the end of the day, Davun had met a few people around the camp. He discovered the camp extended further than he thought, and the amount of people didn't dwindle the further he went. Most people were excited to see him, many of which were hushed 'discretely' by Kalavud. Some folk didn't share the same enthusiasm as others. They appeared to be withholding something back and looked at Davun and Jethro judgingly. It made Davun feel more uncomfortable than he already was and felt like he was being put on trial for something he wasn't even made aware of.

He wondered if Jethro was feeling the same and made an excuse about being tired so that they could retreat to bed. He wasn't certain of Jethro's feelings, but decided it might be best for his brother to get some rest, it had been a long day. Once they reached the tent they would be staying in, they both immediately undressed to sleep. It was a relief to be able to lay down after days of travelling, and a day of meeting new people. The amount of information was beginning to feel overbearing to Davun, and the thought that he still didn't know everything made him feel worse. He glanced over at Jethro, and you wouldn't be able to tell if the situation was affecting him much at all. He seemed like his normal self, but Davun knew he must be more stressed than he lets on. Once Davun was ready to lay down, he moved his bed over to Jethro's and lay down next him.

"What a day, huh? I wasn't expected to meet so many people. I think the worst bit was having to meet Feyra. Though it does make me want to be way more cautious about possible dangers now, just to avoid having to make another trip to her tent," Davun laughed to himself. Jethro let out a small chuckle before letting out a sigh.

"We did a lot today. Especially what Wayne put us through. When he first started showing us the weapons, I was confused. I didn't know why he was showing us. Does he expect us to…fight?"

"I don't think he expects us to fight alongside him. To be fair, I'd be more afraid of his backswing if I was fighting alongside him. We should learn to defend ourselves I suppose. I don't really know why, but I guess it's a useful thing to know?"

"Yeah. It would be. I just keep thinking about yesterday and how…how I didn't know what to do when you got hit with that arrow. I froze. At first, I didn't know what happened, but…when that passed away, I still didn't move. I didn't know what to do. You fell to the ground bleeding and these creatures were around us but…I didn't do anything. And now that I'm thinking about it, I don't know what I could have done at all."

"You couldn't have done anything Jeth, it's fine. We weren't expecting something like this to happen, we couldn't have known. Don't blame yourself for not knowing how to fight?"

"I know, but…You don't know how to fight either. And you still did something. That day the Lakkerfel attacked us. You jumped in front of me before I even knew it was moving. And…and I couldn't do the same for you."

Davun could hear Jethro holding back tears as he spoke. This had clearly been something that had been bothering him for a while.

"Jeth, I'm glad you didn't do anything. Whenever something like that happens, your priority should be yourself. If I get hurt, that's one thing, but I think I'd feel a lot worse if you were hurt. I'm bigger than you, I'm more likely to get through something like…well I guess like getting hit by an arrow," Davun tried his best to console his brother. He didn't want Jethro feeling like that he should be the one protecting him, that's not how being the little brother worked. He especially didn't want him to recklessly put himself in danger just because his older brother wasn't strong enough. Without being able to see his brother, Davun was unsure if his words were having any effect on his brother. He felt guilty that Jethro felt this way and wasn't sure what else he could say. It was obviously out of Jethro's ability to do anything, neither anticipated being attacked at all, yet he was still putting the burden on himself.

"Jeth. You have to trust me when I say, it's not your fault. It was out of your control. Don't pain yourself over what happened. Besides, if you wanted some courage then maybe learning to defend yourself will help with that. Give it time Jeth, you're still just a kid," Davun wasn't sure if he believed the last part himself. Jethro has gone through a lot for someone of his age. Parents deceased, worked from a young age, seen more fights than a child should have, and now being told he's a part of something as important as world saving. Jethro was getting thrown into the deep end, and Davun knew it was going to build up. He mulled over what to do before gradually falling asleep.

***

The boys woke up to the rustling of armour, clatter of weapons hitting each other, and a man yelling about. Davun began to panic. He hadn't fully woken up yet, and couldn't understand the man shouting, but seeing all the shadows run by his tent was enough to send enough of a shock for his body to react, and he was over at the tent flap before realising he'd even gotten up. He saw everyone in the campsite moving in the same direction. All of them looked to be in a hurry, except for one man who was walking around shouting, stopping at each tent to open the flap. He was young, not much older than Davun. He had a small amount of facial hair that looked to be growing back, short brown hair, but despite how young he looked he was ordering everyone around with certain authority.

"Training time! Training Time! Everyone to the fields!" the young man was yelling, which Davun could hear now that he could focus. He caught Davun looking at him and made his way over.

"You're one of the new guys, right? Well, I'm Nim. I'm the Chief Assistant, which is just a fancy way of saying I run messages and fetch their drinks. Even if it's just a crappy title, it still means I outrank you, so just remember that. Wayne wants everyone over at the field for training, so get at it," he commanded.

"Okay," is all Davun could muster out before Nim moved on to tell others. He was not only stunned at everyone attending the warmups, but the confidence the young man spoke with. At such a young age, he stood with authority and when he spoke, he expected obedience. Davun decided that it would be best to follow his orders and head over to the field. He went to wake Jethro but saw that he had already woken and begun getting dressed. He seemed oddly reserved, not mentioning anything as the two got ready and made their way to the field. Davun wasn't sure what to say, so all he could do was give his brother a one-armed hug as they walked. He wasn't sure if it had helped Jethro, but he didn't shrug the arm off. He decided to just keep an eye on him during training rather than pushing the issue for the moment.

After warmups, they all split into separate groups. Each group was designed for a different training exercise. Wayne put the boys in a group of other inexperienced members. Davun noticed a few others that didn't seem like the fighting type, but then again, neither was he or Jethro. They practiced unarmed defensive manoeuvres, which Wayne explained was essential for everyone to learn. After a while, Wayne had everyone split into further groups to train with different weaponry. Jethro was excused to help with food preparation, while Davun was brought to a group to learn sword and shield. Wayne led the group at first, practicing basic sword techniques without a shield, before moving on to teach a specialised group how to use a greatsword. His replacement was an older gentleman who was obviously a Northerner. He had light brown hair that was turning grey, pale blue eyes, and despite his age he seemed athletic and toned. He carried a shield that was smaller than the one Davun had picked out, but he carried it effortlessly. He took off his circular spectacles and placed them in the pocket of his shirt.

"Right lads and ladies! Put your swords back in the cart," he bellowed out. As expected, he had a thick Northerner accent, and just like Kalavud, he smiled a lot.

"For those that are new, I am Hadik. For this training, we won't need a weapon. When taught correctly, a shield is both for defence and offense. Obviously, it won't kill as easily as a sword, but I'm not teaching you all how to kill. I'm teaching you how to stay alive. You will be taught not only how to use a shield proficiently, but how to use it to disable your attacker by...well, by knocking them out. That simple. Now, there are different types of shields, but for now we'll all learn the same one. If you wish to learn different types, you'll have to find your own time for it I'm afraid. We've got a long way to go and probably a short amount of time, so I can't teach everyone individually. Try to learn quickly so we're all at the same level," he spoke as he spanned across the group, taking in the newcomers. His smile never faded as they all dropped their weapons into the nearby cart and walked back to formation. It truly made Davun feel uncomfortable. He wasn't sure why such an innocent, friendly gesture disturbed him so, it's not like the way they smiled was creepy. It just seemed like there was no real reason to smile, so why did Northerner's do it? Davun tried to distract himself from the thoughts by losing himself in the lesson, which Hadik was apparently going to make it easy as he approached Davun.

"Brought your own shield from home, did you?" Hadik chuckled as he nodded to the shield Davun was holding. Davun looked around and noticed that everyone else's shields weren't as nearly decorated as his. He felt a little humiliated, but he didn't want to give up the shield either.

"It's alright lad. It's a fine shield. Obviously, you trust it, which can be quite difficult for some people," Hadik then raised his voice so that everyone could hear, "An important lesson every shield wielder must learn, is to completely trust your shield. If you do not trust your shield, then your shield will fail you. Your shield is only as strong as your resolve to hold it. For example..." without pause, Hadik spun around to Davun, who instinctively raised his shield. A loud clang sounded as Hadik's sword clashed against Davun's shield. Davun slowly lowered his shield, to see Hadik smiling. He stared at Davun a moment longer, before swinging his sword the person next to him. The person didn't react fast enough, as Hadik's sword swung directly into the lowered shield, causing the person to stagger backwards before falling. Hadik sheathed his weapon, and helped the man to stand, apologising for using him as an example.

"Trust between you and your shield, is a matter of life and death. Your instincts must always be to put this big chunk of metal between you and the other metal that wants to kill you," he looked around for a moment, making sure all had heard. "That's enough talk for now. Let's begin with some basic techniques to get everyone up to speed."

Davun easily lost himself in the training. He immediately became enthused with everything Hadik had to teach. He picked up most of the techniques with ease in the hour that Hadik taught them. There were times where Davun instinctively helped his sparring partner, making small gestures to let the other know where to hold his shield. His partner didn't speak but followed Davun's mute instructions. Once the training came to an end, everyone was placing their shields back in the cart, when Hadik placed a hand on Davun's shield. "Not you, lad. Instructions from Arkarn that you were to keep that if I thought it suited you. You're not great, but you've got some natural instincts with it. With proper training, you could do well. Keep it in good condition. I don't know where he retrieved it from, but it's obvious that he went through efforts to get it. You don't recognise it, do you?" Hadik stared at Davun with curiosity which quickly changed to disappointment as Davun shook his head. "Shame. I was hoping what was special about it. It's good quality and all, design indicates it's from the North," Hadik talked with a low voice, before regaining his composure and smiling. "Well, maybe that's all it is then. A shield. Your shield. Consider it a gift from Arkarn."

Davun was a little reluctant to be the only one taking a shield but accepted it. Hadik gave him a nod and walked off to return the shields and attend to his other duties. Davun strapped the shield to his back and walked back to his tent.

CHAPTER SIX

"My companions who traveled with me are no longer able to provide any of their wisdom. Each has chosen their own path, one that I either cannot follow, or choose not to follow."

In the kitchens, Jethro sulkily chopped vegetables. He thought he had gotten away from this kind of work, but he knew he had to help. He just wished he could help with something else. He continued to idly chop the carrots, pondering his situation and possibilities to work elsewhere. The cooks had stepped out not long ago to talk with one of the messengers to order more supplies, leaving just Jethro and three other kids to do prep work. The others seemed to know each other already, talking as they did work. The oldest, a boy around the age of fifteen, had dark brown hair tied into a tail. He had few hairs on his chin, showing he was starting to go through the transition. He would tease the other two, a girl who was about twelve, and a boy who was around eight, even younger than Jethro.

Jethro wanted to speak with them, but he wasn't sure how. He'd really only spoken to Davun, both in and out of work, and didn't know what to say to them. He'd played with other kids his age sometimes in the village, but taken out of his familiar environment, he was left feeling lost. He snuck looks whenever the kids would laugh, wondering what it was about. The older boy would mock the girl, and the younger boy would join in. They continued no matter how much the girl whined and protested, but she would laugh along with them. She would knock their potatoes off the board, forcing the boys to rewash them every time. Jethro was surprised they didn't appear to be worried about preparing enough food in time. They weren't taking their job seriously, having not done much since the cooks left. Maybe Averly was overly strict with her business than normal. Or the cooks here just didn't care enough, so there was no real punishment for slacking off.

***

The kids were laughing loudly, when suddenly Jethro heard bowls spilling over. He turned to see that one of the kids had knocked over a cart of vegetables, spilling the contents all over the dirt floor of the tent.

"Look what you did, Crella! You made a mess!" the oldest boy exclaimed, though Jeth was pretty sure he was joking.

"It wasn't me! I was over here the whole time! You two knocked it over because you're clumsy, can't stand on your own two feet!" the girl retorted, her voice obviously reflected her annoyance.

"It wasn't me! I was over here the whole time!" the younger boy imitated her, while also mocking her stance and hand gestures.

"Shut up!"

"Alright, c'mon now, let's clean this mess before the chefs come back," the older boy ordered, starting to pick up the potatoes that rolled further away. "I hope I don't fall over though, my feet are really hard to use," he smirked, looking at the girl to see her reaction. Jethro couldn't see her because she was faced the other way, but whatever her expression was amused the two boys as they began laughing. Their laughter kind of lifted his spirits, but he still felt the weight of not being a part of the laughter. As he snuck another look with the corner of his eye, he noticed someone else. He had short, light brown hair kept in a mess. His clothes looked plain and ragged, but most suspiciously was that he was hiding behind another bench, peeking over at the other three kids. He turned to Jethro, and they both stared at each other wide eyed. The crouching character had bright blue eyes, and his face contorted into a smile as he pressed a finger against them to signal Jethro to keep quiet. He beckoned Jethro over, before stealthily running out of the tent without making a sound, the other kids taking no notice. As he ran, Jethro noticed something hiding in the pantleg of the peculiar boy. Curiosity and cautiousness battled inside Jethro, but curiosity ultimately got the better of him as he followed the figure out of the tent. The boy was waiting just outside the doorway so that he wasn't visible to the others inside. He smiled at Jethro, before producing an apple from his pants and taking a bite of it.

"I don't usually get seen when taking a snack. I guess I messed it up this time. Thought you would help them pick up all the vegetables that spilled," he sounded both disappointed and amused. The boy was about Davun's height, and possibly around the same age.

"So, you knocked over the cart?" Jethro asked, trembling a little as he did. He was nervous, both talking to a complete stranger, and wondering what he should do about someone sneaking in to take food, even if it was just an apple. The stranger grew a cheeky grin while nodding.

"Yeah, it's best if I have a distraction. I thought you would head over to your friends to help them, that's what the others usually do. Oh well, my mistake. I should be more careful next time. Assuming, there will be a next time?" he leaned closer to Jethro while his voice lowered. "You won't tell anyone will you? No harm in taking a small snack, right?"

Jethro froze for a small moment. Jethro wasn't certain if the boy was doing it on purpose, but Jethro felt a little intimidated. He felt he couldn't protest even if he wanted to, so he simply shrugged and went along with whatever this boy wanted. The shrug seemed to please the boy as he smiled and ruffled Jethro's hair.

"Excellent! I'm Delavun by the way. Hopefully you'll be seeing more -and sometimes less- of me. I like you, though you're a bit quiet. Sometimes quiet is good though," Delavun was trying to reassure Jethro, and it did help a bit.

"I'm Jethro," he managed to squeeze out before laughter from inside caught his attention. "I should go back to work before they notice I'm gone."

Delavun looked at him, puzzled. "Surely, they should have noticed by now, just make sure you have a good lie when they ask. Maybe something like…you saw a pretty bird, or…even better! You went to find the chefs to tell on them for slacking. That should scare them into not asking any more questions!" Delavun got excited at his idea, obviously proud of the thought. Jethro wasn't too comfortable in lying but wasn't quite sure what to tell them, so he didn't have to confess he saw someone taking fruit. Delavun looked inside the tent and watched for a moment. After a moment, he pat Jethro on the shoulder and gestured inside. "Now would be the best time, they're just about finished with picking up the mess. Good meeting you, friend" he smiled before dashing off, disappearing into the crowd of people going about their business. Jethro turned and walked inside the tent. The others were washing the fallen vegetables in a nearby basin and preparing their bench to continue working. Jethro noticed their smiles had gone and they were no longer joking around. It's as if something had happened while he was gone, their attitudes had completely changed.

Maybe they had an argument? No, I would have heard it. I was only gone for a moment, and they were still laughing. I wonder what got into them.

The three other workers remained oddly quiet. Jethro had only been working with them for a couple of hours, but they seemed different when they weren't talking. To his relief however, they didn't ask him about his absence. Whether or not they didn't notice, or just didn't care, Jethro didn't know. The four of them continued to prepare food until the cooks came back and began showing the kids how to make the stew that they would serve everyone in camp that day. Jethro took interest in learning it but wondered about some choices they made or didn't make. They were using spices Jethro wasn't accustomed to, so the process was just different for him. In the end, the stew was nice, and everyone seemed to enjoy it. At least, it seemed that way to Jethro. No one complained, but no one really complimented the cooking either. They said their thanks and separated into groups to chat, not exactly the response Jethro had expected. He pondered on if the stew just wasn't that good, or if there was something wrong amongst the people. He'd only been here for a day, but he imagined the camp being higher in spirits.

When he saw the amount of people that had joined for a common goal, he had imagined everyone working together, talking, laughing, and most importantly, a well-run camp. He anticipated everything being organised, but he can't quite figure out which tents were for sleeping or which tents were for cooking, medicine, or even storage. It appears that you must ask others for directions if you want to find anything. It seemed disorganised to him, but maybe this was a planned layout that he just couldn't figure. He was still new here, so maybe it was still his inexperience that made no sense of the layout. The cooks didn't wait for everyone to be served before they began eating. They dished themselves a bowl and sat down to talk with their respective friends.

Davun waited for Jethro to return from his training before eating. The stew wasn't what he expected. It didn't have a bad taste at all, it was just different to him. He ate slowly, debating on telling Davun about the odd boy he had caught sneaking an apple from the kitchens. He had promised the boy not to tell anyone, but he didn't feel comfortable not telling Davun something. They had rarely kept any secrets from each other. Ultimately, Jethro decided it wasn't worth telling, as he'd probably not see the boy again, however if he did happen to catch the hungry thief again, he would inform Davun about him. He would have to tell someone, it wasn't right to keep taking stuff from the kitchens, but he didn't want the boy to get into any serious troubles just because he was hungry.

Jethro noticed that Davun was also rather quiet during their meal but put it down to being tired from the extra training he had gone through, although he was becoming increasingly curious about the shield Davun had strapped to his back when he arrived. It was now placed against the log they sat on, and Jethro stared at the design of it, recognising it as the shield Wayne and Kalavud had shown them previously. He finished his food first and resisted the urge to blurt out the question that was on his mind but managed to hold it in until Davun placed his bowl down.

"Dav, why do you have that shield?"

Davun looked at the shield, then at his little brother and shrugged. "I'm not sure myself. Everyone seems to think I should have it, but I don't know why. This one was the only one of its design, and they pretty much handed it to me. The only one who seems to know about it is Arkarn, but I haven't seen him to ask him about it yet."

Jethro noticed his brother looked at the shield warmly. Despite not knowing about the shield, or even having held one before to his knowledge, even Jethro could tell his brother was attached to the newly attained item.

"What is the symbol for? Does it mean anything?"

"I also have no idea. No one explained it to me. I'm not sure if they even know themselves, honestly. Arkarn is the one who organised it, and he apparently hasn't told anyone why."

"So, you only got a shield? No sword, or anything else? I wanted to hold one again" Jethro looked around the shield to see if there was a sword that he hadn't noticed Davun place down. To his disappointment, Davun nodded.

"Yeah, just the shield. Apparently, it's better for me than a sword. I suppose I'm less likely to be shot by an arrow when I'm holding a shield and not a sword," Davun chuckled, instinctively rubbing his wound. It had become tender from the training, but ultimately didn't impact him much during the exercises. It did flare in pain when he moved in a particular way at times, but whatever Feyra had applied was working wonders. He had been injured before, remembering the bite he received from the Lakkerfel, but the arrow wound seemed like a papercut in comparison thanks to the salve. Jethro put on a small smile, not wanting to recall the memory of the blood pouring from his brothers wound that day. He never liked seeing Davun bleed, obviously, but since the rabid Lakkerfel bite he took that his brother received while protecting him, he knew that Davun would do it again for his sake. Jethro didn't know what lay ahead, but the fact they were both being taught self-defence tactics indicated that they would be seeing more trouble. Though he didn't know how these tactics would help avoid arrows. At least Davun had a shield that could protect him, but Jethro had been given nothing.

Maybe they don't plan on taking me. Maybe I'll be taken back to the town. Back to Averly. Without Davun.

They wouldn't separate us…would they?

The thought scared Jethro. He had always been with Davun. They did everything together, as far back as he could remember. Their parents had died shortly after his birth, and with no living family members they knew of, they had only each other.

And now that things were changing, now that they were on an unexpected and nearly unbelievable path, they may not be together much longer.

No, they wouldn't. Why else would they teach me to defend myself? I must be going with them. I'll refuse if they try to leave me behind or take me back.

Jethro began breathing heavily. He was panicking at the thought of having to be distanced from Davun. Davun was still waiting on a response from Jethro and noticed his brother's expression change. Jethro's eyes widened a little, and his breathing was noticeably louder.

"Jeth, it's okay. I was only kidding. Well, sort of. A shield is better than a sword when…sorry, I shouldn't have brought it up. I'll be fine, I promise," he tried to reassure his brother. He wasn't certain why Jethro's demeanour changed. He could only guess it was related to his arrow wound that had shocked the both of them.

Neither of them could have foreseen such an event happening, especially so soon after leaving home. What turned into a small trip away from home had quickly turned into something unexpectedly dangerous, and from the sound of it, it would only get progressively more so. Davun did his best to try change Jethro's thoughts to something more pleasant, so the brothers spent the rest of the meal break talking about the possible changes Averly was making in their absence.

CHAPTER SEVEN

"How much damage will the truth do to the common folk? Perhaps it is better to believe a lie, to keep the peace. Now, more than ever, I wish I had my friends by my side. The questions continue to toil within me."

The captain turned out to be a woman called Demoria. She wasn't particularly tall, standing around average height for a woman, but that didn't stop her from intimidating most people around her. She stood with an air of authority and purpose, her dark brown eyes demanding focus. Her black hair was kept short at the top that it barely reached halfway down her shaven sides. She was wearing mismatching armour, the top half being bronze, bearing what appeared to be an emblem but it had been painted over with a symbol of three hands clasping an arm to form a triangle. Her hands were plated in black gauntlets, whereas her legs were equipped with scratched, grey iron. When she spoke, it was loud and dominating, as if to make sure everyone within earshot knew she was talking and not to interrupt her. When Wayne introduced the boys to her, she seemed unimpressed. She eyed them both, looking them over, before dismissively throwing out a greeting and turning back to the table that people were seated around. Arkarn, Wayne, and Kalavud were the only ones the boys knew who were participating in the meeting. Four others sat around, excluding the captain.

"And this is our Commander, Barith" Wayne gestured towards an older man, who gave a small nod in return. He had short grey hair, neatly brushed to look presentable. His matching steel armour was neatly polished, which also proudly bore the painted symbol over a different emblem. "He's in charge of our troops. Organises their training and leads them on a battlefield. Next to him we have our Quartermaster, Serena," Wayne moved onto the girl sitting next to Barith. She had red hair, and glasses that covered bright green eyes. Her skin was a little pale, and she appeared to be a little gaunt as the definition of her skull was obvious. She politely smiled and waved as she was introduced.

"Next, we have our Scout Master, Tervu," Wayne directed their attention to across the table, where a man with green-yellow eyes sat. He had a dark green bandana that covered the top of his head, and his clothes clung tightly to his body revealing a slim and athletic frame. His face was clean shaven, showing various small scars on his otherwise clean skin.

"And lastly, we have the Doctor," Wayne introduced the last man with a grin on his face. The man was grinning until he had been introduced, where he adopted a more embarrassed expression.

"I've asked you not to call me that. What if Feyra heard me? I don't want to have to deal with that. I keep telling you all I'm not a doctor," he spoke calmly, his voice revealing no signs of aggression or demands. He looked to be in his thirties, brown hair tied behind his back that fell down to just below his shoulders. His glasses had slipped slightly down his nose, and his light brown eyes felt soft and caring. "My name is Thedan. It's lovely to meet you both."

"We've told you, your name is Doctor. When will you learn, honestly?" Kalavud teased. The man just smiled, not troubling himself to argue.

"He's called that because after talking to him, you feel better," Wayne continued, smiling along with Kalavud.

"I oversee the people here in our resistance. I oversee recruiting and settling any differences between our members. I also try to help wherever I can. Please call me Thedan. Though if you insist on calling me Doctor like the others, please do not call me that in front of Feyra. She is the head of our medics and would really be upset if she thought I was as qualified as she was," Doctor continued, choosing not to respond to Kalavud's bait.

"It's nice to meet you all," Davun spoke to everyone at the table. Demoria had finished rummaging and organising her papers, so she cleared her throat to grab the attention.

"We can continue the pleasantries after. Take a seat so we can get on with this meeting," she ordered, clearly not allowing anyone to debate. Jethro and Davun sat next to Kalavud, while Wayne took the open spot next to Arkarn on the other side of the table. As the boys sat, that could see the papers Demoria had been moving around. They were various maps and letters that appeared to be reports of some kind. She grabbed a pile next to her and began spreading them across the other papers.

"These are the reports from the scouts about the surrounding area. None of them mention any Ratling sightings, or anything out of the ordinary. The ambush on Arkarn's group on returning to the camp had not been detected. If the Ratlings appeared after our scouts' patrol, it means they knew exactly when they would leave, and when Arkarn's group would be returning. If this is the case, it may finally be proof we have a spy amidst us. The other possibilities are the Ratlings are even better than we thought at hiding themselves, Tervu's Scouts aren't worth the food they eat, or they just got lucky. Whichever way, the enemy seems to know what Arkarn's is up to. Which, I hope that Arkarn will now level the field with. Tell us how these two boys are going to help us win this thing. Do not leave us in the dark any longer. I have let you do as you wish since you convinced me to start this, now you owe us all an explanation," she scowled towards Arkarn, clearly unhappy.

It seemed there was some tension between the two, which made Jethro feel a little uneasy. He felt like he could tell how much annoyance and frustration Demoria had towards Arkarn.

Davun, on the other hand, became a little annoyed that Arkarn wasn't revealing everything, even to the people he was supposedly working with to overcome an enemy that Davun was still unsure about. He figured everyone here knew what was going on, and they had a well thought out plan they were putting into action, but it seems that not even the Captain of this resistance was aware of everything she needed to be. Arkarn sat silent for a moment, before rising from his chair and placing his staff against the table.

"Firstly, I am sorry about keeping particular things from all of you. I had reasons that ultimately led me to believe it was better if I kept it quiet until the young boys arrived here safely and were at least willing to hear us out. Now that that is the case, I can tell you all what the plan from here on out is," he looked around the table to make sure he had everyone's attention.

"Second, I know who is organising the Ratlings. He has most likely manipulated them with promises of food, they're simply creatures. The man we are looking for is Artruis Valitirian. I don't know his exact reasoning, but his plan revolves around the Balkyeros Egg, otherwise known as the orb of the Phoenix," Arkarn took a moment to pause to let everyone process the information. The boys were vastly confused, not having heard of Balkyeros or even the orb that was mentioned. They had heard stories and legends about the Phoenix from travellers at the inn from time to time. The Phoenix was said to be a bird of flames, that would appear to save innocents in their time of dire need. That's all it was, however, just a story. No one who told these stories claimed to see it personally, or at least they weren't very believable when they claimed to have. Davun looked around the table to see if others were as confused as he was. Expectedly, Jethro looked at Davun hoping for an answer, but Davun just shrugged. Wayne and Kalavud looked thoughtful, and Barith didn't seem surprised at all. Tervu, Doctor, and Serena all looked a little shocked to hear such a thing, which only confused Davun further. Captain Demoria, on the other hand, didn't change her expression at all. She stood, waiting for Arkarn to continue explaining. Arkarn's gaze shifted to the boys and seemed to understand their confusion.

"For those who do not know, I will explain. There are powers that exist in this world that many think are legends. These powers have been sighted throughout time, and due to exaggerations and mistaking what they've seen, most are thought to be creatures. However, they are real, and they are no creature. Humans hold them. Humans who have their own intentions. Some have used them to gain a position of power. Some seek them out to gain the strength they need to dominate. These powers can be terrifying, but even more frightening is what the human who holds it in their hand can choose to do with it," his face began grim, as if recalling a horrifying memory. Davun could only wonder what Arkarn may have seen, if what he was saying was true. Arkarn looked up and continued his explanation.

"Balkyeros is the title given to the holder of a particular power. The power is the ability to create fire, and with enough skill, achieve flight. Only one person may possess this power at a time, and the power passes on when the holder dies. People have seen multiple Balkyeros many times before, and through their stories a legend was created. The Phoenix. The wings they sprout to achieve flight are pure flame, so people have mistaken them for a bird on fire. When the holder dies, the power is transferred into an orb, where it remains until the rightful heir makes contact with it. It contains a self-defence mechanism to punish those who try to claim it for themselves. A person who touches the orb, and is not the rightful heir to its power, is stricken with pain. In most cases, it has resulted in death. Artruis does, and doesn't, hold this power. He struck down the previous holder a few years ago, Darian Ferdin. With Darian's death, his powers transformed into the orb, and now await their next owner, the rightful heir that Darian had chosen. Artruis is unable to access the power without the heir, so he seeks that person out. Unfortunately, I believe he has discovered who that person is, and that is why an ambush was laid for us on our journey back. His goal, the heir, and the answer to our predicament, is you, Davun. You have been chosen as the next

Balkyeros," his eyes locked onto Davun, trying to look as calm as possible to ease the effect of what he said on Davun.

That didn't stop Davun from feeling the immense pressure suddenly placed upon him. He hadn't ever considered that it was possible for someone to possess anything beyond human capabilities, and now he is told that his father – a man he couldn't even remember – had left him a power that had gotten himself killed.

Why would he have done this?

If he really was around until Jethro was born, then he would have known how old I am. Why would he leave something so dangerous to me?

This doesn't make any sense. I can't do this. This is for someone else, stronger than me, more prepared than me, like Wayne or Kalavud. I can't do this. I can't d-

Davun felt small arms wrap around him. He looked down to find Jethro had embraced him. He suddenly became aware of the fact that he was breathing heavily and sweat had begun pushing itself to the surface of his forehead. All eyes were on him, some showing concern, others stared as if judging his response to the news, but it was Arkarn's expression that stood out most to Davun.

It looked like regret.

Davun locked eyes with Arkarn for a short moment, before Arkarn registered the situation and shuffled a little where he stood to regain composure. Arkarn took a deep breath and spoke out. "I know it's a lot to take in right now, but he fact of the matter is the situation we are in requires your complete cooperation and understanding. I am sorry to be the one to tell you about the reality of your position, it's a lot to bare. We'll give you a little time to process everything, but please be aware that we are here to help. Don't hold onto your thoughts to the point you begin spiralling down, you'll cause yourself a great deal of stress. Speak to us. We can and will help you, Davun," Arkarn spoke with sincerity. Davun knew that Arkarn meant what he said and would be the first person to try and help, but that did little to comfort him as reality began to seem distant. He began to feel a little numb, the only feeling left was his brother's arms around his waist. He needed to leave the tent, the eyes on him expecting a response felt like walls surrounding him, suddenly making him feel claustrophobic.

"I need to go to my tent," Davun announced, abruptly standing up and walking out without looking back, though he still knew Jethro had followed him. He hurriedly walked to his tent, ignoring the looks he received and the occasional greetings. His only focus right now was to reach his tent. Jethro rushed after his brother, weaving between the busy people going about their own business. He ran past several people trying to introduce themselves, including Delavun who was trying to start conversation, but he didn't look back when few called out to him, worried that something may be wrong.

Davun began to stumble a little as he stepped. His vision blurred, and the noises began merging into one fading amalgamation of sounds.

Pain shot through his right arm. Before he could even grip his arm in pain, the pain won the internal battle, knocking Davun unconscious.

***

When Davun woke, he found he was alone, laying in what seemed to be the medical tent. It was dark, with only small flames from the night patrols flickering between the cracks of the tent door as it wavered slightly in the wind. He was a little sore, but mostly he felt relieved that no one was around. He could fix his muddled thoughts and take his time without anyone bothering him or silently demanding an answer. The night soothed him a little, reminding him of his view of the moon shining bright enough to show the full view of the mountain he would stare longingly at. Davun struggled coming to terms that what Arkarn said was true. He was still a stranger to this operation that seemed to be going on long before he arrived. How was he supposed to believe that all this was just waiting for him to arrive? Why would Arkarn not have come to him in the beginning if the situation was as bad as he made it seem?

The questions continued to pile on the longer he thought about it. He was still uncertain if he trusted in Arkarn's story enough to even believe if it was real. There was still so much he needed to know before he could put his mind towards it, and possibly risk his life. The power of fire did seem tempting, but baffling that one could control such a thing. His curiosity was getting the better of him, slowly waning his decision.

I wonder what it would be like to control fire...It would come in handy. Maybe I don't have to return back to Eraton if I had such power. I could travel more, maybe help people who need it, and...

And be hunted down for the rest of my life for the power. If the previous holder was killed for it, then people will come after the next person who holds it and will only continue doing so until they get it. This isn't safe for me. Or for Jethro.

As if his thoughts were being read, Arkarn entered the medical tent to see Davun already gazing at him. It was still dark out, but Davun could see the surprised expression Arkarn had upon seeing him.

"I thought you would still be asleep. I only came to check if you were alright. I shall leave. I don't wish to cause you any more stress than I already have," Arkarn spoke softly, a slight hint of regret in his voice.

"Then stay and answer some questions I have," Davun replied as Arkarn turned to leave. Arkarn paused, before facing Davun and silently nodded. He walked over to Davun's bed, pulling a nearby small table that held a candle closer.

"Let me just light his candle for some sight. Though I can't seem to find the sparker," Arkarn continued speaking quietly. Davun wasn't sure if it was due to other patients possibly resting, or that Arkarn was about to answer some questions he may not want to. As Davun shifted in his bed to sit up, Arkarn had apparently found the sparker as light emitted brightly in the darkness, showing the pair as they sat on the bed.

"What is it you wish to know?" Arkarn waited patiently as Davun shifted through many questions to decide where to start.

"If what you say is real, why now? Surely you have been working against this man for a while, so why only retrieve me now instead of ages ago where I could have been training for it?" Davun blurted out, almost forgetting to lower his voice in case there were indeed other patients, but he couldn't see any within the glow of the small candle. Arkarn took a deep breath before responding.

"It is true, I have been working hard for a long time, longer than you may expect, against Artruis. Everything I have said is very real. I did want to send for you earlier, but two things were stopping me. The first being this resistance army. I needed to be here to help build it up and get everything in running order. I joined them early into their development, and it isn't easy trying to operate a small army without seeming like a threat to any of the kingdoms. The second was your age. Both of your ages, rather. I was worried that if I sent for you while you were too young that it would only scare you, and I wanted to avoid any notion to Artruis that you were here, as he will come after you when he discovers it. His Ratlings may not be the greatest of spies as they stand out pretty well, but they do see, and he does have others working for him. It is very real someone, or possibly several people, work for Artruis within our camp. You must also be careful with who you speak to here. I wish I could guarantee that no one would betray you, but there is no such guarantee for something like that."

Arkarn didn't rush his response. He took his time with each sentence as if heavily deciding each word. Davun listened, paying attention and trying to understand Arkarn's position, when something Arkarn said stood out to him.

"You said both of our ages. Why did you need to drag Jethro into this?"

The question looked as if it had stabbed Arkarn, hitting a nerve that he wished remained untouched.

"Jethro will play a bigger role than you may think. Being the older brother and the sole caretaker for him, I thought it would be best if he were here, with you, in our camp and under our protection. If he were left at the village, you would have been worried about his wellbeing. When Artruis reveals that you have a little brother, he will definitely attempt to use him to manipulate you. He will try to take Jethro as leverage and bring harm to him to wound where it would hurt most. It is best if he remains in your sight, and with people you can trust."

The last word sounded bitter to Davun. He had rarely trusted people with such a task. He had left Jethro in Averly's care before when he needed to rest from being sick, or running an errand for her, and his brother's wellbeing was always on the back of his mind. It was something he couldn't shake off. He was the caretaker for his brother ever since their parents died and he will always be so. It's not a responsibility he could easily share with someone else. He shifted a little where he sat, before turning to face Arkarn again.

"How do you know I am the heir of this supposed power? I never knew my father, even if he was around before Jethro was born. I have no idea what he even looks like, so why would he leave something so valuable and so much responsibility to me?" the words tasted bitter as he asked. He may not have known his parents. The feeling he was getting was that at least his father had still been alive for a while after Jethro's birth. Arkarn seemed to be internally debating with himself about how to respond. Davun considered if he was trying to think of a good enough lie to avoid answering truthfully, so he perked up a little to see any changes in Arkarns' posture in an attempt to catch him in a lie.

"I knew Balkyeros," Arkarn responded slowly. The news shouldn't have surprised Davun as much as it did, but what had caused his mind to run was that Arkarn had knew his father. Or at least claimed to have known him. The man sitting before him could answer so much more than Davun originally expected. It seemed like Arkarn held all knowledge that Davun wanted to know so badly. He wanted to know how his parents died. He never believed in the answers anyone in the village would give on the few occasions they actually answered. They never wanted to discuss it, always trying to end the conversation as quickly as comfortable. It had always made them appear uncomfortable and Davun didn't know why.

Maybe now he knew.

Maybe they tried to hide that his father had such power and tried to hide his and Jethro's relation to the man for their safety. If that were the case, it had worked. No one ever came looking for them.

No one.

No other family members had come for them either. Maybe it was all to protect them.

Or maybe it was because there was no one else.

If his father had really been murdered for his power, maybe other living family members were also targeted. Any connection to Balkyeros would be dangerous, and once the enemy becomes aware of his existence, Davun would be in the same trouble. Trouble that gets people killed.

And people they were connected to.

Arkarn sat in silence, waiting for another question. When one didn't come, he decided to continue talking.

"I knew him many years ago. Before the two of you were born. I was an adult who was indecisive and unguided. Despite being the same age, Balkyeros was the opposite. He knew where he was headed, he chose his own path and accepted any consequences with a calmness and wisdom I still haven't seen in one so young. He became my mentor in life. He brought me out of the maze I placed myself in and showed me the world. He told me always think about my decisions carefully, considering every possibility, and most importantly, don't live in the regret that may come with them. Move on. Assess the situation you are in and make what you consider to be the best decision," Arkarn talked fondly of Davun's father. Memories were brought to the surface of Arkarn's mind that he hadn't recalled in a long time. He reminisced in them for a moment longer, before realising that Davun still remained silent.

How many of our family died for this secret?

Scenarios raced through Davun's mind. He became aware of the size of the impact his decisions would have to himself and his brother.

I can't let anything happen to him.

"Balkyeros knew what he was doing when he chose to pass his power to you. I know it isn't worth much to you in saying this, but trust in his plans. He was not a man who carelessly place a burden on someone who he didn't think could handle it, or a power that he thought didn't deserve it. He knew he was going to die. It was inevitable for him. He couldn't stop Artruis, but we can. We need to retrieve the orb from him. We can't let him achieve his goal," Arkarn continued talking softly, attempting to reassure Davun that the right decision was to let the resistance help him to recover the orb.

"What are his plans? Power? World domination? Or he just really wants to be a flaming bird?" Davun blurted, not wanting to make light of the situation but the frustration was really digging into him and he lost his patience for a moment. Arkarn didn't face Davun, instead choosing to stare at the floor.

"He is after its power, that is true. It's what he wishes to use that power for I am unsure of. He isn't a man that would gain power for the sake of power. He has a purpose. He is driven towards something and nothing will stand in his way. He's a powerful, cunning, and manipulative man. To him, nothing is too dire or impossible if it means he gets what he wants. No matter what happens, Davun, you must absolutely not deal with him alone. There is more yet that I have to tell, but it is something for everyone to hear, and right now you need some more rest. I can't have Feyra coming after me for keeping you awake after you fainted from the stress earlier," Arkarn chuckled a little at the end, trying to lighten the mood. It didn't seem to have much effect as Davun clearly expressed disappointment in his face. Arkarn stayed a moment longer to see if Davun had anything left to say but sitting in awkward silence he decided to tell Davun to get some rest and blew out the candle. Arkarn anticipated Davun calling out in the darkness to pry for more answers, but as he slowly left the tent it remained as quiet as when he had entered. As he departed, he noticed Demoria standing just to the side of the doorway.

"You sure move around quietly for someone who wears nothing but clinking metal all the time" Arkarn commented, not turning to face her knowing full well what her face would show. It was always the same when she looked at him.

Suspicion. Judgemental. Uncertain.

"I suspected you would be having a little chat with him. It's nice to know you trust him with information that you can't entrust to your captain. I suppose she wouldn't mind you holding back that kind of important information though" she spoke, clear irritation in her voice cutting into Arkarn. The guilt of hiding sensitive information from her was brought back to the surface, something he constantly tried to suppress when he saw her.

"There is much I still haven't told him that you know, so no need to be jealous" he tried lightening the situation with small humour, but to no avail as Demoria's tone didn't change.
"It's good to know that my advisor is playing his own game in amidst our dire fight for survival using the very information he is meant to be providing," she stepped up to Arkarn as she spoke, she stood with a straight back, head lifted slightly to meet his gaze with a stern scowl. "I don't know what your goal is, stranger, but I hope you tell us all before it's too late for anyone. Now is not the time for secrets, but you already know that, don't you?" she stormed off without waiting for a response, emphasising her anger at Arkarn. He hated when she referred to him as a stranger. She used it when she wanted to drive home how Arkarn treated her, despite everything they had built and accomplished. He could only imagine the stress he was piling on top of her already existing mountain of burdens, but there were some things that she mustn't know yet.

Or ever, if possible.

Davun approached the next day with determination. He had spent most of the night contemplating the situation and ultimately came to a decision. He had a goal set before him, a path he thought was best for both he and his brother. First, he had to continue his unfinished conversation with Arkarn. There was still more that had to be explained, and some other things that were bugging Davun after the information Arkarn revealed in the night. After getting the all clear from Feyra, Davun sought out Jethro and the pair continued their daily training routine with the other members of the camp. Wayne was a little hesitant at first to let Davun train, but after insisting that he was fine, Davun was allowed to stay. The training began getting easier to get through, beginning to keep up to pace with the other students. However, that didn't stop them from feeling sore after, their bodies may be used to hard labour, but not rigorous daily training. When the boys settled down to eat the midday meal prepared for the camp, they were interrupted by someone clearing their throat behind them. They turned to see Nim, looking impatient.

"Captain wants you two in her tent now. A meeting has been called," he relayed the message, turning to hurry off elsewhere. Having not waited for a response from them, Davun evaluated that the matter couldn't wait for them to eat, so the boys carried their bowls to the captains' tent. They discovered they were the last to arrive as everyone else was already seated – except for Demoria of course. She stood at the table in her usual authoritative stance, impatiently waiting for the boys to sit as she tapped her fingers on her crossed arms. Without a word, they took the seats next to Kalavud.

"Now that we're all here, let's go over some stuff that *some* of us missed last night," she pointedly looked at Davun who looked back sheepishly. "The scouts reported no signs of enemy troops within ten miles of our encampment. In saying that, now that we've retrieved what we travelled here for, it is time we pack up and get moving towards our next step. We'll travel at a slow pace, allowing time for our soldiers to continue their training and not be put through a lengthened, strenuous march at the same time. The enemy is on the move, we have to track down the location of their main operations. That is where Artruis will be and where we will strike. We will first head North. Our long-distance scouts returned with a report this morning, another village was attacked. We will

pick up the survivors and continue advancing North-East."
Demoria continued, speaking each word matter-of-factly, but that
didn't stop Barith from cutting in.

"Our troops are not ready for a large-scale attack, especially if
we keep picking up new stragglers. They won't have time to train
before we throw them to the rats. They'll only die, slowing a
single soldier each at best. If we truly wish to utilise more soldiers
then we need to give them time to become soldiers," his voice was
stern, but still held an air of respect that one does when speaking
to their superior. Demoria turned to Barith, expression not
changing.

"They'll become soldiers as soon as we give them a weapon.
The survivors willing to fight are not weak. Their spirit will carry
them as far as they can in the battlefield. They may not make it far,
or slay any of the rats, but we cannot let the enemy continue
growing in number, nor can we deny any of the survivors'
vengeance if they wish it. We promise them that much when they
choose to join us," Demoria retorted. Barith was obviously
displeased with the answer, opening his mouth to argue back
before Arkarn cut in.

"Though I agree with Barith that giving a peasant a sword and
throwing them to the pits doesn't make them a soldier, I'm afraid
we do not have much of a choice in the matter. The more recruits
we receive, the further training will be extended, and the further
damage the enemy will do, which will only create more potential
recruits. It is a cycle we need to break if we wish to progress," he
tried to reason, though Barith still held a frown. The old soldier bit
his tongue on the matter, allowing Demoria to continue with the
next matter.

"As usual, Tervu will have his scouts run ahead and make sure
the way is clear. Thedan, you need to do another political run on
our behalf. The direction we are heading will take us closer to the
Kingdom of Vanguinar. You need to speak to the crown and try to
convince them that our matter exists. I am hoping that the
combination of being a small Kingdom and villages being attacked
near their border will help to convince him, but…" Demoria

sighed, and her face relaxed for a moment, showing both fatigue and sympathy, "I know we've had no luck in receiving assistance. I do know that this tarnishes your reputation, spouting about 'nonsense that doesn't exist', but we can't give up now. Even if a portion of anyone's army were to aid us, then we can stop this invisible army and reveal it to the world. Do what you can, Thedan. We won't blame you if the outcome isn't in our favour."

This was the first time Demoria's demeanour changed in front of Davun, and it happened so suddenly he was caught off guard a little. Thedan looked at Demoria and smiled. "I know the strain of not being believed is causing us all headaches, but I will do my best, of course. King Tarveyin is an incredibly selfish king, but I believe he may be able to be persuaded if we promised him the right things, thought it will be highly unlikely we can offer them." he made sure to lock eyes with Demoria, somehow reversing their roles and demanding her attention.

"Even if I am unsuccessful, Captain, our situation will be no different. We have ventured this far without any aid from outside sources, we can still go further. We will achieve what we must without anyone else if we must. We have no other choice." He spoke sincerely, raising his voice just a bit to emphasize his words. Demoria stared for a moment, before returning to her usual expression and nodding to him.

"Grab your usual guard and horses and set off when you can. We will camp West of the Glistening Meadows, hiding in the forest that covers the borders of the two kingdoms. Good luck, Doctor." Demoria stood proudly as she gave the order. Thedan stood and nodded to her, smirking a little as he left the tent to begin preparations for his journey. Davun was uncertain if Demoria referred to him as the Doctor out of respect, or humour. He found it hard to believe it would be the latter. His deciphering was interrupted as Demoria cleared her throat. "The rest of us, give out the orders to pack camp. You all know your sectors to cover, we'll set out after morning training tomorrow."

Everyone nodded in return, except for Barith who stood and saluted. They all set out of the tent with their orders, each turning a different direction and began yelling instructions. The camp turned from a leisurely hangout into a frantic mess as people began to try and follow what was being yelled. It now occurred to Davun that this camp was not filled with properly trained soldiers, but rather a disorganised, inexperienced group of ordinary people. The reality of the situation broke through the illusions he gave himself about the camp. He now realised how many women and children were around, not the usual sort you would expect to see in an army. Most of them didn't look like the fighting sort, showing not much muscle or athleticism, and revealing a lack of discipline. Now that the smoke was out of his eyes, he could see what was causing it.

CHAPTER EIGHT

"Even though we've kept the truth a secret for now, we continued to delve deeper into its mysteries. Each story we follow reveals two more."

Everyone in the camp, no matter how small or confused they might be, were putting in all of their effort. They were doing their best to try and follow the orders being shouted and organise themselves. No matter where he looked, he saw people trying to complete something that was abnormal to them, outside of tasks they were used to. The more experienced members were training the newer recruits who seemed to be struggling with tasks that would be instinctive for a well-trained soldier. A group of people were struggling how to take down a tent properly, stepping over each other to try complete what they each individually thought was the next step, only confusing one another further. Another group he could see were struggling with crates, unable to find the right tents they had been instructed to clear out and attempting to sort out the mess.

He even noticed a group of men and women rounding up the children to keep them occupied so they wouldn't hinder the rest of the camp. Everyone had roles, and whether they knew what role that specifically was or not, they still tried their best to work together to get the job done. This was just a group of ordinary people trying to better themselves in ways they hadn't planned on purely out of necessity. That's when a few things mentioned in the meeting struck Davun. He shifted through the busy encampment, weaving between people as they walked by and doing his best not to slow anyone down, making his way to Wayne. He found the muscle of a man continuing his orders at the edge of the campsite.

"Wayne, I need to ask something," Davun shouted, trying to get his attention over the growing communications of the people heeding the orders. Wayne took notice and looked down at Davun, the commanding face melted into a smile as he awaited the question.

"No one here is a real soldier, are they?" the words became a struggle to release as his lips quavered. He already knew the response, but he still dreaded having to hear it. Wayne's smile didn't change as he stared at the people bustling about.

"Right now, they are all soldiers. But that isn't the answer you are looking for, is it?" he looked back down at Davun. "Some are former soldiers. The rest are survivors. Their homes destroyed by Artruis. Fortunately, quite a few survive his attacks, but not all of them join us. Everyone here has lost something. Their life savings. Their homes. Their family. Their friends."

Wayne looked down, the smile nearly faded as his eyes reflected an unspoken thought.

"We promise them vengeance. We offer them a weapon and call them a soldier. We train them as best we can before letting them willingly run into battle completely unprepared," he looked back at Davun, expression unchanged, "but that is completely their choice. We merely offer the opportunity and a means. It is entirely their decision if they wish to join us or not, and when they do, they are free to leave at any time. We do not force anything upon them that they do not want. This entire little scrambled army of people we have are desperate to not let this man continue destroying others' lives as he has done to them. You would be surprised by what someone who holds such a thing in their heart can do on the battlefield."

The words struck Davun. He had thought this was an army of soldiers, perhaps belonging to a few lords as a means to protect their lands, not as a band of people who lost everything that meant something to them. Normal civilians. He felt his body break into a cold sweat, thoughts continuing to scramble to piece together this reality he was dragged into.

As if knowing how to break Davun out of the trance, a horn sounded. Everyone froze in their tracks as they waited, staring in the direction the horn sounded from. Not a moment later, a second horn blew, and the camp was thrown into chaos. Wayne immediately began trying to regain some order as the nearby group of children were being escorted in a frantic push. Davun shouted, trying to demand an answer about the situation but he wasn't stupid. Despite never have heard it before he knew what the horn meant.

An attack was coming.

He attempted to get information from Wayne who was trying to command a group of people to throw on what minimal armour they could and head to the front lines but was unable to grab any details before feeling like he was in the way. He decided to hurry back towards the captains' tent to find Jethro. He knocked into a few people who were trying to strap helmets and weapons to their bodies while making a run towards the front of the camp. He managed to stumble his way to the tent, barging in to find Doctor and Serena scrambling the remains of the papers left from the meeting. Thedan looked surprised to see Davun but decided to take advantage of the situation.

"Davun! Good, we need your help, please! Take these papers, we need to move them, so they don't get taken!" he rushed over with the scrolled papers in a bunch and shoved them into Davun's arms.

"I can't, I need to find Jethro," Davun tried to argue, but Thedan wasn't taking no for an answer.

"I'm sorry Davun, your brother is fine, I am sure, but we need the help. The sooner we get Serena to the safety box the sooner you can look for your brother," he retorted. Davun opened his mouth to try and convince Thedan to find someone else, when Thedan grabbed the back of Serena's chair and pulled it out from the table. He then pushed her passed the table and towards Davun who was still standing near the entrance. This was the first time Davun had seen Serena not seated at the table and what he saw was another item to add in today's list of surprises. Serena was bound to a wheelchair. She desperately grasped a pile of papers laid on her lap to stop them from falling off as she was hastily pushed. Davun knew he had stared longer than he should have and began to feel guilty as he stared at the empty space where the bottom half of Serena's legs should have been. She either took no notice to him or chose to ignore him due to the situation as she made no comment or response when Thedan wheeled her passed Davun and out of the tent. Davun got his nerves together and chased after them. He clung onto the papers Thedan had given him as he wove between people rushing about, still keeping a desperate eye out for Jethro who was nowhere to be seen near the captain's tent. The ground was uneven as Serena's chair rocked bumpily along, dropping a few papers that Davun paused to pick up. He swiftly caught back up to them and looked ahead to see where they had been running. There were a few cages made out of wooden logs of various shapes and sizes. All three had doors that were wide open, and several people were ushering the children into them. It appeared to be some kind of protection box designed to contain those who couldn't fight until the battle was over. There were others rushing over after obtaining their gear to stand on guard in case enemies reached the cages. As Thedan and Serena approached one of the containers, the usher made room to allow Serena's chair to gain entrance. Thedan quickly wheeled her inside, then returned to Davun to grab the remaining papers. "I know you won't listen to me advising you to enter the safety box with us, so I will advise that you quickly find your brother and both of you rush here. He might already be in one of these so don't delay if you can't find him. Trust in the people of the camp to take care of each other," Thedan rushed his words so he could return to the confinement of safety. Davun hadn't considered that Jethro may already be in a safety box and out of harms way, but that didn't matter to him. He didn't know for certain if Jethro was safe or not, so he set out to search the camp on the chance his brother hadn't yet made it. As he run, he instinctively grabbed his shield off his back. He didn't think he'd be running into a fight, as he currently had no weapon, but he knew full well that the rats could use bows. He ran aimlessly around the captains' tent, quickly peeking inside each surrounding tent to search for Jethro. As he rounded to the last side, he caught sight of Kalavud aiming his bow at something Davun couldn't see. He released it and expertly retrieved another arrow and knocking it, though this time his bow was lowered and not taken aim at anything. Davun took this opportunity to run towards him.

"Kalavud! Kalavud! Have you seen Jethro? I can't find him anywhere!" Davun yelled, refusing to not be noticed this time. Kalavud took a quick glance at him and then back to where he had been staring. As Davun got closer, he couldn't find what Kalavud was staring at amongst the trees, or if there was anything at all. That's when Kalavud turned to Davun wide eyed and stretched out his arm, opening his hand towards Davun.

"Hand!" Kalavud shouted. Davun didn't question it and grabbed it without hesitation.

"Shield!" Kalavud yelled again, and tugged Davun, which caused him to spin and stand in front of Kalavud.

A clang was heard as Davun's already raised shield deflected an arrow he was unaware was flying towards him. Davun remained in his defensive stance as Kalavud stood back up from taking cover behind him and let an arrow fly into the leaves of a tree. A moment later, a bow fell from the tree, followed by the corpse of a Ratling. Davun surprised himself that he followed exactly what happened. At least, he thought he followed it all.

"Mighty handy that thing is. Thanks for the save, friend!" Kalavud smiled his usual smile, that quickly disappeared as he reassessed the situation around him. Davun now noticed a few unmoving bodies of humans around him, all with arrows protruding from their torsos. He anticipated feeling sick at the sight of seeing a dead body, but instead a heat rose inside of him. He felt himself getting angrier and more upset the more bodies he saw. He turned to Kalavud with a reinstated resolve.

"Have you seen Jethro?" he asked. His shoulders dropped a bit as the hope of finding his brother shrunk when Kalavud shook his head.

"Sorry, mate. I'll keep an eye out, though most of my attention is towards the trees at the moment. I've a few more archers on their way here, so why don't you keep looking for him and get yourselves somewhere safe," Kalavud responded, scanning the nearby surroundings again. Davun simply nodded before running off to the front lines. He figured other people he knew would be there, either fighting or giving orders. He was hoping one of them may have seen Jethro somewhere.

As he approached where the main fighting line was formed, he saw some people on horses running down Ratlings that tried to run around the signs, and archers trying to pick each other off on both sides. He noticed a horseman fall to an arrow, toppling over to the ground as their horse ran off into the forest. A couple Ratling archers took notice and ran to cover the ground where the horseman fell, taking aim at an archer at the end of the line. Davun saw Demoria running as hard as she could toward the Ratlings to try stop them before they could fire, but she was too far. Davun could see she would not make it in time before both of them fired at the unsuspecting archer, who was struggling with her bow. She looked as if she had never held a bow before, fumbling around with the arrow trying to set it right, but it kept falling to the side, inevitably falling to the ground. Davun sprang into action, racing towards the archer who still hadn't noticed what dire situation she was in.

"Duck!" he shouted as loud as his voice would allow. This clearly caught the wannabe archer off guard, as she suddenly looked up and saw Davun full sprinting towards her. She toppled over as her balance was already off from having to scrape her arrow off the ground. Davun took his stance again, raising his shield as the two Ratling archers loosened their arrows. One flew off to the side, hitting no one, but the other hit the shield directly. Before they could reach for another arrow, Demoria was upon them, swiftly and precisely striking her sword to cut down both Ratlings without damaging their bows. Davun turned to the woman to see if she was okay. She sat on the ground trembling as she stared at the enemies' arrow that had landed a few metres away after bouncing off Davun's shield.

"If you can't hold a bow, run to shelter! You'll only get yourself or someone else killed," Davun yelled, feeling guilty for having been so crude but he felt it was necessary. He didn't want to see more people die, and he couldn't justify leaving her side after seeing what a mess she was. He made sure to stand with his shield raised while she picked herself up off the floor and ran towards the safety boxes. He then proceeded to walk to Demoria who had already began dashing towards a group of soldiers fighting for their life trying to fend off Ratlings that were beginning to swarm them. He decided it would be best not to try delay her, he would have to find someone else, but as his eyes scanned the front lines, he saw everyone was preoccupied in fighting.

Wayne stood nearly twice the size of the Ratlings, easily towering over them as his greatsword cleaved its way seamlessly through multiple Ratling bodies. Beside him were Barith and Hadik, organising the front-line soldiers into their formations. They were doing their best to prevent the enemies from their archers who were being instructed by Tervu, as he was simultaneously shouting where to aim and dismissing any who were still too inexperienced to be of any assistance. Davun thought it best not to bother any of them and decided to continue his search for Jethro alone.

He ran off to the side of the camp where he had begun his search after being satisfied that Jethro was nowhere near the main fight. He hurried his search, checking each tent as he passed by and still no sign of his brother. He noticed a group of cavalry fighting off a group of Ratlings who had tried to circumvent the main fight but had clearly been blocked from advancing.

Davun frantically looked around having done a full lap of the camp, when he noticed the leg of a person disappear into the Captains' tent. His immediate first thought was his brother returning to the tent in search for him, but then remembered that Thedan and Serena had cleared the important papers from the table beforehand in case of someone infiltrating and attempting to steal their plans. He considered that someone with malicious intent was going after those plans. Either way, he needed to check it out, but as he cautiously advanced, a horse not far from him let out a painful whinny.

He turned to see a horseman heading towards him trying to desperately control his horse as it staggered, struggling to remain upright. It bled from multiple wounds and was attempting to reach safety, but it succumbed to its wounds and toppled to the ground. The rider managed to fall off the horse before his leg was crushed under the weight, but in the process, he lost grip of his sword and it landed a few metres away. At the same time, a single Ratling managed to break through the defence that the cavalry were valiantly working hard to put up, and it darted right for the prone rider. The prone rider shook off his moments daze and immediately saw the Ratling, dagger in hand and running to take his life. He stood, hesitating between running for his sword for protection, or running away for his life. The hesitation decided for him, as the Ratling covered more ground and retrieving the sword was no longer a valid option. The man turned to run, fear in his eyes. Davun pushed the thought of a potential spy to the side and ran to intercept the Ratling from reaching the man. He was already short of breath as he had been running around the entire camp in search of Jethro, but the adrenaline helped him break through the burn of his lungs as he forced his legs to push harder to reach the man in time. The Ratling, apparently tired of chasing, threw his dagger at the fleeing man. It embedded itself into the man's side and he fell, the Ratling not pausing for a single moment during his attack was almost upon him. Davun didn't stop running and lifted his shield, bashing the Ratling as its outstretched hands reached for the dagger that had pierced the man. The Ratling and Davun rolled over each other before coming to a stop and separated. Davun recovered quickly, standing in preparation for an incoming attack but the Ratling was only beginning to shake itself off from the attack.

Davun saw the man, still laying on the ground with the dagger sticking out like a thorn, but he was moving. Davun had no weapon to properly take care of the Ratling, but that didn't stop him charging on top of the rat creature and pinning it to the ground, using his shield to crush the rat into the earth as hard as he could. The Ratling screeched and hissed, flailing its limbs in a frantic mess in an attempt to break free. Davun was surprised how easy it was to hold it down but could do nothing else about the situation without a weapon or a means to disable his enemy without moving. The Ratling managed to free one of its arms enough that it could reach around the shield and it began trying to scratch Davun in any place it could reach to cause harm.

It was successful in drawing blood from Davun's arm and face, as it continued to claw and grab whatever it could, tearing apart Davun's shirt sleeve. Davun wasn't sure how long he could pin the creature down for, he looked over to see if the man was in any shape to run but the man was struggling to even crawl let alone stand. However, Davun noticed something else. Behind the man, Nim was running for him, sword drawn, and yelling something that Davun hadn't taken notice of until now.

"Hold it!" Nim was yelling but stopped when Davun gave a nod in response. Nim leapt over the wounded man attempting to crawl away and continued his mad dash towards Davun. The pinned Ratling had also seen Nim running towards them, weapon drawn, and began struggling even more. Its screams of anger turned into high pitched screams of fear as Davun did his best to hold the creature down. Just before reaching them, Nim raised his sword with both his hands. Davun quickly rolled to the side as Nim swung down with all his might, cutting into the frightened Ratling. Davun lay on the ground, panting heavily to catch his breath while Nim pulled his sword free of the fresh corpse.

"Thanks," Davun said softly between breaths, hoping it was loud enough for Nim to hear. Nim didn't show any indication of having heard it, instead walking over to the wounded man.

"This is going to hurt, bite down on your sleeve," he said to the man, little sympathy in his voice. Barely giving the man enough time to register and comply what he had said, Nim gripped the handle of the dagger and pulled it free from the man's body. The wound oozed blood, but Nim had bandages on hand and quickly wrapped it a few times around the man who was doing his best not to show his pain. After finishing the quick patch job, Nim turned to Davun who had gotten back up on his feet.

"Help this man, and yourself, to the safety boxes," Nim ordered, clearly in the state of mind that he was above Davun. Davun was in no position to care about the attitude right now, and let it slide.

"I'm looking for my brother. I also saw someone heading into the Captains' tent. I don't know if it was him or not, but I was on my way to find out before…" Davun felt no reason to finish the sentence, as the situation was obvious. Davun couldn't tell for sure as Nim turned away, but he was fairly certain that the boy who was not much older than him had rolled his eyes.

"I'll check the tent, and if It's your brother I'll send him after you, but now is not the time to be playing hide-and-seek. Get yourself and this man to safety," Nim dismissed the conversation, heading towards the Captain's tent as promised. Davun really wanted to continue looking for his brother, but after doing a quick search of the grounds and not finding his brother, he decided to take the man to the safety box. He would at least do that, though he wasn't entirely sure if he would stay himself. He was pretty sure Nim had no actual authority over him, but he also didn't want to make him more annoyed than he already was, and Nim appeared to have more experience in this situation. Once the man was successfully escorted to safety, Davun took a look around, before complying to Nim's order and entered the safety box himself.

They waited anxiously, listening to the sounds of battle until the signal was given that the remaining Ratlings had fled.

CHAPTER NINE

"We have discovered many truths and met many more who keep it a secret. Upon learning of our departure, they pleaded to us to join their society of truth keepers, but do they speak from reasoning, or paranoia of a human's true intent?"

That night, the Captain called for a quick meeting to discuss the results of the battle. The battle hadn't lasted long after Davun had reached the box, but to him it seemed like hours. He experienced firsthand that not being able to see what is going on around you, waiting in anticipation for it to end, hearing all the sounds of the battle wondering if each one meant another death. It was still a traumatic experience for anyone inside, especially the children. After the battle had ended, he met up with Jethro who had thankfully been safe inside a different box. He claimed that Delavun had found him and brought him to the safety boxes as soon as the fighting had started. He apparently also left to try find Davun at Jethro's request but couldn't locate him. Delavun chuckled when hearing that Davun had been searching for Jethro and put it down to both of them running around like mad and not crossing paths, though Davun hadn't found it as amusing. He was relieved to have discovered Jethro was safe and was in no laughing mood after spending so long be worried. He realised his thoughts were distracting him from the meeting that had just started and returned to the conversation that was taking place.

"We lost a few soldiers in today's skirmish. Artruis is toying with us. He is trying to dwindle our numbers down while throwing his thousands at us, piece by piece. I don't know what his aim is, and it would help a lot if we did," Demoria spoke with bitterness in her voice, and pointedly looked at Arkarn who simply shrugged in response. Demoria sighed, losing hope of obtaining a much-needed answer. "Thedan and Serena, good job on recovering our papers, I'm glad you got them and yourselves to safety. Nim reported to me that Davun saw someone entering the tent but discredited it when he ventured here and saw no one. I'm not as quick to dismiss such a thing, so as long as you are sure you saw something Davun, I will keep it in mind," she looked over at Davun, who nodded.

"I know I saw someone enter. I had been searching for Jethro so I believed it may have been him, but after the battle I discovered Jethro had been inside a box since the beginning. I couldn't chase after them myself, I had to go help a horseman who fell," he explained, feeling uncertain as to how Demoria would judge his actions.

"Speaking of which," Barith interrupted before Demoria could continue speaking, "I received a few reports that this young man saved as many as three people. I would say two, seeing as one of them likes to exaggerate a little."

"I would never exaggerate about such a thing!" Kalavud feigned hurt after the Commander had clearly indicated he was referring to him. Kalavud then changed to a more serious tone. "He honestly did save me. I mean, sort of. He blocked an arrow that I probably could have avoided anyway, but he did allow me to spot the archer and take him down without having to move!"

Barith seemed to accept the answer. "So, we'll just say three. Kalavud, an archer woman who was having some issues handling her bow, and a horseman whose horse fell in battle. That's three more that remain to fight another day thanks to him, but…" Barith took a short pause and looked over to Davun, "For his supposed first battle, he sure didn't seem to have taken on the effects I would have anticipated. Most young people would cower at the sight of bodies. Freeze, lock up, their minds jumbled, but Davun did none of that. He saved three separate people at three separate points where there would have been the stench and sight of death. He's a natural fighter," what had sounded like concern turned out to be a compliment from the old soldier. Davun wasn't sure if he should, or even how to respond and so he stayed silent as few people looked at him in a mixture of puzzled, proud, and curious expressions.

"He'll be a great defender for Hadik then. Have Hadik put him to good use for the next fight, Barith," Demoria spoke, trying to carry the conversation to the next step. Barith nodded in return.

"A few horses fell, lowering the number of horsemen we can have. We'll have to send for more when we near a city or ranch. Thedan," she turned addressing the polite man who gently smiled at her in response, "Your mission will be held off until midday tomorrow. We will skip tomorrow's morning training, instead making as much distance between here and our next resting spot as we can. There is something amiss with our reports or scouts, they should have reported a small band of Ratlings headed toward us, but their reports state no such thing within our searching distance. They couldn't have cleared that much ground in time without being seen. Tervu, take responsibility and find out what is going on. Now." Demoria was beginning to grow visibly angry at the idea that someone in their scouting parties had betrayed them. Tervu reflected the same unspoken thoughts and immediately stood up to attend to the matter.

"I'll have the remaining scouts in camp send for the ones out in the field for questioning. I'll handle the interrogations personally," the last words were spoken through seething teeth. Demoria didn't respond to the Scout Master as he left, accepting his response and moving forward with the meeting.

"Arkarn, we need Davun to be put into action soon. We need to find where Artruis is, send everyone we have to storm his grounds and retrieve the orb that is undoubtedly close to him at all times. We are running out of time. Our resources will only be consumed at a higher rate the more we recruit, and as stated during the last meeting, we are recruiting at a higher pace the more villages that are destroyed. While I welcome any and all help, we can only last so long. Find this man, Arkarn," she almost sounded like she was pleading rather than ordering. Arkarn adopted a grim expression.

"There is one means I can take verify his location. It is not an action I wished to take, but it is one I will have to. You are right, we cannot let this continue until everything we have built dwindles down to nothing. I will set out in the morning."

Demoria's response was annoyance, but that quickly softened into a defeated look.

"We must do what is necessary to ensure more villages are not destroyed. With no military help from any lords or kingdoms, we are on our own. We must sacrifice anything to ensure this man is stopped, Arkarn. But like we promise anyone here, we cannot make you do anything you do not wish."

"I know, Captain. My decisions are my own. Let us have a talk tonight, before I depart tomorrow."

Arkarn looked serious. Demoria nodded and turned back to the address everyone.

"The enemy seems to know where we are at all times. We must be prepared for a fight at all times. From now on, we must be vigilant. We'll have to plan more fortitudes for our next campsite. Ratlings may be generally weak, but they are great in number and we still have a large number of inexperienced fighters. I'll have Tervu send scouts ahead to pick a suitable location for us and I'll begin planning defences. Stay prepared, there could be more out there."

Davun sat silently, feeling like he had been put on a pedestal in the centre, but still somehow being talked around. He decided to bite his tongue and not make any comments this time. He figured he just had to spend more time here and learn more before he could have any valuable input.

After the meeting ended, Arkarn and Demoria went off to have their private conversation. Each other of the leaders went about their own business, continuing the packing of camp in anticipation for leaving in the morning. Davun was motivated to begin learning things he thought would be essential, and to begin with he thought he needed to learn more about how myths and legends were a twisted existence if he were to be a part of that contortion. With most people busy, or having personal conversations, he found Thedan who was preparing his own departure from the group the next day.

"Doctor, I was wondering if you had a moment to help me," Davun interrupted the man as he was busy packing a satchel. He looked up and greeted Davun with a warm smile.

"Of course. What would you like?"

"What do you know about these mythical creatures? Which ones are real, which ones exist through powers, and which ones are just plain made up?"

Thedan pondered on the question for a moment. It seemed as if the question may not have been as easy to answer as Davun first thought.

"Well, it is quite complicated and I'm afraid I don't have all the answers, but I suppose I do have some. When I was first brought into this camp and told about their tales and origins just as you were, I set out trying to figure out some of it for myself. For example, the phoenix was obviously a key creature I wanted to discover more about," Thedan decided to take a seat on a nearby crate, gesturing for Davun and Jethro, who had followed Davun here, to do the same.

"The phoenix has many tales and iterations, but they all have some common elements. The first is whether or not the creature was actually a bird, it had wings. The second was that it used flames in some way, whether it called upon it to burn its enemies or wore it like armour. And the last was that in each and every story of people recalling their encounters with the phoenix, is that it protects people. I have not discovered a single story in which the phoenix is portrayed in a negative light. It's always showing up to save innocent villages or individuals from a danger beyond a normal humans' capabilities. Some talk about taking down entire bandit raids on its own, a couple refer to it warding off large beasts from potential victims. One story even talks about it fighting off a manticore, another mythical beast whose winged body has the tail of a snake, mane of a lion, but the face of a man. If some of these stories really do come from seeing humans with powers, I am a little frightened at the idea of laying my eyes on whoever holds a power of a manticore, it doesn't sound too pretty" Thedan chuckled. "But there are a few that Arkarn has confirmed that exist through powers. The Phoenix, the Dragon, the Wendigo, and the Chimera."

Both Davun and Jethro had heard of several mysterious creatures, such as the Dragon, from tales of travellers at the inn. Many of these creatures were explained as if they were to be feared, so the thought of the Dragon existing through a power that belonged to a human gave Davun mixed emotions about it. Glad, because such a large and powerful creature didn't actually exist, but scared because these tales derived from somewhere, so whoever was seen using such powers were portrayed with such destructive power.

"What about unicorns? Are they real?" Jethro asked, recalling one off the stories he had heard. For some reason the question caused Thedan to laugh loudly.

"By far, that has been my favourite discovery. I will tell you the tale another time perhaps, but I will tell you that unicorns were made up by a philosopher whose plan to awaken people's minds backfired drastically. To return to the original topic however, I'm afraid I haven't the time to explain all my findings to you. Arkarn is the man to speak of about this topic, but I fear he is also journeying on his own tomorrow. I will allow you to read the books I have kept though, if you wish to read stories about them. I haven't many unfortunately, we must travel light so I try to keep as little books as I can. All I've left is a few stories on the Phoenix, one on the Wendigo, and one I have yet to read more about, the Minotaur. They are available to you at any time, including my absence," Thedan smiled at the curious boys. Davun was a little disappointed that there wasn't enough time for them to talk more, but the books would have to do. They boys thanked Thedan and wished him luck on his mission, before departing with the books that Thedan obtained from his personal belongings. Davun set about to his tent, lighting a candle to provide light and began reading through the books that spoke about the Phoenix. Averly had taught Davun how to read, expecting him to be able to take more responsibilities in the inn as he was getting older. Jethro was interested in the book as well, so after trying to read over Davun's shoulder unsuccessfully as he didn't have the ability to read fluently, Davun began to read the stories out loud.

A story he read was about the phoenix appearing in the middle of a night as if it were the sun itself and setting ablaze a group of a people referred to as 'Daritians'. They were a darker skinned, tribal people who attacked a village to purposefully lure out the phoenix in an attempt to capture it to devour it. However, they failed in their plans as the phoenix proved too strong to be caught, saving the remaining villagers and burning the entire Daritian trapping party to a crisp. Another story talked about the Phoenix, this time it was portrayed as large as a whale, a bird of monstrous proportion, as it protected an entire city from being devoured by a ravenous horde of demons craving human flesh. The third story was written by a fisherman who recalled his tale of seeing the phoenix. He had set out for his daily fishing trip as any other, when suddenly the phoenix swooped over him out of nowhere and fought off a predator hidden in the water that the fisherman had unknowingly become its prey. The fisherman never did see what the phoenix had fought, but after its fight, it disappeared from as quickly as it had arrived.

Davun noted that Thedan was right that all three stories had the same elements, but he missed out on one detail, or at least hadn't considered it a big enough issue to take note of. No story states that the phoenix interacts with any person, only that it appears to defend innocents from attacks, and then promptly disappears. If the phoenix really were a person who had the power over fire, why did it seem to avoid any contact with people? There was clearly more that Arkarn had yet to explain. Davun contemplated forcing Arkarn to speak more on it when he returned from wherever he was going, which was another thing that bugged Davun. Why was it not publicly stated where Arkarn was travelling to? Why was it that it had to be a secret to everyone?

Or was it only a secret to him and Jethro?

Is it because they still see me as a child? If they really wanted to give me the responsibility of being a holder of power, then why treat me like I couldn't even handle small amounts of information?

Davun felt his attitude lowering, his motivation to continue researching had disappeared. He decided it would be best if he and his brother got some rest after the many events of the day. He waited for Jethro to get into his makeshift bed, blew the candle out, and waited for sleep to come.

CHAPTER TEN

"The amount of people we have met who are connected to the myths in some way is remarkable. Who knew that there was already a civilisation of people, mostly unknowing of one another, that have been keeping the stories just what they are. Stories."

The next day proved as arduous as Davun had expected. The camp was woken early to finish packing their tents and were set to march. Barith did his best to try keep some organisation amongst the civilians, but many lacked the discipline and kept breaking formation. They took many short rests to let children and elderly catch their breath. Arkarn had kept his promise and left before they had even begun to pack, whereas Thedan awaited until later in the day until the camp got closer to the location designated by the scouts before departing, making sure to say goodbye to the brothers before he did so. Wayne and Kalavud travelled with Davun and Jethro, keeping them entertained and motivated by telling stories of their previous ventures. Davun really couldn't tell which stories were true, exaggerated, or simply made up, as Kalavud emphasised nearly everything in his story. One thing that was clear was that the pair had known each other previous to joining this band of survivors.

"Have we told them about the time we scared the group of bandits so much that they ran with their tails tucked between their legs, leaving all that they had stolen behind? That was so much fun!" Kalavud could barely contain his excitement with each telling of a story.

"I am still convinced they were only hunters, Kal, and I still feel bad about it!" Wayne didn't sound as happy to recall the event Kalavud had referred to.

"Nonsense! They were bandits! They had some gold, stolen weapons and way too much food for three people! Besides, why else would they run instead of telling me they weren't bandits?"

"Just because you call them bandits doesn't mean they were actually bandits! Maybe it had to do with you scaring them by pinning the piece of chicken hanging from one guy's mouth to a tree by throwing a dagger!"

"Like you're one to talk about scaring people! When they got angry at me, who was the one who snuck up behind them looking all intimidating and furious?!"

"I wasn't meaning to sneak up on them, I was only walking! It's not my fault they didn't notice me, and my face isn't intimidating! I was trying to be friendly to them before things got out of hand!"

"If I had a creature more muscle than man suddenly appear behind me with stupidly wide grin on his face, I'd have been so scared I would have had flashbacks of someone else's life flash before my eyes!"

The way the pair bickered was causing everyone within earshot to laugh. No one took their arguing seriously, as it was obvious that Kalavud and Wayne liked to tease each other often and neither of them would ever have taken anything to heart. In fact, Davun thought that they wouldn't take anything negative anyone had said about them too seriously. The pair were too optimistic and wouldn't be let down by words. They were either too simple minded that only actions would have effect, or they were some of the most strong-willed people Davun had ever met. He was envious at the concept of it being the latter. Not that he reacted negatively to the way people spoke to him, he just hadn't had much of a social life growing up while taking care of his little brother, so it left little chances to shape him in such a way. Davun began to reflect on his upbringing, or the lack thereof while growing up to be the sole carer of his little brother. So much of his life had been given to making sure Jethro was kept well fed and sheltered that he felt he had missed out on having a life of his own. Not that he regrets anything, just saddened that he was ultimately stripped of having a proper life because their parents had been supposedly murdered. Davun began to sink deeper into his thoughts, each one spiralling into the next, causing him to feel demotivated into even continuing the march. He simply wanted to lay down and ponder on his life instead of having to keep up the pace off walking with the rest of the army, but he knew that there was no choice in the matter. As if reading his thoughts, Kalavud placed an arm around Davun, wearing the large grin that had begun to grow on Davun.

"Laddies, you need to hear this one," Kalavud pulled in Jethro with his other arm then raised his voice loud enough to make it obvious he wanted Wayne to hear, "When the meat man tried to flirt with a bar maid and ended up with the guards nearly arresting him!"

The people near grew closer to hear the story clearer, taking obvious interest in the story that Davun already had doubts about the truthfulness behind it.

"Really, Kalavud? You're going to tell that one to everyone?" Wayne called out from where he stood a few paces back. "Maybe I should tell them about the date your mother set you up with that you were so attracted to."

"Oh, hush Wayne, no one is going to believe your nonsense anyway."

"Nonsense? I'm fairly certain that you still write him letters."

The crowd around broke into an uproar of laughter and whistling. Kalavud didn't look embarrassed, nor did he drop the smile for a moment. Davun looked up at him and it seemed that the threat of the story hadn't bothered him in the slightest, but rather he revelled in seeing everyone's joyous reactions. It was difficult for Davun to admit himself that he admired Kalavud in that moment.

"You can tell your short story that you've been working so hard on for the past few months in a moment, Wayne, but right now I need to tell them that you're attempts at flirting are a literal crime."

Even Davun couldn't help but laugh along, his spirits immediately lifting and his depressive train of thought abruptly forgotten. The rest of the march was filled with stories and laughter, making the long trek seem not so arduous.

***

The camp was set up along a cliff that stood roughly fifty metres high. Not the highest of cliffs, but still provided an obstacle if the Ratlings wished to attack from that side. The safety boxes were among the first to be set up, along with some defensive measurements along the perimeter of the encampment on all sides, including the cliff as wooden spikes were jutted out horizontally to hang over the edge. It seemed as though Demoria was taking extra precautions, which reassured Davun that she had more experience than he is aware of. The days training had been called off to properly set up the defences in time for any attacks that may occur, leaving Jethro free to help with cooking again. Davun had little or no experience in anything that needed to be done during the camps' setup, but he was wanting to help so he did his best to help with the manual labour of transferring freshly chopped logs to the camp to be made into more spikes and barricades. When night fell, making it difficult to continue any form of work, the camps' defences were mostly completed. Jethro and Davun retired to the small tent designated to them, this time it had a couple of guards posted at the entrance. They waved to the brothers as they approached. Davun waved back, confused at the sight of them. "Uh, hello. Is there something wrong with the tent?" he inquired, donning a worried look. The guards only wore a helmet that had no face coverings, and a chest plate that bore the symbol Davun had learned was designed to represent the army of survivors. The female guard smiled, hand resting on the hilt of her sword that sat in its sheath on her belt. Her eyes were bright blue and the torchlight the male guard held revealed her freckled face. Her blonde hair was tied back, and the bottom half had been dyed pink. She was definitely older than Davun, but she still looked young, not much older than twenty. The male guard had dark brown eyes, black hair that had also been tied back, but the flickering light exaggerated the obvious scarring of burns on his right cheek.

"Is someone coming for us?" Jethro looked around as he instinctively hid behind Davun.

"Oh, no, no! We're here just in case there is another attack. As you know, once the enemy knows who you two are then…" she trailed off realising where her explanation was getting her, her expression changed into a mixture of worry and confusion as she tried to think of a better explanation.

"You'll be fine, kid. No one's coming for you now, we're simply protecting you two in case an attack happens during the night. Nothing to worry about," the man spoke, kindness in his voice. His face remained serious, but his eyes were soft.

"Well, thank you. I wasn't expecting anyone to be stationed at our tent, but we appreciate it," Davun did his best to sound polite. In truth, having them there made him feel more tense about the situation rather than safe. It reminded him that he was sought after by a dangerous man who led an army of rat creatures. He was sure that it also had a nerve-wracking effect on Jethro, so he took his brother inside the tent to get some rest. As they entered the tent, the female guard held the flap open.

"If there is anything you need, just ask us! I'm Rekura, and this grouchy guy is Vincent," she smiled. Davun thanked her and she closed the flap door to return to her post. Davun and Jethro prepared for bed, going through the bags they had brought to pick out the next day's clothes, knowing they would have to get ready fast after being woken up.

"Dav…" Jethro began, hesitating a little as he debated on continuing his sentence, "I don't feel right. I think something is wrong. Maybe we aren't meant to be here. I trust Arkarn, but I don't know if…" he stopped.

"If?" Davun prodded him to continue, worried what was going through his brothers' head.

The poor kid has been through quite a lot of change and pressure a kid shouldn't have. I have to do something.

"If by the end of this, you'll be okay. You're supposed to go and get this orb thing from a man who sounds really scary. I don't want you getting hurt, Dav. I don't want to have to deal with Averly on my own."

Davun smiled fondly at recalling Averly. Despite her demanding nature, she had provided the opportunity for the boys to live proper. Davun didn't realise he could actually miss someone yelling at him for making a small, insignificant mistake like using the wrong tablecloths during the wrong season.

"I'll be fine, Jethro. I honestly don't think I'll be doing much, other than maybe getting this power that apparently lets me control fire," Davun was getting excited at the idea of obtaining such an ability, but then felt wrong for thinking it. Having such a power would only cause Jethro more issues in life, if more dangerous people were to come after it. He was conflicted between wanting to have power, the price of that power, and if that power truly even exists.

"Then why did you get the shield? They expect you to be attacked."

"They haven't given me a weapon yet, so obviously I won't put up much of a fight. I did get shot by an arrow, so maybe it's to help with that."

"That still means you're being attacked. You can't stop all the arrows if they shoot them at you from all directions," Jethro began getting worked up as his imagination ran through deathly scenarios.

"Jeth, calm down. I'll be fine. Everyone here is set on protecting us, they won't let anything happen to us. Don't worry about it, okay? I know what I'm doing. You'll have to trust me that everything will turn out fine," Davun did his best to de-escalate Jethro who had begun showing signs of having a panic attack. Davun had made a decision on what his path forward would be, and the highest priority was keeping Jethro safe. He decided it was time to move his plans forward, especially while Arkarn wasn't around.

Tomorrow, he would take Jethro back home to Eraton.

***

The next day the training regiments began again. No change to the schedule, but everyone was pushed to work harder to make up for lost time. Everyone was expectedly more exhausted than usual after the training and allowed a little extra time to eat and rest before having to return to their assigned duties. Davun ate his meal with Jethro in silence, before excusing himself to find Kalavud. He had decided that it would be safer to convince Kalavud to join them on his mission to return to Eraton. He decided it would be best so that Jethro wouldn't be a target as long as he wasn't seen in the company of the army. Their village should only be a couple days travel, but Davun wasn't confident that he could navigate back so easily, it would be best if Kalavud could guide them. He wasn't sure how he could convince Kalavud about his idea, or if Kalavud would try and stop him, but having someone who knew the land and knew how to fight would be a great asset to have if he wished to return to Eraton safely. He just had to hope that if he couldn't convince Kalavud to join him, then to at least ask him not to tell anyone in camp about his plan. He had doubts about Kalavud keeping a secret, but he needed someone more experienced than him to ensure his brothers safety.

He didn't find Kalavud eating his meal with Wayne as he had expected, but instead was informed that the pair were having a private conversation in a nearby tent. Davun walked over to the tent, and as he was about to push the flap aside, he could hear angry voices arguing in hushed tones.

"...can't do that. Leave it to Arkarn, please. It's his fight, not yours."

"I can't change my mind, Kal. What that man did to everyone here, he...he shouldn't be allowed to live anymore. No King or Queen will see him hanged without any proof, and they won't even acknowledge his existence! I don't trust Arkarn to do what needs to be done. He might be able to kill Ratlings, but I feel like he'll be too soft on Artruis. He needs to be taken down, one way or another. If I see him, I'm going to kill him."

"You know you shouldn't, don't you? You know the man is dangerous, but that's what you're hoping for, isn't it, Ryan?"

"I told you not to use that name, you know what it-"

"I know precisely what it means and how it affects you, which is why I'm using it. She wouldn't want you to do this, Ryan. You meant so much to her, don't throw that away for over a personal vendetta. It's obvious from how Arkarn speaks about him that he's no ordinary man, he's got to be a power holder as well. Don't do it, Ryan."

The tent fell silent. Davun decided it would be too obvious to anyone looking that he had been eavesdropping, so he entered the tent. He saw Wayne and Kalavud facing each other, both with frustrated expressions, though Davun saw no one else in the tent. Kalavud quickly changed to a smile, but Wayne took a bit longer to visibly shake off his emotions.

"Davun! Wasn't expecting you to find us in our little party tent. Well, you caught us doing our secret little dance that we do. We trust you won't spoil the surprise to anyone?" Kalavud asked, though Davun couldn't quite tell if he was speaking in code or only joking to avoid the awkward tension.

"Is your name not Wayne?" Davun asked, choosing to dance around Kalavud's question. Wayne was obviously reluctant to answer the question, his usual upbeat demeanour hidden beneath a layer of contemplation. After a moment, Wayne shook his head.

"No. My name is not actually Wayne. It's Ryan, and I don't want to talk about it, nor do I want you telling anyone," he spoke in a serious tone that Davun hadn't heard from him before. Kalavud smacked Wayne's chest.

"Lower your shoulders, poor kid thinks you're trying to intimidate him."

Wayne took a deep breath and loosened his stance. "Sorry, Davun. I wasn't trying to intimidate you, I was just a bit tense. Please don't tell anyone. I'm not hiding anything that affects our plans, I'm not some kind of spy, I just don't want to talk about it."

Davun looked at Wayne, conflicted on how to interpret the uncovered secret. It really didn't matter what his name was, but it did feel like he was hiding stuff. It made him question what else he could be hiding, as well as what Kalavud was possibly keeping secret as well. He knew Arkarn kept secrets from everyone but hadn't expected it from either Wayne or Kalavud.

I expect too much from people I barely even know. Besides, I came here trying to keep a secret myself.

Davun realised it would have been contradictory for him to hold anything against Wayne for having a secret. It was clearly something personal, and Davun found himself believing him when he said that his secret wouldn't affect anyone at the camp.

Davun also realised something else. If he wanted to trust people, they would have to trust him as well.

"Can I ask you both something important, and I also need it kept a secret."

CHAPTER ELEVEN

"In a way, it is poetic. Keeping these legends alive, telling of their tales under the guise of a children's story book. It is a lovely tribute to those who have earned it, while not revealing anything at all. The world reads the truth, and yet they remain unsuspecting."

Arkarn set off from the camp on horseback, riding in the early hours of the morning. He was confident that the camp could run without him. After all, they had done so several times before. He was forced to travel often, having to track down particular people and gather information when the situation called for it. The people he needed to meet from time to time were meant to be kept secret from the world unless they wished to be seen.

Their powers would be sought after if they were discovered.

He needed to discern Artruis' location. For whatever reason, their scouts were unable to find the enemy army, let alone Artruis himself. It didn't seem possible that the Ratlings could evade their search for so long, so Arkarn had to take drastic measures he wished to avoid just to find out where they were hiding, so that they could then take a bigger risk by amassing an attack to retrieve the orb.

He hated having to deal with the chimera.

The chimera was greedy. Never letting go of something without something in return. He knew that Artruis had met with the chimera at least once. It was possible that he knew where the survivor army camped and where it was headed. The chimera could communicate with the animals of the forest, anything that happened within he would know about. Arkarn knew that Artruis and the Ratling army were moving in the forest. All the villages that had been attacked were mostly near the outskirts, so it seemed logical they had been chasing Arkarn in circles within the forest.

Arkarn was tired of chasing Artruis, being in his shadow every step of the way. Now that he had Davun and Jethro in camp, it was finally time to bring this secret war they were having to an end. Artruis would only continue to drag things out, destroying villages in an attempt to find something that no one seemed to know what it was. It couldn't have been in search of the brothers, he was certain Artruis knew where they were and that they had been in camp recently, there was no reason to continue causing chaos. Artruis was more subtle than that, so there must be another motive to destroying small towns, and somehow passing it off as bandit attacks. Many things weren't adding up to Arkarn, and that made him frustrated. He was constantly berated for hiding answers and information that would greatly benefit their cause, when in truth he didn't have all the right answers to give them. There were still things he kept secret until the right moment to tell them. It was for him to dwell on and resolve, he didn't want to add to Demoria's burdens and problems that piled themselves on top of her with each passing day.

Today he would answer one of, if not the most, important question that they needed. It was time to stop playing cat and mouse, and to find Artruis and his army. Arkarn knew this would mean having the inexperienced survivor army that he helped build up put their lives on the line, most likely ending in mostly casualties, but it was necessary to recover the orb. This was all to recover the orb, have its power unlocked, and taken away from Artruis.

Or take Artruis away. Permanently.

It was an option he had been considering, but he knew that the strategic man wouldn't be easy to take down. He didn't like taking lives, but he knew better than most that sometimes it must be done to prevent more lives from being taken.

Arkarn slowed his horse to a stop. He had approached the bright yellow ladian flowers that signalled he was close to the chimera's lair. The ladian's were also known as blood eyes, for the dark red centres that the yellow petals surrounded, which made them easy to spot out but were seen as a bad omen amongst travellers.

Arkarn dismounted, trying his horse to a nearby tree, a generous amount of slack in the rope to allow his horse to wander the immediate vicinity.

He made his way between the trees, his destination was a large boulder covered in moss, a few plants finding life near its base. He rounded the large stone until he came upon the carved opening that led down to a natural cave. He took a deep breath to calm himself, knowing that losing his emotions may cause him to let slip information he couldn't afford to give. He began the descent into the dark pathway leading into the earth. The sun was placed on the opposite side of the rock, so it didn't illuminate too far down. He had travelled this path before, however, so he placed his hand along the wall and walked confidently forward, expecting the couple of turns it would take to reach the end of the cave. He had been here once before, the experience was so impactful that it had burned the details of the cave into his brain. He had really hoped to avoid returning, but now was not the time to be selfish.

After the third turn, Arkarn could see the dim light that the torches lit inside produced this far. He rounded the last corner and it opened into a large room. The room was filled with furniture as the chimera had made its home here. A bed placed against the far back wall, surrounded by an assortment of knick-knacks and valuables. A table sat with several plates placed onto one side, the remnants of the food eaten had yet to be cleaned off. There was a bookshelf only half-filled with various literature, and a couple of barrels he knew would have food and water. He was still uncertain as to how such furniture found its way down into the cave, as one man wouldn't have been able to carry them so far from a village. He had debated if they were given birth here from extracted materials of the local environment, but the chimera was hardly the type to put in such effort.

A large desk sat on one side of the room with paperwork, gems, and bones scattered about. A solitary man stood in the middle of the room, dark blue eyes fixated on Arkarn and his lips contorted into a crooked smile. He stood slightly below average height for a man, his back slightly arched, letting his loose, tattered robe dangle. His head was balding, revealing the top part of his skull, the grey hair that remained beginning to thin. Despite the crooked man's appearances of age settling in, his frame indicated he was healthy, no signs of sickness in his face.

"Arkarnryus! What a lovely surprise to see you here! To what do I owe this surprising pleasure?" his voice crackled slightly.

"Requiss. How have you been?"

The man's face immediately changed to annoyance, his demeanour following suit. "I told you not to call me by that silly Daritian title. My name is Pallinor, damn you!"

"I apologise. You know I've been raised to use the appropriate titles when necessary. I'll make sure to refer to you as Pallinor from now."

Pallinor rolled his eyes but seemed to accept the apology. He looked at Arkarn, still expecting an answer to his original query.

"As you more than likely know, I'm here for information."

Pallinor's face changed back into a smile, but his eyes were shouting greed. He relished in these opportunities when they arose.

"I can't give anything away for free, but you knew that before you came here. Your payment will depend on how heavy the information you seek will be."

Arkarn prepared himself, expecting the old man to ask the world of him in return.

"I know Artruis is within this forest. I've also surmised he may have visited you. I want to know his location."

This piqued Pallinor's interest as his eyebrows raised in curiosity.

"Ah, seeking to end your little dispute with him, are we? Well, the information of such an important person is surely worth much to you. I do have the answer, but I'll need something of equal value in return."

Arkarn met his eyes as they tried to burn through him in search of something worth giving.

"Who are you, really? I know that you aren't an ordinary man with no name and helping lead an army by banding together survivors out of the goodness of your heart. Who are you?"

The words drove their way into Arkarn's brain like metal spikes. This was something he couldn't give a man who traded information with his enemy.

"Perhaps there may be something else I can give you in return?"

"Afraid not for this kind of information. I already know of other things that would have been of equal value, and this is something for my personal interest, not something I seek to trade. Unless it can bring me something even greater, of course."

"Then do you still trade with Artruis?"

"Tsk, tsk, tsk. Another question would require another payment. Are you sure you want to know?"

"Yes"

"Then first tell me this. What is the purpose of the shield you gave the young lad?"

Arkarn was surprised that Pallinor knew of the shield but realised who he was dealing with. His creatures of the forest must have seen it and reported it for some reason in some detail.

"Hope."

"Elaborate."

"He is a beacon of light for us. Seeing him on the field will bring comfort to the other soldiers. Having him fight alongside them, and they know they will be safe. The shield is simply his flag, if you will. The symbol he bears to give the other survivors hope."

Pallinor tapped his chin, thinking about the information he just received. Arkarn kept that symbol in his head. He reminded himself why he was here, and if he could act fast enough, perhaps he can take care of Artruis before the information became a problem.

"Yes," Pallinor finally spoke, "I still trade with Artruis. In fact, I'm going to finish one last trade with him before I collect the debt he has been accumulating. It's not often I let someone repay me later, but he has something I truly desire."

Arkarn wanted desperately to know what it was that Artruis had that someone like Pallinor would want badly enough to let him create a debt. Pallinor was not someone who liked being owed, as the person could run off causing a hassle for Pallinor to chase them down, or they could die before being able to return payment.

"Well, you have your answer, now the original payment if you wish to know more."

Arkarn was beginning to regret coming here in the first place, but he knew he had to reveal more than he wanted to in order to end the battle.

Arkarn raised his hand, palm facing Pallinor. Fire wrapped itself around his extended arm and shot out towards the unexpecting man, missing him by mere inches.

Pallinor was sent into a panic, his body jerked backwards away from the fire and parts of his body began to change itself. His back grew feathery wings, his mouth grew large, pointed teeth, his hair grew to wrap around his neck and the top of his head, and his feet formed hooves.

"Danger! Danger! Fire! Pain! Hurt! Kill! Run!" Pallinor's voice changed with each yell, accompanied by various growls, yelps, and whimpers. Arkarn's arm lowered, and the fire disappeared.

"Stop!" he shouted, now furious, "You have been given your answer, now give me what is mine."

The now abomination of creatures that was Pallinor lowered to all fours, his face no longer that of a man. He began to shack, as if wrestling something inside of himself.

"Artruis…resides…in the…north…amidst the…Green…Heaven…" the words were a struggle to release from his throat, as saliva spilled from Pallinor's mouth. Without another word, Arkarn turned and left, leaving Pallinor to frantically run around the room in a panic, knocking over various things as he did so. Arkarn didn't care, he got what he came for and left with more than he wanted. He needed to act fast if he was to reach Artruis before he could trade for that information.

Arkarn walked up the stone slope and headed out to the surface. He stewed in anger while contemplating Artruis' supposed location. Their scouts had been to the Green Heaven multiple times, but all had returned, reporting no activity there. There was a piece to this puzzle he didn't have, and that frustrated him to no end. He knew that Artruis was a dangerous man, but Arkarn was convinced now more than ever that his enemy was most likely in possession of a power already. He just didn't know which one, or what he could do. It was time to return to camp and begin their preparations. Arkarn rubbed his hands through his tied hair, causing a few strands to fall loose. For each thing he discovered, another question replaced it. It was an endless cycle that he was determined to put an end to, even if that meant it would end on a question.

Arkarn untied his horse and mounted it. It would take almost a day to reach the camp on horseback, giving him plenty of time to think things over.

After a couple hours of riding, Arkarn stopped to let his horse rest. He filled a bowl with water from a spare waterskin and allowed the horse to drink. As he waited for the horse's thirst to be quenched, he heard another set of hooves hitting the ground in a sprint. He turned to see a man riding a horse, heading straight towards him. The man raised his arm when he got close, revealing their army's symbol.

"Sir! I've an urgent message from Captain Demoria!"

CHAPTER TWELVE

"Reading over the tales and legends of creatures with the newfound perspective has changed the way I view how they're told. What stories are alternate truths, and which were made by a drunkard who had too much ale one eventful night?"

The cloudless sky allowed the sun to shine its rays to illuminate the forest, giving the plant-life a healthy green glow, the speckle of flowers displaying their bright colours amidst the green canvas. Despite the beautiful scenery, Davun was feeling no better about his actions.

"Davun, are we really going back to Eraton?" Jethro asked his older brother with a sense of worry in his tone. Davun had explained they would return to Eraton to avoid the upcoming fight, having no place in such a battle.

"Yes, Jeth. We'll go back to the way things were, nothing for us to worry about. On the chance they recover the orb on their own, they're more than welcome to visit us and who knows, maybe having the power of fire will really speed things up in the kitchens."

Wayne and Kalavud chuckled at Davun's off-handed joke. Davun had managed to, surprising even himself, convince them both to guide them back to Eraton safely. They anointed one of their underlings to take over their roles while they were gone, hoping no attacks would come in the few days it would take to return. They had questioned Davun's intentions initially, but ultimately agreed with him that it would be the best option to head to Eraton.

"Are you sure they won't need you?" Jethro asked. Despite wanting Davun out of danger so that he wasn't harmed, he still thought that his older brother was essential to their plans, given how important the role he is meant to play is. It was true that Davun had no idea how needed he would be in any coming fights, his only combat ability was to put himself behind a shield, but his little brother's safety came first. He would see to it that Jethro remained safe and non-existent to the enemy.

"They won't need me, Jeth. They're capable on their own, I can't exactly help them much by being inexperienced and uneducated on these powers that we still have yet to see. They'll be fine, as long as they have Demoria leading them, and these two clowns help when they're not trying to out-embarrass each other."

"Clowns? Now I take offence to that," Wayne spoke out in a loud tone, his face mocking a hurtful expression.

"I agree, we're not clowns. We're jesters. Entertainers. Story tellers!" Kalavud continued Wayne's thoughts, reflecting the same pseudo-expression.

"Royal entertainers, at least!"

"I agree, the high crown would love our conversations and stories about our travels."

"How could you say that about us, Davun? I thought we were friends?"

"Clowns...he called us clowns! I don't know if I even want to continue walking anymore," Kalavud exclaimed dramatically, closing his eyes and falling forward, landing on the ground with a thud.

"Now look what you've done, you've taken his will to even stand upright. Honestly, Davun, words can hurt you know. We might be professional mercenaries, but we still have feelings. In fact, I think my legs are being sapped of their strength as well..."

Wayne started to feign losing control of his legs as they exaggeratedly wobbled, "Oh no!" Wayne pretended to lose his balance and began to fall on top of Davun, who instinctively stepped back to avoid being crushed. As he stepped back, Kalavud grabbed his ankles from where he lay on the ground and Davun fell backwards. The fall didn't hurt him, but he was momentarily stunned at the unexpected trip. Wayne and Kalavud began laughing hysterically, and once Jethro registered what had happened, he didn't attempt to hold back his own laughter and joined in. Davun felt the blood rush to his cheeks in embarrassment but gave a short laugh at his own humiliation. Wayne offered a hand and helped Davun stand back up, giving him a short pat on the back. Davun did his best to wipe off what dirt had accumulated on his back while beginning to think of ways to get back at them.

***

The sun began to hide itself below the horizon, their journey mostly completed as they neared the mountain that Davun would stare at often from his view in the kitchen window. They decided it would be best to rest for the night and finish their walk in the morning. They debated about setting up a fire for warmth, as they were no longer confident about where the enemy troops were. The other days attack was a surprise, no scouts had reported enemy movement in this area. In the end, they chose not to have a fire, instead trying their best to warm themselves with their blankets and clothing. As the last of the day's light dimmed, a cool breeze caused Davun to shudder. He huddled closely with his brother, doing his best to keep Jethro protected against the cold. The pair of guides were uncharacteristically quiet as Davun looked over to them. They seemed unaffected by the cold, making Davun feel envious. Davun tried to get cold off his mind, so he decided to start conversation by asking what had been on his mind recently.

"So, why did you two join the army?"

Wayne immediately looked down, recalling unwanted events. Kalavud looked grim as well but decided to answer Davun's question regardless.

"Wayne and I were mercenaries for hire long before the army even formed. We had no knowledge of these mythological beasts existing through powers, and I still don't quite understand it, but we had heard of attacks on some villages. They were reported to be bandits that had been captured, so when the army began, we naturally declined their offers to hire us as we didn't believe them either. Something I am still ashamed of. It wasn't until…" Kalavud trailed off, his eyes darted to Wayne whose gaze was transfixed on the ground, as if staring into a fire that wasn't there. "A certain village was attacked. That is when we decided to join them. Free of charge."

"I'm sorry," was all Davun could think of saying. He felt bad for bringing the topic up, it was something he should have guessed when Wayne said everyone who had joined the army was a survivor, but curiosity clouded his thoughts and got the better of him.

"It's fine, lad. It's a reasonable enough question," Kalavud gave a small smile. Jethro shifted to sitting upright from leaning on his brother.

"Did you lose your family, Kal?" Jethro asked, shocking Davun that his brother would ask such a question outright. Kalavud didn't seem offended, instead shrugging.

"Haven't seen them since the day I left the North. So, in a way, yes, but I'm not sad about that. They were holding me back from living my dreams. I did lose someone though, who I felt was my family, but I don't think we sho-"

"My little sister," Wayne interrupted, eyes still focused on something that no one else could see. "My home was the village that was attacked. I was a mercenary, so I travelled most of the time, but I would frequently return home. Not long after rejecting Demoria's offer for our services, my hometown was attacked by Artruis' swarm of rats. My parent's death was one thing, but my little sisters was another. That is why we are here today. To see to it that Artruis doesn't get what he wants, and to help everyone in that camp seek the vengeance they deserve," his words became steel. It was clearly difficult for the large man to recall whatever he had seen.

"I-" Davun began, but Kalavud held up a hand.

"While we're on the topic, and so it isn't brought up again, his little sister was only five at the time. She was a little slow in learning to speak and couldn't pronounce Ryan properly. Whenever she tried, it sounded like Wayne, so he adopted the name to remind him of home. I was also attached to her. The big lug is like my brother from another Southerner. I went with him on his trips home and his sister was the reason I kept going. We each have the same goal in this army, and it's not something I think we should talk about further. We want Artruis dead, stripped of everything he tried to accomplish, which begins with making sure the power he seeks is brought to its rightful owner. Hopefully right before his eyes, but that's just a bonus."

Even if Davun could think of how to respond, he was too afraid to say anything. The matter was clearly difficult to bring up, which was no surprise given how painful his own thoughts were of losing his own brother. He was glad he asked though, as not only did he feel like he could completely trust the duo, but it strengthened his resolve that returning to Eraton was the right thing to do.

***

Davun woke from the low light at the crack of dawn, having had only a few hours of sleep from the cold. Jethro was still leaning against him, eyes closed in a blissful sleep. Davun looked around and became startled when Wayne and Kalavud were not where they had been asleep, their blankets left disturbed on the floor. He woke Jethro up in a panic, and barely gave his tired brother the time to open his eyes before jolting up to look around. He was relieved when he saw the pair not far away, talking to another man he didn't recognise. They shook hands with the stranger before he began jogging away from them. The pair watched him for a moment before turning to see Davun staring at them, Jethro just to his side rubbing his eyes.

"You're up early. Just as well, we can finish the walk before midday then," Kalavud called out as they got closer.

"Who was that?" Davun didn't hesitate in asking, still in a shocked state at seeing the empty resting spots.

"A scout from the camp. Demoria sent them to have us return to camp. We told him what we were doing, and he agreed to relay the message to Demoria, so we've still got time to finish the trip before being yelled at," Wayne explained, trying to calm Davun. Davun nodded, taking a few breaths to straighten his thoughts that were scrambled as soon as he woke. Jethro yawned, causing Davun to yawn. The night would take its toll on him, but he was determined to return to Eraton as fast as possible.

They retrieved their belongings, had a light meal and continued on travelling to Eraton. They took the same path through the mountain, and as they trekked down the slope on the other side, Davun caught view of their hometown. He was relieved to have not been tracked down by the Ratlings, as he believed there was no way they knew where he hailed from and so there would be no ambushes between the mountain and the town. As they got fairly close to their town, Davun called everyone to a stop. He was dreading this moment, and so he took a deep breath to resolve himself.

"Wayne and Kal, you stay here. Having a couple of strangers return with us might seem a little odd, and I'm trying not to get into any long explanations before I leave."

Jethro looked up at Davun, confused.

"Leave?"

Davun sighed, feeling a bead of sweat starting to push itself to the surface of his forehead. He hated lying to his brother and would feel guilty for a long time about it.

"I'm not staying, Jeth. I'm sorry, I know I lied to you, but I couldn't have you causing any kind of fuss before we left," Davun found it hard to look his little brother in the eye. He didn't think it would be difficult to have lied to a ten-year-old, but his brother was different. His brother looked up to him, being his sole protector. Jethro looked betrayed at first but realised what it meant that Davun would be returning. Tears immediately began to build in Jethro's eyes. Not wanting to leave his brothers side, he clutched onto Davun.

"You can't go back Davun, I thought you were going to stay so you wouldn't get hurt," Jeth cried out, no longer able to hold back any tears. Davun hugged his brother.

"I'm sorry, Jeth. Try to understand that they do actually need me there. I need to be there when they try to retrieve the orb so that its power will not fall to Artruis. It's only a matter of time that he discovers where I live and then he'll come for Eraton. If I bring myself right to him in the final confrontation, then he'll have no reason to ever come here. I'll be fine Jeth. It's something that must be done and cannot be changed," Davun did his best to try get his brother to understand, but he knew it would have no effect. His brother was too young to accept that there were such things that were inevitable. Arkarn had been wrong about having Jethro at the camp. Artruis would track Davun down at no cost, so having Jethro close would only cause him to get in the way of harm. If Davun stayed away from his brother and Eraton, both would be protected as long as he revealed himself before Artruis discovered either. Davun knew what he was doing, and both Wayne and Kalavud agreed with it.

"You can't Davun, you'll get hurt! You can't go back now!" Jethro continued crying, refusing to let go of Davun as if he would disappear the moment he did. Davun was feeling guiltier by the second, so he pried off Jethro's hands and held them in his own.

"I promise I'll see you again Jeth. Nothing will happen to be. I'll come back, with the power of fire, and then we can do a bunch of cool things with it. But right now, our biggest issue is figuring out how to deal with Averly," Davun tried to lighten the situation, but neither he nor his brother could find the strength to smile. Davun knew Averly would not easily accept taking care of Jethro and letting Davun leave again. He held his brothers' hand and through both of their tears, they made their way to the village.

By the time they reached the inn, the boys tears had dried, and it left their eyes red. Davun had finally came up with what he was going to say to Averly to convince her to take care of Jethro in his absence. With one final deep breath to calm himself, Davun pushed the inn door open and stepped in. Despite not being away for very long, the inn felt nostalgic to him. The familiar tablecloths and cleanliness to the place felt like home to him. So did the Averly's yelling as her voice preceded her around the corner.

"If that is the weekly delivery of my vegetables then you are much too early to be-" she stopped as she caught sight of the boys. "Oh, it's you two. You're back from your luxurious trip. Where are my cloths that I ordered?" she asked, seemingly not interested in the small break that she was still under the impression the boys had taken. Jethro ran up to her and hugged her, tears finding their way back down his face.

"Stop this! You'll ruin my fine garments with your salty eye fluids! Davun, what is the meaning of this?! What did you do?!" she yelled, and Davun was unsure if she was more furious about the fact Jethro was crying and it may have been something he did, or that her clothes would be potentially ruined very slightly.

Davun panicked and decided to take no chances facing her wrath.

"Take care of him, I've gotta go," was all he managed to blurt out before running out of the door and out of the village. He could hear her attempts to get him to return, but all he could do was run, the carefully planned out speech disintegrating at the sound of her voice. He ran until he was well out of the village, and even from where he caught up with Wayne and Kalavud, he swore he could still hear her shouts of displeasure.

**

The sun was halfway through its descent as the trio forced their eyes to remain open from a sleepless night as they walked. They had made it most of the way and surmised that if the moon would light their way then they could travel at night and reach it before the moon hit its peak. Wayne and Kalavud chatted idly, Davun not paying attention to them as he pondered his thoughts, feeling incomplete without Jethro nearby. They had never really been split apart, and each step only drifted him further away. It was an odd feeling for him, and it was something he would have to adapt to. He knew Jethro would be kept safe in Averly's care, but he did feel bad for not being around to deal help with Averly's yelling. Davun just had to hope that Jethro was capable of dealing with it on his own. He had considered that Averly might go easier on his little brother than she had on him, but quickly dismissed that idea knowing full well that Averly didn't care about age.

Age. Jethro was still young.

Davun's spirits dampened when he realised that a ten-year-old child might consider what he was doing as abandonment. He stopped in his tracks, facing back, considering if he should return to the Eraton and get his brother back. Or maybe stay with his brother and avoid the fight entirely.

I don't really have the will to fight. It's not my fight anyway, it's theirs. They can find me once it's over if they want me to unlock this orb or whatever you do with it.

Wayne and Kalavud, having been silent for a moment when the conversation died down, turned to see that Davun had stopped walking. He tapped Kalavud's arm, pausing them both so that they could see what Davun was doing.

"You okay, Dav? I know it's tiring, but we need to keep going if we want to make it back tonight. No time to go back on any decisions. He'll be fine, right Kal? Kal?" Wayne repeated himself, turning to his companion whose eyes had narrowed at something that Wayne couldn't see, but knew exactly what the look meant.

Wayne pulled his greatsword from where it was strapped on his back. Kalavud pulled out his sword. Davun turned to respond to Wayne and panicked when he saw them draw their weapons. He quickly pulled out his shield and started darting his eyes around to try and locate what they had seen.

Then multiple Ratlings burst out of the bushes.

They rushed straight for Wayne and Kalavud as they were in the front. Wayne ran to meet them head on, Davun lowered his shield and began to run forward to help in any way that he could without an actual weapon. Kalavud remained still, his sword only half risen, his stance indicated that he expected another Ratling to burst out and attack him. Davun was about to rush past him when he suddenly turned around, his other hand flinging a dagger that Davun hadn't even seen him draw. The dagger flew into the torso of a Ratling hiding on a branch, bow and arrow in hand and aimed directly at Davun. It was as if Kalavud knew where he had been all along and had been waiting for him to make a move by attacking Davun when he lowered his shield. Davun stared for a moment in wonder as the body fell unmoving from the tree.

"You start to learn a few of their tactics when you've been fighting them for a while, laddy," Kalavud spoke, continuing to scan the nearby trees, "Now go give Wayne a hand. Just a bit of advice, don't stand too close to him."

Davun realised he had stopped moving and sprinted forward to help Wayne who had felled a couple of Ratlings as even more broke through the bushel. Wayne was truly terrifying with his weapon. He swung it around effortlessly, one attack leading into another, a sidestep to avoid an attack while swinging, it was as if his blade never stopped moving. Davun could see why Kalavud gave him the advice not to get too close, Wayne was in full control of his immediate area and getting close would only get in his way. It seems that some of the Ratlings weren't as dull as Davun had thought, as one stopped its advance after more of its kin fell before the giant of a man. Davun foresaw that it was preparing to do something and started running towards it. The Ratling pulled a dagger from its belt and pulled its arm back in preparation of throwing his weapon. His arm swung forward at the same moment Davun collided with it. The dagger was knocked off course, gaining nowhere near the momentum it needed to reach Wayne who appeared unaware of what was happening. The Ratling rolled over but quickly regained its footing, standing to face Davun.

Davun had his shield raised, eyes locked onto the Ratling. The Ratling produced another dagger and gave an animalistic screech.

"Youse is in the way. Youse all must be killed. Youse is stealing all our food," the Ratling seemed to struggle to get the words out. Davun was stunned. He had not anticipated the Ratlings to have the ability of speech, and so the Ratling speaking to him had caught him by surprise. At that same moment, the Ratling lunged, sensing the moment that Davun's defences lowered slightly. Davun tried to raise his shield but was just shy of reacting in time as the dagger managed to cut him in his shoulder. The wound wasn't deep, but it stung. Davun winced at the pain but had no time to deal with it as the Ratling gripped onto Davun's shield in an attempt to wrestle it out of the way to allow the dagger to find an important organ. Davun contested with the Ratling for his shield, using all his strength to keep himself from being stabbed. The Ratlings' scrawny arms showed a surprising amount of resistance as Davun couldn't shake it off. The Ratling pushed itself forward, Davun taking a step back in the sudden surge. The Ratling was giving a growl of effort as it kept trying to move the shield enough to create an opening.

"Duck!"

The shout had come from behind Davun, and by reaction he turned to look. Kalavud was moving towards him with great speed, dagger in hand. The Ratling took this moment to push against Davun again, this time causing him to lose his balance and stumbling over backwards, Ratling landing on top, the shield still remaining between them. The Ratling raised its arm to strike at Davun who was in a difficult position to manoeuvre his shield properly as it was still being held by the Ratling. At that moment, a dagger landed into the torso of the Ratling, and it collapsed on top of Davun. He quickly pushed the corpse off and rolled over to be on all fours, catching his breath. Kalavud approached him and offered his hand, helping Davun to stand.

"Not quite what I meant, but still works."

Davun noticed Kalavud had resumed a calm demeanour, but he was still anticipating a fight, instinctively raising his shield to rush back in. What he saw, however, was bodies littered around Wayne, who was now cleaning off his blade with a rag.

"It's alright, laddy. Pretty sure the big guy got all of 'em."

"We should quicken our pace back to camp. It won't be safe for us to camp out here. I'm also worried about what happened to our scouts to allow the Ratlings this close. We have to report it to Demoria."

Davun nodded as Wayne approached them. Davun looked down at the Ratling that had attacked him. Its ragged shirt had raised slightly when he pushed it off, revealing its scrawny frame. Its ribs were clearly defined through its fur, and its waist was half the width it should have been.

"We know, lad. We think that, for whatever reason, Artruis isn't keeping them fed. Could be he is simply that cruel, which I am inclined to believe, or just doesn't have enough food to feed them as they multiply."

"Considering that the villages he raids are devoid of all food, I'd say it's the former."

"It spoke to me. It said that we were stealing its food."

Wayne and Kalavud look puzzled as they all now stared at the body.

"They have said a few things to our soldiers before, such as wanting our food, but never claimed we were actually stealing their food. All the more reason to head back tonight and report it to Demoria," Wayne was eager to leave. They returned to their course, hastening their pace to avoid any more attacks before nightfall.

CHAPTER THIRTEEN

"The stories have also been an adequate motivation for my ventures. Discovering a tale inspires me to find its origin, learn of any truths behind stories meant for imaginative minds, and to see if any of the published historical books have any traction to the words they claim. I wonder what these humans have done to be portrayed as vicious and grotesque as some articulate."

The moon was fortunately bright enough to light their path long enough for them to return to camp. Thankfully, it had remained untouched during their absence. Unfortunately, that meant Demoria could focus her attention on scolding them. She was furious, brushing past the details of the report of the ambush they suffered, her face red from yelling insult after insult, sputtering as she tried to comprehend what they were possibly trying to accomplish. They remained silent unless Demoria asked them a question directly. Once she was tired of screaming at the top of her lungs at them, she slammed a piece of paper on the table.

"What is this?" Wayne asked, staring curiously at the parchment that must have had some importance for Demoria to produce it during her rant.

"A letter from Arkarn. I sent a messenger to inform him off what you were doing as soon as I found out. If you think I was mad, then you best find yourselves some suitable armour for what Arkarn is going to do to you."

Wayne grabbed the letter and his face had somehow dropped further than what it had been during the yelling. He passed it onto Kalavud who had a similar reaction, and then to Davun.

***

Idiots. They're complete idiots.
Just idiots. That's it. Idiots.
Your scout won't convince them because they're idiots.

My business here is finished. I have been graciously given Artruis' location. I'll fill everyone on the details, but first I have to go retrieve Jethro from where those idiots are going to leave him.
Idiots!
They don't understand anything!

Punish Wayne and Kalavud even if it means they'll be unable to fight for us ever again!
I'll have a chat with all of them when I return.
Idiots!

***

The writing was hastily written, several lines had been crossed out as if he couldn't figure out how to begin. One thing he had been certain of though, was that he believed the three of them were idiots.

"The messenger who delivered it had trouble expressing the reaction Arkarn had when receiving the news, but he scared his horse well enough that it took the better part of an hour to get it calm again. Which of you geniuses came up with the bright idea to leave Jethro all alone?"

Whilst Wayne and Kalavud had taken the scolding with regret for their actions, Davun had slowly begun growing angry instead.

He did what was best for his brother, so why was everyone else so angry that his brother was now safe?

"It was me," Davun announced loudly, not quite a yell but still audibly loud enough that his emotions became obvious. "The enemy is after me. Having Jethro with me would only cause him to be in the way of harm. Keeping him away from me is the best option!"

Wayne and Kalavud went wide-eyed as Davun loudly explained his actions. They sat in shocked silence, no one had ever spoken to Demoria like that. They sat motionless, expecting Demoria to somehow become angrier than she already was. To everyone's surprise, however, she instead sighed, dropping her shoulders as she laxed her stance.

"May the harpy steal your voice, Arkarn," she cursed under her breath, barely perceptible enough for Davun to hear, though he wasn't sure if he was meant to have heard it or not. She stood for a moment, gathering her thoughts together.

"Arkarn will explain it to you when he returns. I will see to it personally that he does. There is more he hasn't told you that should have been essential in the first place instead of playing his games. I wish I could tell you now, but it is not my place. Just know that you've all made an idiotic decision, though I can't exactly fault you for not knowing it."

She wasn't making any sense to Davun, though there was clearly some importance of having Jethro at the camp he hadn't been told. In addition to being angry he was now also confused, which just lead to frustration. There were still crucial things that Arkarn had yet to tell Davun, and now it seemed that information involved his little brother which only sent him deeper into frustration. He knew full well that these adults only saw him for his age, but they had no idea what he has been through, having to take responsibility for Jethro his entire life. He could handle so much more than they assume and wouldn't have to unknowingly be put in a situation where he left Jethro alone, who apparently has more of a role to play than simply being kept safe. He felt the frustration grow and grow, his fingers turning red from where they were tightly gripping the table.

"Wayne, Kalavud, labour duty. I'll find a more fitting punishment for you later," Demoria ordered, no sign of her usual demanding voice she spoke with. Wayne and Kalavud didn't utter a word as they rose from the table and quietly left the tent, not turning back. Davun felt unable to sit still, fidgeting constantly as he tried to find a comfortable position to sit. He found himself wanting to push the table over and storm out, when a hand fell lightly on his shoulder. Demoria had sat herself beside him, her face soft, devoid of any anger that was previously there.

"Take a breath. Don't let your anger get the better of you. It leads to rash decisions that you could come to regret," she spoke in a calm and sweet tone. Davun looked away from her, not wanting her to see his face as he felt the tears wanting to crawl their way out of the sockets of his eyes. He didn't respond, but that didn't stop Demoria from continuing to try.

"You know," Demoria spoke, her voice lightly cracking as the sadness attached itself to her words, "My son would have been just younger than you are now. I was young when I had him, so I took in all the information I could on how to be a good mother to him, and if I want to be honest with myself, I think I was looking forward to his angsty teenager stage. I felt like I could have helped him with his issues and rebellious stages of finding himself, but…" she trailed off, so Davun turned to face her, seeing something he never thought this woman had been capable of.

Tears.

They trickled down her cheeks and passed her still lips, landing on the cold iron of her armour.

"I can no longer help him, Davun. So please, let me help you instead."

Davun couldn't hold back anymore. He burst into tears, letting go everything he had held onto for years out all at once. Not feeling like he had a childhood, being forced to mature much earlier than he had to just to ensure that his younger brother could survive, working each day to earn shelter and food instead of playing games with friends he never made, and the added responsibility of being the sole heir of a power that had danger surrounding it, rushed to the brim of his eyes in the shape of tears, accompanied by its audio counterpart in the form of wailing. Demoria let her tears fall freely as she pulled Davun into an embrace, letting him bawl his problems out and just making sure he didn't feel alone in the situation. Davun didn't care about the wall of metal, the simple act of her arms around him gave him a great deal of comfort as he finally let free of something that he never knew had built itself up.

***

Davun did his best to distract himself with physical labour. After the daily trainings and midday meal, he helped cart fallen trees into camp to be stripped and carved into spikes to enhance their defences. Rekura and Vincent helped alongside him, having been given orders to keep an eye on him in case he tried to leave camp again. Davun knew it was for appearances' sake, Demoria had trusted him when he told her he wouldn't leave without her permission again, but the rest of the camp had been shaken when they discovered that he had vanished. He hadn't realised that everyone in the camp fully believed he would be the end of Artruis' plans and having him suddenly disappear caused a panic he hadn't considered. He felt guilty for having everyone worry about their situation, but he now understood what his mere presence meant amongst everyone at camp. He let Rekura and Vincent tag along without any issues, and even chose to create conversation to get to know them better. He discovered Rekura hailed from the North in one of the few villages that had been attacked there. She was recruited a few days after the attack when their army discovered the village and found Rekura among the survivors. Unfortunately, none of her family had made it, and only a few of the survivors had chosen to join. Vincent didn't speak much, but Rekura stated that she had found Vincent during a Ratling attack on his village. The army had successfully scouted the enemy before the attack and managed to make it in time to help defend it. She discovered Vincent lying motionless underneath a burning wooden beam that had pinned him to the ground after landing on his face. Davun could have only imagined how that would have felt, and despite his situation, thought it fortunate that Vincent had been unconscious during that event. He was also informed about how much the army really moved, having visited various nearby borders while chasing down the army. It seemed that no matter where they were, the enemy was able to keep tabs on them and stay ahead enough to constantly remain out of sight. It seemed Artruis was a fearsome opponent, having the upper hand since the army formed. It seemed like he was stringing them along, but Davun had no idea what his reasoning doing that would be, though he had no idea about Artruis' intentions at all. No one in camp seemed to know either. Either Arkarn didn't know, or it was another secret that he kept in his collection.

"Davun?" Rekura asked, cutting into his thoughts and bringing him back to the situation. He had forgotten he was in the middle of conversation, having gone on a tangent of thoughts after hearing Rekura talk about where the army has travelled since she joined.

"Sorry, got distracted. What did you say?"

"I asked you the same thing. I know how you were brought here and why, but what is your story?"

Davun sat on the question for a moment, causing Rekura to wonder if he got lost in his own thoughts again.

"Honestly, not much. Didn't know my parents, they died around when Jethro was born, and I have no memory of them. I only remember being taken care of by the woman I worked for. I worked in an inn from a young age so that my brother and I could live, and that's about all there is to me."

Rekura looked a little disappointed. "That can't be all there is to you. There has to be more. What are your interests? What are you good at? What do you enjoy doing?"

Davun was honestly not sure how to answer. He hadn't had much time to explore his own interests, but he knew that telling Rekura that wouldn't be a good enough answer for her.

"If you had asked me before I knew any of this, I think I wouldn't have been able to think of an answer for you, but now I think I would like to find more about mythical creatures. If I'm meant to be a part of them in a way, I'd like to learn about what others are out there. See what stories were really true or not."

Rekura became visibly excited, even whilst dragging her cart with Vincent, who seemed to take little interest in the conversation.

"That sounds amazing! There are sure some scary ones, I wonder if they are real or just some person with the strong abilities. Like the minotaur! A large beast with the head of a bull, protecting a labyrinth for eternity. That would be boring, I feel bad if that one turns out to be true. Oh! Do you reckon the leviathan is real?"

Davun looked at her and shrugged. He had heard the leviathan once before from a passing sailor, but he didn't elaborate on it and they didn't get many sailors passing through the inn to ask them about it. It was supposedly a large creature that dwelled in the ocean, about ten times the size of a passenger boat. He didn't know much more than that, such as if it had any abilities, only that the sailor was scared to talk about it, it seemed like a bad omen to even mention it.

"I don't know much about that one. A frighteningly large creature like that is difficult to believe it ever existed, and it makes little sense that someone saw a person with abilities and somehow saw a monstrous creature."

"Doesn't it send shivers down your spine just thinking about it though? Like, what kind of terrifying destructive power would this person have to make people see such a hulkingly large creature? It can probably hide beneath the surface of the water, making itself appear bigger to scare people off? What do you think, Vince?"

"I don't want to know. I don't like the ocean."

Davun was surprised that Vincent had been listening at all. He was under the impression that the gloomy man simply ignored everything, but he had responded straight away without hesitation.

Davun wanted to get him to continue talking, enjoying the moment that Vincent participated in the conversation.

"Don't like the ocean? Any reason?"

"Don't know. Too vast and open. Too deep, maybe. Can't see anything below the surface. Too many possibilities."

Davun hadn't considered that what he saw as an adventure and wonder, some others might see as scary and dangerous. It was true that many things could happen on the seas, but he felt his sense of adventure would overcome the fear of it if he ever had the opportunity to travel on a boat. At least, he hoped it would. Vincent had brought up some good points about the ocean that Davun was beginning to second guess traveling on a boat.

"That will be really fun for you, discovering all these other powers that exist like your own. When you get it, I mean," Rekura smiled at Davun. Davun blushed a little when she smiled and pretended to focus on his cart to avoid showing his cheeks. She seemed to genuinely believe that Davun would travel the world to seek other powers, which is something that definitely appealed to him, but the truth was he had no idea what he would do after obtaining the power. It was attached to some sort of responsibility, given that all the phoenix stories were about protecting innocents. He had no idea on his future obligations, but he knew that his top priority would always be Jethro. If he did decide to travel the world in search of powers that were hidden to the general public, he had no idea if he would bring Jethro along. Who knew what other powers truly existed, and what kind of person held them? If someone like Artruis were to gain control over something such as fire, he could truly wreak havoc if that was his wish. If someone just as destructive held a similar or even stronger power, then he would be putting himself and Jethro in danger. He couldn't leave Jethro behind again, but he couldn't sit in the village forever either.

"What do you two plan on doing once this is over?"

"I can't quite decide! On one hand, I'd like to research which mythical creatures are real, exist through people, or were simply made up. On the other, I'd like to settle down and have a family, maybe in a quiet village or at the edge of a city!"

"I don't know. I haven't thought about it."

The contrast of their two characters really put things into perspective for Davun. There really were a wide variety of people in this camp who have the same goal. What was even more surprising was that someone as cheery as Rekura had willingly become a soldier after a traumatic experience. Someone who was so positive, and innocent had chosen to join an army over vengeance. He found his hatred for Artruis grow just thinking about how someone could do something so devastating to someone like Rekura. He pulled his small cart alongside them as Rekura tried to convince Vincent to think about what he would like to do once they could return to their lives.

***

A day later, the camp was attacked by Ratlings. It was no larger than the last attack, and with their added defences they managed to lose only a few members. Hadik had Davun stand near the front lines this time, wanting him to experience what it was like, so he knew what to expect. He didn't let Davun actually join the formation, but he did have Davun run off to archers or fallen horsemen when they needed it. It was easier to learn from the smaller fights before joining the larger ones. Davun was also given a weapon this time, a shortsword, so that he could appropriately defend himself if no one was around to help. Davun heard a few stories about other soldiers experiencing their first kill of a Ratling, so he felt himself shaking a little in uneasiness for having to slay something, even to the point he began to feel queasy. When the time came for his first Ratling, however, he discovered he hadn't hesitated for a moment. A Ratling broke free and had darted right for Demoria, who was preoccupied assisting the archers as she tried to get them to hide behind cover from the enemy's arrows. Davun didn't wait for Hadik's order this time, and intercepted the Ratling, driving his shortsword through the creature's abdomen before he even realised he had even pointed it.

From there, Hadik no longer called out anything, instead focusing on keeping the shields at the front in formation, letting Davun cover any loose enemies that filtered through. Barith commanded the soldiers who were in the fray of battle, unfortunately suffering a non-severe wound to his side as an arrow struck him. He continued fighting, seeking medical attention after the Ratlings were defeated, and earning himself a scolding from Feyra for worsening his wound instead of immediately attending to it. With Thedan out of camp, Davun was given the task of escorting Serena to and from the safety boxes. She was quiet, the only time she spoke was when Demoria asked for an update on their supplies where she then spoke in great detail. Davun escorted Serena to her tent at her request, when Wayne and Kalavud stopped him shortly outside of it.

"Hey, Dav, take this to Serena for us," Wayne handed him a plate of bread and cheese, and a cup of water. Davun was confused but accepted the food.

"She's been down ever since she joined, lad, for obvious reasons. Keep her company, make sure she eats. She's been avoiding it as much as possible and we're worried about her."

Davun nodded, putting on his friendliest smile before entering the tent. He found Serena staring at her table, her papers neatly stacked to the side. Her arms remained in her lap as Davun placed the food in the open space she was staring at.

"Brought you some food, Serena."

"Thanks," she replied but remained still. Her gaunt face showing no emotions.

"Not hungry?"

"No."

"Okay. Well, do you mind if I sit here for a bit? I don't think we've spoken much before."

"You're welcome to stay. I'm afraid I don't have much to say, unless you want to hear about how many supplies we have, like the exact number of plates and cups we have."

"Oh, wow, you really know that?" Davun chuckled lightly, hoping to create conversation even if meant talking about medial things.

"Four-hundred and fifty-nine plates, and only thirty-two cups."

"You mean to tell me I gave you a cup that probably has four other people's saliva all over it? I am so sorry."

Serena gave a slight smile but didn't respond. Davun smiled to himself, having seen her smile for the first time since they had met. He quickly tried to think of something to say to before the creeping silence became awkward.

"How many spoons?"

Serena turned her head to face him, surprised that he asked such a question. "What?"

"Well, if you know the plates and cups, then you should know how many spoons, right?"

"I, uh..."

"It's okay if you don't, I just thought that you had to know absolutely everything we had here."

"No, I do. Two-hundred and ninety-six spoons. Though that number seems to go down every time we seem to eat. Somehow, we keep dropping them and not noticing."

"Pretty soon we'll have to try eat our soups with forks then."

Serena chuckled, which was music to Davun's ears. He was happy to see Serena's mood change, even if it was just slightly.

"I'm pretty sure we'll just drink them from the cups at that point" she joked back.

"I hadn't thought about that. I'm glad you're here to solve our problems when we inevitably become spoon-less."

"Oh certainly, just don't expect me to help much if we run out of forks."

"Oh, what would we do if we had no forks? We'd probably starve to death at that point. No way I'm drinking soup out of cups every day," Davun flailed his hands around in exaggeration, as he tore off a piece of Serena's bread and ate it to emphasise his point. She laughed louder this time. Davun couldn't hold back his own smile, and really had to hold back from showing any outward celebration when she followed him in tearing off a chunk of the bread and slowly ate it. He was surprised that the methods he used on Jethro to get him to eat would work on any adult, but he was glad that it had.

"I think we'd truly be lost if we had no plates though. I couldn't imagine what we'd put our bread on."

"Oh, especially because of all the soup in the cups, right?"

"Exactly! If only we had someone appointed here that kept track of exactly how many plates, we had at all times to ensure we'd never run out."

"Oh, I don't know, that sounds terribly boring."

"Yeah, you're right. Good thing no one has to do that then."

She continued to laugh along with him, idly picking at the bread and cheese as she did so. Davun would pick at it at some points so that she didn't think he was there to make sure she ate. He may be using the same tactics as he did on a child with her, but he certainly didn't want her feeling like one.

Once the food was mostly eaten and they continued to joke with each other a little, Davun grabbed her plate and cup and headed to leave when she grabbed his arm.

"Thanks, Davun. Come by again sometime."

Davun blushed a little as she pulled him into an embrace. He accepted the hug with a smile.

"Anytime, Serena. In truth, this helped me a lot more than I had expected."

"Demoria filled us in with what happened. She was pretty irate, but she didn't seem half as much today. I'm guessing you had a mouth sewn, horn to the ear conversation when you returned. I can't say I agree with going against Demoria and Arkarn's wishes, but I know you did what you genuinely thought was best for your little brother, and I can appreciate that. You're a good older brother, Davun."

The words melted off some of his stress. His dutiful care for his brother had never been acknowledged by anyone other than Jethro. It made him feel happy, something he had to admit had been scarce for a long time.

"Thank you, Serena. We should eat together again soon"
Davun gave her a large smile.

"Careful now, if your mouth grows any larger, it'll get stuck
and turn you into a Northerner," she teased him, smiling back.

Davun left the tent with the dishes, nearly bumping into
Wayne as he stood just outside with Kalavud, clearly having
eavesdropped on what transpired.

"You handled that like a true Northerner, laddy."

"I'm not a Northerner, Kal."

"Well, you've certainly got some of the blood in you, lad, just
look at you!"

"What he means to say, is that you did well in there Davun.
Good job. We can't tell you how much it meant to us to hear her
laugh again," Wayne placed a proud hand on Davun's shoulder,
giving a gentle smile.

"It helped me a lot, too."

Wayne gave Davun a pat on the shoulder. He nudged Kalavud,
and the pair walked away, leaving Davun to pile the dishes where
they were to be washed.

***

Davun had just settled into sleep when he was gently shaken
awake. He forced his eyes open, flinching at the candlelight that
Rekura held.

"Hey, sorry to wake you but Arkarn has returned, and Demoria
has called all officers to attend an emergency meeting," she spoke
in a rushed tone, making the urgency of the message clear. She
placed her candle on the table and left the tent. Davun hurriedly
dressed, choosing not to take the time to put on his boots, and was
escorted barefooted to the Captain's tent. There, all the officers
were in attendance, including Arkarn. The only person he couldn't
find was Jethro.

"Davun. Sit," Demoria commanded, her voice somehow more
serious than normal. Davun quickly seated himself, looking
around once more for his brother but not finding him.

"Where is Jethro?"

Arkarn looked at him, failing to hold back a scowl.

"He's gone."

CHAPTER FOURTEEN

"Which of the powers are truly controlled by the human that wields them, and which are merely using the human as a vessel? Do these minds have any form of sentience, able to take control of a human once bonded? Many of these powers have the ability to change one's nature.
Take the Harpy, for example."

Jethro begrudgingly peeled the potatoes, dipped them in a bowl of water to clean them and placed them aside to be later chopped. Averly had spent almost no time sending him to work since he had arrived in the early morning. The night was bustling with visitors and the cooks worked like mad to ensure that every dish was up to Averly's refined standards. The big rush had ended, and now Jethro prepared vegetables so that the remaining cook could make the workers a well-earned dinner. He began to despise not only Averly, but even some of the friends he had made recently, for thinking his only use was to prepare vegetables. He hated the task, but he had quickly learned that whining to Averly got him nowhere. He knew it was better to bite his tongue and get the work done rather than complain about it, but he couldn't help but feel like a tool and that everyone around him thought he was slow minded by setting him to a tedious task that no one else wanted to do.

Maybe all I am good for is peeling potatoes.

The thought slithered into his mind as he held back a tear. He wanted to learn more, particularly about flowers and the possible applications they had when used in various methods. He was fascinated by plant-life, as there seemed to be such a wide variety that existed that each could have their own use, like being made into a strong-smelling liquid that could waken animals from hibernation, or even used to alter the taste of food. He wanted to explore what other plants existed that he was unaware of.

But that will never happen. I'll be peeling potatoes for the rest of my life.

A loud crunch of someone biting into an apple broke his thoughts, causing him to snap his attention behind him. Delavun stood, smiling as he chewed, apple in his hand. Jethro, understandably shocked at seeing him, also hadn't noticed that the remaining cook had left the room. Delavun, not saying anything to Jethro, began snooping around the kitchen in search of more food to eat. Jethro stood in stunned silence, watching him shuffle things around, opening small crates where they stored the majority of the vegetables and fruits. Delavun seemed dissatisfied with what he discovered, choosing to pocket a few carrots and apples. He turned back to Jethro, handing him a mixture of carrots and apples.

"Here, we need these for our trip back."

Jethro just held his hands out and Delavun shoved the food into them.

"Well, come on. We better go before someone comes back," Delavun spoke casually, heading towards the window that was already open.

"What are you doing here?" Jethro finally managed to speak.

"I'm here to get you, of course."

"Why? I haven't even been here a full day."

"Trouble at camp. Some emergency. I wasn't really paying attention honestly. I was sent to get you back. Come on, you can ask me questions on the way, I don't want to have to speak to anyone who might come in," Delavun spoke nonchalantly and jumped out the window without waiting for a response. Jethro stared for a moment longer, before stashing what he could into his pockets and holding the rest, and climbed out the window after Delavun, who hadn't waited for Jethro and had already begun walking away.

"Well, that was much easier than I thought."

"What was?"

"To convince you to return to camp."

"I don't like peeling potatoes. Can I leave a note for Averly?"

"Best not to, we've got to get a move on, lad. There really is some kind of emergency. I'm sure this Averly will be fine. She'll find someone else to do the boring stuff."

Jethro felt bad for leaving Averly without saying anything, but he was worried that something had happened to Davun, as they sent someone else instead.

"Do we have to walk back, or did you bring horses?"

"We're walking. I don't really like horses, honestly. Too temperamental."

Jethro was disappointed at the idea of having to walk for a full day again, but he reluctantly accepted the answer as there was no other choice.

He stopped in his path, turning back to face the inn, debating on quickly running back to tell Averly. Delavun grabbed him by the arm and spun him back around.

"No time. Let's go. Emergency and all."

"Is Davun okay?"

"Yeah, he's fine. No one's hurt, I think. I wasn't told details, I hope, just to get you and return to camp as soon as possible. I even got permission to knock you unconscious and drag you if you chose to resist, but I knew you wouldn't."

Jethro was a little surprised that they had given him permission to do that, clearly Davun wasn't told about that part. He glumly followed Delavun out of the village, the guilt of not letting Averly know of his departure following him.

***

Since they left after the sun had set, they chose to rest not too far out of the village. Delavun clearly did not wish to stay there longer than he had to, getting what walking they could do before having to stop to let Jethro sleep. Delavun took off the pack he was wearing and handed it to Jethro, which he now recognised as his own pack. Delavun had already been to his room before their meeting to retrieve it, not wanting Jethro to waste the time repacking things. Jethro pulled out his blanket and wrapped himself to ward off the cold, but it couldn't keep it away completely. He shivered throughout the night, waking several times when a particularly cold breeze would blow.

The sun began to rise, peeking over the horizon to brighten the lands, but Jethro was in no mood for it. He faced away and covered his head with the blanket to shield himself from the light, desperate for more sleep. He wasn't too certain if he had slept further when Delavun pulled the blanket off to let the sun in.

"Time to go. Come on. Places to be and such."

Jethro wanted to resist against the abrupt order, wanting to persist in trying to get more sleep, but recalling that Delavun had been sent to retrieve him with a sense of urgency, he decided it best to comply.

Something was happening at camp, and for whatever reason that meant Jethro had to return, which to him only meant something had happened to Davun and that he was being lied to so that he would walk without having to worry. Delavun packed the blanket back into Jethro's pack for him, handing it over with a smile. He then took out a carrot and began to take bites of it. Jethro chose to do the same as they continued their walk.

Several hours into their walk, Delavun called Jethro to stop. Jethro thought he was calling for a rest, but the young boy stood on alert. He then grabbed Jethro and dove into a nearby bush, the branches scratching Jethro in various places from the unexpected movement. Jethro lay on the ground as Delavun sat next to him, peeking out of the bush.

"Stay there. Don't move," Delavun whispered in a harsh tone. Jethro's heart began to pound, his ears perked open to try pick up anything that could be deemed a threat. He heard the gentle rustle of the leaves as the wind swayed them. Other than that, there was an eerie silence as Delavun placed a hand on Jethro's stomach to keep him laying down. Jethro was growing terrified, the addition of not being able to look for the possible danger only accelerated his fear. That's when he heard what they were hiding from.

A series of pattering along the ground became audible near them, followed by what sounded like a singular set of horse hooves, as if in chase. Jethro barely caught sight of the Ratlings' feet running from his obscured view from the ground. He then saw the horse charging towards them, and a Ratling fell from an unseen attack. The horse didn't slow its momentum, running past each Ratling, and each one fell to something Jethro couldn't quite see. Once the last Ratling that Jethro could see collapsed the ground with a newly formed gushing wound, the horse slowed to a stop. Jethro couldn't see the figure on the horse and wanted desperately to stand to see who their saviour was, but Delavun held a firm hand on him. Jethro glanced up at him, but Delavun had a scowl on his face as he stared at the figure out of Jethro's view. After a moment, the horse continued its gallop. Delavun remained watching until they were completely out of view before easing his hand off Jethro. He then exited the bush to take a better look around for more enemies. Jethro sat up and made his way through the branches as they tried to scratch him once more. Once he left, he saw the aftermath of the mysterious horseman's work. Each Ratling bore a large cut on their backs that slowly oozed blood.

"Why didn't we come out when they were dead? The horseman would have been on our side," Jethro asked, confused as to why they couldn't meet their saviour. Delavun looked back, his scowl unchanging.

"That wasn't an ally. He is no friend of the Rats, and he is no friend of ours."

Jethro looked even more puzzled, but now realised that Delavun's scowl was trying to mask the fear that was set in his eyes.

"There is someone killing these Ratlings, but also doesn't like us?"

"He likes the camp, sure, but he's not an ally. It was best if we remained hidden, I couldn't have dealt with him. We better move before he decides to turn around for whatever reason."

Delavun spoke dismissively and began walking, clearly not wanting to talk about it any longer, but that didn't appease Jethro's curiosity.

"Who was it?"

"You don't want to know, so just leave it!" Delavun snapped. Jethro became ashamed as he clearly had upset the person who had come to return him back to camp, and back to his brother.

"Sorry. I'll be quiet for now."

Delavun took a deep sigh, put on a smile and turned to Jethro.

"No, I didn't mean to yell like that. I am sorry. That man just brings out a fear in me that I loathe, I shouldn't have released it onto you. Let's just keep walking so we can get as far away from him as possible."

Jethro nodded, doing his best to hold back the tears but was unsuccessful as a few managed to escape. He wiped them as they trickled down his face, wondering what man could bring out such fear in a soldier of their army. The only man he thought could possibly do that was Artruis, but the way Delavun had described the mysterious horseman, and the fact that he had cut down Ratlings, proved that it wasn't the leader of the enemy. That meant that there was someone else out there he feared crossing paths with, and not knowing who he was or what he looked like caused the fear to escalate. He would have to ask someone at the camp more about it, as clearly Delavun did not wish to discuss it further.

Night fell upon them after a day of walking, and they had yet to reach the camp. The surroundings seemed unfamiliar to Jethro, but he thought he just hadn't taken down the scenery as much as he thought he had. Jethro had been tired and exhausted but sleep still had not come easily to him. He tossed and turned against the cold of the night and couldn't escape his thoughts. He was scared for Davun, wondering if something had befallen him to have to return to camp so soon. Eventually, sleep claimed him for a couple of hours, before being woken by Delavun to continue walking.

Midday came and went by, and they still had not reached camp. Jethro was becoming concerned, his legs sore from having travelled for such a long period of time.

"How far are we from camp? I thought it was closer than this."

"Well, we might be there if someone didn't have to keep resting his tiny little legs," Delavun teased, "but we aren't too far now. Should reach it by nightfall. The camp had to move locations again, but it wasn't too far."

Jethro recalled the camp site that had been chosen deliberately by their scouts and wondered why they had to move from it. They had taken so much time to prepare a wall and a solid defence against the attacks, so it didn't make much sense to him to have to move so quickly.

I don't know anything about war, so how should I know why they had to move.

Jethro chose not to question Delavun further, he would have to wait until they reached the camp and ask Demoria, or Arkarn. Maybe even Davun would know. If there had been an attack, surely Delavun would have told him by now, unless he was still keeping that part a secret to avoid being asked questions. He didn't seem like he enjoyed answering all of Jethro's questions as they walked, but they did have idle conversations about topics such as food and the scenery. Delavun liked munching on carrots and apples as he liked the crunch they gave, and for some reason he seemed to have great joy in talking about it. He described the feeling he got with a surprising amount of detail for what seemed like such a small thing for Jethro, but he let Delavun talk to try and understand why he seemed so fascinated about it. In the end, Jethro remained unconvinced that the crunch was as appealing as Delavun made it seem, but Delavun insisted that Jethro might understand one day. Jethro talked of the local fauna they saw, rather than asking questions directly about them. Delavun either didn't know much about the plants or had chosen to not speak much about the topic to avoid encouraging Jethro to ask questions.

Throughout their conversations, Jethro was no more aware of the reason he had to return to camp immediately. The reason was bothering him, but the camp was not far off, so he did his best to not ask again, instead waiting to ask it of Davun. Having only seen him earlier that day, Jethro missed his older brother a great deal. They had parted ways, fully believing they wouldn't see each other again until it was all over and Davun would return with the newly acquired power of fire, that Jethro was discretely envious of. He wanted a cool power like his older brother, but he knew that it didn't belong to him. He would just have to relish in Davun's abilities and was still excited to see what he could do with it.

Maybe he can find another power for me, and then we can have some fun!

Jethro delighted himself with the concept of both of them obtaining a power. He obviously couldn't have fire because that belonged to Davun, but maybe they could find something just as fun for him.

Maybe water? No, I don't want to put out Davun's fire when he's using it. Maybe I could fly! I can take us both in the air and- oh wait, I think Davun said he'll get to do that too. What else is there? I hope there is something to make walking easier, I don't like walking so much. Or maybe a power to instantly peel vegetables, that would be nice. I could get it all done really quick and then have time to play with Dav.

Jethro spent a while contemplating new ideas that would make his life easier.

"Okay, we're here," Delavun called out, coming to a stop. Jethro had distracted himself that he hadn't realised the camp was in view. He excitedly snapped back to reality, preparing to rush forward into camp to find Davun, but his attitude immediately dropped when his eyes set upon what was in front of them.

Just more trees. Trees and a large rock. There was no camp.

"What do you mean? I don't see the camp? Where are w-"

"Hey, we're here!" Delavun cut off Jethro, yelling even louder this time, as if calling to someone Jethro couldn't see.

Jethro continued to search around, still seeing no sign of the camp and no one else in sight. The only thing of any interest to Jethro were some yellow flowers with a nice red centre.

CHAPTER FIFTEEN

"We discovered the Harpy amongst an older tribe of Viktavians. She could sprout feathers from her arms, and her singing was truly captivating. She could not speak Tellish, so we could not understand what she said.

That did not seem to bother her. She watched our mouths whenever we spoke, as if our voices captivated her in turn. She somehow understood what we spoke, despite not sharing a language."

Davun woke up in the medical tent once again. He was greeted by the morning light of the sun shining through the fabric of the tent. Feyra was tending to another patient nearby, wiping their forehead with a damp cloth. He rubbed his eyes to help wake himself, trying to recall what had happened. He recalled being in the emergency meeting with Demoria and the officers, and remembered Arkarn saying tha-

That Jethro was gone. He was no longer in Eraton, where he had just arrived two days ago. Arkarn had rushed to the village from where he received the message of their intent and arrived in Eraton a day after them, only to discover Jethro was already gone.

That's when his memory stopped. He must have blacked again from the stress. Guilt rushed back to him, swelling up inside and crawling its way up his throat, lodging itself there and refusing to move. He seated himself upright as the guilt threatened to make him hurl the contents of his stomach.

"You're awake. I suggest you prepare yourself. Arkarn will speak with you and he was furious once he found out," Feyra spoke out, not turning to face Davun. Davun laid his head back, sweat beginning to emit from various places. Feyra grabbed a fresh cloth and her bucket of water and seated herself next to Davun. She dipped the cloth, squeezing out the excess water and wiping Davun's forehead. The coolness soothed him a little, not realising that he had begun feeling increasingly hot.

"He found out about your little bite. Turns out that it wasn't an infection after all, so my medicine did little if anything at all."

Davun looked at her confused. "What is it then?"
"Poison," Feyra answered grimly. "Poison that is out of the realm of my abilities. I cannot cure a poison that shouldn't exist."

"What do you mean? How could I have been poisoned? Are you sure that the dog wasn't just rabid, and I got its disease?"

"Don't be stupid. If it were something as meagre as a rabid dog, you don't think I could have aided with that? When I say it is poison, I mean that it is poison. I have no idea what kind of species of mutt is able to induce such a potent venom, but my theory is it is a dog of legends. Why not? Everything seems to be nowadays." Feyra was growing increasingly frustrated, though Davun wasn't entirely certain if it was due to his idiotic question. He looked at his arm that had its bandages removed, exposing the wound he had received before he had ventured out from Eraton. The wound was a mixture of black and a dark shade of green. A yellow tinge surrounded each puncture mark, causing it to stand out. The thing that troubled Davun the most was how much the green had covered. It had now grown to what seemed double the original size of what he had thought was bruising. He touched the infected area, inspecting the troubling wound that he had been ignorant about, passing it off as an easily treatable disease that Feyra had already cured. Panic ran through his body as soon as his hand made contact with the area.

It was numb. He couldn't feel a thing where the grotesque colour had spread to. He tried to hold back tears as things began to stack upon him once again. His brother missing, and it was his fault for leaving him completely alone. He had been poisoned, which was not only causing him a fever, but had killed nerves in his arm. He could still move it, but he felt nothing. He cried a few tears at the prospect of losing his arm, when Feyra gave him a light tap on the head.

"Crying will get you nowhere, boy. Things happen and sometimes we can't control what happens. You have more things to worry about, like having to deal with Arkarn when he realises you've woken. He was livid once we took off your bandages, raving on about how you could keep the poison a secret."

"But I-"

"I know, you didn't know. Arkarn knows that too, I believe, but I think it was how he chose to deal with your supernatural poison. He seemed to recognise it and told me there was nothing I could do about it. And he was right," Feyra looked defeated as she stared at his arm. She gave a small sigh before turning away and continued to speak. "He wanted to speak with you as soon as you woke, so one of your friends ran off to get him," she gestured towards the tent flap that had been pinned open, and there Davun could see Vincent standing on guard. He hadn't realised someone had opened the flap, and now he dreaded having to deal with Arkarn.

"I don't know what creature could have done this, but it seems like we're not only trying to recover a power that shouldn't exist, but we are also trying to survive against one. Our situation just became a lot more dire, it seems."

Davun was opening and closing his right hand. It still functioned as it should, but he also discovered that he couldn't feel anything in his hand. It seemed the poison had the same effect on everything passed, and including, his elbow. He tried picking up various objects around him. His blanket, his pillow, the small candle holder with the waxy remains of a burnt candle. All had the same result. He could pick them all up as normal, but he felt nothing. Sweat dripped again from his forehead, the shock of realisation that his hand was numb combated the heat of his fever, causing him to feel numb all over.

"You'll have to get used to it. The arm has succumbed to the poison. I don't know how far the poison will spread, but I imagine if it reaches your heart, you'll die. We can only hope that Arkarn knows the cure."

As if his name summoned him, Arkarn appeared in the entrance. His expression already showing frustration and anger before his eyes laid upon Davun.

"Can you walk?"

Davun nodded.

"Then come with me," Arkarn spoke with a sense of urgency, leaving as quickly as he had arrived. Davun swung his legs off the bed, grabbed his shield that lay against where he had rested, and he followed Arkarn's hurried path. Rekura and Vincent followed them, as they were ordered to, all the way to Arkarn's tent. Arkarn didn't speak a word to anyone as he made his way inside. Davun had never been inside Arkarn's tent, but it was smaller than he imagined it. He hesitated, unsure if he was expected to follow Arkarn inside, before deciding to enter anyway. Inside the tent, the number of possessions had not met Davun's expectations either. A makeshift bed lay on the floor, some books strewn about it, and a singular table was placed in the room that Arkarn was now standing at. It appeared to have a couple of plants growing in small pots as well as an assortment of glass jars and tools for measuring and stirring.

"You should have told us about the poison, but now it has spread much further than anticipated."

Arkarn spoke, sounding angry and not turning around as he began arranging the things on the table.

"I didn't know it was poison. Feyra took a look at it, and I told her a dog bit me, so she thought it was an infection of some sort," Davun had to hold back his own volume, not wanting to get into a yelling match with Arkarn. He reflected the anger that Arkarn was showing him.

"Did the dog have a missing ear?"

Davun startled at the sudden question. He was expecting Arkarn to throw more accusatory remarks at him.

"Yeah, but how did you know that?"

Arkarn plucked one of the plants from the table and began to crush it in a mortar and pestle. "Lakkerfel's are resilient things. Their hides becoming so tough that they become prime war dogs, and as such have been banned as pets. Lakkerfel's may be resistant to damage and are ferocious in battle, but they are not venomous. Nor was the one that attacked you from the army's litter. I do not know by what means, but Artruis has obtained a Lakkerfel and managed to turn it venomous" Arkarn plucked the other plant as water began to heat over a small fire that Davun couldn't see as the back of the man obscured his vision.

"There is no true cure. Once this poison enters your blood, it immediately begins to attack your insides, killing off anything that allows you to feel. If acted upon quickly, I can stop the spread, leaving the affected area to a minimum."

"If there is a treatment, why did you tell Feyra there was nothing she could do? She might have been able to produce it if you had shared that information with her."

"Don't try to get smart with me, Davun. Feyra could do nothing about it, she doesn't have the knowhow or the core ingredient for it."

"What would that be? She has many supplies, I'm sure."

"This" Arkarn nearly shouted, producing a small chain that sat around his neck out from beneath his shirt, exposing a torn dog ear. Davun immediately recognised its tough hide as part of the Lakkerfel that attacked him.

"How did you…but that was before I was even attacked, how could you have known?"

Arkarn didn't respond straight away, instead focusing on his task. He removed the ear from the chain and began to heat it over the fire as he placed another plant into the now boiling water.

"I've known of his mutated pet for a while, so I began my preparations as soon as possible. I lured his pet into a trap, and through a great deal of effort, I managed to grab one of its ears. With it, I can produce a treatment that will stop its growth but will not eliminate the poison itself. I'm afraid that would require something even beyond my abilities."

"So, you've been carrying an ear around until someone was bitten by it? What happens when more people are bitten?"

"No one else will be bitten. I have a theory that the Lakkerfel does not actually produce the poison itself, rather it was somehow infused into it. It seems to not be able to use the poison more than once without that infusion again. I also knew that it would be targeting you, which leads me to my next question that you absolutely need to be honest about," Arkarn paused, stopping his task and walking over to Davun, lowering himself slightly to match Davun's eye level.

"Where were you when the Lakkerfel bit you?"

"In Eraton."

Arkarn's face immediately dropped as if he had expected that answer. He turned back to the table and grabbed the flask that contained the ear and the odd bluish-green liquid that he had made. He fished the ear out with his stirring instrument and set it on the table. He held the flask in his hand, inspecting it.

"That means that Artruis knew who you were, and where you were, before I was even able to meet you," Arkarn spoke softly, the realisation cutting through him deeper than he expected. Davun stood still, uncertain how to interpret the information.

"What…What does that mean for Jethro?" he managed to speak through a shaking jaw.

"It means that he is almost certainly in Artruis' grasp."

Davun felt dizzy, losing his sense of balance slightly as the fear for his little brother sent him into a daze. Arkarn placed his hand on Davun's shoulder to grab his attention and handed him the oddly coloured concoction.

"It has cooled a little, but you must drink it while it is at least warm. And try to keep it down, I know it's not the most pleasant of tastes."

Davun grabbed the flask, trying his best to steady his shaking hand. He stared at the liquid while trying to process the situation his little brother was in. The odour of the drink hitting his nostrils with a powerful stench that caused him to reel back.

"Hold your nose, if you must, but down it quickly. It's best to try get it all in one go."

Davun held his nose, and inwardly counted to three before downing as much as he could. The taste was worse than the stench, as the warm liquid felt thick and gooey as it dripped down his throat. He gagged and coughed as he tried to force it down. It had tasted worse than he imagined chewing a rusted nail felt like. He managed to down most of it, but Arkarn insisted he consume the remains and so Davun reluctantly swallowed the rest. The taste glued to his tongue and throat, unable to be rid of it.

"I know, Davun. I know you are worried for your little brother. I am afraid I do not know where he is. We know Artruis' location, but there is no telling if he is truly in Artruis' possession, or if he will be hidden away somewhere. But all is not lost. We will not sit idly when we still have options. This time, I will not journey alone. You will accompany me, and whoever else we may be able to spare. If our first option doesn't quite pan out, then we have a second, which will take considerably more time. As long as our options exist, we will find him at any cost, Dav."

Davun was slowly beginning to feel better. He felt his pain subsiding as he guessed the tonic was taking its effect throughout his body. He nodded in agreement with Arkarn, and Feyra's words echoed to the surface of his mind. Now is not the time to sit and cry about the situation. Now is the time to do whatever you can to change your situation.

As long as his brother lived, he would find him.

CHAPTER SIXTEEN

"The Viktavian's tribe leader spoke broken Tellish, so communication was poor, and I possibly have been unintentionally misled due to mistranslation, but I took in what they said as factual. It appeared that before the young woman obtained the power of the Harpy, she had been deaf. Now, she hears all, and goes beyond that by somehow understanding a language she does not know.

Is the girl's hearing restored by the power of the Harpy, or is it the Harpy's hearing in a girl-shaped receptacle?"

Davun was having difficulty sitting on his horse correctly. He hadn't been taught how to ride aside from Kalavud's helpful advice of 'sit on the saddle and don't fall off'. He couldn't quite find the right position to be comfortable. Every which way he sat would make something sore from the horse's movement. Arkarn took the lead as he guided Davun, Wayne, and Kalavud through the forest. Rekura and Vincent had volunteered to accompany them along their journey but had been convinced to stay to help defend the camp. Wayne, Kalavud, and Arkarn were enough to keep Davun safe. Demoria was reluctant to let three officers depart camp, in addition to Thedan being gone, but was persuaded when Wayne and Kalavud appointed capable soldiers to take their places in their absence. Wayne and Kalavud found themselves frequently needing to leave the camp, so they had been training people to take their positions when necessary. Their journey would either take a few days, or possibly a half a week, depending on how their first destination's events would transpire. Arkarn hadn't told them where they were headed, only that it was where he had been during his last leave. He didn't wish to tell anyone during their time in camp, as he didn't want anyone to overhear or eavesdrop on the information. The location was meant to be a secret and showing just the three of them would put him in a worse situation than he had already made there.

"So, Arkarn, just making some light conversation, but where in the minotaur's labyrinth are we headed?" Kalavud called from his horse. He was smirking as he watched Davun shift position again on his horse.

"Well, if everything goes well, you'll have your first real encounter with a power of legends. The Chimera." Everyone perked up to this. Wayne and Kalavud shared a pleased look.

Kalavud, despite being part of an order whose goal it is to seek out a particular power, had yet to see any with their own eyes. They became visibly excited, smiling to each other. Davun had momentarily forgotten the discomfort riding a horse brought him, as he pondered on what to expect, before realising that the answer was just in front of him.

"What kind of power is the Chimera? Should we be worried?"

"Worried? No. Not unless he is provoked, scared," Arkarn's voice quietened to be barely audible, "Or if he is still a little upset with me"

"What did you do Arkarn? Do we need to have another chat about your anger issues?" Wayne called out in a voice that sounded like he was speaking down to a child.

"I wasn't very happy with our bargain, and things may have gotten a little…heated."

"Great. Not only may we not find our answer to the missing lad, but we might also go missing ourselves. Lovely."

"No need to be dramatic about it, Kal. We'll be fine. Probably. The Chimera has the ability to transform any part of its body into a beast. Truthfully, I don't know the full range of what it can turn into. I also think that when he transforms, part of his mind is replaced by the animal parts he takes on, and over time that has taken its toll on him. I'm not certain how stable he is mentally when he is in his normal state, but he definitely loses some control when he transforms. So, in the unlikely event that you see him sprout claws, wings, hooves, or Kalavud's face, then probably best we take our leave at that point."

"Wow, cheap shot Arkarn."

"I think it was very descriptive and informative."

"I didn't realise Wayne and Arkarn were in this together. I hope you're at least on my side, laddy."

"I think I'm more impressed that some beasts can speak the human tongue."

Kalavud feigned hurt, grasping his chest as if he was wounded. Davun smiled, but immediately felt guilty for having joked around while Jethro was missing. Wayne and Kalavud's antics were a great distraction from reality, but now was not the time to be distracted. They had to push as hard as they could to find his little brother as soon as possible. The thought of what Artruis would do to his brother in order to get to him sent shivers down his spine.

He'll most likely want to trade me for Jeth. What should I do if that happens?

He of course would do anything to save his brother, even if it meant giving his own life, but from what he understood about the situation, it was more than just his life that Artruis would be getting. Give a man like that the power of legends, there would be no boundaries to the pain he could cause.

But could Davun really trade his brother's life to prevent that from happening?

Did he have the strength to prevent more lives being lost if given that opportunity?

"Dav?" the Northerner's accent called out from beside him, breaking him out of his thoughts.

"Everything okay, laddy? You went quiet all of a sudden. And I'll be honest, being grim is not a good look on you."

Davun smiled slightly as the Northerner poked his insult at him. It was funny to him how a well-timed insult from a friend could mean so much.

"I'm fine, Kal. Just worried, that's all."

"I know laddy, but there aint no point worrying about it if we're already heading towards him. He'll be fine. Artruis won't harm the little fella if he still wants you, so as long as you stay alive and focused, we'll get him back no worries."

"He's right, Dav. With a mug like that, Kalavud could pose as the Lakkerfel and sneak in to get Jethro without being seen."

"How about we paint your body grey, and you can pretend to be a rock? You would be good at it, y'know, since rocks don't have any hair."

"Well, what about Arkarn, then? The way he's always frowning when he's angry or thinking, he may as well just disguise himself as a Ratling. He's got enough hair to cover his entire face, I reckon."

"Do not drag me into this game of hag and witch. I am happy with how long my hair is, thank you."

"Hag and witch? What kind of Southerner logic is that?"

"Because you are both being ugly by casting insults at each other. Is it really a phrase you haven't heard before?"

"Never in my fourteen years below the border. You Southerners have some odd phrases, honestly."

Davun was surprised to discover that it was a Southerner phrase. He had heard it a few times from passing parents as they scolded their children, and assumed it was a common phrase everywhere.

Wayne and Kalavud argued for a while about different phrases that Northerner's and Southerner's used, before finding something else to argue about. They could talk for hours about irrelevant things that weren't worth the time it took to debate, but it seemed that was how they passed the time. Davun eventually got the hang of riding the horse, and so they picked up the pace a little. They could only go as fast as Davun could handle his horse, slowly increasing their speed over time. By the time night fell and they had to set up for camp, Arkarn informed them that they were at least halfway there. They chose not to light a fire as it may cause attention from unwanted visitors, so they sat huddled against the trees, waiting for sleep to find its way past the clod breeze blowing against their skin.

"Things will be alright, Dav. I want you to know that. I can't guarantee it, but Jethro should remain unharmed as long as you are hidden from Artruis. Once we have confirmed his location, we'll begin our attack against the Ratlings and break into Artruis' base. We won't let him be alone for long," Arkarn spoke loud enough for all to hear but directed it at Davun. Davun found it hard to trust Arkarn's words. The mysterious man still produced an aura that was doing its best to pull Davun in to bridge that gap of trust, but Davun actively resisted. For all he knew, Arkarn always knew where Artruis was and had been holding off the attack for his own intentions. There was something both genuine and shady about him that would only confuse Davun whenever he tried to figure the man out. His emotions would fluctuate about Arkarn, but he decided to accept Arkarn's words, wanting to believe that the deceitful man really did have Jethro's well-being in mind.

"Though, I feel that we should talk about a possibility that may arise. And I know you will hate me for it, but please allow me to explain before you all attack me," Arkarn's voice shook slightly. Everyone shifted to place their backs against the tree to face Arkarn's darkened frame as the last of the day's light was fading.

"In the event that Artruis will hold Jethro hostage in an attempt to trade him for you, Davun, I am ashamed to ask that you agree to it."

This stunned Davun, numbing him even to the bitter stings of the cold winds. This was not something he had expected one of his protectors to say. He hadn't made up his own mind about what to do in such a situation, but it appeared that Arkarn had already come to that decision a while ago.

"Before you all interject with your own questions and opinions, please allow me to explain why I think it is best. If you disagree, please voice it," even in the dark, Davun could tell that Arkarn was uncomfortable by the topic. He was sitting there, asking the heir, the reason people are fighting against an enemy unknown to the world, to sacrifice himself.

"Firstly, I believe that in being Artruis' hostage that you will fare better than your brother. If he uses a method of torture, you will be able to bear more than Jethro. Second, Artruis is manipulative and cunning, but above all he is cold-blooded. There are no limitations that he will adhere to in order to achieve this phantom goal of his. If he believes that you will not trade yourself in for Jethro, then he will not hesitate to discard your brother. Artruis is resolved and acts as if everything he does has no consequences, and that is what makes him truly fearless. If he claims that he will kill Jethro if you do not turn yourself in, then I am in full belief that he will do so. Thirdly, he cannot kill you right away, Davun. It is not how he obtains the power of Balkyeros. Though I do not know his plans of how to achieve that, by all reason he shouldn't kill you before you have claimed the power."

Davun listened to every word carefully, ignoring the sounds of the nocturnal animals beginning to wake. Wayne and Kalavud remained silent for a moment, uncertain if they agreed with Arkarn or not.

"How can we trust that he will hand over Jethro even if I agree?"

"Artruis may be cold-blooded, but as I also said, he is a man of resolve. He will do whatever it takes in order to unlock the orb. I get the feeling that none of this is personal to him, and we are merely obstacles that are in his way. If he has the means to be rid of the obstacle, then he will do so by any means. I'm certain if we could be bribed that he would have done so the moment we began to form ourselves into an organised group. It is even possible that if you had asked him to disperse his Ratling army in promise of handing yourself over, he would have done so, though that was never an option of course. The only reason I ask you to do it now, is for your brother."

Wayne was growing agitated, the darkness doing nothing to hide his emotion in his voice. "Arkarn, you can't possibly ask him to do such a thing. We'll save Jethro by other means, we have other options."

"I can trust you guys, right?" Davun cut him off with the unexpected question. Everyone sat silently, trying to decipher the reason behind the question.

"Of course," Arkarn responded with full sincerity.

"Then I'll do it."

"Lad, think about it a bit more before you agree."

"I trust you guys. I have full belief that once you have Jethro, you will all do what you can to save me. Once Jethro is safely escorted out, then come for me. I'll survive until then."

"Dav…you don't have to rush to the decision," Wayne tried to persuade him, but to no avail. Davun shook his head, forgetting they were in the dark.

"You guys can save me. Jethro will be scared. I can't have him stay in the clutches of that man longer than I must."

"This is all assuming that he indeed does have him. Though, I fail to think of another possibility."

"But Dav, think about it ple-"

"Wayne, the lad has made up his mind. Let it go. We'll just have to go through all the effort to make sure we get him back safely so that we can scold him then."

Wayne gave a defeated sigh, clearly unhappy with the decision, but didn't debate it further.

"I am truly sorry to ask you of something so large, Davun. I am in your debt for this," Arkarn spoke, a slight quiver in his voice. Davun wasn't certain, but he thought he saw Arkarn wipe away a tear from his face as he moved in the darkness.

"Making sure Jethro is safe will repay that debt."

Arkarn nodded silently. He wrapped himself in his blanket and faced away from the group to rest. Wayne and Kalavud also laid themselves down to sleep, accepting the matter resolved. Davun pulled the blanket up to his chin as he sat against the tree, unable to find the effort to sleep. He weighed the decision he had just made for a while before he could no longer keep his eyes open.

***

Morning arrived to wake Davun, who was surprised to see that he had slept better than he had before while camping without fire. Wayne and Kalavud were still resting, but Arkarn was already awake and staring at the leaves as they gently swayed. His bag was already packed, and the horses were chewing on some carrots that he had placed for them.

"Everything okay, Arkarn?"

"It will be. I just enjoy watching the leaves dance with the wind. I find that it calms me to immerse myself in these small things."

Davun looked up to see what Arkarn was talking about. He did admit that the leaves were mesmerising as they bellowed back and forth, as if thousands of tiny dancers were putting on a performance just for him. He wanted to turn away to wake Wayne and Kalavud, but he found himself immersed in the pattern more than he had anticipated. He wasn't sure how long he had been staring at the leaves with Arkarn when Wayne and Kalavud stirred awake. Once the bags were packed, and they fed themselves, they set off on their travel once more. With Davun having some experience in riding, Arkarn decided to push them harder to cover more ground. They reached their destination around midday, though it wasn't quite as Davun had expected. He imagined seeing a cabin in the middle of the woods, possibly even a hole in a tree for someone to live out here, but instead he discovered it was a rock. A large rock that acted as the entrance to an underground cave.

The group dismounted from their horses and tied them to the nearby trees and gathered at the entrance of the rock.

"When we go down, please do not say a word. In no way should you answer any of his questions. The only way to get information from him is to ask him a question first. Answering his questions first are seen as donations and won't achieve anything for us. I am not certain what else I can offer him, so he may wish information from one of you, or even an object if he deems us unable to answer any of his questions. I am hoping that in me asking the questions that I must make the payment, but I am not certain that is how he works. We will see what happens, however, so just be prepared."

Arkarn explained as he stared down the dark slope. Everyone nodded silently, and took a step forward after Arkarn, before Arkarn abruptly stopped.

"Oh, and one more thing. He may not enjoy seeing me again, so prepare to evacuate if we must."

Wayne opened his mouth to say something but Arkarn had already begun descending, so Wayne chose to roll his eyes. They formed a line at Arkarn's direction, grabbing hold of the person in front of them as they traversed the pitch-black pathway. After a few turns, Arkarn stopped, causing them to slightly bump one another.

"Something isn't right," he spoke out into the darkness.

"What is it, Arkarn?" Wayne called out from the back, anxiousness in his voice.

"There should be light. We have entered his quarters, but there are no lights."

"Well, he is part animal so maybe he can see in the dark? Call out his name, perhaps."

"Stay here," Arkarn told Davun as he unhinged his hand from his robe. They heard Arkarn walk a few paces before hearing the sound objects being shuffled around. After a moment, light was created as Arkarn light a candle that he had found. It wasn't terribly bright, unable to brighten the entire room. From what they could see, things were a mess. Random objects were littered across the floor, the table that Arkarn had retrieved the candle had torn books and papers, with scraps of food left on various plates and the table itself. Arkarn walked deeper into the room, shedding light on a bed that was empty but showed signs of use.

"He isn't here," Arkarn announced, clearly upset at the prospect.

"Where would he have gone?" Wayne called out while searching through the books.

"I am not sure. He very rarely leaves his cave, usually only to collect debt or restock on food."

"Well, I can assure you it isn't the food one," Kalavud called out as he held up a dead rabbit from a crate that he had opened, holding his nose against the smell.

"Then he is off to recover a debt then. Though, I have no idea who from. I know he has had dealings with Artruis, but I doubt that Artruis would have left himself in debt to the Chimera of all people."

"Artruis has been dealing with this Chimera?" Wayne called out, surprised at the fact.

"Yes, it was part of the information I was to reveal to you all, but other matters took precedence. No point in worrying Demoria and the soldiers with that information while we leave them to defend themselves. The Chimera is able to communicate with the animals of this forest, which is how he knows everything that goes on within it. I was hoping that he would have known Jethro's whereabouts, but clearly that is no longer an option for us."

"What now then?" Kalavud asked, wiping his hands from the animal carcass.

"Now, we go with our second option, which I'll admit I was going to have us go anyway. Maybe I can now convince them to provide us with military assistance, but they will none-the-less have the location of Jethro."

"Who are 'they'"? Davun asked, as Arkarn seemed to be talking more to himself than the others.

"Old friends of mine. And now, our only hope of knowing where Jethro is."

"That doesn't explain who 'they' are, but how would they know where Jethro is?"

"Truthfully, I have no idea. Some of their ways are beyond my understanding. I always put it down to having a hunch, or instinct, and disguising it with some fancy tricks, but they have always been correct."

"Is he just going to keep avoiding on telling us who 'they' are?"

"Probably, lad. We'll have to find out when we get there."

The group left the cave, twisting through the darkened path again, and emerged to the surface as the light stung their eyes that had begun to adjust to the darkness. Arkarn ordered everyone to mount their horses and to prepare to travel for another day. Davun inwardly groaned at the idea of riding the horse for another day, his lower body already sore from riding so long, but knew it was necessary to find Jethro faster. He grabbed his horse and rushed after the others as they began the next length of their journey.

It took them over a day to reach where they were being led, and Davun couldn't believe it when he saw where it was.

They stopped at the base of the mountain near Eraton. The one that Davun would stare at while he idly worked, and the place where he had met Arkarn.

"Leave the horses here, we'll travel up by foot," Arkarn ordered, and the others followed.

"Are we really going to climb this mountain? It looks dangerous, Arkarn. Especially if the kid has to carry his shield up, maybe he should leave it here."

"Do not worry. The climb may be strenuous, but it is not dangerous. There is a path they have hidden to reach the top to make it easier upon themselves. Follow."

Arkarn guided them to a pile of large rocks located at the base of the mountain. He walked up to the pile and then stepped to the right of it. He placed his hand against the slope of the mountain and pushed. A doorway revealed itself, leading into yet another dark passageway. The door tried to close itself, but Arkarn placed a hand on it to hold it open.

"Inside. Come on."

Wayne and Kalavud were hesitant to enter, but Davun wasted no time before walking in. The others soon followed, and the door closed behind them, completely preventing light from entering the tunnel. Arkarn produced a candle that he had taken from the Chimera's room and lit it to spread light upon some stairs that led up.

"It will be a strenuous climb up the stairs, there are many of them. There is a small opening nearly halfway up that we can rest at."

The group began to trudge themselves up the stairs. It seemed endless to Davun, as the light only travelled so far and didn't allow any sight past five or six steps. Davun's legs began to burn as he took one step after the other, his breath becoming heavy and sweat dripping from his forehead. He began to feel like asking to stop so that he could rest, but the stairs finally led into the small opening and Davun immediately collapsed against the wall. Wayne and Kalavud followed by sitting themselves down and massaging their legs, while Arkarn remained oddly still in the centre.

"Aren't you even remotely tired, Arkarn? What kind of monster can climb those steps and not want to rest," Kalavud joked, but genuinely curious as to why Arkarn didn't appear to be relaxing. Arkarn turned to face them, an upset look on his face.

"I am sorry. I thought they would leave you be if you were travelling with me. Do not panic. No harm will come to you."

His words sent them all into a state of panic, as their eyes darted around the room to see who he was referring to.

"What do you mean? What's going o-" Wayne fell silent as his unconscious body collapsed to the floor, a dart sticking out of his neck. Before Kalavud could react, another dart pierced the skin of his arms. He angrily pulled it out and reached for his sword before fainting. Davun looked at Arkarn, who held his remorseful expression.

"Sorry, Davun. It'll be a little unpleasant."

Before Davun could respond, he felt a small sting in his neck. He felt the sensation of falling as sleep forcefully claimed him.

CHAPTER SEVENTEEN

"If these powers have the ability to change the body, what stops them from changing the mind? Which of these power holders have their personalities nurtured by the use of the power, and which were changed as soon as the power was given?

Are their minds their own? Or do they simply think their mind still belongs to them?"

Jethro followed the two men through the forest. Delavun had taken him to meet one of his companions, an old man who tried to appear refined, but would periodically lose the guise and act a little erratic. He claimed to be able to help Jethro resolve the war, but the words seemed menacing at the time, and so did everything else this man had said. Delavun avoided the few questions that Jethro could muster the courage to ask about where they were going, and when they would reach the camp. Jethro walked a few paces behind them as they had a whispered conversation that the man called Pallinor would randomly raise the volume of his voice before seeming to force himself to bring it under control. Jethro wasn't an ignorant child, he knew something was amiss, but he wasn't sure what to do. He didn't know if Delavun was a part of the ruse and could be trusted anymore, nor did he know where the camp was to run away.

"Where are we going?" Jethro managed to ask again, but he was scared of what their reaction might be so it hadn't come out as loud as he thought it would be. Pallinor became visibly irritated as he clenched his fists beside his body and strained his neck as if trying to control his anger. Delavun spun around, walking backwards so that he could face Jethro while still keeping pace with Pallinor.

"Now, now, Jeth. I thought I said it's a surprise and that you shouldn't ask. Pallinor here was close to spoiling it for you, and I don't think any of us would want that."

Jethro looked disappointed at the response, despite it being what he was expecting. Delavun's demeanour had changed since meeting with Pallinor. He became more confident, but it appeared that the unstable man was most likely his superior, though Jethro did not know him from the camp. Jethro continued to walk in silence, debating on what he should do. He didn't feel right following these guys, and his chances of surviving out in the forest while searching for the camp, that he wasn't even sure if it really had moved, were slim. They changed direction of their course, as if an obstacle were placed in front of them that they needed to skirt around. Jethro began to feel scared. Without someone here that he could trust, he had no idea what to do. He was used to being told what to do, and now that he was in a situation where he was uncertain about the people he followed, he had no idea what to do. He missed Davun. Without him, Jethro was lost. He was dependant on his brother making the choices, and wouldn't hesitate to trust the likes of Kalavud, Wayne, and Arkarn.

But none of them were here. He had to make his own decision. He slowed his pace a little, drifting a little back to create more space between them. When he had doubled the distance between them, he turned and ran. He ran as hard as his legs could take him, the fear of being chased sending adrenaline through his body in an attempt to help his body escape. He wasn't sure if the blood had swelled to his ears so that he misheard, but the yell that the old man gave when he realised, sounded a lot like a large beast trying to intimidate its prey. He continued running, not turning back to see how close they were to him. His only objective now was to find the camp, and Davun. It felt like he was running for his life, though neither Delavun nor Pallinor indicated any wish to harm him. His body began to feel the burn of running as fast as he could, and the cold sweat of fear. It gave him a weird sensation that numbed his body. He was running for his life, and he would have to push past the limits of his body in order to achieve that. He continued to run, inwardly praying that the camp was just hiding behind the next tree, or that someone would appear to save him.

He felt something knock his foot and sent him tumbling down. He received a minor scrape, but his mind set that aside for a more urgent matter. Delavun was standing above him, panting heavily.

"I forgot how fast you kids can run, gees. That took a lot more effort than I thought," he spoke as if nothing was wrong, and that the situation was funny to him. He pulled Jethro to his feet and pushed him towards where Pallinor was standing in the distance, where he had run from.

'Go on, back we go."

Jethro didn't move, not out of defiance but because he was afraid of what was going to happen to him if he did. Delavun gave another small shove, but Jethro still remained unmoving.

"Look," Delavun spoke, rounding to Jethro's front and crouching to meet him at eye level, "I was really hoping that you were just going to follow us like you obediently follow your brother, but it seems I need to give you more of an incentive, so how about this. You willingly walk with us, and I promise that I'll kill you with this if you piss off Pallinor again," he produced a small knife that Jethro was unsure where he was keeping hidden.

"Trust me, it'll be a lot quicker than what Pallinor will do, so it's a good deal. He'll toy with you like a predator would to a much, much smaller prey. Do not make him angry again. It won't end well for either of us. Now that you have your incentive, let's go," Delavun stood to the side, his arm extending out as if politely letting Jethro walk first. Jethro took a hesitant step forward, the fear that Delavun was trying to invoke into him working as intended. Jethro was uncertain if an old and scraggly looking man could really catch him if he tried to run, but he figured that Delavun would simply catch him again and hand him over. He didn't know what Pallinor was capable of, but he didn't want to find out firsthand.

Jethro once again followed the men, who revealed themselves to be his captors rather than saviours. He was ordered to remain next to Delavun that was accompanied by another threat of what would happen to him if he tried to run off again. Now that Jethro was closer, the discrete conversation that they were having died down, the few words that were spoken no longer in a whispered voice. They talked about going to collect a debt beyond anything that Pallinor was ever owed. Jethro had no idea what kind of person would be indebted to a man like Pallinor, or how such a situation would ever arise. He decided it wasn't monetary, as Pallinor looked like he owned very little, so it must have been some kind of favour. He pondered on the idea that they had been hired by someone to retrieve Jethro, but the only man he could think of that would seek him out is Artruis, but it was only speculation. If Delavun really was only hired to retrieve him, then why was he already at camp before either Davun or himself had arrived? And why had he not been ordered to take Davun instead? Or try to lure him out of the camp during their time there? They seemed to wait for the right moment to go after him, though he didn't know how Delavun knew where to find him when he was hidden away in Eraton. He knew he was just going to be kept in the dark even if he tried asking questions, and he decided it would be best not to speak. He didn't wish to draw their ire more than he already had.

They travelled for a few more hours before stopping to rest for the night. They gave Jethro another warning about attempting to run away whilst they slept. Delavun gave Jethro an apple to eat while Pallinor went off into the woods to find himself some food, stating that he wanted to eat meat. When he returned, however, he appeared to be unsuccessful in his hunt as he carried nothing. Jethro wondered if Pallinor had caught something and cooked it on his own, but Pallinor hadn't been gone long enough for that to be feasible. Jethro had secretly wanted something other than the apple given to him, but obviously couldn't state it as he was in no position to ask of anything. The others placed themselves next to Jethro to reinforce the point that they would be keeping their eye on him during the night. Sleep was elusive for Jethro. He was afraid to move into different positions, not wanting to give the others the impression that he was trying to escape. He pondered where he was being taken to, and to whom. He wondered if Davun would ever discover that he was no longer in Eraton, and if it was going to be too late when he did. Davun had no intentions of returning to Eraton until the battle was over and they had reclaimed the orb, so there was no telling when Davun would know. It was already too late to find him easily, as he had no idea how they would even find him at this point if they did find out earlier. Jethro felt a sudden wave of fatigue hit him, and not wanting to think about anything anymore, he wished for sleep to claim him.

They arose in the early hours of the morning and didn't wait to properly waken first before setting off again. Delavun produced another carrot for Jethro to eat whilst they walked. They travelled through the forest, taking seemingly spontaneous turns at random intervals. Once they had walked half a day, Pallinor gave out the order to stop.

"We have arrived," he spoke. Jethro looked around, seeing only more trees. There were no buildings, landmarks, or anything out of the ordinary to him. Delavun looked equally confused has he searched the surroundings.

"Tell your master that I have business with him. We will remain here," Pallinor called out into the empty forest. Jethro had no idea who he had been speaking to, but Pallinor sat himself down as if waiting. Delavun followed suit and gave Jethro a signal to do the same. Jethro sat, puzzled as there had been no reaction to the old man's calling out. After a moment of complete silence, leaves rustled above them, and a Ratling dropped to the ground from a branch it had been hiding on.

"Yes, we recognise you's. We will gets master. You wait," it spoke in a high-pitched voice, almost a shriek as if speaking were difficult and a strain on its throat. The Ratling scurried off, disappearing in the distance behind some trees. Jethro knew that this was the outcome, but he still feared it none-the-less. He was to be handed over to Artruis, most likely in an attempt to blackmail Davun into coming. Afterall, Davun was really the one he was after so that he could unlock the power of the phoenix. They waited for almost an hour before a band of Ratlings marched over to them from the direction the original Ratling had went. Amongst them stood out a singular human, standing well above the shorter creatures. He had long black hair, brushed neatly back, his skin was a pale white, and he wore a black shirt and pants. His overcoat was also black but had green embroidery along the edges. Jethro couldn't quite tell if the green pattern were symbols of some kind from where he sat. His attire contrasted with his pale skin, but the most peculiar thing about the man was that he wore a cloth around his head that covered only his eyes. They marched until they stood about fifty paces away, and Pallinor rose once they had stopped. Delavun and Jethro stood as well. Jethro's legs began to shake as the band of Ratlings vastly outnumbered them, and the man in the middle was especially intimidating.

"You have brought the latest thing I asked for, I assume?" the man spoke, his voice slightly deep and even.

"I don't normally take requests to fetch things, but how could I resist what you promised to give in return. This is the brother of that Davun character I've heard so much about," Pallinor smiled as he spoke, clearly happy at the prospect of their deal.

"Allow me to inspect him."

"Inspect him all you want once he is yours. First, you must give the information to me."

"I only wish to ensure that you have the right person. I trust that you believe that you have it correct, but I have no use for someone who has no connections to Davun."

Pallinor rolled his eyes, placed his hand on Jethro's should and pulled him to stand before him. The Ratlings moved aside to allow the man to walk forward. When he got close, Pallinor tightened his grip on Jethro's shoulder. The man walked up to Jethro and without any words or hesitation, he grabbed Jethro's arm and rolled up the sleeve, inspecting the arm up and down. He then did the same thing with his other arm, both his legs, and his torso.

"Young man, are you the brother of someone called Davun?" he spoke evenly, almost in a monotone voice. Jethro remained silent, the cloth that covered the man's eyes intimidating him into silence.

"Please answer me. I do not wish to drag this out longer than it must go," the man's voice didn't waver. Jethro nodded, too afraid to lie in the situation.

"That is satisfactory. I will accept him."

"Uh, uh, uh! You must answer me my question first. I also have other information that you might be interested in if you wish to make another trade," Pallinor tried to entice the man, who showed no reaction, instead walking back to his Ratlings.

"You may have the information once my business in this forest is complete,"

"That is not what we agreed on, Artruis!" Pallinor growled.

"If it appeases you, I will even provide more than what you have already asked. Anything you desire, in fact. Once my business is done, I will present myself to you and answer any question you wish of me."

Pallinor pondered about it for a moment, clearly intrigued by the offer. "No, I don't think so. You've accumulated enough debt as it is, and now it is time to pay. Before I can even consider handing over the child, you must answer the most important question we have already agreed upon. What is it that you seek from the Balkyeros orb so eagerly? What could be so important about it that you have done what you have done in order to unlock it? I must know that in the least!" Pallinor grew increasingly frustrated as he spoke, clearly not having an answer to the question bothered him greatly. Artruis remained silent, Jethro could only assume he was staring at Pallinor from behind the cloth.

"You may have that answer, and more, once my busine-"

"Do not give me that! Who knows which way this fight will go! You could die or run off once you've achieved the power of flight, and I do NOT like chasing down my debts. You give me the answer now, or I will hide the boy from you until I get twice the payment!" Pallinor pointed at Jethro, his hand now a claw. Jethro took a step back, surprised to say the least. He had definitely not expected this old man to have claws, he was certain that he had human hands before. He looked up at the man, who apparently had grown more hair than he had before, and at a darker shade. Jethro looked around to see if anyone else was as surprised as he was, but no one other than the Ratlings seemed to react. The Ratlings shifted where they stood, now on edge as Pallinor was becoming hostile.

"Do not do anything rash. Let us come to –" Artruis tried to reason, but Pallinor let out a growl, his face now formed into a lion. The Ratlings lowered their weapons, ready to attack if the hybrid of a creature lunged at them.

"You must give me what is mine!" Pallinor roared, his voice now more beast than man. Artruis remained still, seemingly not intimidated by the display before him.

"Retrieve the boy," Artruis commanded, and the Ratlings surged forward. Pallinor yelled, growing a tail made of a snake's head. Delavun grabbed Jethro and pulled him back out of the inevitable fray. He put himself in front of Jethro, producing the knife he had on his person to threaten any Ratling who came close. Pallinor swiped his powerful arms that were now covered in fur, and knocked down several Ratlings, at the same time his tail managed to bite a Ratling, the stricken creature giving out a screech of pain. Jethro couldn't take his eyes off the creature Pallinor had become, afraid that it might turn towards him at any second. It continued to strike down the Ratlings as they tried to swarm him. Artruis remained unmoving from his position, watching the events unfold before him. He raised his hand, giving a signal to more unseen Ratlings as arrows flew from nearby treetops. Few found its mark and pierced Pallinor's flesh. Pallinor roared, scaring a few Ratlings as they cowered in preparation of being attacked. Pallinor crouched to all fours, staring at Artruis who was now in his sights. Artruis gave no reaction to the beast of a man, continuing to face him as if nothing were wrong. Pallinor fiercely roared once more. Artruis continued to stare him down from beneath his cloth. Artruis took a single step forward. Pallinor turned, facing Delavun and Jethro, and began to charge at them. Delavun grabbed Jethro in an embrace as if covering him from an oncoming attack, and Jethro prepared himself for death. He fully believed that Pallinor was in a rampage and would easily strike down anyone in his path. As the stomping of Pallinor's heavy body grew closer, he felt talons of a large bird wrap around him, and his feet lifted off the ground. He thought himself dead, his soul having left his body and now floating away to evaporate into nothingness. He felt the rush of wind blow his hair, and he opened his eyes. The reality was nearly as shocking, as he realised that he was now high above the trees. The creature that Pallinor had become now had talons instead of claws, large wings sprouted from his back as they flapped, continuing their ascent to escape from Artruis and his Ratlings.

CHAPTER EIGHTEEN

"Through many of the tales, I understand why the minute percentage of the world's population fears the truth being revealed. Despite the number so diminutive in comparison to the overall number of humans that fill the world, there are still those who seek the powers for personal gain.
And they will do almost anything to obtain it."

When Davun finally opened his eyes, he saw the clear, bright blue sky. He lay upon a soft blanket that acted as a barrier to the ground, which was a carved stone slab, shaped into a rectangle as if it were a bed. He looked around, seeing movement on all sides, but his mind was still addled from the effects of the dart that he had been struck with. He sat up, holding his head as the world seemed to swirl around him for a moment.

"Please, do not push yourself," a soft voice spoke to him. He focused his gaze on the floor below him, waiting for his mind to piece itself together so that he could make sense of his surroundings. After a moment, he was able to stand with little effect to his balance. He still felt a little muddled, but sensible enough so that he could process his surroundings.

What he saw was some kind of settlement. There were small shelters made from a combination of wood and stone, with peculiar red and gold symbols painted on them. Dark skinned people were walking about in a variety of coloured clothes – many of which were robes - and all were lined with wool at the shoulders, wrists, and ankles. Their feet were covered in what seemed like wool and leather, to soften the hard ground they lived upon. Many bore woven patterns that sat around their necks, displayed over the brim of their clothing, and closely resembled the symbols that Arkarn wore on his own robe. Even though these people vastly differed in the described attire and manners of the book he had read, Davun recognised them.

Daritians.

The only similarities between the book he had read and the people before him were the dark skin, and the patterns they proudly displayed about their neck. He turned to face the person who had spoken to him, now on edge knowing who these people were and what they might be capable of. They had once had the intention of hunting down the Phoenix, and now that he was before them, he was afraid they were still in pursuit of the power. Not that he had it yet, but they would surely hold him prisoner once they knew, if they didn't already.

The person who spoke to him was a woman who sat next to the stone slab he had woken on. She wore a yellow robe, lined with the same wool as the others, and woven, red fabric that made a pattern he couldn't quite discern around her neck. She smiled at him, unmoving from her seated position.

"Give yourself a moment. The air is thinner than you are used to, but you will adjust," she spoke, each word clear and precise, with only a slight accent. Davun had not realised it before, but she was right. He was finding it slightly harder to breathe, every breath he took felt like it wasn't inhaling the amount of air it should have.

"You are scared of me. I see that. It seems that your false history has reached you before the truth has. We must give the unnamed man a talking to," she stood as she spoke. She was nearly as tall as Wayne, and somehow just as intimidating despite her pleasant smile.

"You can ease your mind. I do promise we are not a threat to you. What version of false history have you been led to believe?

That we eat our own? That we are savages who attack villages? Perhaps it is the one where we kidnap children during the night so that we might feed them to the Wendigo?" she smiled as she spoke, amused at her own suggestions. She certainly didn't appear threatening, but Davun knew that some appearances were not to be trusted, just a mask hiding true intentions. He tried to steady his own breathing, but remained keeping an eye on the Daritian, who was waiting patiently for him to speak.

"I…Do you know who I am?" he decided to ask, before revealing anything he wished to keep hidden.

"I do, young one. You are an ally to the unnamed man and said to be the next Balkyeros."

Davun felt his heart sink. He had hoped that they hadn't known about who he was. The smiling Daritian took notice of how Davun reacted, and a flash of realisation entered her eyes.

"Ah, I see. You think we wish to hunt you. Still a twisted story, but at least there is some truth to that one. Please trust me, we do not wish you any harm. The Daritian people hunted a Balkyeros once, yes, but it was not to capture or slay him. It was so that we could speak with him, that is all," she explained, her hands clasped before her. Davun wanted to trust her, but he couldn't believe everything he was told, which included the book he had read. He was inclined to trust in some of her words, however, as Arkarn brought him there on purpose. Seeing that Davun remained hesitant and on edge towards her presence, she continued explaining.

"We Daritians can be trusted by the likes of you, heir of Balkyeros. Our people now exist to protect and guide any who claim that title. We are the protectors of the Phoenix. We are her flock."

In that moment, he wanted desperately to believe her. He wanted to believe there were more people wanting to help him with his powers, rather than seeking to take it from him.

But he couldn't completely trust in the words. It seemed too good to be true.

"Where is Arkarn?"

"Arkarn?"

"He was the one who brought us here."

"Oh, I see. My apologies, I had not realised he had given you his title to call him. I thought he had given you his name in your tongue."

"My tongue? Wait, is that who you meant when you said unnamed man?"

The Daritian woman nodded. "Arkarnryus is a title he bears with our people now. It is one that he chose himself. In our language, it means to be never given a name, or that you have discarded your own name."

Davun wasn't sure how to react. He knew that Arkarn had kept secrets, that much was obvious to everyone, but to not even give his real name? Why was he trying to hide his identity?

"Who was he before?"

"The title he now has was selected by him, I am afraid I do not have the right to tell you who he once was. It is something only he is allowed to say, but people who claim that title have reason behind it. You must trust that the unnamed man. His title only eradicates his name, it does not change who he is."

"Unfortunately, who he is, is what I am worried about. He keeps information from the people who should know it most. It makes it a little difficult to follow him blindly."

"Yes. Somehow, I do believe that. We Daritians do not believe in hiding the truth, it is not who we are as a people. We try to deal with situations as best as we can, and to do that, everyone must be aware of the situation so that we might help one another. I do not know why the unnamed man chose to adopt a different method. I guess we did not have an impact on his personality as much as we had hoped."

"What do you mean? Was Arkarn actually raised here?"

"Here? No. But with we Daritians, yes. We guided him for many years, but it has been a while since we last laid our eyes on him. He has been off doing the work of—"she cut herself off from the sentence, and Davun couldn't tell if she was thinking of the translated words or thinking of something else to say entirely.

"He has been doing his own work. He is a busy man, it seems. But I am glad to see that he has kept you well."

"I'm not who I am worried about. My brother has gone missing, and we came here to apparently find answers on his whereabouts, though I honestly don't know how you will help."

"Me? I am afraid I cannot help at all. My name is Shardian, but to my people I am Nyamyt. In your tongue it means…head mother"

"Head mother?"

"I take care of the people here. If someone becomes sick, I will see to it that medicine is provided. I make sure that we are fed, healthy, and warm, and are able to continue life."

Davun nodded to show he understood. He took another look around and noticed that Kalavud and Wayne were not far away, speaking with a small group of Daritians. They seemed to be having some difficulty with the language barrier, as he noticed Kalavud exaggerate his words with his hands to try and get his message across. The Daritians didn't appear to be hostile towards them, and they didn't seem to be worried either. Davun decided to relax a little, though he still felt the need to be cautious.

"I see two of my friends, but I don't see Arkarn. Where is he?"

"Follow me, heir of Balkyeros. I will take you to him," Shardian gestured as she began to guide Davun. The ground here was not what he had expected from the top of a mountain. It seemed that the Daritians smoothed out an area to live upon, though many slopes still remained. As he walked past, many Daritians glanced in his direction, but their faces were unreadable as they showed no sign of recognition or interest in him.

"We have lived here for many years now. Shortly after you were born, I would guess. We are but one of few Daritian groups left in the world. We fear that by producing too much, we will need more land, which increases our risk of being seen. It is best we remain hidden from the world below, so please do not tell anyone of our existence," Shardian narrated as they walked. Davun continued to look around, everything he saw piquing his curiosity. They seemed to display small symbols or pictures wherever they could fit it. It brought colour to an otherwise grey environment, and obviously had some deeper meaning than mere decoration. They climbed the last slope and reached Wayne and Kalavud, who smiled when they saw him approaching.

"That was a bit rough, wasn't it Dav?" Wayne greeted him, as the surrounding Daritians moved to one side to allow the newcomers to merge with the group.

"I think it was quite a pleasant sleep," Kalavud chimed in, finding any opportunity to input a joke, "I was just asking these lads here for their recipe so that sleeping in the forest will be a lot easier."

The three Daritians looked at each other and spoke in a language that Davun assumed was their native tongue. They ran off unexpectedly, Kalavud calling out after them.

"No, I was only kidding around! I...and they're gone. Well, I at least hope they write it down in a language I can read."

Wayne laughed, and Shardian smiled along.

"I am bringing your friend to meet with the unnamed man. Perhaps you two would like to join him?" she offered, and the two men happily accepted. They had yet to see Arkarn since they had woken as well and were just as eager to find out why they had come. As Shardian walked up a steep slope, her three followers in tow, they began to hear shouting up ahead. It was in the Daritian language, but it was obvious to anyone who heard that the man yelling was angry. As they reached the top, a man burst out of a shelter, thrusting the curtain that acted as a door aside. It was a Daritian, dressed in a purple robe with yellow trimming, and a red and white woven fabric around his head, his hair fed through the gaps of the pattern. He was carrying a large branch, with a dull orb at the top that the branches' limbs held in place. He was gesticulating wildly, and at one point even pointed a finger at Davun. Arkarn had followed the angry man out of the shelter, not saying anything, rather just listening to the man go on a rant about something unknown to Davun.

"What is he saying?" Davun asked Shardian, who lost her smile and seemed annoyed.

"Arkarn. Your friends have woken. Perhaps you wish to fill them in. I will calm Takas down."

"You will not be so eager to calm me once you realise what this man has done, Nyamyt!" Takas shouted at her in Tellish. Shardian raised her hands to try calm Takas down and spoke to him in Daritian. Takas stormed back into the shelter he had come from, and Shardian followed, disappearing behind the curtains. Arkarn looked exhausted as he approached them and sighed deeply.

"What was that about?" Wayne asked, curious about what had transpired.

"That was Takas, the man who is able to find Jethro for us. He is their Balkynys, which roughly means that he can see that which is out of our vision. He was able to locate Jethro. Kind of," Arkarn explained, staring at the ground as if deep in thought.

"Where is he?" Davun asked after Arkarn had stopped talking, too impatient to wait for Arkarn to continue.

"He is still within the forest, but he is not with Artruis, that much is known."

"Then where is he?!" Davun was getting worried. Not being with Artruis should have been a good sign, but Arkarn didn't look happy about it.

"Before Takas started going on a tangent with his own opinions, he did manage to tell us that Jethro is travelling with the Chimera."

"Well, that's good isn't it? You know them, so you can find them and just get Jethro back?" Wayne seemed hopeful, but Davun already knew it wasn't going to be that easy. Arkarn shook his head, his face reflecting the same disappointment in the rest of them.

"We went to the Chimera's home and he wasn't there, so he's travelling. The issue is I do not know where he is going, or even why he has Jethro. He could have easily handed him over to Artruis, but perhaps Artruis had nothing to offer him. Pallinor could be finding someone else to trade with, or possibly already knows someone who is interested, but I can't think of anyone else.

I do not know Pallinor's intentions, and that is what frightens me. With Pallinor on the move, it will be even harder to locate Jethro."

"But you just said that Takas knew where he was? Why don't we just go and get him now?" Davun was growing irritated from worry, only wanting to find his brother as soon as possible, but it seemed a new obstacle would place itself in the way every time they tried to move around the previous one.

"Not that easy, laddy. He said the Chimera is travelling, so right now we might know where they are, but by the time we get there they would have moved," Kalavud surmised, and Arkarn nodded in agreement.

"Unless we know where Pallinor is going, it is going to be very difficult to find them, I fear. Especially if they leave the forest. I hope that Pallinor's fear of civilisation will keep him within the forest, but there is still the possibility he'll go somewhere else."

"Then why don't we just get Takas to come with us? Could he track Jethro while we travel?" Wayne suggested, and Davun perked up to the idea. Arkarn thought about it for a moment, debating something internally.

"No. Takas will not travel with us. But there may be someone who can, though I don't know if they will agree to it. It will make the Daritians angry, but it might be our only option," Arkarn spoke quitter than normal, as if he didn't want to be overheard. The curtains slide open behind them, and Takas and Shardian emerged, walking towards them. Takas still looked annoyed, but at least had stopped yelling. Shardian approached Arkarn, and the two spoke in Daritian, clearly not wanting the Teldarian folk to be part of the conversation. Shardian seemed to be speaking down to Arkarn, but it was hard to tell when Davun couldn't understand. She then turned to face them all and changed her language to Tellish.

"As much as we wish for you all to stay with us, time is of the essence. You must all set out to find the young one as soon as you can."

Davun assumed that's what they had planned on doing anyway, so he interpreted what she said as more of a dismissal to leave. It didn't seem in her character to do that, in the little time that Davun knew her, so he was confused.

"Arkarn, we haven't had a chance to speak yet. It has been a while since you last arrived, and there is something that you must know," she continued, this time facing only Arkarn, but continuing in Tellish so that everyone understood. "A while ago, we discovered that the Vykurius was slain. We do not believe its power returned, but that is only a guess."

It seemed that every time Arkarn was involved in a conversation, new information was revealed. They had only been here a short time, and yet Davun had already been informed of so much, even if it was indirectly. Some of it only created more questions, like who or what Vykurius was, but at this point he had so many questions to ask, he wasn't sure where to begin. Arkarn caught the look on Davun's face and turned to address him.

"I know, Davun. I know. Please allow our business here to finish and I will answer questions on our way to find your brother. Is that alright?"

Davun nodded silently, already annoyed that more information was presenting itself from Arkarn despite having been there such a short time.

"How long ago did he die?" Arkarn asked, returning the conversation.

"Our best guess, weeks before we discovered him, and that was several months ago. We unfortunately have no leads where the power may have gone."

Arkarn looked grim, the news clearly not a good sign.

"Nyamyt, I know I have lost much of my respect due to my actions, but I must request something of you. Of all the Daritians. The upcoming confrontation with Artruis is not in our favour, and with an unknown Vykurius out there, it is very possible that we will be attacked from within before the fight even begins. I must request that the Daritians aid us in our battle. At least long enough for us to reclaim the orb, then we call a retreat. I will deal with Artruis personally, before the orb is retrieved."

Shardian sighed deeply, her face showing regret for what was coming, telling Arkarn all he needed to know before she even spoke.

"You know that the Daritian people cannot be seen by Teldarians anymore. We risk too much being discovered by them again. They have been influenced too much by the lies and we are no longer safe. Our presence may only serve as a new threat to your people, we cannot risk ourselves or risk distracting your army from fighting. I fear I only see negatives when you ask me of this," Arkarn raised a hand to stop her, and then bowed his head.

"I know what I ask you to risk, and I would not ask it if I didn't know the full complications of it, but I understand your reasoning. I will do my best, as I always have, Nyamyt."

Shardian smiled, her eyes still saddened. She spoke to Arkarn in Daritian, causing the man to guiltily smile as he responded to her in kind.

"Then," Arkarn returned to Tellish, speaking to everyone this time, "Let us share a meal once this is over. It has been too long, my friend."

"You are all welcome back. Once the new Balkyeros claims his title, we shall feast," Shardian smiled. At that moment, the trio of Daritians that Wayne and Kalavud had been speaking to hurried back, seemingly excited. One of them carried a small wooden box, trying to hand it to Kalavud who was simply confused. He accepted the box and opened it, revealing a few darts carefully placed inside.

"I was only kidding! I didn't really want the darts so I could sleep!" Kalavud tried explaining to them, but it seemed these Daritians weren't versed in Tellish as they continued to smile and gesture to the darts. Kalavud insisted on returning them, but the Daritians were stubborn and wouldn't take them back. Kalavud sighed, admitting defeat, and thanking them instead.

"I'll find another use for them."

Wayne laughed. "It isn't often that I see you give up Kal, but it gets funnier each time."

"I think I've already found another use for them."

Arkarn and Shardian laughed along as well. Davun could only manage a smile, not quite feeling up to laughing while his brother was in an unknown situation. Nobody seemed to know what Pallinor's intent was, and that made Davun nervous. Without knowing the intent, it would be hard to track him down. They did not know where he was going and would have to scour the forest to find him while still avoiding Artruis and his Ratlings. The situation was glued in Davun's head, any form of positive feeling being suppressed as he pondered on how they would go about tracking down his little brother. He couldn't muster the strength to laugh, or even properly admire what lay upon the mountain that he would view most days.

"Nyamyt, I thank you for your hospitality in letting my friends stay. We will depart, we do not wish to bother you any further."

"Have you told them about the custom they must partake before they may leave here?"

"Of course not, Nyamyt."

"Excellent. Then we shall say our goodbyes," Shardian turned, and ordered Wayne, Kalavud, and Davun to stand next to each other. She then called all the Daritians with a loud shout. All of the Daritians stopped what they were doing to respond to the call, and after moments they surrounded the three Teldarians as they stood confused. Davun looked to Arkarn for answers, but he was nowhere to be seen.

"Friends of the unnamed man. You have been brought here and revealed the only secret that the Daritians keep. Our existence. It should be obvious to you why we must remain hidden, and so you must convince us that you will not tell any other of our existence," Shardian announced, as Takas appeared to be repeating her words in Daritian so that everyone could understand.

"You must make with us a bond of truth. You must not break it. If you do, then lives will be lost. To form this bond, you must look me in the eyes, and promise from deep within your inside that you will not tell any. The words may be easy to say but know that they carry with it much weight. A promise to a Daritian must not be broken. If it is, your soul will be torn asunder by Ulkinys, your light given to Balkavyros, and your physical body fed to Anyty. Stand tall, look into my eyes, and bear unto me your promise that supports many lives upon them."

The Teldarians remained silent as Takas finished the translation. Shardian took a step forward, her posture remaining upright as she awaited the words. Wayne uncrossed his arms and stared right into Nyamyt. He pointed a finger to his chest, a southerner tradition that signified plunging a dagger to your heart should your words be a lie and made eye contact with Shardian.

"I, Ryan Baleforn, promise I will not reveal your presence to any, even should it save my own life."

Shardian seemed satisfied with the words, smiling and nodding to Wayne.

"Ryan Baleforn, your words are accepted. The promise has been made and cannot be broken."

Kalavud straightened his back, preparing to make eye contact with Shardian, but stopping to grab a handful of gravel. He rubbed it between his hands for a moment before letting the loose stones drop to the floor. He revealed his hands to show the small grey marks that some of the stones left behind.

"My name is Kalavud. My hands are dirty, but my tongue remains clean. I promise you that I will not tell a living soul about your existence on this mountain. Should it be broken, may the harpy take my tongue and voice. In addition to what you said, of course" he smiled his infamous smile, and Shardian nodded in acknowledgement.

"Kalavud, your words are accepted. The promise has been made and cannot be broken."

Shardian then faced Davun in turn, awaiting his response. Davun hesitated for a moment, uncertain if he should make some sort of gesture as the other two had. He decided against doing anything extra, hoping that just his words would be enough.

"I, Davun, promise on my own life that I will not reveal your home here, or your presence in our world. I have no grand gesture to accompany my words but know that I would do nothing to betray the people who can promise me my brother back."

Shardian stared at him, and time seemed to stop as Davun awaited her response. After a moment, she smiled and nodded.

"Davun, your words are accepted. The promise has been made and cannot be broken. You three Teldarians of both the North and South are free to leave our home and return to it as long as your promise remains unbroken. Travel safe, my friends, and I do hope that you are able to recover Jethro."

"We thank you again for your warm welcome, and your permission to depart, Nyamyt. Goodbye to you all," Arkarn spoke from behind them. He bowed to Shardian and turned, leaving between a gap that the crowd created for them. Wayne and Kalavud followed, but Davun didn't move.

"Thank you again for locating my brother, Balkynys. Without your help, we would be aimless."

Takas didn't speak but did nod to him in acknowledgement. Davun turned to leave, chasing the others who were headed for the stairs.

"Goodbye, Davun. I hope you are prepared for the role that you play," Shardian called out to him. Davun turned, smiled and waved to her, then returned to following the others as they began their descent down the stairs, on their way to rescue Jethro.

CHAPTER NINETEEN

"Almost no truth we uncovered was without a tragic tale that took place sometime within the powers' timeline. Betrayal, murder, deception, blackmailing, force. The list of sins, crimes, and foul behavior goes on with each story.

If such a small percentage of our population suffers so much, what would happen if that percentage was raised?"

The ground did not provide any cushioning as Jethro and Delavun were dropped to the earth as Pallinor was landing. Jethro landed on his front, the wind escaping from his body as he slid and rolled. Delavun tried to land on his feet, but the momentum was too much, and he was sent forward, tumbling until he lay on his back. Pallinor landed near them, spouting a mixture of grumbles and growls escaping his lips as he slowly began to return to his human form. Jethro desperately tried to breathe but began panicking as the air proved difficult to intake. He moved to being on all fours, breathing as fast as he could in an attempt to get more air to enter his body. Delavun walked over and crouched beside him.

"Calm down, you got the air knocked out of you, it's alright. You just need to slow down, let the air come to you. Try to pace yourself," he guided Jethro, who did his best to try and calm himself. He did slow down a little, but it was difficult to remain calm when you couldn't breathe. He breathed as patiently as he could, and after a moment, the air began to circulate into his body as if there was somehow more of it. Delavun patted Jethro on the back and helped him to stand. He looked over at Pallinor, who was spouting nonsense mixed with creative curses as he paced back and forth.

"Sorry about that, Jeth. Pallinor gets a bit rough when changes like that, but at least we got out, right?"

Jethro wasn't certain how to respond so he just nodded in agreement. He was staring at Pallinor, who was now completely human, no signs of any animal traits to be seen. Delavun noticed Jethro's quietness and saw that he was staring at Pallinor.

"Ah, right. You don't know. Well, Pallinor is the Chimera. Heard about it?"

Jethro nodded. "Only a little,"

"Well, the bottom line is he can turn into animals and you don't want to see him angry. Or scared. Or upset, annoyed, and even some cases, too happy. Don't cross him and you'll be fine. Best to stay away from him while he processes what happened."

Jethro realised what was meant to happen. He was going to be handed over to Artruis. The man he was supposed to be fighting against. The man Delavun was supposed to be fighting against.

"How could you, Delavun?"

"How could I?"

"Betray the camp like this. What did Pallinor offer you? Money?"

Delavun chuckled at the prospect and sat down next to Jethro. "Not quite, but you were almost there. I was working for Pallinor before the camp was even formed. Someone, this Artruis guy, visited Pallinor one day asking to be informed when a certain boy entered the camp. Pallinor sent me in to keep watch for when Davun arrived and find any leverage I could use against him so that we didn't really have to use force. Well, you both arrived, and both of my tasks were solved on the same day, so that was convenient for me. I reported to Pallinor who told me to stay and obtain information before anything happened. So, you see, I never really betrayed the camp. To be quite honest, I doubt they even really knew I was there," he spoke, amused by the situation. Jethro became angry at Delavun, mostly towards his attitude about what he'd done.

"So, the entire time, you weren't actually part of the camp?"

"That's right. You'd be surprised how much people don't notice when they're focusing on other things. Or how much you can gain someone's trust with a fake name," he snickered at Jethro, clearly aiming the latter comment towards him. Jethro looked at him, puzzled and angry. This was all a game to Delavun, and now Jethro had been taken as part of it. He was supposed to be given over to Artruis, who would have used him to lure Davun into a trap, and now he had no idea where he would end up, all the while his brother was probably still searching for him. They might even attack Artruis, thinking that he was there only to find their deaths in battle. Jethro was furious but knew lashing out at Delavun would only make things worse, especially if Pallinor became involved. He turned away in a huff, not wanting to look at Delavun. Jethro tried to hold back tears of frustration, which became more difficult as Delavun began laughing.

"Oh, come on! Delavun? Awfully close sounding to someone's brother. It hits you unconsciously, your instincts telling you to like and trust me simply based off a name. I'd say don't take it personally, but quite honestly, I don't know if it was. It was pretty fun watching you believe in everything I said. That kind of power gives quite a thrill."

Jethro was trying his best to not lash out at Delavun, but every laugh that came from that boys' mouth struck a nerve in Jethro. It became too much for him, and he turned to Delavun and lunged at him, pulling a small kitchen knife that he had snuck from Averly's inn. Delavun was quick to react, grabbing that hand that held the knife the moment it pierced his skin, only drawing a slight amount of blood. Jethro struggled, trying to drive the knife deeper into the other boys' stomach, but his strength was no match for Delavun, who twisted his arm, causing his grip to loosen and drop the knife.

Delavun followed it up by pushing Jethro backwards, knocking him down in the process.

"Wow, a knife? That's a pretty dangerous thing to carry around. You could have killed someone," he mocked Jethro, picking up the knife and walking over to him. He crouched beside Jethro, who now sat upright, and stared at him with a smile.

"Maybe you aren't quite aware of what these things can do. Would you like me to show you?" his voice was low and creepy. Jethro couldn't respond, the look on Delavun's face had become slightly twisted, intimidating Jethro into shock. Delavun took his silence as his answer and grabbed Jethro by his shirt, pulling him close. He then took the knife and slowly began to draw it along Jethro's cheek, who was struggling to get loose. He tried to grab the arm with the knife, but Delavun kept his arm strong, drawing a small line of red on the side of Jethro's face. Jethro began to cry, the cut no less than a scratch and producing little pain, but the look in Delavun's eyes scared him. It was like nothing he had seen before. They were eager. Hungry for more pain. He was truly enjoying this.

"Enough!" Pallinor barked from where he stood. Jethro wasn't certain if he had seen what Delavun was doing or was simply tired of hearing him cry out. Delavun let go of Jethro, who quickly scrambled backwards, away from the insane boy. Delavun stood, keeping his smile. He then threw the knife as far as he could, not caring where it landed. He stared at Jethro a moment longer, relishing in the look on the young boy's face, before turning to speak with Pallinor.

"So, what's our plan then?"

"I'm thinking, so just shut up for a moment!" Pallinor snapped. He clearly had not planned on his deal falling through with Artruis, and now was panicking about what to do next. Jethro sat, tears still falling down his face, breathing heavily, his eyes not straying away from Delavun. He was still shocked by the look Delavun had, like something inside him was hungry to see the pain he was inflicting on Jethro. Even though Jethro now knew the truth about Delavun, and everything he had been at the camp was a hoax, Jethro just hadn't thought him capable of such a thing. The boy must have been hiding a personality beneath a personality. Despite revealing what his intentions were earlier, he still had much the same personality as he displayed in camp, with a little impatience mixed in. Whatever was festering beneath the surface of Delavun scared him just as much as when he'd seen Pallinor's transformation. He was beginning to wonder if he was better off with Artruis.

***

Jethro was once again ordered to walk alongside Delavun. The proximity of the boy now gave Jethro chills, and made him paranoid that the boy would suddenly strike him. He walked, doing his best to keep an eye on Delavun while not trying to make it obvious. They walked through the forest, though Jethro had no idea what their destination was. He wasn't even sure if Pallinor knew, or they had just started walking in hopes of coming up with an idea along the way. They still had to avoid the Ratlings, and possibly anyone who came searching for Jethro from the camp, if they had discovered his absence. Pallinor walked, his face in a scowl, clearly annoyed at his situation.

"So where are we headed, Pallinor?" Delavun asked, not wanting to walk aimlessly.

"I have a few ideas, so just keep walking. I'll decide in a moment,"

"Well tell me, maybe I can help."

"If you haven't figured out the possibilities based on the direction we are headed, then you likely don't know that they exist, so you're of no help."

The response clearly bothered Delavun, who now had a slight scowl of his own. Wandering aimlessly didn't appeal to anyone, but it at least seemed that Pallinor had an idea of where they were going, though Jethro still didn't know what Pallinor's plans for him were. Right now, he was an item to be bought, and the only potential buyer was now pursuing them instead. He wished there were a way to contact Davun or leave any indication of where he was or was heading, but he knew his brother was still most likely back at camp, training to fight and retrieve the orb.

Maybe Artruis chasing us is a good thing. Without Artruis to lead the Ratlings, they can recover the orb easier. I don't think Artruis would have brought it with him.

The idea grew on Jethro. Maybe if they could lure Artruis long enough, it could benefit the camp. He knew that either way, he would be a prisoner, so why not let both sides distract each other? Not that Jethro had much of a choice in the matter, but he decided it would be best if he appeased Pallinor and Delavun's orders to increase their chances of evading Artruis and the Ratlings.

At that moment, an arrow struck the ground in front of them. They all turned to see Ratlings, most of them charging while the others with bows lined up their shots.

"Pesky vermin can be so quiet when they want to be!" Pallinor growled, beginning his transformation into the amalgamation of creatures. An arrow flew by Delavun's head, who quickly ducked to the side and took his position in front of Jethro. The Ratlings began to swarm Pallinor, this time more cautious to his attacks, some keeping their distance and waiting for an opportunity to strike. A few Ratlings broke off and began heading towards Delavun who was shielding Jethro. The first Ratling died to Delavun's thrown dagger, and Delavun met the other Ratling unarmed. He caught the Ratling's wrist and twisted the weapon out of its hand and shoving it aside long enough to retrieve the dropped sword, plunging it into the Ratling's guts. More Ratlings swung around Pallinor and made their way towards Jethro. Pallinor gave out a roar, pouncing on the flanking enemies.

"Delavun!" the creatures voice spoke, with barely any human left in it. "Take the boy and escape to the North! Flee towards the ruins of the Idrani!"

Delavun followed the order without hesitation, retrieving his thrown dagger and grabbing Jethro's arm, pulling him along as he ran. Pallinor struck down the Ratlings as they tried to follow, his snake head that acted as his tail biting the loose ones not caught in his swipes. Delavun kept a tight grip on Jethro, as if letting go would cause him to vanish. Jethro did his best to keep up, not wanting to be caught by the Ratlings. As if predicting what they would do, a group of Ratlings broke out of their hiding places in front of them, heading straight towards them.

"Oh, Gods' blight!" Delavun cursed, letting go of Jethro and preparing his dagger. The first Ratling dashed forward, aiming to slash Delavun as it raised its sword. Delavun ducked under its swing, impaling it in the chest with his own weapon. Another two surged forward, both aiming to take down Delavun. Delavun avoided their attacks, waiting for an opportunity to strike. He danced around their swings and managed to stab one in the neck as it missed and extended too far forward. As Jethro watched them, hoping that Delavun would strike down the second, tiny claws grabbed his arms. A Ratling had used the distraction to approach him from behind and began dragging him away. Jethro kicked and yelled but was unable to get loose. He then planted his feet on the ground and pushed himself into the Ratling as it continued dragging him back. The sudden surge of force sent the Ratling over, one hand still managing to remain clamped onto Jethro's arm. Jethro took the free moment to go for his knife but held back a curse when he remembered he no longer had it, so he tried his best to pry the claw off. The Ratling stood up, pulling Jethro to his feet and attempted to reclaim Jethro's other arm. Jethro struck the claw around his arm, but it appeared to have no effect on the creature, who successfully managed to grab Jethro's arm again. The Ratling continued trying to drag Jethro away, but now Jethro had a better position to resist. He pulled against the attempts to be dragged, refusing to go willingly. The Ratling gave a small screech, almost sounding like it was annoyed, and wrapped its tail around Jethro's leg. Jethro hadn't anticipated the Ratling to use its tail as it lifted Jethro's foot, causing him to lose balance. The Ratling took the opportunity to drag Jethro quickly, not giving him a chance to try and stand again. Jethro was dragged a short distance, still lashing out at the Ratling and flailing his legs to impede the movement, but he couldn't completely stop himself from being taken. The Ratling tightened its grip on him, his claws drawing traces amount of blood as Jethro wriggled and twisted.

Then Jethro suddenly stopped being dragged. He looked up at his attempted kidnapper, who was now unmoving. The claws around his arms loosened, and Jethro fell to the floor. The Ratling toppled over a moment later, blood pouring from a fresh wound on the side of his neck. Standing over him, Delavun pulled him to his feet by his shirt.

"Let's go, before more come," Delavun ordered, his voice oddly calm, and began to run the direction they were headed. Jethro took a quick look around and chased after Delavun. They ran past where they had been ambushed, where all that remained were Ratling corpses. Jethro looked ahead at Delavun and noticed a trickle of blood making its way down his arm. He hadn't gotten through it completely unscathed, but it didn't appear to be a serious wound if he could still run without it impeding him. He continued to follow Delavun as they wove through the trees, avoiding the occasional Ratling that came searching for them. Jethro began to understand how Delavun hadn't been caught at camp. He had a knack for being unseen, at times Jethro had difficulty registering where Delavun had ducked into to hide, despite actively following him. Delavun reacted fast at the slightest movement or sound from a Ratling, and they managed to evade the scouts that were sent after them. Once Delavun was comfortable that they wouldn't be found, they decided to take a short moment to rest. Delavun looked back in the direction they had come, as if expecting to see someone come after them. Once they had caught their breath, they began walking with a hurried pace, to increase the distance between them and the Ratlings as much as possible. Once the adrenaline from running settled down, Jethro began wondering about where they were headed. He had never heard of the ruins of the Idrani, and so he had no idea where it was.

"What are these ruins of Idrani Pallinor told us to go?"

Delavun didn't answer immediately. He continued walking, while frequently checking their surroundings for any pursuers.

"I don't know," he answered eventually, his tone not hiding his annoyance.

Why would Pallinor tell us to go there then?

"How are we supposed to go somewhere if you don't know where it is?"

"North."

"Yeah, but if you do- "

"North," Delavun's voice was stern, clearly not wanting to discuss it. Jethro let it drop but wanted to know more about it. It must have meant something to Delavun if Pallinor had directed him towards it. Jethro could only hope that these mysterious ruins, that not even his guide knew where they lay, would make an appropriate hiding spot from Artruis.

CHAPTER TWENTY

"Then there are powers that truly terrify my core, should the wrong person be capable of obtaining them. Some are powerful enough to destroy villages, potentially even cities. Others can manipulate their way into leadership, governing a kingdom with ease.

If the wider population were made aware of these powers, would they be more perceptive in who they follow as a leader, or would they instead seek the power to lead for themselves?"

The mountain stairs proved to be tiring, though not half as much as climbing up them. Davun reached the bottom exhausted, breaching into surrounding forest from the exit that Arkarn had opened for them. They took a moment to stretch their legs and take a break to eat. The sky had begun to dim, indicating that night would soon fall upon them. They sat around, the silence becoming a bit eerie for Davun's liking. Kalavud reached into his backpack and fetched out a cloth and began tying knots into it. Wayne and Davun watched with interest as Kalavud fashioned a belt-like holding device for the darts he was given. He slotted the darts into the knots he had created and discarded the box. Wayne looked at him, eyebrow raised.

"What? The box was too clunky if I actually wanted to use them."

"I thought you didn't want them?"

"Well, it would be rude to throw out a gift. You Southerner's and your lack of manners."

"Says the person who likes to dance on furniture."

"You love the eloquent display I put on when I'm on a table."

"I love eating food on my tables. What I don't love is putting your feet, that are covered in dirt and filth, where I put my food."

"Oh sorry, I didn't know that Southerner's hadn't invented plates yet. Don't worry, you'll get there."

Wayne rolled his eyes at the comment, but his smile expressed his amusement. Arkarn seemed to have not noticed any of it, as he continued to sit on the ground, facing the mountain.

"Shouldn't we make our way towards Jethro now?" Davun spoke out, standing up. He was eager to go after his brother and wanted to begin before it became too dark for them to see. Wayne and Kalavud nodded, standing in unison.

"We must wait here until night falls," Arkarn spoke, remaining seated.

"What for, Arkarn? We know where Jethro is now, or at least some kind of indication. We can still make some ground if we leave now," Davun argued, confused as to why Arkarn didn't want to immediately leave.

"We don't know his exact location anymore, so we are aiming our arrows without a target. I have spoken to a Daritian, and they have agreed to come with us and guide us toward your brother. They should be here any moment. I know it is difficult to have patience in a time like this but waiting for them will be worth it."

"How can they track my brother? You already said Takas won't travel with us, so it isn't him."

"They are in training to be the next Balkynos. They have some aptitude towards the vision and will take us directly to Jethro. Even should Jethro move, we can discern his location anytime we need to, as long as our new companion travels with us."

"The vision?"

"It is how Takas managed to track Jethro. I can't quite describe it, as the teachings of it are not easy, and I haven't had the time to learn. I'm not even certain if I can learn it, truthfully."

"So, it's not another mythical creature's power?"

"No. It is something the Daritian's discovered how to do a very long time ago. I'm not too knowledgeable on its history or applications, but I do hope to learn more about it once I have the time."

Davun let the conversation drop. He was annoyed they weren't making their way towards his brother but did his best to convince himself that the Daritian was worth waiting for. He had trouble believing that a Daritian would actually come down the mountain. After making him promise not to tell anyone of their existence, why would this supposed tracker risk being seen? The Daritians had already stated they would not leave the mountain under any circumstances.

"Arkarn, are they really not going to help us fight Artruis? If they're supposed to be guides to this Balkyeros, why would they not aid in retrieving the orb?"

Arkarn sighed, pondering the question to himself for a moment before answering. "In truth, I do not know. I want to believe that they did not mean those words and that they will come and aid us when it is needed, but a Daritian does not lie. I know I have asked them to risk their lives, but I would not have asked if the situation did not call for it. I can only hope they realise the error of their choices before it is too late."

Davun also wanted to believe that the Daritians were going to aid them. The survivor army were not great in number, nor were they disciplined soldiers just yet. Many could fight, and they were improving, but the sheer number of Ratlings would most likely overwhelm them. He wasn't sure if the Daritians could fight, but just having more bodies willing to fight would greatly aid them. The vibe he got from the Daritians were that they were dedicated to assisting the Balkyeros in any way they can. Perhaps it was because he was not yet the Balkyeros, but they knew he was the next to claim that title, so that should have been good enough.

Davun stewed on it for a while, before remembering Arkarn had promised something else.

"Who, or what, is Vykurius?"

This time, Arkarn glanced over to him. His face a mixture of seriousness and worry. Davun immediately got the feeling that whoever – or whatever – it was, it was a danger that could not be ignored.

"Vykurius is the Daritian name for it. In the land it was born, it is known as the 'Colo-Colo'. It is another power, much like the chimera or the phoenix. We do not know the full extent of its powers, but we do know that if left unchecked, it can cause serious harm to an entire city. We do know that whoever holds it becomes a master of subterfuge. They become hard to see, as it toys with emotions and minds. It has the power to sap one's spirit, lowering their willpower to do whatever task they are doing. It is not a power that we can simply ignore, and it took a great deal to track down the current holder. We do not know the exact means that the power is transferred, each one has its own method, but they all have a resting place they return to should no one claim the power. The Daritians kept an eye on the current holder, but that user has now died, and we do not know where the power of the Colo-Colo has gone. It frightens me not knowing who has it, or where they are."

"Is it possible that they are within our camp?" Wayne asked from where he sat, chewing on a piece of bread.

"Very possible. If they work for Artruis, it would explain a lot of how he seemed to get our information. My main concern is if Artruis has it himself. It might be why he alone has been so elusive."

Davun hadn't considered that. He assumed that it had been someone in their camp, but Artruis being a power holder made things worse. With this particular power, it sounded as though Artruis himself could walk through the camp unseen if he wished, but Davun did not know how the power worked. No matter how he looked at it, Davun was convinced that the Vykurius was at their camp, or at least had visited it. He had no proof, but it was better to act as if the Vykurius were a threat involved in this secret war of theirs. Letting them roam the camp, freely gathering information was too great a risk for them to not consider.

"So, how do we find out who it is?" Davun asked Arkarn, who had returned to facing the door with his eyes closed.

"I'm afraid I don't know. It is theorised that the Vykurius has a tail of a rat but appears to be human. I cannot confirm if this is true, however. The last user was very careful about not being seen, and it was luck that he was discovered."

It was not the answer Davun had hoped for. Arkarn seemed to be giving up on finding the Colo-Colo already, before even beginning the search. If they were in camp, they could move about freely, gathering information from everywhere, potentially even from the meetings with the officers. Wayne and Kalavud were quiet, most likely thinking the same things as he was. He judged from their silence that neither of them had a solution either. It was another problem they had to work out, but that could be worked on once they recovered Jethro.

CHAPTER TWENTY-ONE

"How would we even find out about anyone who would hold these powers?
How could we prove it? Would anything even change if they were exposed? Or
would their powers simply protect them from people remembering their
exposure?
Has it happened before?"

Night fell as the group waited patiently. Davun had no choice
but to believe the person they waited for would more than make up
the time they wasted by waiting. They sat in silence, the
conversations had died down as each person lacked the motivation
to talk. The situation began to weigh upon them heavily as they
grew tired. The lack of movement only adding to their thoughts,
feeling demotivated by remaining still.

Finally, the sound of the stone door opening cut through the
silence of the night, everyone perking up to pay attention. Light
from a torch filled the cracks the door created, before coming into
full view as the door swung open. Standing behind it was a young
girl, around sixteen, holding a torch in one hand, and what
appeared to be Takas' staff in the other. She wore a violet robe,
and her head was adorned with a thin white pattern woven of
cloth. Arkarn stood to greet her, arms open as he invited her into

an embrace. She accepted the offer as she exited the pathway, the door closing behind her.

"I am so glad that you accepted my proposal. Your help is most welcome and needed," Arkarn spoke as his arms closed around her.

"Takas would never have left. He is too stubborn to realise that this is something worth risking your life for."

Arkarn let go of her and turned to invite everyone into the light of the torch. The Teldarian's complied to the request, eager to meet the person they had been waiting for.

"This is Shayarv. A Balkynos in training. She will aid us in locating Jethro along the way. This is Wayne and Kalavud."

"It is a pleasure to meet you both," she smiled, giving a slight nod in greeting.

"And this is Davun, heir to the Balkyeros title."

"I see. It is a pleasure to meet you too, Davun," she greeted him the same, though Davun got the distinct feeling that she had not entirely meant it. He smiled, wondering if he had imagined her smile was a little different to how she greeted his companions.

"Thank you for helping us find my little brother. I may not know a lot about the Daritians, but I gathered enough to know that you are leaving against their will," Davun expressed himself, just thankful to be able to begin searching for Jethro.

"Do not think that I am lying to them. I didn't tell anyone I was leaving, and I am only doing it because I believe they are in the wrong for not willing to leave the mountaintop to help the next Balkyeros," her tone was a little bitter, and her eyes did not leave Davun as she said it. Davun wasn't sure what he had said to offend her, he only wished to extend his thanks.

"Shayarv, no one here thinks you a liar. We are all grateful you have listened to reason. You will aid us immensely. We should walk away from the base of the mountain before we rest for the night. The Daritians might search for you, but I doubt they'll go far into the forest," Arkarn explained, defusing her attitude, though it still left Davun wondering what he had done to offend her. Arkarn gestured for Shayarv to lead by torchlight. They mounted their horses, Shayarv sharing with Arkarn, and rode for about an hour into the forest, before stopping to rest the night. They chose to not light a fire, opting to remain as hidden as possible, which meant having to fight the cold to increase their chances of remaining unseen.

Morning broke out, and Arkarn woke everyone up to get an early start on their journey.

"Shayarv, would you please discern his location for us?" Arkarn asked politely. Shayarv nodded, finishing her bread and wiping her hands clean of crumbs.

"I'll need a few moments undisturbed," she declared as she sat herself down, closing her eyes. She laid the staff across her lap, and began to utter something in Daritian, not audible enough to make out even if Davun had spoken their language. Arkarn gave everyone a signal to move away to give Shayarv some space. They walked far enough away so that their voices would not disturb her, and they watched her with curiosity. She kept her eyes closed, and her hands still. At one point, she reached out and grabbed the crystal-like ball at the end of the staff. No one spoke a word as they were all transfixed by what Shayarv was doing. After about ten minutes of watching Shayarv speak to herself, occasionally removing her hand from the orb and placing it back, she opened her eyes and stood. Her audience approached her, seeing that she had finished.

"He is somewhere in the north part of this forest. He appears to be alone, though I can only detect someone in his immediate vicinity," Shayarv sounded tired, and a little disappointed.

"That is more than enough to get us started, Shayarv. You have done an excellent job," Arkarn complimented her, a smile appearing on her face. Davun was motivated more than ever to start walking, now that they had a general idea of where his brother was. Davun immediately grabbed his pack, ready to set off, when Arkarn raised a hand.

"I know you are eager, Davun, but locating someone takes quite a bit of energy. Give Shayarv a moment to rest and then we will depart," he spoke, handing Shayarv his waterskin to drink from.

Shayarv took a mouthful and handed it back, looking a little guilty as she did so. Davun's heart sunk a little, but he knew that he couldn't ask someone to push themselves if they were already exhausted because he was impatient.

"Sorry, Davun," Shayarv spoke, and now Davun looked guilty.

"No need. You're doing me a huge favour by...doing whatever it is that you do in locating my brother. I didn't realise it was exhausting for you, so I apologise," Davun immediately responded, not wanting Shayarv to feel bad for doing a good deed. He placed his pack down, and sat beside her, gesturing for her to sit as well. She obliged to his request, taking another drink from her own waterskin. Davun noticed she had been sweating a little, and her breathing was noticeably heavier. He wondered what the process entailed if she was this drained from sitting and chanting, though he didn't ask. He doubted he would get any answers if it were meant to be a Daritian secret.

After another short rest, Shayarv announced she was well enough to begin walking, and so the group set off North, following Shayarv's instructions. She reiterated that she did not know exactly where he was, and that he may move by the time they get closer, so she would need to locate him again before night fell. They walked along with Shayarv and Arkarn in the lead. Wayne and Kalavud began their usual banter, and Shayarv would chuckle at some of their comments, though she was trying to keep her amusement hidden. Davun still felt guilty for having made her feel bad for delaying them and recalled that she already seemed to be a little agitated towards him, so he gave his horse the order to speed up, pulling his horse alongside the one she shared with Arkarn.

"I'm sorry if I made you feel a little bad before. I was a little impatient, I didn't realise how much your...uh...technique took from you."

"It is not an easy thing for me to do, so it takes a lot more from me than it would from someone more experienced like Takas. I appreciate your apology."

"So why did you decide to help us? I mean, Shardian seemed resolved when she said they could not help."

"Nyamyt means well, but she is frightened for our people. Teldarians no longer take kindly to our people, and she fears we will be attacked if we are discovered."

"Why would our people want to harm your people?"

"You have heard stories, no? I do not know the entire truth myself, but it seems to all stem from a misunderstanding. Our people were thought to be attacking villages, so the King of the land at that time declared us as aggressors and sent his army after us. We tried to defend ourselves as best we could, but word reached the ears of the surrounding Kings, and so they also sent their armies. We were outnumbered, so we retreated into hiding. For many years, we sent emissaries to clear the situation, but each time we were attacked. Eventually, our people accepted that we must hide from the world, so we hid in the mountains, away from where eyes might accidentally find us."

Davun listened with interest. He never knew that his people had any other kind of conflict other than the general animosity between Northerner's and Southerner's, though there was still a lot he didn't know about the world he lived in.

"If it was such a long time ago, perhaps the situation has changed? Surely your people still aren't outlawed?"

"We do not wish to risk it. Even if Nyamyt changed her mind, she would have to change the minds of the other Nyamyt and Nyafyt. She cannot make a decision that affects the entirety of our people."

"Nyafyt?"

"Head father,"

"Oh, I probably should have guessed that," Davun was a little embarrassed.

"Probably," chuckled as Davun's cheeks turned a slight shade of red. Davun was happy she at least laughed a little from their conversation, it meant that she didn't have a general disliking for him as he originally considered.

"So, why are your people dedicated to aiding the Balkyeros? They all seem to know that these powers even exist, whereas I am sure my people only think of them as stories."

"Our people believe that these powers were bestowed to humans by the gods. It is said the gods sacrificed themselves in order to give their powers to the people, so that the people may have the ability to sustain themselves and survive. Our people found the resting place of the Phoenix. We protected it, but people kept arriving, seeking to obtain its power, wanting only to fulfill their greed. Once we saw what humans were truly capable of if given a power that places them above others, we dedicated our lives to protect the power that had been placed into our hands. We would ensure that at least one of the powers would not be tainted, so we sought out the users of the Phoenix, and protect its resting place as it awaits the next heir."

"Arkarn also mentioned a resting place. What is it exactly?"

"It is different for all of the God's powers, but for the phoenix I hear it is a large nest of some sort. Should the Balkyeros die before declaring an heir, the power returns to this nest, lying dormant until its next holder comes to claim it."

"If there is no heir, how can anyone claim it?"

"Of that, I have no idea."

"I have an inkling of what it might be" Arkarn chimed in, having listened in on their conversation. "I have the theory that it no longer has an heir, rather it chooses someone based on the ideals and moralities of its previous holders. Anyone may place their hand on the orb and be judged, but if you are deemed unworthy then the same fate exists as if you weren't an heir now."

Davun wondered about Arkarn's concept. It would mean that the power had some level of sentience if it could choose who could obtain its power. Maybe that's how the wrong person laying its hand on it would suffer, the orb already knew who it belonged to, and punished those who weren't. Shayarv also had gone quiet, pondering the possibility of Arkarn's words.

"So, all powers have a resting place?" Davun asked, curious to learn more.

"Yes, all of the powers have a place to go if left unclaimed. I do not know where they lay, however. I'm not even sure how most of them are passed along, but the Daritians have already proven that they don't all follow the same methods. The Vykurius for example, is not left to an heir such as the Balkyeros is. They believe it can be taken somehow, but they do not know by what means. There is another power that they have learned how it is transferred, and it is a rather gruesome and grotesque ritual." Arkarn's face contorted slightly as he recalled the process.

"What is it?" Davun asked hesitantly, not sure if he really wished to know based on Arkarn's reaction when he spoke.

"In our tongue, the Wendigo. A creature of death. It's a disgustingly twisted creature, more monster than man. It feeds upon the flesh of the dead, and its legends state that it appears to feed on any prey that enters its domain. A creature so cruel has an equally cruel method. To claim its power, you must cut out its heart and eat it," he spat the words out as if they had a bad taste on his tongue. Davun nearly gagged at the idea of eating a heart, the mental image of the blood and taste was unsettling his stomach that still held his morning breakfast.

"A vulgar method. Despite having the wrong person almost instantaneously incinerated, I'm glad the Phoenix's egg is a much simpler procedure" Arkarn added, his face still reflecting the thoughts of such drastic measures to obtain a power. Davun agreed, resisting the urge to allow his food to come up the way it had gone down. He would have welcomed not picturing that mental image, having trouble getting the imagined taste off his tongue, but he also did wish to learn more about the powers. He hadn't imagined any would have required something so barbaric, thinking they would all be as simple has designating who the next heir would be. He wondered if any other power could be worse than the Wendigo's transference, but he wasn't entirely sure if he wished to know if there really were any.

"I don't think I want to know what happens when the Wendigo's power returns to its resting place, waiting to be reclaimed," Davun commented, imagining that its resting place had a worse method than directly passing the power.

"Just as well, we do not know its resting place or what is involved in that procedure," Arkarn responded, finally shaking off the bitterness of recalling the hideous procedure. Davun wanted to take his mind off the images, so he tried to change the conversation.

"Shayarv, could you tell if my brother was well?"

"I'm afraid I'm not quite skilled in sensing his emotions, but from what I tried to discover, he is unharmed."

Davun felt a little relieved. He was worried that his little brother may be roughed around in order to get him to comply. He knew that Shayarv's vision of him may be incorrect, but he wanted to believe that she was accurate. It meant that his brother may not be in any immediate danger, and there was still time to save him.

They group walked, idly chatting to pass the time, when they heard a voice in the distance. They turned to see a man, running towards them while continuing to shout.

"Arkarn! Arkarn!" the mans' words became clearer as he drew closer. He raised his arm as he came within distance, revealing the emblem of their camp.

"One of our scouts! How fortunate," Arkarn exclaimed, realising who the man was.

The man ran up to the group, panting from his rush. After taking a few breaths, he eagerly spoke between breaths.

"Arkarn, I have some reports from the other scouts you would be interested in. One scout has discovered a group of Ratling corpses that were not attacked by our soldiers. Upon further inspection, the scout reported that the wounds looked as if a bear got to them, but that's simply speculation. There is no way the entire group of Ratlings would have died to a bear."

"I could guess what did it," Arkarn interrupted, letting the man breathe.

"Also, I have news from Captain Demoria. We suffered another attack just yesterday, and scouts are now reporting sights of various groups of Ratlings moving about the forest. They still do not know where they are coming from, but they don't appear to be heading towards the camp. They seem to be in search of something, but we still worry that they may be organising a larger scale attack than before."

Arkarn processed the news, trying to piece the information together. He stood, staring off to the distance, lost in thoughts. After a moment of silence, he took in a deep breath and faced the scout.

"Has Tervu uncovered anything from his interrogations?"

"Many of our long-distance scouts who sent word back through our messengers were discovered dead. We fear that their messages never contained any factual information, having no idea how long they have been dead for. He recalled the remaining long-distance scouts, worried for their safety and the possibility of further false information."

"Good. I have been given the location of the Ratlings main base of operations. Green Heaven. I know our scouts have reported it empty before, so I'm not sure what is happening there, but something is keeping it hidden from our scouts. I am certain it is there. Return this information to the Captain but tell her not to launch an attack until we return. Understood?"

The scout nodded, and Arkarn dismissed him. The scout saluted him and the other two officers and began running towards camp to deliver the message.

"Well, that was rather fortunate," Wayne commented, his tone insinuating that he didn't entirely believe in the coincidence.

"I made sure we remained within the perimeter of our scouts, hoping that one would see us," Arkarn answered the unasked question. Wayne nodded, as if the answer was expected.

"We shall walk for another hour before I must ask Shayarv to locate our Jethro again, in case he has changed directions," Arkarn announced, continuing the path they had been walking. Shayarv nodded in an acceptance.

The hour passed, and they sat down in silence to allow Shayarv to discern Jethro's whereabouts. This time, they remained closer, and her ritual was even more complex and confusing up close. The words were still uttered too quietly to be heard from where they sat, not that it mattered to Davun as it was in Daritian, but she seemed to place her hand upon the clouded crystal ball at specific moments. The times she removed her hand from the ball, it was as if it had grown searing hot and threatened to burn her skin. As she completed her ritual, she broke out in deep breaths and a sweat, her face expressing panic that she had not shown the previous time.

"What is it Shayarv? What happened?" Arkarn rushed over to her, inspecting her and not liking his discovery as she appeared drained and frightened.

"Death. So much death, unpleasant deaths. He is scared, and alone. In a place where the unhappiness of the dead reeks."

"Green Heaven? He is at Green Heaven?" Arkarn asked her, impatient for an answer. Disappointedly, Shayarv shook her head.

"We know of Green Heaven, it is not as unpleasant as this place, I hope. I do not know this location, but the dead were trying to interfere with my reading."

Arkarn thought for a moment, trying to think of any other place similar to Green Heaven.

"Is it North?" he asked her, his voice now calmer. Shayarv nodded, slowing her breath.

"The only significant location at the Northern edge of the forest from here are the ruins of an old village that once tried to prosper within the forest. I thought it had simply been abandoned for a better location, but it is possible that something far more tragic occurred there."

"It's our only lead at the moment, it's better than looking nowhere," Davun spoke, trying to urge a choice in direction and Arkarn nodded in agreement. They allowed Shayarv to rest, before heading North to find Jethro.

CHAPTER TWENTY-TWO

"I tried to lose myself in more research before coming to a decision. I figured the answer would either come to me in the form of sudden clarity, or an event would occur that would answer my dilemma for me.

In hindsight, it was cowardice of me to think someone else could answer my own morality."

The Ratlings were smaller in number, but patrols were more frequent. It seems they split up into more groups to cover more ground. Jethro was frightened, but still followed every order that Delavun gave so that they wouldn't be caught. They had been discovered at one point, the Ratling giving out some kind of screech that must have alerted the other Ratlings, as more joined in the pursuit as Jethro was dragged along by Delavun. They managed to create enough of a gap to lose sight of them for a moment, so Delavun threw Jethro into a bush, telling the frightened young boy to remain hidden as he lured their pursuers away. It wasn't long before he returned, having lost the Ratlings. They hurriedly walked, still keeping an eye out for any patrols that came back their way. It was late in the day when they finally arrived at their destination.

Remnants of houses were strewn about, made of wood, and at first glance appeared to have vines growing over what was left of the shelters, but upon further inspection, the vines were intertwined as if they were intentionally apart of the structures. They remained healthy, still connected to the earth, but they stood out as Jethro had not seen any vines grow in this forest. He did not know how nature worked, so he surmised that this end of the forest must be able to support them, but he could not see any outside of what was left of the village. Delavun appeared to be just as interested in their location, also wandering around, inspecting the remains. He allowed Jethro to walk around on his own, trusting that he wouldn't try to escape again. Whether it was because his threats of harm worked or running off alone into the forest while packs of Ratlings were hunting for them was suicide, Jethro wasn't certain. Whatever the case, Delavun seemed to relax once they reached the ruins, acting as if the Ratlings wouldn't be able to discover them there. Jethro continued walking around, curious by the history the place must have. It was clear that people had put time into building their houses, but some looked incomplete while others appeared to have been intentionally destroyed. The houses all appeared empty, save for the occasional chair or table. The village looked as though it had been abandoned, but there were signs of an attempt to collapse the few buildings that had debris in or around it. A cold breeze blew over Jethro, and he shuddered as it found its way up his back. He was trying to shake off the cold when he noticed the only stone structure of the village. At first glance, it appeared to be some kind of floor, mostly covered in dirt save for a patch that looked as if it had been dug out, but the uncovered patch revealed the stonework to be a ceiling instead, as it revealed a hole into a chamber below. The hole was twice the size of a person, crumbling at the sides as if it had been smashed open. The hole dimly lit the chamber below, the only stuff that Jethro could make out were what looked like statues at all sides of the room, though it wasn't visible enough to make clear what the statues were of. He saw no way down, nor did he have a torch to brighten the room even if there were. He backed away from the hole, turning back towards the remains. He couldn't see Delavun, so he continued to look around. Aside from the occasional furniture and debris, nothing remained in the leftover foundations. Jethro wandered around in circles, speculating what had happened to the village. There were no bodies or bones, so he guessed that the villagers had abandoned the village. The houses that were broken must have collapsed from poor craftsmanship.

"Jethro," a voice called out from behind him, causing him to jump. He immediately turned to see Delavun standing not far behind him, his face serious.

"I was only looking around," Jethro responded, feeling like he had been caught doing something he shouldn't have.

"I know, but I think we should hide for now. We have to wait for Pallinor, no point in being caught by the Ratlings before he does. We'll hide out in one of these scraps of a building," he ordered, nodding towards the empty beginnings of a house that Jethro had been looking at. Jethro hesitantly stepped onto the floor of the building, expecting the untreated wood to break beneath is weight. Once the wood proved secure, he confidently walked in and seated himself against a wall. Delavun followed him not much longer, seating himself beside Jethro.

"What is this place?" Jethro asked curiously, knowing that he might annoy Delavun by asking questions.

"I don't know, but Pallinor told us to come here so this is where we'll wait."

Jethro chose not to respond, Delavun's voice already indicated that he was annoyed at their situation. Jethro grew bored of looking around the empty house he hid in, the walls standing barely taller than himself when he stood. Delavun didn't appear to be in a conversing mood, his face holding onto the serious expression. Jethro had only seen this expression once before, when they had hidden in the bush after they'd left Eraton. Then, it was due to the unseen horseman that got Delavun worried, and now Jethro guessed he was worried that Artruis might appear. Or that he was worried for Pallinor's safety. After seeing what Pallinor was capable of, he doubted even Wayne could take him down. Pallinor grew large when he began transforming, Jethro had trouble telling what the main shape of his transformation was, and everywhere he looked Pallinor seemed to be taking form of a different animal. It also didn't help that Jethro had not actually seen many of the animals with his own eyes, only descriptions from stories, travellers at the inn, and the occasional artists interpretation. Pallinor was truly terrifying when he turned into his combination of creatures. His speech seemed to be a struggle for him, possibly due to no longer having the formation of a human. He imagined a lion would have difficulty trying to talk and smiled slightly to himself at the idea of it.

He then wondered how his brother was doing, and if he had yet received word that he was missing, and if he was looking for him. He was conflicted about the idea. He wanted everyone to take advantage of Artruis being gone by chasing him down, assuming he still was, but he also wanted to be saved. He wanted to be by his brother's side again, not running with someone he once thought of as a friend but had been a fake. He then grew mad at himself for being gullible, allowing himself to fall into the trap. He began questioning if other people he had met at camp were also lying, only there to try and use him to get to Davun. He found it hard to believe that Wayne or Kalavud were capable of such a thing, but he had once believed in Delavun, so he couldn't rule it out as a possibility. His emotions grew unstable as situations ran in his head about all his new friends lying to him. The only person he knew he could trust was Davun, and he may not see him for a long time. Jethro struggled to hold back tears as he continued growing frustrated at himself. Delavun either didn't notice, or simply didn't care, as he didn't react to Jethro's tears that made their way down his scrunched-up face. Jethro sat for a while, trying to control himself but failing miserably, but eventually his emotions played themselves out. He sat quietly, now resisting the urge to sleep as he felt a wave of fatigue creep over him. Delavun had not spoken a word, and Jethro wasn't even sure if he had moved at all. Suddenly, they heard a branch crack under the weight of a foot, and Jethro suddenly became aware of how quiet his surroundings were. Delavun perked up to the sound, turning to Davun and giving him a signal to keep quiet. Delavun crouched and peeked over the wall.

"You can't hide from me like that, come out," the familiar voice yelled. Delavun relaxed his posture and stood up straight, giving Jethro a tap to follow him. They emerged from their hiding spot to meet with Pallinor, who appeared to be a little scratched and grumpy, but in his normal form. He looked around at the broken down and incomplete buildings, inspecting each one as if to find something they had not seen before.

"You made it here alright?" he asked, not facing them as he continued to scan the area.

"A little trouble, but the boy got through without any injuries"

"Good. We'll stay here for a while so I can try to think of what to do next," he ordered, returning his gaze to them as he seemed satisfied from his search.

"I take it you found the place this village tried to hide?"

Delavun nodded, knowing what Pallinor was referring to. Jethro also surmised they were talking about the hole he had discovered earlier but hadn't ventured down. It certainly seemed like a place that was trying to remain hidden from the thick layer of dirt that covered most of it.

"I should have tried to cover it. You didn't venture in, did you?" this time the question seemed to be directed at Jethro, who shook his head. Pallinor squinted at him, as if to try pierce a veil of lies that wasn't there.

"Neither of us went in," Delavun stated as Pallinor stared. This seemed to satisfy him as he turned away from Jethro. He looked around once more, this time his expression had eased. It was obvious even if he hadn't stated it, but Pallinor had been here before. Perhaps even once lived by the way he looked at the remains.

"Let us find som-" Pallinor began but stopped as he stared off at something behind them. Jethro turned to see what it was, and it was the last thing he was hoping for right now.

Artruis. He was standing at the uncovered stonework, his head facing the hole as if trying to see what was below.

"How did you find us so quickly?!" Pallinor yelled through clenched teeth, clearly not expecting to be discovered so quickly.

"Will you accept my answer as payment in place of your other question?" Artruis spoke in his usual calm manner, though there was a slight tinge of sarcasm in his voice, indicating he already knew what the answer would be. Pallinor blurted something unintelligible but sounded a lot like a curse.

"My question is still what we agreed upon, and you must give me what is mine!"

"Yes. I thought you would say that. Unfortunately, you trade in information, and now that I know you have been contacted by the people I am fighting against, I'm afraid I can't let you have such valuable information to freely trade. Should my opponents discover the answer, it would create difficulty for me."

"You should have considered that before agreeing to the terms!" Pallinor was growing furious, hair noticeably growing on his head hands. Artruis didn't appear to be bothered by what was transpiring, not turning away from the hole in the stonework roof.

"I'm afraid things have changed. I am more than happy to answer a question that won't cause me any complications in my mission. Either ask something else, or hand over the boy and receive all the answers you request and more once I have achieved my goal."

Pallinor sputtered, as if choking on his own words. He became flustered, unsure of how to release his frustration through words. Artruis turned to face them, and even from the distance between them, Jethro could tell that Artruis remained oddly calm, his facial expression in its neutral state. There was something about his calm demeanour that sent shivers down Jethro's spine. Pallinor changed from trying to speak to simply growling as his limbs began their transformations. Artruis raised a hand, and Ratlings appeared at the outskirts of the village, most armed with bows.

"Protect the boy. I'll deal with them," Pallinor struggled through his command, his transformation now complete, taking on a defensive stance. Delavun grabbed Jethro by the shirt, and dragged him back into the building they had hid in.

"Stay low, and stay quiet," he snarled, drawing out his dagger and left the incomplete building. Jethro couldn't resist peeking out, worried about what would transpire. Pallinor roared, and Artruis gave the signal to attack. Ratlings swarmed into the abandoned village from all directions, seeking to flank the twisted beast from all sides. Arrows rained in from various sides, but only a couple found the strength to pierce the beasts hide. Pallinor charged, running into and knocking over the first group of Ratlings. He continued pathing towards the archers on one side as they scattered, spreading themselves out so that it would be harder to take them down quickly. Pallinor chased them one by one, as more arrows and Ratlings headed in his direction. Jethro was unsure where Delavun had gone, unable to see him from where he peeked over the wall. Artruis remained still, watching the events unfold. Pallinor continued thrashing about, killing anything that was caught in his path, while more arrows pierced his sides. He gave no mind to them as he continued to bite, slash, and trample any he could reach. The Ratlings appeared more prepared this time, constantly spreading the distance between themselves so they wouldn't all be taken down in a single lunge. Pallinor decided to change tactics, rising back to stand on his hind legs, his arms that had changed into legs, now instead took shape of tentacles, much like that of an octopus. He grabbed and flung Ratlings, towards the archers, managing to make contact with a few and sending them sprawling. The Ratlings didn't retreat, only continued to bait Pallinor further along, allowing time for more arrows to find their marks. Jethro had been distracted watching Pallinor rampage and change forms that he hadn't noticed Artruis had stopped being an observer, now making his way towards him with a casual walk. Jethro began to panic, unsure what to do. Delavun had told him to stay, but that was only making it easier for Artruis. The calm man continued making his way towards Jethro, apparently in no hurry, keeping his pace slow and even. Jethro decided that his hiding place was no longer safe, so he darted out of the entryway and began to run. He wasn't sure where he was going, only that he wanted to get farther away from Artruis. He couldn't let himself be captured today, they hadn't even distracted Artruis for an entire day, that was no time for the camp to be able to attack his base in his absence. Jethro was determined to keep Artruis occupied for as long as he could, so he continued to run, darting between the remains of what once were buildings. He heard Pallinor's continues roars of battle, be he was too preoccupied with fleeing to take a look at how the beast was fairing.

A hand reached out and grabbed Jethro but the back of his clothes, yanking him back with enough force to knock him off his feet, falling prone on his back.

"I told you to remain still!" Delavun complained from his hiding spot, crouched behind some debris. He peeked over his hiding spot, searching for Jethro's pursuer. Jethro rolled over to his stomach and scrambled to his feet, fearing that Artruis was close by and that he had to prepare to run. He took a quick look around, noticing various Ratling corpses spread about. It was clear that Delavun hadn't simply been hiding himself the entire time.

"He's coming. Get ready to follow me," Delavun demanded in a low tone. Jethro was too frightened to emerge from their hiding spot to take a look at where Artruis was, instead trusting Delavun to decide when to run. Pallinor still roared, though the tone had noticeably changed as if it were a different animal.

"Now!" Delavun shouted, darting off without turning to see if Jethro followed. Jethro panicked as he chased after Delavun, not able to keep up to pace with the older boy. Jethro didn't have to look to know where Artruis was, he could sense the man's frightening aura that had been close before they abandoned their hiding position. He followed Delavun as they twisted and turned between the collapsed houses. Jethro was able to see Pallinor standing well above what was left of the village, arrows had been added to the collection that was growing on his back, though he still continued lashing out his tentacles, his now bear head biting some who were unfortunate enough to be caught. Delavun stopped in his path, Jethro nearly colliding into his back from the unexpected halt. Jethro turned to see what Delavun was staring at, seeing Artruis further down the path and facing them. The creepy man's sword had been drawn and held at his side. He faced them for a moment, before sprinting towards them, sword in tow preparing for a strike.

"Run!" Delavun yelled, panic in his voice as followed his own command. Jethro followed, tears beginning to fall as he felt the approach of death coming swiftly from behind.

"ARTRUIS!" Pallinor roared with all of his might. Delavun and Jethro stopped running when they saw Pallinor in the sky with newly sprouted wings, tentacles now powerful claws, and speedily swooping towards them. Jethro braced himself, crouching and placing his arms over his head the moment before Pallinor forcefully landed behind him.

The ground gave in from the impact, collapsing and sending them all down. For a moment, Jethro felt himself leave his own body as he unexpectedly descended into the unknown. He didn't fall far, landing on a patch of dirt that did little to cushion the stone beneath it. His wrist flared with pain as instinctively tried to brace his collision with the rubble. The sound of stone breaking and smashing together was all that was heard before silence took over, a layer of dirt filling the air for a short moment before dissipating. Jethro groaned in pain, bruised in various places, but that was nothing compared to the pain in his wrist. He gripped it in an attempt to deal with the pain before realising the situation he was in. He forced himself to stand, though one of his legs ached when he tried to put weight on it. He looked around, the crumbled stone and dirt covering most of the floor, but the statues that hadn't been broken in the process told him where they had landed.

They had been standing on the stone roof he had discovered earlier.

Now that light shed through on what remained, Jethro could make out the statues. They appeared to resemble various animals, some carved from wood while others from stone. All had been painted in a mixture of colours that didn't quite seem to match the animal that it shaped. There were few objects that remained affixed to the statues after the collapse of the roof. It seemed that some animals were adorned with wooden beads, feathers, and what appeared to be bone.

The sound of stone falling demanded his attention, as he snapped around to see Pallinor shaking off dirt and stone that had landed on him. Near him was Artruis, who must have been closer than Jethro realised before they had fallen. Delavun stood near Jethro, wiping off the dirt from his face, no apparent serious injuries. Jethro went to call out about Artruis, who was beginning to rise, when he noticed that Ratlings had begun gathering around the edge of the giant hole that had formed, bows drawn, and arrows pointed. Pallinor growled low, stepping away from Artruis and rounding behind Jethro and Delavun. Artruis rose to his feet, his half-covered face looking upwards at the lip of the hole, and back down to the three that had just become his prisoners. Despite the cloth covering his eyes, it was apparent that he could still see.

"Danger.... dangerous.... danger..." Pallinor was muttering, as if trying to think of a plan while trying not to panic.

"It seems that the minotaur has finally cornered those lost in his maze. Will you now hand over the boy without any complaints?" Artruis spoke, a hint of relief in his voice. Delavun searched for his dagger, but it had been lost beneath the dirt and rubble.

"Danger...NO! ANSWERS! Must get safe....ANSWERS!" Pallinor spoke at an inconsistent volume, swapping between yelling and muttering under his breath. It was clear that he was becoming deranged, Jethro now fearing his proximity to an unstable monstrous creature. Artruis sighed with disappointment, lowered his head, and began to untie the cloth that covered his eyes.

"DANGER! MUST ESCAPE! ANY MEANS!" Pallinor cried out, panicking as his eyes darted all over as if looking for an escape, landing on Delavun. Delavun stared back at him, confused.

"ANY MEANS!"

Pallinor's large, sharp claws tore through Delavun, blood splattering on the dirt and stone. The claws stained red, dripping the blood of the defenceless boy. Delavun fell backwards, making no sound or movement. The attack had instantly rendered his life from him. Jethro stared wide-eyed, the pain in his wrist forgotten, as the young boy's body collapsed to the ground with no resistance. He continued to look upon the lifeless body of his captor, mouth open, aghast at the sudden act of betrayal. By the time his mind registered what had occurred, Pallinor had gone, flown off without making a sound. Artruis had stopped untying the cloth, staring at the sky as if watching Pallinor flee. He turned his gaze toward Jethro, who became numb as the realisation of his situation settled in.

He had been captured by Artruis.

CHAPTER TWENTY-THREE

"Only two of my closest friends went on discoveries with me. We hired a boat and its crew when necessary, sometimes even mercenaries should we be worried about our wellbeing. It was always my two friends that were by my side whenever I discovered another truth.

Even should I not show the world my work for the many past years, I am happy that those I cared about were by my side when it happened."

Davun walked at the front of the group, eager to keep moving as they neared his brother. The last reading Shayarv performed had shown that the situation was worsening. Jethro was still alone, but his emotions were spiking with fright. His brother was in danger, and he wouldn't rest until he reached him. Arkarn had stated they were nearing the village he thought might be the location where Jethro had been taken, so Davun wanted no delay in reaching it. He could feel his brother drawing closer, motivating each step to lessen the gap. They walked in silence, pushing themselves to quicken their pace without tiring themselves too much. Each person knew how driven Davun was to find his brother, and they would do anything in order to help him recover Jethro.

Finally, the remains of the village fell into sight. Davun could wait no longer, and ran ahead, not bothering if anyone followed. His spirits were high, his brother just ahead of him, somewhere within the village. As he drew close, his hopefulness dimmed slightly as his eyes fell upon the corpses of many Ratlings. He stopped at the outskirts of the village where the bodies began, everyone else stopping with him as they had followed him in running.

"What does this mean, Arkarn?" Davun asked, hearing the group stop beside him. Arkarn looked about, following the trail of corpses that ranged all around this side of the village. He bent down, inspecting the corpse of a nearby Ratling.

"It definitely seems like Pallinor's work. Large claws, torn to shreds, broken bones, some even appear to have chunks missing as if they were bitten. I'm afraid I don't know what it means just yet. Artruis could have your brother, or even Pallinor. I cannot discern that from looking at a corpse, however."

"Then let's search the village," Davun announced, walking over the corpse and heading into the ruins.

"Be careful. If this was Pallinor, he might be out of control. I doubt that he is still here, we would have heard him by now, but always proceed with caution."

The others silently followed, spreading out slightly to search the collapsed village. They searched in silence, doubt in their minds but their hope not yet diminished. The village certainly matched the feelings of death that Shayarv foresaw. The Ratling corpses decorated what appeared to be broken houses. Buildings that used to be homes, but seemingly abandoned. No remains of people were found, so it didn't seem like the village had been attacked. It's just as if the people creating their livelihoods here had simply vanished. Davun continued to search each of the remains he passed, slightly shifting the rubble on the off chance that one of the piles of debris would uncover his brother, though he hoped not to discover him that way. The buildings seemed to be intertwined with vines, which Davun was curious about, but he had no time to admire or inspect the structures, his search for his brother took priority. He became slightly more annoyed and impatient with each collapsed building that didn't contain his brother, causing him to grow frustrated with worry.

"Now, what do you guys think this means?" Kalavud called out from where he stood on one side of the village. He was looking down, so Davun couldn't make out what he was talking about, but immediately rushed over in hopes that his brother had been found, though he already knew Kalavud would have called out if it were. As the group began arriving at Kalavud, each in turn were surprised by what they saw, save for Shayarv.

A large hole revealed the room below, filled with rubble, dirt, and statues.

And the body of Delavun.

They had not expected to find a human corpse, bearing the symbol of their own, in the ruins of a village far out from their camp.

"I don't recognise him," Wayne stated, sighing at the sight of a dead ally. Kalavud crouched down, as if getting a closer look, placing his hand on his chin as he tried to figure out the situation.

"I do not know him either, though he bears our mark," Arkarn responded in turn after scanning the deceased boy's face.

"It's Delavun" Davun informed them, worry causing his voice to shake slightly.

"Delavun? Not a name I recognise," Wayne muttered after giving it some thought. "You knew him?"

"Sort of. He was a friend of Jethro's. I only met him once, but I had seen him talking to Jethro a few times. Jethro was fond of him, I know that much," Davun idly spoke, trying to figure out the situation for himself.

Did he come here in search of Jethro? But how would he have known? This doesn't make sense.

He came to the village expecting to find his brother, only to discover more questions that weren't accompanied by their answers. He walked off from the group, continuing his search around the village hoping not to discover another familiar corpse. Kalavud pulled out a rope from his bag and handed it to Wayne who took it without question. Kalavud lowered himself down into the collapsed chamber, using Wayne as his anchor to the earth above. He landed softly on the rubble of dirt and stone and took a look around. He took note of the various animal statues and their decorations, before moving over to inspect their ally's corpse further. He noticed the splatter of blood that lay near, indicating that the attack had a great deal of force behind it based on the distance it reached. The most curious thing about it was that it matched the wounds several of the Ratlings received.

"Looks like more of your pal's handiwork, Arkarn. Can't quite figure out what he was doing here though."

Arkarn reached to his side, grabbed his wineskin, and tossed it to Kalavud.

"Test his mark."

Kalavud nodded, opened the wineskin and poured some of its contents onto the tattoo located on Delavun's arm. He then rubbed the water against the skin, turning it black in the process.

"Paint" Kalavud called out, sounding bitter. The tattoo had been a fake, meaning that this boy was not one of their ally's.

"Gods take me with them," Arkarn cursed, earning himself a scowl from Shayarv.

"Arkarn?" Wayne asked, curious as to what Arkarn realised.

"I think he was working for Pallinor."

Wayne and Kalavud were shocked at the allegation. They had considered a spy within their camp, but not one who wasn't working for Artruis. They didn't know what Pallinor's involvement was in this war, and it only worried them that they had to consider another threat.

"Got the information from animals…what a joke!" Arkarn began losing his temper, kicking a loose rock to vent his anger.

"No point in losing control of yourself, Arkarn," Wayne tried to cool him down.

"Like you're one to talk," Kalavud casually yelled out from the pit.

"Not now, Kalavud!"

Kalavud remained quiet, instead choosing to inspect his surroundings further, letting Arkarn curse away. Kalavud and Wayne were also stewing in their own anger, knowing that a spy had successfully infiltrated their camp and they hadn't caught them. They had no idea how long this boy had been gathering information on them, or even why Pallinor wished to know. Arkarn had mentioned that the mysterious man trades in information, which they surmised he was selling that information to Artruis, the only one who had any interest in them. A third party wasn't involved in this war, the nearby Kings and Lords ignoring their requests for aid. To their knowledge, Pallinor was not after anything in particular, simply just a trader, but that did not mean he couldn't change his mind after uncovering the right information. They also had no idea how much Artruis had obtained from Pallinor, so they simply had to assume that he knew everything, but if he already knew everything about the camp, why did he not choose to destroy them earlier? It seemed entirely possible for Artruis to destroy the camp from within, simultaneously sending his army of Ratlings to attack with the knowledge of their fighting formations, weaknesses, and supplies. He could have tried taking Davun by force, but for whatever reason, he hadn't.

Kalavud continued trying to lose himself in the peculiar statues, while Wayne had given up on trying to ease Arkarn's anger, instead remaining quiet to try and quell his own. Things were unravelling fast, facing complications they had been avoiding for so long, no longer able to pretend like it didn't exist. The exclusive meetings with the inner circle of trustees had not been enough to prevent valuable information being taken and sold as if it were a common business.

Shayarv watched as Davun continued inspecting buildings, shoving debris aside, in no mood to be delicate in his search. She decided to follow Davun around at a distance, making herself obvious to him to show that he wasn't entirely alone. She needn't have talked to him to understand what he was feeling. His actions spoke more than he like could have spoken if she had tried asking. He continued the shove things aside, kicking remains as he cursed at them for not hiding his brother alive and well. He eventually exhausted the remaining ruins, walking off from the village as if in search of other hiding spots. He stood amongst the trees that encircled the village, facing away from Shayarv who he knew had followed. He tried to hide the tears that were surfacing, actively trying to prevent his face from scrunching in sadness and frustration.

"Can you track him?" he called out to Shayarv, not turning around to face her.

"I am sorry. The lingering of death is too powerful here. It interferes with my reading. Perhaps we should leave."

Davun sniffled as his nose began to leak along with his eyes. He nodded, not able to find his voice to call back to her.

"I shall retrieve the others. I will be back in a moment," she turned and left, knowing that Davun wanted to be alone. She didn't rush herself to allow him more time to deal with his emotions. Davun sat down as she walked away, burying his face in his hands. Shayarv hesitated, wanting to console Davun, but chose to grant his unspoken wish to deal with it alone, instead heading towards Arkarn who was still trying to deal with his own frustration. She could see him in the distance, pacing around impatiently, hands fidgeting as he ran through different ideas in his head. Wayne remained watching Kalavud in the pit, who she guessed was still discovering new things in there. Arkarn eased himself at her approach, taking a deep breath and slowing himself down.

"What do you think it all means?" Wayne called down into the pit. Shayarv stood on the edge, peering down at Kalavud who was brushing off dirt from a statue of a goat.

"Wouldn't a clue. Whoever created this really liked animals, enough to make statues and dress them up all pretty. They also wanted to keep it hidden. The piles of dirt and rock were the roof, probably collapsed from age I'd wager. There are also some stairs over there, but that seems to have its own blockade, I can still make out a stone roof that's still intact above it."

"It looks like a ritual," Shayarv examined, Wayne nodding in agreement.

"I thought so as well, lass, but I wouldn't have a clue what for. The way they painted and decorated these things are giving me a creepy vibe, but it doesn't seem like anything inherently evil."

"All rituals are not evil."

"I know lass, I was just stating that I don't think this one was. Just creepy, that's all. You don't know anything about the people that used to live here by chance, Arkarn?"

Arkarn gave it some thought, but eventually shook his head.

"I know that people once tried to live outside of the kingdoms rules, trying to create their own village within the forest. No books exist to historically dictate their attempt that I know of, so I thought they had simply given up and returned to merge with other villages. From Shayarv's reading of this place, and this supposed ritual site, I'd say I guessed wrong. Something else happened, though I can't say what exactly."

Everyone knew that Arkarn likely did not have the answer, but they still felt disappointed when he could not provide it.

***

Davun sat alone, the urge to cry away his pain and frustration rising as he actively tried to suppress it. He thought back to the time he had let go with Demoria, but he wasn't sure if letting it all out while he was alone would have made him feel any better. Now was not the time to let his emotions control him, however. Jethro was still missing, and he could not tell for certain where he had gone, or even who with, until they distanced themselves from the village far enough for Shayarv to perform her observation. Davun's head remained in his hands as he finally gained the strength to calm himself enough to find the willpower to return to the group. Once his head regained awareness of his surroundings, he noticed things that he was sure hadn't been there before.

Silence and cold. He hadn't realised how cold it had gotten as he now shivered against the sudden change, the silence in addition making Davun feel uncomfortable. The wind did not blow as the leaves above were given no movement, standing uncharacteristically still, not even providing the slight rustling sound that could fill the void.

Davun felt another presence.

He immediately stood. He was not sure how he knew, but he could feel someone else to his side. He turned, expecting to see someone, but what he saw was beyond his expectations.

A monstrous creature, wreaking of death.

Even from where it stood, Davun could tell it was nearly twice his height. Its arms were nearly as long as its hunched over body, its fingers forming into points as if claws. Its face was covered in a skull of an animal Davun didn't recognise; its torso also donned bones as if it were armour. Its uncovered limbs were covered in black fur, yet it somehow still had a feminine frame. There was only one thing he could think of that had similar features.

The Wendigo.

Davun stared at it, too scared to move or speak, locked into its gaze as pale blue eyes glared in return through the sockets of the external skull. Time felt like it had frozen. The overwhelming feeling of death suffocated Davun's senses, becoming unaware of how much time had passed as they stared at each other.

"Brother," it spoke, a contrast of a young female and the deep growling voice only a monster could have, speaking in unison. Davun did not respond, too scared to have registered what it had said.

"Brother," it called out again. This time it reached Davun as some of his senses returned. He looked at it, confused and scared, as if uttering a response would give it permission to kill him.

"Brother?" it spoke out again, this time as if it were a question. Davun hesitated, not sure how to interpret its message.

"Me?" he placed a hand on his chest, as if needing to direct who he was referring to.

"Brother. Gone?" each word was distanced by a slight pause as if it were struggling to find the words, its breathing now audibly loud as it almost sounded like panting.

"My brother? Yes, he is gone," Davun responded, still uncertain what it was asking.

"Artruis," it spoke as if it were an answer. Silence filled once again as Davun questioned what this creature knew about his brother, Artruis, and even himself.

"Artruis," it repeated when Davun did not respond.

"Artruis…has my brother?"

The creature nodded slowly. Its eyes remained fixated to Davun's. Davun had no idea how the creature knew, or why it was even telling him. The Wendigo was meant to be a force of death, a mindless being only existing to feed on others. He was not sure if the creature was trying to lure him into a trap, but that's not the feeling he got. Through the sheer terror the mere sight of this creature brought him, he could still feel that the Wendigo was trying to help. He had no idea why it felt the need to, but it was clear that it was at least trying.

"Are you…the Wendigo?"

The creature did not respond, continuing to only stare at Davun who began to relax his stance a little. Davun dared not get any closer, however, it was clear that the Wendigo wished to keep its distance.

"Did you kill all those Ratlings?"

It shook its head.

"Did you kill Delavun?"

It shook its head once again.

"You're trying to help me, then?"

It nodded.

"Why?"

It remained silent and unmoving. Davun thought it had chosen not to respond again, before its voice struggled once again.

"Stop. Him."

"Stop Artruis?"

It nodded.

The Wendigo wanted him to prevent Artruis from obtaining the power of the Balkyeros, but why? The question ran through Davun's mind, finding nothing but a wide variety of possible answers. The creature knew him by name. It knew what he was doing. It knew what he had done. It was either observing him, or it had a connection to him.

But why would a creature of death wish to prevent someone else from potentially obtaining a power that could bring even more death?

The only answer that Davun could think of was that even the Wendigo was terrified of what Artruis could achieve once he obtained the power. Something so horrific that it scared the embodiment of death.

"Why do you want me to stop him?" Davun asked, fearing what the answer would be, but the creature did not respond. Davun's fears remained unconfirmed, the creatures silence had only brought with it more questions.

"Are you frightened of what Artruis will do?"

Davun stiffened as the creature nodded. The fear beginning to truly settle in of Artruis' plans that still remained unknown. Davun knew the creature would not tell him if he had asked.

"I will do my best to stop him."

The creature again remained silent, continuing to stare with its pale eyes. Davun felt the conversation had ended, but was unsure if he should leave, still frightened that any sudden movement would cause the creature to attack him despite it being illogical. The creature simply continued to stare at him, no longer speaking or moving. Davun took a hesitant step backwards, holding his breath as his foot landed, waiting to see what the creature would do. When the creature showed no signs of moving, Davun took another step back, before gaining the confidence to turn around and walk.

"Maldimon," its voice called out once Davun turned his back. He spun around upon hearing its voice, only to find that the creature was no longer there. He looked around, not able to find it between the trees. He gave up on his search, returning to the ruins to inform the others, the familiar sound of rustling leaves accompanying him.

CHAPTER TWENTY-FOUR

"We travelled many wonderful years together. Without them, there may have been some things that I would have missed. It was always useful having others to collaborate with, providing a different perspective to the same situation. Providing comfort in the few times that journeying can feel lonely. Though now I continue the research alone."

Jethro willingly walked beside Artruis, encircled by his Ratlings. The man had remained silent after asking Jethro to travel with him. He had ordered his underlings to not give chase as Pallinor flew away, finally able to claim the key that he had sought. Jethro followed in silence, quietly accepting his fate as an eternal prisoner. He had tried to escape from Pallinor and Delavun once, and that had resulted in threats. He did not want to know what Artruis would do if he attempted, not that he could escape the ring of Ratlings around them. They marched toward what Jethro could only guess was their base, the night sky slowly taking over the day's light. The Ratlings did not speak to each other and remained in formation. Their discipline and obedience were above what Jethro had thought them capable of. Scouts had gone out in front but had not returned to report anything. Jethro guessed they were well away from the camp and that the scouts did not travel this far frequently.

He was truly alone. Alone with the man who was the cause of many deaths, many lives ruined. Everyone in the survivor's army had joined as a result of Artruis' actions. Jethro could not even find the energy to feel hatred towards the man, feeling drained from his capture once again. It seemed that he now only existed as bait for his brother, no longer a person but an object. He was just a piece on a playing board that his enemies now controlled, and he had seen no sight of any allies in days. He continued to wonder if they even knew he was gone, and what he was going through. They would have to wait until Artruis inevitably sent the message that he had captured the Balkyeros heir's brother and offer a trade.

Jethro couldn't let that happen if it came to that. He considered making a run for it, knowing full well that he would be caught again and anger his new captors. If they did, he would only run again. And again.

And again.

He would run until they were forced to start beating some sense into him. Using more drastic methods each time that he would try to escape.

Until he would succumb to the wounds from the threats they followed through on.

He knew it was a way to stop Artruis from getting the upper hand and having Davun willingly walk into his grasp.

But he was too cowardly to do it.

He could not find the will to run, to be hunted and attacked. The feeling of a knife or arrow entering his body scared him. He would not be able to resist the pain. He would be caught the first time, probably beaten or scarred to teach him a lesson, and he would not run again.

He was a coward.

He was weak for having even being caught in the first place, gullible to the words of one of the first people to befriend him at camp. Running wouldn't accomplish anything unless he had the resolve to follow through with it.

And he knew he didn't.

***

Jethro followed Artruis without complaint until they reached their base. It was a large meadow, though the night sky was blocking the light from shining down on its beauty. Jethro noticed the Ratlings had a variety of shabby looking tents built, and even in some cases he noticed they had dug holes to hide underground. The only thing that appeared to be of any decent craftsmanship was a small house made of wooden logs built at the back of the meadow. The Ratlings that escorted them broke off once they reached the perimeter, and Artruis walked without hesitation or word towards the house at the back. Jethro obediently followed, glancing around with worried looks at the sheer amount of Ratlings that occupied the area. He heard that the Ratlings were great in number, but he hadn't expected this many. He noticed Ratlings sitting in groups, fighting over scraps of food. It seemed that they were starved, not enough food supply to satiate the amount of Ratlings.

They reached the solitary house and entered it, candles already lit on the inside. Artruis held the door open for Jethro before closing it behind him. Artruis gestured towards the next room where a table sat, and Jethro seated himself onto one of the chairs. Artruis brought a second candle over to the table and seated himself opposite of Jethro.

"Thank you for complying on our way here. You will be given food and a comfortable place to sleep in this room, but if you feel like answering, I have some questions in mind."

Jethro didn't really believe he had a choice, so he quietly nodded. Artruis faced him, cloth covering his eyes, but the candlelight revealed that the cloth was thin enough for Artruis to see through it, probably with some difficulty.

"Do you know why you are here?"

Jethro nodded, too nervous to verbally respond.

"Why?" Artruis probed, wanting a complete answer.

"To make sure Davun comes."

"In a sense, yes. Davun will inevitably arrive here. Your friends will discover this location, I will no longer keep it hidden. You are here to entice Davun in coming to me with as little hassle as possible. I only wish for this to be over as soon as possible."

Jethro had a hard time believing that Artruis wanted the fights to end. He had been sending Ratlings to attack undefended villages, killing most of the people who had made homes there. He created his own enemy and continued to add to their numbers even after discovering their existence.

"Do you know what it is that I seek?"

"You want the power that's in the orb."

Artruis did not respond. Jethro wondered if he had gotten it wrong, but if he had, it meant that everyone in the camp had gotten it wrong as well.

"Good enough for now. I will tell you in due time, but for now you may eat and then rest. A bed will be made, and food will be delivered. Ratlings are easily scared, try not to make any sudden movements when they arrive," he spoke, rising from his chair and leaving the room, sliding a furnished piece of wood that acted as a door across. Jethro sat in the room, alone, the candles' flames dancing in the still air. The room was empty save for the table and chairs, and soon a bed. His situation wasn't what he anticipated, expecting to have at least been tied up, but the ordinary room did little to disguise the fact that it was his prison.

The Ratlings entered a short time later, skittering about, constantly eyeing Jethro as if he would attack them at any moment. They placed a box that held his food on the table and piled up blankets in one corner to act as his bed. Jethro remained as still as possible, not daring to move to avoid accidentally startling them. They were interesting to watch when they weren't trying to attack his friends, moving about silently, seemingly in a sort of rush as everything they did seemed hastened. They were either uncomfortable in the room with Jethro, or it was just their nature. Jethro should not have acted as a threat to them, being shorter than they were and unarmed, but that didn't seem to affect their behaviour. The Ratlings left, and Jethro slowly ate his meal of salted meat and bread, accompanied by a wineskin of water, and then lay down in his bed. Sleep did not come easy when you were a prisoner, but Jethro was beginning to get used to it, slowly accepting his fate as a prisoner to be traded like gold.

* * *

Jethro was woken by the sound of the wooden barrier being moved. Artruis entered the room, looking at Jethro as if inspecting him. He moved to the windows, opening the shutters to let the light enter. Jethro winced a little against the bright light, guessing that he had slept longer than he had during his sleeps in the forest based on the lights' strength. He rubbed his eyes, allowing them time to adjust to the lit room, as Artruis waited patiently. Once Jethro could see properly, he arose out of his bed.

"You might be here against your will, and I am sorry that I was forced to use you this way. But I am willing to hear your requests and fulfill them if reasonable. Perhaps you would like a walk of the meadow now that light is upon us?" he talked with his usual calm tone, though this time it was accompanied by a small amount of emotion, clear that he was trying to be polite. Jethro wondered if Artruis had an ulterior motive to the offer, but still feeling like he had little choice in the matter, he accepted.

Walking around the campsite in the daylight was an entirely different experience. The Ratlings had not changed, still fighting over themselves for scraps of food, tents just as poorly built as they appeared at night, though there were more holes than Jethro had originally thought. The difference came in how the meadow somehow glistened from the light, its lush green grass looking soft and inviting. The meadow would have been a soothing sight to behold if it weren't sullied by the sea of Ratlings who had created their home here. He watched them as they scurried about, the only sounds coming from the grunts and hisses as they desperately fought over scraps. He saw them enter and exit the various holes they had created, curious as to what was below.

"Do you know what this place is?" Artruis asked, walking alongside Jethro around the perimeter of camp.

"No."

"It has many names. The Meadow of Silence. The Forest's grave. The Place of New Beginnings. To most, it is known as Green Heaven."

The names all sounded foreboding, attached to death in their own way. He was about to ask Artruis the meaning behind it, but the man had already intended on telling him.

"It is a place many people believe is a portal to a meaningful or pleasant afterlife. They have their deceased loved ones buried here, in hopes they will be blessed with a blissful afterlife. It is now eternally tied to death, and I think that's where its beauty comes from. This place has an energy that I bask myself in everyday."

Jethro eagerly listened, though had become a little distracted once he heard that bodies had been buried here. He stared at the many open holes that the Ratlings had dug, wondering what had happened to any of the bodies if they had discovered any.

"Do you fear death?"

The question came out of nowhere, and Jethro felt Artruis' foreboding presence lingering over him, as if the question had been a threat. Artruis had asked it as if it were a casual conversational piece, but that didn't stop him from being intimidating.

"Y...Yes," Jethro answered, wondering where the question was leading. He was too frightened to look at Artruis directly but kept the man's figure in the corner of his eye, wary of any sudden movements that the man might make.

"You shouldn't be. Death can be beautiful, welcoming you with open arms. You need to live a life worth living, have someone waiting for you on the other side. You are still young, hopefully you will understand one day."

Artruis spoke as though death were a being. It seemed as if it were an accomplishment to have died, provided that you had something to look forward to after death. Jethro had no idea why

Artruis chose this topic for conversation, but it only made the man scarier in his eyes. Someone who does not fear death must fear very little.

They walked further around the glade in silence, Jethro pondering what to expect after the man had talked about death quite openly. He tried to watch the Ratlings to distract himself, watching them gather various tools that Jethro recognised were used for cutting down trees. He only now realised that the camp here had no defences like the survivor's camp. They were completely open on all sides, showing either confidence that they wouldn't be found, or arrogance in their own ability to defend from an attack.

"Do they interest you?" Artruis asked, noticing Jethro had begun staring at the Ratlings once again.

"A little. They're different, but they're dangerous."

"Only truly dangerous if they become organised. Without leadership, the Ratlings are little more than scavengers looking for their next meal. They serve as excellent minions should one be able to persuade them to lead them. Ratlings are many, but they are all dull, unable to establish the intellect to coordinate on their own."

"So, you managed to convince them to listen to you?"

"Yes. Ratlings are susceptible to the promises of food. It was much easier than I had anticipated."

Jethro wondered at how the simple offer of food was able to convince an entire army's worth of creatures to allow someone who was not their own to lead them.

He was also curious at how Artruis was keeping his end of the deal, having seen multiple Ratlings fight over mouthfuls of food. The Ratlings were thin, clearly from not eating enough. It was truly a wonder how Artruis planned to feed all of the Ratlings, and how they continued to obey him when it wasn't enough. They finished their journey around the camp, once again heading inside the sole building.

"I have things I must do. I will be departing from camp for a couple of hours. Please wait inside your room until I return. If you are hungry, just ask any Ratling for food and they will provide. Your cooperation will be appreciated in my absence," Artruis spoke to Jethro as if it was for his own safety, implying that Jethro shouldn't try to escape. Jethro had not planned on escaping, already knowing it wasn't possible to escape the multitude of Ratlings that were just outside of the building. Jethro walked into his room without resistance, and the wooden barrier was slid into place. The windows remained open and unobstructed, allowing view of the hundreds upon hundreds of Ratlings that guarded his room.

CHAPTER TWENTY-FIVE

"We had always expected to find danger around every turn. We never knew if anyone would be following us, waiting for the moment to silence us before the opportunity to scream the truth from the mountaintop could arise. I still don't know to this day if I am being watched. We had to trust that whatever power holder we discovered would not instinctively slaughter us for finding them.
In this regard, we were fortunate."

"**M**aldimon?" Arkarn asked after listening to Davun's retelling of his meeting with the Wendigo. They all remained sceptical that it had been the Wendigo, its described personality not matching with their interpreted vision from stories and history.

"The only Madimon I know is Garthin Maldimon. He was an explorer and scholar, but now I believe he works as an advisor somewhere.... hmm...I think he actually works as an advisor to King of Vanguinar."

"The King that Doctor is meeting with?" Wayne asked, a small amount of hope in his voice. Arkarn nodded to confirm.

"Though, he should be back by now. Let's head back to camp, resupply and meet with Doctor. His mission likely won't have been successful, but he can at least inform us if my recollection is correct. We can decide what to do from there."

"So, it means we have to wait longer to save Jethro," Davun spoke in defeat, the energy draining from his body as he admitted the fact. Arkarn sighed knowing the toll it would take on not only Davun, but Jethro for each moment they didn't rescue him. Wayne placed a comforting hand on Davun's shoulder. They all had to leave it to their own imaginations how Jethro would be treated as Artruis' prisoner. They knew he was the top priority, but they also knew that they had to do whatever they can to increase the odds of defeating the Ratling army in battle. If finding this Maldimon would give them answers, or even if he were able to provide them troops with his position, then it would make the delay worth it.

***

It took them a day to reach the camp on horseback. The walls set up showing signs of attacks, but the camp still looked lively and happy to see their return. Arkarn called them to a halt, wrapping a blanket around Shayarv to hide her clothing so that no one would ask questions before continuing. They pulled their horses into the designated area, leaving them with the handler to take care of, and made their way towards Captain Demoria's tent to call a meeting. It didn't take long for the remaining officers to appear, each greeting them in turn, pleased to see them unharmed. Once they had all gathered and seated, Arkarn stood to speak.

"Our journey was eventful, but unfortunately we were unable to recover Jethro. We learned that he was most unlikely taken from his home in Eraton by Artruis. The trader of information who lives in this forest, Pallinor, likely had a hand in Jethro's disappearance. We were able to find a friend of mine, Shayarv, who was then able to track Jethro to the ruins that lay in the Northern part of the forest, not too far from the Green Heaven. There we discovered a group of slain Ratlings, not killed by any of ours. Amongst the bodies, however, was the body of a human. A boy named Delavun, who bore a fake symbol that resembled ours. Both Davun and Jethro had met this boy in camp, but I don't believe any of us would have. The boy was sent in as a spy, though I am still unsure who for. I believe that he had been working for Pallinor, but I don't have any evidence that speaks to that. Whilst we were at the ruins, Davun had an encounter with something I had not expected in the slightest. The Wendigo,"

There was a range of shocked expressions mixed with worried ones.

"I've heard of the Wendigo. The boy shouldn't be alive if it really had been the Wendigo, surely he was mistaken," Tervu commented, in disbelief that it had occurred.

"The description matches the stories, but the nature of it does not. I will not doubt him when he says it was the Wendigo." Arkarn responded, firmly believing that Davun had been correct in what he had seen.

"I must agree with Tervu on this. The stories of the Wendigo always entail people being torn to shreds and eaten. Most even recall seeing it on the verge of death, as an entity trying to drag them to the beyond," Thedan joined in, recalling the various books he had read on the Wendigo.

"What have I been trying to teach each of you about these stories?" Arkarn spoke out, almost as if he were talking to a child.

"That the stories we read and hear aren't entirely true," Thedan admitted, sighing as he did so.

"The physical description of the creature might match, but the personality certainly doesn't. I haven't the slightest of clues why the Wendigo wishes to help us, but I will accept any help that we can get at the moment."

"It was helping you? Even if the stories aren't very accurate, I still find that hard to believe," Tervu retorted.

"I do as well, but it told us where Jethro had gone, and it gave us a name that I believe is someone it wishes for us to seek out."

"Where is the boy?" Barith interrupted, wanting to get to the main issues without further arguments.

"With Artruis. In Green Heaven."

"We did receive word from you that Artruis was there, but our scouts indicate that it's empty. We have yet to send anyone else since the messenger arrived. Tervu's thorough interrogations revealed that some of the scouts never actually returned from that area, and the ones that did claim there was nothing there. If it is inhabited, we'll need to confirm it before I can pack up our entire army and march over there," Demoria stated firmly. Arkarn gestured to Shayarv, who then removed the blanket and revealing herself.

"This is Shayarv, a friend of mine. She will be able to locate Jethro on our behalf. All that I ask is that you keep her presence here a secret, and that you do not question her."

"That is a bit much after just discovering we had a bloody spy among us," Tervu angrily spoke, more upset about the spy that had successfully infiltrated them rather than having to accept Shayarv as an ally.

"I know, but it is the requirements for her assistance. If we give her a private space, uninterrupted, she will be able to tell us if Jethro is truly in Green Heaven, and hopefully if Artruis is there too."

Everyone remained silent, accepting the conditions without further questions.

"Arkarn…is she…" Demoria began to ask, staring at Shayarv who began to feel uncomfortable.

"Yes, Demoria," Arkarn answered dismissively, not wanting Demoria to finish her question.

"Right. Well now that we can confirm the missing boy's location, and hopefully the enemy's at the same time, what is this name that the Wendigo gave you?" Demoria asked, turning to Davun.

"Maldimon."

"Maldimon? As in Garthin Maldimon?" Thedan asked curiously.

"I don't know," Davun shrugged, feeling a little guilty for not being able to answer it accurately.

"Thedan, was he still advisor for King Tarveyin?" Arkarn asked, hopeful that he had the right answer.

"Yes, he is. I didn't personally get to meet with him. My meeting with King Tarveyin was short. As soon as I mentioned the name Artruis, he became…unstable. Almost as if he was arguing with something I could not see. He became irate, yelling about things that had nothing to do with me. I'm afraid he won't be offering us any aid either."

"As expected, but we will need to return, gaining an audience with his advisor instead."

"Why would the Wendigo want us to meet with Garthin Maldimon? He is a well-known man, famed for his writings and discoveries of old civilisations. He has no stake in this war from what I can tell."

"I have no idea, but it wouldn't have appeared before Davun to tell him without a reason. It will delay our fight and recovering of Jethro by a few days, but it seemed important enough for the Wendigo itself to tell us."

The group thought on the message and its implications. Delaying the final fight by a few days meant having more attacks to defend from, losing more troops. They always slew more Ratlings than they lost members, but the Ratlings didn't appear to be dwindling in number like they were. Having discontinued their recruiting of attacked villages, they had a set number of troops to take on the Ratling army. Their chances of success were already risky as any fight would be, but each day that passed with attacks on their camp drained their resources, increasing that risk each time. Demoria slammed her fist into the table in frustration.

"Gods damn us all! I don't like it, but we have no other choice if we want to get any upper hand we can. This Maldimon better be worth the attacks we'll have to suffer while you're gone."

"We'll travel as hard as we can, Captain Demoria," Arkarn spoke, nodding to Davun to rise so they could prepare to leave.

"Thedan, you go with them. Wayne and Kalavud, remain here this time to provide battle support."

"I will gather my things at once," Thedan rose, dismissing himself from the table with a courteous nod.

"Shayarv, perhaps it is best if you returned to your home," Arkarn called out to the girl who had been preparing to follow him out of the tent.

"That…might not be the best idea right now," she replied, embarrassed and worried.

"Why would…what did you do?" Arkarn groaned, not wanting to deal with any more hassle or surprises that would obstruct his current mission.

"Can we speak in private, Arkarnryus?" she asked him in a polite tone, clearly not wanting to speak in front of the current company.

Arkarn rolled his eyes, preparing to listen to news that he didn't want to hear at a time like this. They exited the tent, Arkarn ordering Davun to fetch food for their travels. Davun complied, though he wished to stay to hear why Shayarv did not want to return home.

Davun gathered a bag full of food that would last them more than a few days and made his way over to the horses to attach the bag to his horse. He passed his tent on the way, not daring to look at it, serving as a reminder that his brother was missing. He pushed through the wave of sadness that tried to discourage him, making his way to the mock stables.

It wasn't long before Arkarn arrived, Shayarv in tow. Thedan arrived a short time later, and they set off to the city of Vanguinar.

***

They rode without incident, either the Ratling patrols had ended in favour of attacking the camp, or they simply let them pass for their own reasons. They travelled out of the forest into open plains, passing the remains of one village that had been attacked before Davun had even met Arkarn or Kalavud. It still angered him to see Artruis' handiwork, regardless of when it occurred. They moved past the remains, not allowing time to linger or bathe in their own hatred. Their only focus right now was to reach Vanguinar and speak with Garthin Maldimon and discover why they had been sent to him. something unbeknownst them. Davun wondered what they would have to say to Garthin that would prompt him to reveal what they had to seek him out for.

Simply saying 'Hey Garthin, the Wendigo spoke to me and told me to seek you out, would you know why they would have said that?' would probably only get them thrown out for wasting his time. Davun had no idea how they would approach this man, or if someone who seemed so important would even spare the time to meet with them. Thedan was able to gain audience with the King himself, so he must have a way to at least send a message to Garthin. They continued to ride, Shayarv looking awkward as she rode. Her seclusion in the mountains meant she had no experience with riding. Davun wondered if that's what he had looked like when he first rode, feeling guilty for finding the way she rode amusing. He had no tips to offer her, still trying to find the proper technique himself. When they rested, Shayarv complained about her legs being sore, so Davun suggested that she had been gripping the horse too tightly and offered other suggestions for her to try that he had attempted but hadn't worked for him. He still felt uneasy on a horse, but he was beginning to get used to it from the days spent having to ride one. They reached Vanguinar after a day's hard ride, the horses exhausted from being pushed for so long. Upon seeing the city peek out over its walls, Davun realised that this was his first time visiting any city. He felt elated, the sight of the city truly a spectacle despite being mostly hidden behind its own defences. The stone wall was much larger than he had expected, having heard that most cities built them to repel invaders. They rode up to a set of large doors, half as tall as the wall itself. One of the doors remained open, and a set of guards were positioned out front to bar their entry. As Thedan spoke with the guards, explaining who he was and that the others were his armed escorts, Davun peeked inside the city, admiring its large buildings lit by many torches as people were still wandering about the streets despite the night already upon them. Davun was excited to see such a sight, but the experience was tarnished by the lack of Jethro. He and his brother had first set out together to visit a city, and now Davun was able to gaze upon one whilst his brother was imprisoned. He decided to take in what he could, wanting to give his brother as much detail as possible when he rescued him.

Thedan lead them to the stables where he paid for their horses to have them kept safe so that they may rest and eat. Thedan then sent a message to Garthin Maldimon, requesting a meeting for the next day, too late to request a meeting unless he had been family or already known to Garthin personally. They then entered a tavern to seek rest for the night. They entered the Lion's Pride, filled with the sounds of chatter and drunken laughter from the patrons that filled the seats. Davun's first instincts were how drab the setting was, the tables lacking any cloths and no colour to offset the brown tone of the wood.

Oh no. Averly has done more damage to me than I thought.

Davun stopped paying attention to the insignificant details that the patrons didn't seem to mind as they rowdily tried to talk over each other. Davun noticed Shayarv trying to cover herself from any wandering eyes, so he decided to step in front of her to shield her further. They followed Arkarn and Thedan, who had rented rooms from the tavern owner, and walked through a doorway to enter the section where the rooms were kept.

"Davun, you'll share with Thedan. Shayarv and I will be in the room across from you," Arkarn answered, Davun now only seeing a mug of ale that Arkarn had somehow procured. Arkarn opened his door and Shayarv immediately darted inside. Arkarn didn't question it, sipping at his ale as he wished them a goodnight. Davun entered his room with Thedan, who lit a candle that sat upon a solitary table between the two beds. The room, though poorly lit by the single candle, was lacking in any care for its appearance. The beds had cheap, grey blankets, somehow making the room seem even more dreary. There was no place to place their clothing if they wished to unpack it from their bag, and the only desk in the room didn't match the paired chair, let alone the furniture in the front room. Davun wondered how excessive and punctilious Averly really was with her décor. The bed was as uncomfortable as it looked, but after spending many nights out in the forest with naught but a blanket, Davun was able to fall asleep without much difficulty.

The next morning, they woke and opted to eat from their own supply after seeing what the tavern cook had to offer. They had to wait another hour before sending another message to Garthin to seek an answer from their previous request, Thedan saying that they had to wait enough time to be courteous. Shayarv had ridden herself of the patterns she wore, now wearing more suitable clothing for her environment. Few gave her looks, but none felt the need to address her. Dark skinned Teldarian's existed, but they were rare in number. Shayarv was not worried that they stared at her for the colour of her skin, but rather that one of them would somehow figure her out to be a Daritian. She decided to cover herself again in a hood to shield her from unyielding eyes. Davun walked alongside her, not wanting her to feel that she had to deal with the glares alone, as he stared in wonder what the city had to offer.

They passed many stores that displayed their names with wooden signs and pictures, stalls that set themselves up in a large circle where many of the pathways met. Davun wanted to see what each store had to offer but opted to look for more interesting locations to visit should he ever find himself here with Jethro again. His little brother would to have loved to see the stores and what was shelved for sale. He resisted the temptations to enter a shop that offered to sell different concoctions for different occasions, calling themselves an 'Apothecary'. Davun had no idea what that was, to him it merely looked as if they were selling coloured drinks.

They let Davun and Shayarv guide them for the hour they had to wait, letting them explore the city on their own terms. When it came time, Davun didn't question having to abandon his exploration, progress towards saving his brother was still his top priority and not even exploring new sights would let him forget that. The group made their way towards the largest building in the city, sitting well above any other and easily the widest building Davun had ever seen. A large wall prevented access to the building, clearly not wanting just anyone to be able to gain entry. They walked along the large wall, three times the height of them, and Thedan handed another letter to a guard out the front, asking them to deliver it Garthin Maldimon.

The guard obliged to the request, returning a short time later to escort them beyond the wall. The other side was decorated with a garden of assorted flowers. They ranged in colours, shapes, and heights, Davun recognising only a couple. They stuck to the main pathway while they admired the garden, smaller pathways branching off at regular intervals for those who wished to walk between the fields to gaze upon the entirety of the garden. Some of the flowers grew just as tall as Davun, though he wasn't able to get close enough to judge if they were indeed taller.

The pathway merged into a larger circular pathway that led around a large fountain. The fountain had five platforms that grew in size as it descended, the water dripping down from one tier to the next. Atop the fountain sat a creature that Davun did not recognise, though it definitely appeared to be similar to a fish, water shooting out of a hole in its head to land in the pool at the bottom. Davun wondered how the water was shooting out like it was, seeing no connected devices that could have been the answer. He judged that the device must have been hidden within the statue of the anonymous creature, amazed that someone had been able to create such a thing. They circled around the fountain, and were told to seat themselves on elongated seats, the wooden legs and backs of which were expertly carved and shaped to create loops and curls. They sat before the large building, being asked to politely wait for Garthin Maldimon to appear, apparently having accepted their request to meet, surprising Davun at how easy it had been.

Davun stared up at the large building before him, imagination running wild trying to discern how many floors or rooms it could possibly have. The building spanned out to what seemed like his entire village but knew that was just an exaggeration to himself. It stood taller than any of the trees he had seen and seemed like it was its own mountain in comparison to the houses in Eraton. The enormous building had grey stone walls that appeared to be kept clean and had very few signs of cracking. The many rooves that it had were a dark shade of burgundy, making it appear as though one large house had few smaller houses attached to it. Davun continued to stare at both the building and the garden in appreciation, taking in the new experience, when the doors they sat near were opened by a pair of guards from the inside. In the doorway stood a man, light brown hair kept at medium length, neatly brushed as if the wind had blown the ends of his hair into a complete circle, nearly resembling a crown itself.

His beard only surrounded his chin and mouth, having been shaved at the sides, showing signs of age as it had begun to turn grey. He stood erect, his flowing, light blue robe lacking a single crease aside from the sleeves. His hands were clasped behind his back as he entered the garden where the group had been waiting. They all rose as the man presented himself, Thedan indicating they should bow slightly once he saw them.

"Lord Garthin Maldimon, it is a pleasure to formerly meet you. I thank you for allowing us time to speak with you about an urgent matter. My name is Thedan Vasterdin. These are my friends and allies. Arkarn, Davun, and Shayarv."

The man smiled at them politely, extending a hand to Thedan who shook it.

"Two Southerners, a Northerner, and a young lady with a name whose origin I don't recognise," the man had a smooth voice, oozing with confidence that was apparent to anyone who heard, "A peculiar group indeed."

"She is of mixed blood, but she was born in the South," Thedan responded quickly, trying to steer Garthin away from questioning her further.

"Still a peculiar name. Well, what matter brings Thedan Vasterdin, the man of gentle persuasion, to my home and asking of my presence?" Garthin spoke, keeping up his confident front and pushing the conversation forward.

"It is indirectly related to the matter I spoke of with your King within the past week."

"I believe he has already given an answer to your request."

"He has, Lord Maldimon, but I am not here in attempt to change his mind or try to seek an alternative route through his trusted advisor. I am here to seek you out personally, after we received a very peculiar request of our own to seek you out."

"What makes it peculiar?"

"Well, how should I put this…hmm…"

Arkarn took a step forward, leaning in a little and lowering his voice a little.

"The Wendigo has asked us to seek you out."

Davun was stunned by how blunt Arkarn was, expecting the next words from Garthin to give orders to the guards to throw them all out for being delusional. To his surprise, Garthin kept his smile, keeping eye contact with Arkarn.

"Very well" Garthin responded after a moments' thought. Davun was not sure how to react. The outcome had been in their favour, Garthin at least willing to hear them out, but he definitely had not expected such an abrupt agreement.

"Let's head inside for more privacy on such a delicate matter," Garthin spoke, turning around but pausing halfway, "Besides, we wouldn't want anyone else discovering your Daritian friend, would we?"

CHAPTER TWENTY-SIX

"We eventually grew more daring, deciding to seek out the truth behind the myths that told of more dangerous creatures. We were worried that the tales would show no results, disappointing our curious minds, but we were more frightened at the prospect of the stories being true."

The room was quiet, the boredom having settled into Jethro a long while ago. There was naught for him to do in the room, so he stared out of his window, watching the Ratlings go about their work. At first, it was interesting watching the way they interacted with each other, the way their bodies moved and how they handled normal tasks like transporting fallen trees back to the camp to be fashioned into a barrier. They made little progress constructing the wall in preparation for the inevitable attack that Artruis was confident would come. The Ratlings clearly had little to no experience in this kind of handiwork, struggling with using the appropriate tools and usually resorting to more mundane methods like hacking at the logs with a dagger. They were clearly not bright creatures, but their numbers meant they could do some of the work faster, such as transporting more wood simultaneously, carrying them as a group rather than using carts to bring them back to camp. They had also chosen to avoid any of the nearby trees surrounding the glade, instead walking further into the forest to find trees to cut down. Jethro was unsure why they had chosen to do this, the closest trees would have obviously saved some time, but even a dull creature would have understood that. The most peculiar thing he noticed about the Ratlings was they didn't appear to communicate verbally. He considered that he wasn't close enough to any to hear them speak, but many Ratlings were located close by his window, so he figured he should have heard something by now. The camp was also not filled with idle conversation, instead just the sound of cutting wood and fights over food was all that could be heard. He wondered how the Ratlings could communicate with each other but realised that they were already very akin to animals as it was, and animals don't communicate like humans do.

Night fell and Artruis had not yet returned, his few hours turning into the entire day. Jethro ate the food that had been brought to him, and with nothing else to do, he tried to sleep. It arrived quicker than he had expected but was abruptly cut short as the sound of the make-shift wooden door startled him awake.

"I have woken you. I apologise. I did not think you would have been asleep," Artruis stood before him, holding a candle.

"I had nothing else to do," Jethro responded, not wanting to sound like he was complaining. He knew that he was basically being held in a prison, so he couldn't expect anything else.

"I see. My work took me longer than I had expected, I apologise for returning so late. Perhaps tomorrow I will allow you to walk the grounds should you get bored again. I'm afraid I cannot let you leave the campgrounds itself, but at least being able to move around will eradicate some of your time."

Jethro wasn't sure on what to say, so he simply nodded in agreement.

"I will let you return to sleep. Is your bed comfortable enough for you?"

"Yes, it's fine," he responded, nearly thanking Artruis before remembering where he was. He wasn't sure why Artruis was being so kind as his captor. So far, he had been nothing but polite and respectful while still being silently firm about the boundaries that had been set. Jethro considered that it might be an act, much like Delavun's had been. His mood turned sour at the thought of being fooled once again, turning over in his bed to face away from Artruis.

"Goodnight," Artruis spoke as he turned to leave, hesitating a moment when Jethro did not respond. He closed the improvised door shut, and his footsteps grew silent as he entered his own room to rest. Jethro stewed in his own thoughts for a while, before a realisation dawned upon him.

Does Artruis know where I lived?

The man surely had known by now that he and Davun lived in Eraton. It was possible that his dealings with Pallinor had revealed the location where his brother had been before departing and unexpectedly making his way into the survivor army. Artruis appeared to be a man who knew precisely what he wanted and how to achieve it.

Jethro fell asleep fearful of what would happen to the innocent and unaware people who might become involved should Artruis decide to take his heinous actions even further.

***

Morning came and Jethro stared at the wall from his bed. He had awoken some time ago but felt no need to get out of bed. He knew that his room was as empty as it had been the day before. He wondered on how his brother was doing, or if the camp had yet received the message that Artruis was holding him captive. He got the feeling that Artruis wanted a big confrontation, instead of trying to make a simple trade for Davun. He also wondered if Averly was fretting over his sudden disappearance, or if she just assumed, he had left with Davun again.

That's all he could do now. Wonder about things. Wonder what was going on outside of his confinement. He missed his brother greatly. He missed Arkarn, Wayne, and Kalavud, and the other friends he had made at the camp. He missed Averly, even her constant scolding of him for leaving things dirty.

For the first time since he had been imprisoned in his room, Jethro cried.

A few hours passed when Artruis entered the room, followed by Ratlings carrying the usual meal. He moved to open the windows as the Ratlings hurried out. Jethro stirred awake, having fallen asleep after tiring himself out again. He rose out of bed as Artruis gestured for him to sit and eat his food, seating himself down across from Jethro once the boy had taken his seat. Artruis remained quiet while Jethro slowly ate.

"Perhaps we shall go for another walk today?" Artruis offered once Jethro finished his morning meal. Jethro didn't want to spend more time with the man but was eager for any chance to leave his room, so he accepted.

They began their walk in silence, taking their time as they encircled the camp once again, sticking close to the tree line this time. Jethro stared at the trees, wondering what reason the Ratlings had for not cutting them down. Perhaps they had some sort of defect he had not noticed before. Jethro was no expert on trees, however, and could discern no reason for the trees to be left alone.

"Why do the Ratlings avoid the closest trees?" he asked, once again not able to hold in his curiosity. Artruis glanced about at the trees, his face unchanging and his eyes covered, unable to betray any thoughts or emotions he may have been trying to hide.

"I told them to leave the closest trees alone. These trees create the boundary for what is the Green Heaven. Without them, the energy that I connect with here might be tainted. I do not wish to take that chance," the man spoke in his usual calm demeanour, but it was clear even to Jethro that this place held more of a meaning. Either that, or Artruis was a very superstitious man, but Jethro highly doubted that would have been possible.

"You do not feel its energy, do you?" Artruis asked the young boy who was still looking at the trees.

"No. I don't really feel anything."

"Not surprising. Many factors are probably preventing you from allowing yourself to reach out to it. You are young, you do not see what I see, and you are here against your will, which will taint your emotions negatively."

Jethro wondered what else he was supposed to feel if not negative towards the Ratling campsite. This entire place held the entire reasoning for so much death and lives that had been meaninglessly destroyed. To him, this place meant nothing other than a target to vent his hatred towards. He didn't hate the scenery itself, just what occupied the scenery, which obscured any possible connections he could have held towards the glade. Even if they weren't, this place was meant to be a cemetery, what kind of connection was he supposed to have? Whatever Artruis saw in this place escaped Jethro, it might be something he would possibly never understand. The man was still an enigma to him, meeting him only brought more unanswered questions. The man somehow still held so much mystery, and Jethro was beginning to wonder if Artruis' – even if it were a meagre display – politeness meant that he would still answer some questions.

"Why are you doing this?" Jethro asked bluntly, not expecting a proper response. He hadn't intended to word it that way, but it blurted itself out. Artruis continued to walk alongside Jethro in silence, showing no reaction to the question. Jethro figured Artruis would simply pretend like the question had never been asked, when the man surprisingly responded.

"How old are you now?"

"Ten."

"Still so young. You have never been in love, have you?"

"No."

"Then you will not understand my reasons for why I am doing all that I do."

It wasn't a clear answer, but at least Jethro now knew that Artruis' was trying to accomplish something for someone he loved. Jethro decided to try his luck again.

"What is your goal?"

"That is something that your friend Arkarn has not yet discovered?"

Jethro felt himself beginning to panic with worry. He revealed something to the enemy that he wasn't sure he should have, not knowing that his questions would have had ramifications. Jethro did not respond, afraid he might reveal too much about something he wasn't sure he should even be talking about.

"I cannot answer that question," Artruis continued after Jethro remained silent. Jethro's remaining hope of finding the answer diminished, not wanting to pursue the question should he reveal something else he shouldn't have. They continued to walk without talking, Artruis seemingly enjoying the scenery while Jethro had become too distracted with his thoughts. He was racing through questions that he was deciding to actively avoid in conversation, as well as what Artruis might ask of him and how to avoid answering his questions. Suddenly, a thought that Jethro had been avoiding brought itself to the surface once again, this time in the form of a question. A question that he needed an answer to.

"Are you going to kill my brother when you trade me?" the air felt still as the words crept out of his mouth. It was a question he really did not want to ask, but knew he needed to hear the answer. Artruis didn't respond immediately, leaving Jethro to suffer in the silence.

"Anything that I say will give away the answer. Should I lie, you wouldn't believe me."

The words pierced Jethro's heart, his mind clouded, unable to deal with the wave of mixed emotions. Somehow wanting to go back to confinement, Jethro ran ahead towards the house. Artruis did not call out or give chase, but the Ratlings did perk up at the sudden movement. They watched Jethro run, but did not react, they watched him disappear inside the house, and returned to their work. Jethro tried to slide the wooden panel shut, but it was difficult from his side, leaving it slightly ajar. He threw himself onto his bed of blankets, and for the second time that day, Jethro cried himself asleep.

CHAPTER TWENTY-SEVEN

"Many tales of dangerous creatures exist. Many claim to have sharp talons, claws, or teeth, to provide natural weapons to eat human flesh. We had our doubts that such a creature truly existed, our minds no longer taking the prospects of the stories seriously after our discoveries.
But how long have we believed that these were only stories?"

"**H**ow did you see me as Daritian?" Shayarv asked Garthin. They had been moved into his office, and then through a secret pathway, the door of which had been part of the wall to make it indistinguishable. He assured them that they were now away from prying eyes and ears. He wasn't entirely certain if the King would have sent spies once he learned about their meeting. He explained that the King could be a little paranoid at times and would often distrust his own staff. The room was littered with books and papers, with a quill next to fresh ink for writing. The room also had a desk with only one chair, obviously not designed for guests, so Garthin sat down while the rest stood.

"Your name, mostly. If you are trying to remain hidden, perhaps try to take on a different name. It is similar to some areas of the world, so an ordinary person may not question it as much. However, I have done my research on Daritians, suspecting that they still existed. Your skin tone is darker than most, so I didn't think you were of mixed blood. Your facial features, mostly your chin and cheek bones, match what I have read and seen in the few accurate drawings that exist."

They all listened intently as Garthin explained himself, his smug smile not even attempting to disguise his relishing in revealing how he knew. The man clearly liked to show how knowledgeable he was, though this kind of information might have been well earned to deserve it. Shayarv looked a little ashamed for revealing her identity so soon after leaving her home. She clearly had not been anticipating someone able to identify her so easily. Davun noticed she shrunk into herself a little as she barricaded herself in shame, so he decided to stand next to her to provide comfort.

"You know of Daritians? That is a surprise," Arkarn spoke, suspicious about how Garthin discovered the fact.

"Do not worry, I will not tell anyone. Provided you also keep what I have to tell you a secret. And this room, of course. I can't be worried about spies reaching my research," he gestured towards the piles of paper and books located all about the room, which he then shifted the papers so that they could not be read.

"Incomplete research, I should add."

"You are still conducting your research? I am glad to hear that. Many thought you had given up your thirst for the world's hidden knowledge, taking a comfy position as an advisor to a King." Thedan excitedly commented, clearly with some knowledge about the kind of research Garthin conducted.

"Yes, I am still researching, but it is not in the typical field that I've written most of my books in. I will reveal to you, because I suspect that you all already know seeing as you are travelling with a supposedly extinct Daritian. During one of my unrelated voyages to uncover a different history, I instead discovered the truth behind the mythical beasts told in tales."

This surprised everyone. The truth was not known to many, mostly within the inner circle of their camp, but this man had somehow found evidence of the truth.

"At first, I didn't believe it. Sceptical as any sane scholar would be. So, I read more books, I travelled to more locations, and eventually provided myself the ability to answer my own question. I travelled to where I believe the powers of the Basilisk slept. And I was correct."

"You truly located the place of the fearsome Basilisk?" Shayarv interrupted, clearly surprised to hear the claim. Garthin didn't drop his confident smile, once again eager to bathe in his own achievements.

"Yes. We discovered the remains of what we suspected was the original holder of the Basilisk power, and how the stories began. Whilst his body had long but decayed, sitting in his tomb for centuries on end, his eyes remained untouched by time. The eyes of a snake."

Everyone took a moment to process the information. Sat before them was not only a man who had discovered the truth behind the mythical tales of beasts and legends but had actively researched and discovered the resting place of one such power. Davun had no idea how to even begin looking for such a place without the assistance of Arkarn or a Daritian, and yet this man apparently discovered it without any such assistance.

"If I may ask, if you discovered such a thing, why did you not write about it? You held onto the knowledge yourself?" Thedan asked curiously. Garthin's smile dropped slightly, as he looked at the polite man.

"I became…a little obsessed. The knowledge revealed a whole part of our world that I thought I was the first to discover. The many years of history written in a vast number of books as though it were facts and not mere stories, were a complete fabrication. Or at least mostly fabricated. I became driven to seeing which legends still existed in our world in the form of a power that one could hold, and which were mere stories. I still took notes, but never gave myself the time to write them and reveal them to the world. It is not something you can just throw out there and have people believe you. You need evidence. I am writing my first book now, but it is taking its time. Between my motivation and my..." he drifted off, his smile now almost faded entirely.

"You do not know if the world should be privy to such information," Arkarn added, finishing what Garthin had to say. Garthin nodded, smiling sheepishly.

"I am not entirely certain if it is right to reveal it. Telling the world about these powers would mean that greedy men and women would seek them out, killing each other, going to war, abandoning their own friends and family for some power," he became irritated towards the end. Clearly this was something that he constantly fought over in his mind. To show the world his research that he devoted his life to, at the cost of possibly sending it into chaos. It was not something any person with care for human life could decide easily. They already knew what someone was capable of in pursuit of one of these powers, who knows what would occur should the entire world become aware.

"If I might revert to something you said earlier for a moment," Arkarn interrupted the silence while they all weighed the options, "You mentioned 'we'?"

Garthin took a deep breath. "Yes. We. I did not journey on my own after discovering the truth. I managed to convince good friends of mine to accompany me on exploring a whole facet of our world that was being kept hidden. Seraferan and Artruis."

"Artruis actually accompanied you on your trips? So, there are more people who have discovered the truth, then?" Thedan asked, intrigued that Artruis and Garthin had a connection.

"Just those two. They won't be telling anyone about the discovery. They have each made their choices for their lives and will see it through until the end. That's the kind of people they were."

"Much like yourself, then."

Garthin chuckled slightly. "Yes. Perhaps that is what made me so fond of them."

"Why are you talking about them as if they no longer exist?" Davun asked, wondering if Garthin had thought Artruis deceased and wanting to reveal the horrible things he had been doing.

"Because they no longer exist to me. It has been many years since I last laid my eyes on either one. Well, that is not entirely true. Artruis paid King Tarveyin a visit earlier this year but pretended like I wasn't even in the room. He spoke with King Tarveyin, claiming to have turned in the bandits that were attacking the villages, and left."

"He actually reported that to the King?" Thedan exclaimed, aghast at the idea that Artruis had the gall to do such a thing. Davun began to grow angry again, the hatred returning to the surface, his hand that still had feeling clenching into a fist. Shayarv placed a hand on his arm, attempting to calm him. The villages that Artruis destroyed and all the lives that his Ratlings had taken at his order had simply been ignored by the crown over a simple lie that probably didn't even have any evidence to back it up. The King must be a gullible fool to let a man like Artruis walk right through his doors and lie to his face about the murders of his own people. Davun had no idea what could drive a man to do such a demonic act, but he was certain that Artruis was no longer human.

"That is the claim he presented to the King. Somehow, through no evidence or even explanation, he convinced the King about bandits that I do not think ever existed."

"Of course they don't exist. The villages that were destroyed were destroyed by Artruis!" Davun burst, Shayarv tightening her grip a little attempting to calm him further. Garthin locked eyes with Davun, staring at him as if trying to gauge how much anger was churning inside.

"I suspected something of the sort."

"Then how was he able to convince King Tarveyin about the death of his own citizens without providing the evidence to support it?" Thedan asked before Davun had a chance to outburst again.

"Those damned eyes."

Everyone was confused at the answer, save for Arkarn who grew worried. Garthin responded as if it explained everything, letting people remain curious as to what he meant by the words while he himself seemed to be racing through thoughts.

"What do you mean 'eyes'?" Davun asked impatiently, not wanting to wait further for an answer.

"The Basilisk," Arkarn responded for Garthin through seething teeth. Everyone was shocked, Arkarn's answer confirmed by Garthin's silence.

He...already has a power?

The thought threatened to make Davun shake with worry. The prospect of a heinous man obtaining two powers made their situation much more dire. The powers of the Basilisk remained unknown to Davun, but if they were as powerful as people seemed to think of the Phoenix, then their chances of winning the upcoming battle would drastically drop to near naught. They would have to change their strategy to account for Artruis' abilities, but Davun wasn't certain if anyone knew what they were. Before he could ask Garthin, the man sighed and began to speak.

"A long time ago, Seraferan made a decision. I do not know if I have her permission to reveal what it was, but all I can say is she made a great sacrifice for humanity. Upon one of our research trips, we uncovered something terrifying that was causing the deaths of many. Seraferan made the decision to prevent that from happening further, but in doing so it cost her the wonderful life she had built. I have not seen her since that day. Artruis, at first, was wracked with guilt and sadness for having lost something so dear to him. He and Sera had wed but a year before. He tried desperately to convince her not to sacrifice herself, that there could be another way they could handle it, but Sera was a strong-minded woman. She would not have made the decision if she thought there was another way. Artruis spent some time alone, and after some months, decided to return to assisting me in my research. We travelled together for little longer than a year, before one of our journeys changed him drastically. The last thing Artruis told me before he left was that he was going back for the eyes of the Basilisk so that he had the means to save Sera. I still do not quite know how he intends to do that."

The room went quiet as Garthin stopped talking. His usual confident demeanour had turned into sadness and regret as he recalled the painful memories. Davun had calmed down a bit, Shayarv still holding onto him, but his understanding of Artruis' intentions were no clearer than before. The man might have a goal, to somehow return Sera to him, but how he intended to do that with the powers of the Phoenix was still unknown. Perhaps it wasn't the final piece of his plan, his plan that involved murdering countless innocents who had no idea that what he sought even existed. His passion to return a loved one did not account for the executions of several villages. If he really did manage to return Sera, who Davun assumed was deceased, then surely she would not be content to hear the methods Artruis had chosen in order to return her. The way Garthin spoke of them indicated to Davun that they were not capable of the horrid acts that Artruis had been doing. Wherever they had gone, or whatever they had discovered, supposedly changed this man to the emotion-less monster who had no care for human life.

"This…journey that changed him…what were you seeking?" Arkarn asked, as if he already guessed what the answer would be.

"Before I do, I do not wish to reveal something that you do not know in this area, so I would like for you to tell me what it is Artruis has been doing."

Arkarn took a deep breath as Thedan gave Davun a look to not let his emotions take control and let Arkarn speak for him. Davun took a deep breath and listened as Arkarn explained everything that Artruis had done. He talked of the camp of survivor's that had banded together after the surrounding lands would not aid them, in belief that all the attacks had been bandits and that they had been dealt with accordingly. He explained what Artruis was seeking but chose not to reveal that Davun was the next heir. The explanation was lengthy, but it was necessary to describe all that Artruis had been doing. When he was finished, Garthin remained staring at him, brow deepened in thought.

"So, he even managed to uncover the Rat King's truth…that bastard. That was on our list of legends to explore. However, it does contain the answer of what we had journeyed for that changed him. The very thing that you now go to war to stop him. The Phoenix. We uncovered an old Daritian homestead, and through the various paintings and papers that remained, we uncovered that they sought to protect the owner of the Phoenix powers. I do not know what changed Artruis that day. Nothing that I had uncovered gave me any indication as to what could change a man so drastically in a mere moment. My only guess is that he seeks the power of fire to accomplish yet another hidden goal of his. I can no longer predict what that man will do. The Artruis I knew would never have done such things, especially if Sera were still around. The man discovered a way to fix one of his regrets, but in doing so completely diminishes Sera's sacrifice. You must not let such a thing happen. Sera will despise him if he undoes what she willingly chose to do. For the sake of both of them, stop him by any means."

Davun stared at the man's eyes, thinking he saw a piece of hatred towards Artruis. Garthin spoke adamantly, in full belief that Artruis should not be allowed to achieve his goal that unwinds a great deed of another.

"We will, and for that to happen, I must ask you to describe what you can about the powers he obtained from the basilisk." Arkarn gently added, prompting Garthin to continue.

"As you are probably aware, there are many…dire measures one must take to obtain these powers. In the case of the Basilisk, you must seek out the eyes that lay in the resting place, or in the current holder, and then scrape out your own eyes and replace them with the Basilisks'," Garthin casually described, the description causing all but Arkarn to wince at the idea. "I do not know exactly what the powers are, but from the stories, it definitely gives the holder a kind of poison. It seems deadly as there isn't any recorded word that I have read that speaks of a survivor. The other, which I am more than certain that I have seen during his meeting with Tarveyin, and I assume the other crowns as well, is that the eyes hold a kind of mesmerising technique. They are able to, for what most of the books refer to as a paralysation, hold the victim in a trance. The victim becomes unaware of their surroundings, and even lack the free will to move. During this, the Basilisk may tell the victim a lie, and the victim will believe it. I don't know the exact method or how it works in its entirety, but…" Garthin leaned closer to emphasise his next words, "Do not look into his eyes. He is only able to use that power when you lock eyes with him. Deny him this, and all that's left is his poison, which I'm afraid I am no use for."

"You have given us much, Garthin Maldimon. I thank you for your time and your information. It will be used to prevent Artruis from undoing what you described as someone's noble sacrifice. We will see to it that Sera will remain untouched," Arkarn bowed to the seated man, who smiled faintly in return. They were all truly grateful for Garthin's help, but the man seemed to be lost in his own thoughts to acknowledge their appreciation as they all thanked and bowed him in turn.

"There is something you could do in return for me," Garthin spoke to them after they had finished thanking him.

"Name it, please," Thedan responded, eager to be able to fulfill any request in return.

"I suspect that you already know of the next heir to the Phoenix," he spoke, glancing at Davun and his smirk returning slightly, "I would appreciate it if they would come speak to me once you are successful in retrieving the orb. I would very much like to learn about what they can do."

Davun tried to remain as still as possible while trying to keep his face unchanged so that Garthin could not read it. He did not want to give away anything that Arkarn wished to remain hidden. Garthin's smirk grew larger as he stared at him, Davun worried that he had been unsuccessful in hiding his reaction.

"It might take some years for them to be able to see you, as you may know the Daritian's must find them first to be able to guide them. However, I promise to you that they will seek you out once they have explored their powers first. I am sure you would appreciate more knowledge on what it is they can achieve," Arkarn addressed him formerly, speaking as sincerely as he could.

"That would be splendid," Garthin accepted, standing from his chair and reaching out a hand to Arkarn, who shook it to honour the arrangement.

"It might be time that we leave, the King might become suspicious if he is not aware of my location when he sends his spies to see if I plan on betraying him," Garthin spoke, leading the others out of the hidden passageway and into the main office. Garthin lead them back to the gardens, where he was thanked once more by the group who were truly appreciative of his assistance.

"Oh, Lord Maldimon, if I might ask something," Thedan asked nervously, "What made you decide to stop your journeys and become advisor to a King?"

Garthin's smirk came back in full as he stared at Thedan, pleased.

"Who said I stopped? I am still conducting my research," he answered, turning and walking away without another word.

CHAPTER TWENTY-EIGHT

"Our search eventually led us to uncover one of the cruelest truths. The Wendigo. Not only its abilities, effects of wielding its power, but also the role that no one knew it played."

Jethro had not eaten the prior day. After locking himself in his own prison, he refused any food that was brought by the obedient Ratlings. The food sat on the table, rotted and stale. His stomach growled, longing to be full once again, but Jethro was adamant in convincing himself he didn't need to eat. The thought of food made his throat tighten, threatening to return any food sent down, as his emotions now controlled his body. He now knew the predicament that he had let himself wander into would cause the death of his brother. He did not deserve to eat, the guilt convincing him that he should be the one to perish instead. His previous thoughts of ceasing to exist returned, now a viable option in order to save his brother. He was feuding with himself as he weighed his options and their possibilities. He couldn't let Davun turn himself over and be executed to save him from his own ignorant actions that caused this situation. If Jethro were no longer being held as a prisoner here, then Artruis would have nothing to offer. He wanted Davun to stop Artruis, but that would be arduous as long as Artruis held something precious against him. Jethro needed to do something instead of waiting idly while others would risk their lives just to save him. Davun was the key Artruis needed to his operation, and Jethro knew that he couldn't let that happen. The different ways he thought of eradicating himself from the situation sent phantom pains through his body as he imagined how dire it would hurt to perpetrate them. He chastised himself again, for not having the strength to accomplish what was necessary from his point of view.

Morning came, Jethro dipping in and out of sleep having slept throughout the previous day. He was lying awake as the sun peeked over the horizon. He waited until it was higher in the sky before finally removing himself from the bed to open the shutters. He stared out at the camp where most of the Ratlings appeared to be asleep, forming huddles to use each other as warmth. He waited in his room, knowing that a Ratling would soon come by to present fresh food for him, which he hadn't yet decided if he would eat. His body still threatened to reject anything he tried to swallow, but he also knew he couldn't go hungry if he needed energy. Any plan he could think of required at least some effort to accomplish, and he wasn't certain if he had that within him. Jethro heard footsteps outside his door, a combination of Artruis' and Ratlings, followed by a knocking that clearly wasn't from the Ratling. They simply just entered to drop off the food and left without hesitation or word, they certainly never knocked. Artruis allowed himself in after a moment of silence, holding Jethro's plate of food. He walked over and sat down at the table silently, simply waiting for Jethro to respond to his actions. Jethro had returned to his bed, laying still as he could feel the man's eyes beneath the cloth staring at him.

"Please seat yourself," Artruis spoke, no longer waiting for Jethro to act on his own. Jethro considered ignoring the request, hoping that Artruis would just leave if he lay there long enough, but he decided not to anger the man who would kill his brother. If Artruis would succeed in his plan, he didn't want Davun to suffer because he had annoyed Artruis. He slowly rose out of bed and made his way to the table, seating himself across from Artruis. He stared at the plate of food that was exactly the same meal he had been fed since he had arrived. Artruis sat patiently, waiting for the young boy to begin eating. Jethro stared at his food, choosing to instead fumble around with the bread instead of eating it. Now that the food was presented before him, and the addition of Artruis watching, he felt the difficulty rise from attempting to force himself to down the food.

"Are you not hungry?" Artruis asked, the sight of the other plates of food still displayed themselves on the table. Jethro didn't respond, not entirely knowing the answer himself. He knew that he should have felt hungry having not eaten in almost a day, but the thought of eating the food made him gag slightly.

"Is the food not to your liking?"

"The food is fine," Jethro answered, idly rolling his bread on the plate.

"Then what I confessed yesterday ails you into not eating?"

Jethro hesitantly nodded. He didn't wish to have this conversation with Artruis, knowing there was nothing he could say to convince the man to change his intentions. Jethro could no longer look at the man, the scene playing over in his head whenever he thought about it.

"I know there is nothing I can say to make you feel any better. If you warmed up to the idea of your brother being killed, then you would have lost some of your humanity. However, I do require you to be in full health, so I must insist that you eat."

The man's words had the opposite effect on Jethro. Speaking about the fate of his brother only aided in Jethro's decision to not eat, truly feeling sick. He stopped playing with the bread, placing his hands in his lap instead. He stared at the food as if looking at it were enough to satisfy his bodily needs. Artruis sighed, realising that Jethro had come to a decision.

"This is not something I enjoy doing for such a monotonous task. I must ask you to look at me," Artruis spoke, beginning to unwrap the knot that kept his cloth in place. Jethro's curiosity pulled his eyes up, wandering what Artruis would reveal to him. He wanted to know why the man covered his eyes, or at least the upper half of his face, and now he would be given the answer, possibly to persuade him into eating. The food was all but forgotten as Artruis lowered the cloth to the table and stared at Jethro.

Jethro held back a gasp, his mouth gaping at the sight. Artruis' eyes were not human. They appeared snake-like, yellow with a green tinge in its entirety save for the black line that served as his pupil. Jethro couldn't help but stare into them, the world around him forgotten, no longer aware of the situation that he was in. All that mattered now was the many questions he wanted to ask about the eyes but couldn't find the effort to do so. He stared at them, as they stared in return, as if both were as equally curious in each other. Jethro had no concept of how long he stared into those eyes, the questions disappearing from his mind as he became transfixed with them.

"You will eat your food now," Artruis spoke. Jethro nodded and immediately began to eat his food, the threats his body made completely forgotten and ignored. Artruis returned the cloth to its resting place around his eyes, leaving the room so that Jethro could eat in peace.

Midday came when Artruis returned to Jethro's room. Jethro had eaten his meal to its completion, even requesting more food from the Ratling that remained outside his door. He had no idea what had come over him, the emotions that had controlled him momentarily pushed aside to allow basic human needs to take over. He ate until he was full, the feelings slowly coming back as his thoughts changed from focusing on food to what really mattered. Artruis discovered Jethro sitting at the table this time, staring into it as though a giant hole had appeared holding the world's treasures right before him.

"Perhaps you would like to take another walk today," Artruis suggested to him. Jethro's immediate instincts were to reject the offer, but then remembered that he needed various objects if he were to attempt any of his plans. He decided he should take the offer while it lasted so that he could look around camp, hoping an opportunity would present itself for him to obtain one without anyone noticing. He arose from his chair without word and followed Artruis outside.

They walked their usual circle around the campsite in silence. Jethro had no wishes to speak with the man. He had plenty he wanted to ask, but not only was he angry towards the man, but was afraid of what else he might uncover. They rounded the camp until they reached the opposite side when a Ratling approached Artruis.

"Masters. The boys has been seens thats way," the Ratling spoke as if it were uncomfortable to form each word. It pointed towards the South-East where only trees could be seen. Jethro had not noticed any Ratlings return to camp. It seemed as though the Ratling had come from the campsite to give a report, but Jethro just assumed he hadn't noticed it, too focused on searching for anything nearby that he could use.

"I assume he is not alone?"

"No masters. Threes others are with hims."

"Arkarn?"

The Ratling nodded.

"Do not initiate a fight. Retreat to camp."

The Ratling nodded again, and to Jethro's surprise, the Ratling returned to the camp instead of carrying the message off to the scouts. He stared as the Ratling simply returned to going through a pile of weapons, as if choosing which one he liked the look of most. He remained standing still as Artruis continued their walk. He hurried to catch up to the man, wanting badly to know if Artruis had noticed the Ratling had ignored his orders.

"Do you delay because you wonder about the Ratlings' actions?" Artruis asked when Jethro caught up beside him. Jethro wanted badly to respond but decided to keep his tongue still.

"You are easy to read. I do not need your words to know what it is you wish to say, so I will be courteous and answer your unasked question," Artruis spoke, his voice having a slight tone of annoyance to his usual calmness.

"Many stories of the Ratlings exist. Some say that the first Ratling was born to a woman who had committed a great sin, and it bred from there. One such story even suggests that they were summoned by a man who asked demons to plague the neighbouring city to settle a feud he was having with a rival Lord. Based on what I have observed from my time with the Ratlings, I choose to believe that the Rat King is the most accurate. It is said there was once an enormous rat that walked on its hind legs, attacking cities in search for food. This enormous rat was apparently compromised of thousands of rats piled together, each blow it took only served to kill few of the rats at a time. Eventually, the now titled Rat King, fought a city it could not defeat. Before all of the rats that compromised together to create the enormous figure were slain, they dispersed, hiding from humans, biding their time to repopulate to one day recreate the Rat King. If these rats were to organise themselves in such a way that they could create an enormous creature, they would have to all be of the same mind. That is something I have discovered about these Ratlings. They are all of one mind."

Jethro listened to the story, enamoured at the concept of a large Ratling that could trample cities. The sheer number of creatures it would take to form something that large was impossible to imagine all spread out. He took a look at the sheer number of Ratlings that were at this campsite and imagine them all piled together would not have even come close to the size he imagined as Artruis retold the story. He also couldn't believe it possible for Ratlings to simply band together to form a gigantic version of themselves that could function enough to level cities. It was not the concept of the giant Ratling that Artruis was trying to convey, however, it was that the Ratlings all shared a mind.

"You mean…they all think the same?" Jethro couldn't hold back his question, too bothered by it to leave it unasked while the opportunity was there to be taken.

"In a sense, yes. They are all their own creatures, each having their own instincts and bodily needs such as food, but they all share in one mind. It is the best way I can describe it. If I give one Ratling a message, then all the Ratlings receive that message at the same time."

The concept of sharing a mind didn't seem possible to Jethro. He had completely forgotten that he believed in the power that lets someone create and manipulate fire that now seemed entirely possible to him, but the concept of sharing one mind across potentially thousands of bodies did not make any sense to him.

"Are they psychic?"

"Perhaps, but I do not believe so. I simply think they all unintentionally share the same information with each other. It is simply how they were made. They cannot control it."

Jethro stared at the Ratlings as they were all going about their own business, no form of communication anywhere. It made sense to him how the Ratlings had no need to speak to each other, but the concept was still too surreal for him to completely accept. He also realised that if it were true, it was how Artruis was able to control and direct all the Ratlings on his own. He thought that Artruis would have had some help other than the Ratlings, but he hadn't seen another human during his time here. He continued to stare at the rats, noticing how none of them spoke, the only sounds they made were the growls and snarls from fighting over the food. The Ratlings had so much more to them than he had thought, no longer seeing them as only scrawny, obedient slaves, but rather as one band of manipulated creatures who don't even know their own capabilities. The Ratlings were certainly slow minded, the camp they had made appeared to have no organisation other than the processing area for their log making which he assumed Artruis had informed them how to set up. The barricade had made significant process, surrounding the backside of the camp and logs being placed at each other cardinal direction to provide at least a little cover. The Ratlings continued to work wordlessly, hauling in fallen trees as a group, working together seamlessly. He wondered what these Ratlings would be capable of if they had the intelligence to lead themselves, the story Artruis had just told echoing in his mind before he decided it would be best if they didn't.

Jethro continued their walk in silence, several questions replaying themselves in his mind, urging themselves to be asked, but he refused them, not wanting to make any more conversation with the man who would kill his brother.

At least as long as Artruis held him as leverage.

He eyed around the camp, seeing the pile of weapons that the Ratlings had created, apparently just tossed into one location until they needed them. One missing weapon would go unnoticed, but the difficulty was for him to remain unseen. Their camp was open, leaving scant cover for him to hide behind. His current position was too obvious for him to swipe a dagger unnoticed, and he doubted that Artruis would keep his eye off him long enough for him to do so. He decided against attempting to obtain a tool for his way out, his plan would have to be delayed until a better opportunity arose.

Jethro's thoughts were interrupted as he heard a bark from the forest. It sounded again before he was able to identify the source. A large Lakkerfel was bolting towards them.

A Lakkerfel with one ear.

Jethro froze, expecting the Lakkerfel to charge him again as it dashed towards them. As the Lakkerfel approached, his mind began to function again, realising that Davun was no longer with him to protect him anymore.

It was time to protect himself.

He dashed towards the stash of weapons, the Ratlings he neared becoming wary of him and distancing themselves from him. He picked up the first weapon he could grab and swung around to face the Lakkerfel who would be right behind him with a dinted sword tightly gripped with both hands.

As he spun, he saw the Lakkerfel sitting by Artruis, obediently staring at him with all of its attention. Jethro was confused for only a short moment as the reality of the situation struck him. The Lakkerfel was Artruis' pet. Or rather, another tool for Artruis.

"Release the weapon. He will not harm you unless I command it," Artruis called out, facing Jethro though his expression remained still. Jethro reluctantly lowered his weapon, inwardly scolding himself for not having stashed a dagger while he had rushed for a weapon to defend himself. He let go of the sword and cautiously approached Artruis who was patiently waiting for him to return to his side. The Lakkerfel didn't appear to care for Jethro's presence, its eyes not leaving Artruis for a moment. It sat by his side, patiently waiting for its next command.

"It is safe to be near me," Artruis tried to convince Jethro, who had stopped a few steps away from him, still wary about the Lakkerfel. Artruis seemed to have complete control over it, but that didn't mean that Jethro was convinced that it might break its concentration in an instant and attack him. Artruis was confident in his ability to control the beast, but even he would not be able to stop it if it chose to simply lunge at Jethro.

"If he frightens you, then perhaps we shall complete our walk without him."

Jethro nodded. Artruis raised a hand to the Lakkerfel as if to tell it to wait. He continued walking, the Lakkerfel remaining where it sat, eyes still fixated on Artruis. Jethro stood staring at the beast. Its hide looked thick and durable, he wondered what someone – or something – had to do in order for its ear to go missing.

The Lakkerfel suddenly changed its focus onto Jethro, who panicked in turn and caught up with Artruis as if being near him meant that the beast would not attack him. He turned back and saw the Lakkerfel unmoved from its position, eyes still locked onto him.

They finished their walk, and Jethro returned to his solitary confinement, unsuccessful in his attempts to obtain anything that would have helped his solution to save his brother.

If he didn't think of a way to liberate himself from Artruis' possession before the army arrived, then his brother would only be marching towards his inevitable demise.

CHAPTER TWENTY-NINE

"The method of obtaining the Wendigo's power from the current holder is as disturbing as its appearance and mannerisms. The method of obtaining it from its resting place, however, is even more barbaric."

Davun entered his lonely tent that remained untouched at the camp. They had made it back to the campsite undisturbed, sighting a few Ratlings who appeared to uncharacteristically observe them before running away. He had met with Captain Demoria and all of the captains upon returning to the camp where they were all given a detailed report on what had occurred. Arkarn and Thedan retold Garthin Maldimon's words in its entirety, not leaving out even the smallest of parts. The company sat and listened, uncertain of what to do with the information they had been fortunate enough to have obtained. Demoria suggested time for them all to think it over, sending the travellers off to get some well-deserved rest, another meeting planned for the morning.

Davun settled back into his personal tent. It felt empty without his little brother there to fill the other bed. He placed his pack down, not bothering to empty its contents. He sat down on his bed, hoping that the fatigue would arrive to persuade him to sleep and escape his thoughts. He sat, watching the candle he had lit, eyeing a droplet of melted wax as it raced down the side, landing in the catching tray below to merge with the rest of its kind. Time seemed to move slower the closer he thought he was to Jethro. He was losing himself in the thoughts of what his little brother was potentially being put through while being held captive in Artruis' domain. He wasn't sure how long he had been staring at the candle before his awareness found its way out of the labyrinth his thoughts had created, the candle appearing to not have melted at all despite it feeling like it had been hours.

"Are you guys there?" he called out, hoping that his personal guards had once again been posted outside his tent upon his return. Rekura immediately entered the tent with Vincent right behind her. Davun was happy to see them, welcoming any way to distract himself.

"Do you need something, Dav?" Rekura asked softly, sensing the pain in Davun's voice. Davun didn't turn to face them which he knew had been bad manners, but his eyes couldn't find their way off the candle.

"I just...just wanted to talk."

"Oh, well...we can talk. As part of our guard duties, we have to make sure you are kept safe, so I am happy to oblige in this life saving request," Rekura perked up a little, hoping that her cheeriness would spread to Davun. Vincent rolled his eyes, clearly not agreeing that the method would work, but Davun appreciated the attempt enough to smile slightly. Rekura sat on Jethro's bed opposite the candle, while Vincent remained standing in the small amount of light.

"So...enjoy your trip to the city of Vanguinar?" Rekura asked, attempting to strike up a conversation.

"Yeah. It was nice to finally see a city."

"That must have been so exciting! I remember my first trip to the city. Not Vanguinar, but a city in the North. A much better city if you ask me, you Southerners have your layouts all confused I think."

"Perhaps to Northerner's who have no sense of direction," Vincent chimed in, surprising the both of them with his remark. Davun was unsure if Vincent had been serious, having never heard the young man speak like that before. He was relieved when Vincent smiled embarrassedly, though Rekura raised an eyebrow, a sign that she wasn't about to let the comment go uncontended.

"Perhaps it is because Southerner's use their own made up directions instead of following the ones everyone else has chosen to follow," she raised both eyebrows at Vincent, awaiting his response, ready to retort the moment he did. Vincent looked confused momentarily, wondering what Rekura was referring to.

"How in this world do we use a different directional system?"

"Well, judging by the way your cities are laid out, it's obvious you don't follow the same rules that the rest of the world does, so I can only assume that you've made up your own."

"That's Northerner logic for you. Don't understand something, so therefore it must be either magic or completely made up."

"Look, all I'm saying is that cutting the head off a chicken and building around wherever its panicking body wanders is not a suitable method for building a city."

"How do you even come up with these analogies?"

"Us Northerner's have been watching you Southerners in confusion for a long time, we simply describe what we see."

Davun laughed. "Have you guys been spending time with Wayne and Kalavud by any chance?"

Rekura laughed while Vincent inwardly sighed realising the comparison.

"Besides, we all know that Northerner's haven't quite figured out how to figure out things for themselves yet. They need to watch Southerner's so that they can learn."

Rekura opened her mouth in shock, though her smile was obvious. Vincent laughed slightly at the retort, a sound that was pleasant to hear from the usually quite guard. Davun wondered if Vincent was finally beginning to return to the person he was before all of this happened, happy to see his friend was becoming more interactive. They continued to joke and laugh with each other, eventually shifting the conversation to their childhoods. It didn't take Davun long to forget his worries, dissolving himself into the conversation to forget all matters for a moment.

The positive feelings were short-lived by the sound of the horn, blaring over their conversation to warn them of the incoming attack.

The trio grabbed their weapons, Davun thankful that he was allowed to keep a sword and sprang outside of the tent. Soldiers were rushing to the front gates, fumbling with their armour straps as they hurried to meet the oncoming attack. The officers had reacted quickly, organising the soldiers into formations, as a scout was allowed entrance through the front gate, panting heavily with a torch in his hand. He ran to meet with Captain Demoria, Davun following after him to hear the news.

"Captain! A large group of Ratlings are headed to our front! I'd say a little more than what we're used to! But –"

"Barith! To the front gates, shields up! Wayne, follow them and counterattack once their shields are met! Tervu, get the platforms in place!" Demoria shouted her orders, knowing exactly where each of her officers were to shout in their direction.

"Captain!" the messenger yelled to get her attention in desperation, immediately showing signs of regret but not backing down from what he was trying to relay. Demoria turned to him, annoyed to be interrupted.

"They have no weapons, Captain!" the messenger blurted out, concern written all over his face.

"What?!"

"No weapons at all Captain! I didn't see a single one brandishing a bow, nor sword, nor a stick! They've got nothing to attack us with, but they charge us nonetheless!"

"What in the gods names are they doing…" Demoria spoke through seethed teeth, frustration rising as she attempted to see through the enemies plans. Davun didn't say a word, equally confused as to why the enemy would attack them during the night with no weapons. They were up to something, but no one seemed to know what it was.

"Tervu!" Demoria shouted to the Scout Master, who was in the midst of ordering multiple platforms to be placed along the barricade that would allow archers to shoot from behind cover,

"Take over the archers! Kalavud! Take a small unit and watch the sides, send Nim if you see anything!"

"You got it, Captain! Dav, you and your friends with me!" Kalavud called from his side. He turned to see what friends he had been referring to and saw that Rekura and Vincent had followed him when he'd moved closer to hear the scout. He nodded, following Kalavud who was gathering torches along the way. He moved along one side of the barricade before stopping and staring at the wall as if gauging how long it went on for. He then crouched and unsheathed a dagger, stabbing it into the ground and digging a small hole with it. He then planted the torch into the small hole, jamming it in so it couldn't topple over. He then did the same procedure at regular intervals until all sides of the camp were covered. He then made his way over to the safety boxes where those who couldn't fight were still gathering inside and climbed on top of one. He scanned the surrounding wall, trying to focus on what he could see within the light of the torches he had placed around. Davun stood at the ready, searching for any non-fighters who remained outside of the safety boxes. Nim had caught up to them during Kalavud's torch planting after receiving his order from Demoria. They waited, unable to see how the fight at the front gate that was unfolding. The last of the people gathered inside the boxes, including Shayarv who had been instructed to stay out of the fight, and they were shut and locked, the guards remaining in place to protect from any potential threats who made it this far.

As if the locking of the boxes were the signal, Kalavud spotted movement.

"North!" he shouted, firing an arrow from his bow and pinning a Ratling that was scaling over the barricade. More Ratlings were close behind, too many for Kalavud to take down on his own.

"Nim! Go get help! We've got more coming from the East!" Kalavud called out, his hands moving as fast as they could to fire as many arrows as possible. Nim obeyed the order and ran. The young boy was fast, placing his sword back onto his belt so it wouldn't impede his urgent message. The Ratlings appeared to be well prepared this time, as a Ratling leapt from its hiding place behind a tent, tackling Nim to the ground. Davun didn't wait for Kalavud's order to assist Nim, instead charging for the Ratling that had Nim pinned to the ground without a word. He ran as fast as he could, watching Nim struggle as the Ratling scratched at him with its sharp nails. He pushed harder, determined to save the messenger, when from the corner of his eye he spotted movement lurching out of the shadows of another tent. It was too late for him to react as another Ratling lunged at him, knocking him to the ground. Davun kept hold of his sword and shield, but the Ratling had his sword arm pinned to the ground. He had gotten so close to Nim, who continued to try and fend off the Ratling, blood surfacing from the various scratch marks on his face and arms. Davun tried to push his own Ratling off, but his shield arm was also pinned to the ground. With both arms pinned, the Ratling used its feet to scratch at Davun's legs. Its nails on its feet were dulled from the ground over time, so they weren't as effective at tearing through his clothes to get to the skin, but some did manage to find their way as the stinging began collect from his legs.

He quickly checked on Nim who appeared to be faring no better than he, but at least had caught one of his Ratlings' arms to prevent it from scratching him. Davun wriggled and shifted, doing his best to cause the Ratling to lose its footing or grip, trying to create an opportunity for himself to strike his opponent down. He looked over at Nim again, seeing his raised arm bleeding as it struggled to hold the Ratlings' arm. The Ratling on top of Davun dug its nails slightly into his numbed arm, but without feeling he took no notice. Davun tried to plant his feet on the ground to gain some footing to push, but the Ratling forced its own feet down on his legs. Davun then let his legs rest as if giving in to the Ratling. The Ratling saw an opportunity to strike with its feet again, but the moment it shifted its foot to claw at his victim's legs, Davun lifted his leg as hard as he could, causing the Ratling to momentarily lose balance.

"Nim!" Davun shouted. The Ratling still held onto his arm so he couldn't raise it but did have a moment to at least move it along the ground. He flung his numbed arm, hoping that his body would listen and wait until the right moment before flinging his sword towards Nim. It slid across the grass towards the messenger, who let go of the Ratling arm to clutch the swords' grip. The unsuspecting Ratling took the moment his hand was freed to strike down on Nim again, viciously clawing at him to cause as much damage as it could while unarmed.

Nim struck the sword into the Ratlings side, tossing it off of him in anger. He stood, stumbling slightly as his arms nearly buckled from tiring out against the Ratling. He turned to Davun, ready to return the favour.

"Boy! Take my horse!" Arkarn yelled, jumping off his horse right beside Nim, and using the horse's momentum he collided with the Ratling mid-air, sending them both rolling. Arkarn chose not to hold onto the Ratling, instead rolling onto his feet in an expert fashion, drawing his sword and plunging it into the Ratling before it had a chance to stop rolling.

Nim threw the sword back to Davun and clambered onto the horse.

"Thanks," he muttered, before riding off towards Demoria. Davun gave him a nod before turning to thank Arkarn for saving him.

"Save it for later, Davun. We must aid them!" Arkarn shouted, having turned to face the safety boxes where the Ratlings were getting uncomfortably close. They charged towards the fight, more Ratlings swarming over the walls. Vincent and Rekura were fighting as best they could to fend off the Ratlings, their spears creating a perimeter that the Ratlings feared entering. Suddenly, a group of Ratlings swarmed them, too many for them to slay before passing them and heading straight for the safety boxes.

Arkarn was faster, thankfully, as he swiftly cut down the few Ratlings that had made it through.

"Davun, you cover this area. I'll aid the others in covering the other side!" Arkarn called, slaying another Ratling before rounding the box to attack the Ratlings from the East. Rekura and Vincent tried their best to fend off the Ratlings only for more to scale the barricades to join in the fray. Davun ran to fight beside them, doing their best to form a line that the Ratlings could not cross. They swung their weapons to attack any who dared to get close. Some stayed back, wary of being struck down if they attempted an attack, but their numbers slowly grew, as well as their confidence along with it. They began to slowly surround the trio as they continued swinging and thrusting their weapons to any in range. Davun could see that the odds were stacking up against them, some of the Ratlings eyeing the safety boxes as if thinking to make a break for it. He knew they couldn't defend against them if they all charged, their numbers were now simply too many for them to defend against all at once.

Suddenly Davun heard the hooves of horses, galloping across the dirt in determination. He turned to his side to see reinforcements in the forms of cavalry, led by Nim. They split into two groups to aid the guardians of the safety boxes, trampling through lines of Ratlings as they could do little underneath the weight of the horses. The Ratlings tried to leap onto the horse, only to be struck down by its rider. Eventually the Ratlings simply opted to scratch at the horse's legs as it rode by, so the cavalry were forced to change their tactics, skirting the outside to pick off Ratlings and keep them in formation. Davun was thankful for the help, noticing how exhausted Rekura and Vincent were, but they remained in fighting form, willing to put their lives on the line to prevent these Ratlings from advancing.

Suddenly, a small group of the Ratlings to their left screeched in unison. It wasn't loud by any means, the Ratlings didn't seem capable of it, but it was startling. The trio reacted, expecting that group to rush forward, thinking it a war cry.

Vincent was swarmed by a surge of Ratlings from the opposite side. They piled onto him, depriving him of his weapon and quickly tearing at the straps of what little armour he wore. Rekura and Davun reacted, desperately slashing and thrusting to save their friend from the multitude of Ratlings that were clawing him, tearing the flesh wherever possible. As soon as Davun and Rekura turned, however, the screeching Ratlings took the opportunity to advance. The cavalry intervened, trampling the front runners, threatening to run down any more who dared to advance. The group hesitated for only a moment, before running once more.

Davun felt his blood boil as he watched the Ratlings who were tearing into his friend as he struggled on the ground. He struck down another Ratling, only for another to take its place on top of Vincent. They seemed endless, determined to do as much damage as they could to the one soldier they managed to pin down. They ignored Rekura and Davun entirely, allowing themselves to be struck down without any attempt at defence.

Davun yelled, using all of his force to shove as many Ratlings as he could off of Vincent. He pushed the majority over as the first lost its footing, causing it to fall into the ones behind it and knocking them over with it. Davun and Rekura struck down the remaining couple, as the toppled Ratlings found their footing, readying themselves to rush forward. Davun stood over Vincent, shield raised, intent on letting no more Ratlings reach the wounded soldier. He dared not to look down to see what condition Vincent was left in, not allowing the Ratlings another chance to catch him by surprise. He had completely forgotten about the Ratlings that had charged from behind, turning to see the cavalry dismounted and fighting alongside Rekura to keep their attackers at bay.

The Ratling nearest Davun charged, keeping low as if to grab Vincent by his foot, only to be cut down by Davun's sword as he cut the creatures outstretched hand off, following it by a fatal blow to the chest. He raised his sword to the Ratlings, threatening them to the same fate if they provoked him again. The Ratlings kept their distance, slowly spreading themselves out to surround him once more. Davun knew he would have trouble defending against off all of them, but that didn't mean he would back down. He prepared himself for any sudden lunges, knowing that the next time one rushed forward, they all would follow.

Then the Ratlings did something that no one had anticipated.

They retreated.

Simultaneously, without words or any sound of a signal, the Ratlings retreated in unison. They turned, scaling the wall once more to disappear into the darkness of the night forest. From Davun's perspective, they had the upper hand, he had no idea why they would have retreated instead of taking the opportunity. Perhaps the fight at the front gate had ended in their favour, and so the Ratlings retreated before the rest of the army arrived.

A Ratling rushed past Davun, keeping itself low from any attacks. It had come from where the safety boxes were.

Davun turned to the safety boxes, fearing that something had happened to the people inside.

Instead, he saw an 'X' scratched into the side of the box.

***

"It is a message," Arkarn answered. Captain Demoria held a meeting with the officers after recouping from the battle. The last of the Ratlings had fled, and once determined that it was safe, they rounded up the wounded for treatment. No lives were lost, but many had been scratched by the Ratling claws. Vincent had been the worse, suffering wounds all over his body. The sheer amount of scratches tallied up to put him in a serios condition. He had been bleeding from nearly everywhere on his body, the Ratlings were vicious in their focused assault.

"But what is the message? That we can't keep our own people safe? Why send his minions without any weapons?!" Demoria was furious, confused over the Ratlings tactics but mostly upset that their safety boxes had been reached. It struck a blow to them, though no one inside had been harmed. A Ratling had snuck through the chaos and managed to engrave its message.

"I think it means that it is finally time. He wants this fight to come to its end, but he wants us to go to him."

"So, he can have the upper hand? I don't think so!" Demoria slammed the table.

"He has one of ours that he wishes to bargain with" Arkarn responded softly.

"I know. I know," Demoria admitted. "I just hoped that we wouldn't be playing into his hands but that seems like it's inescapable now."

"He's been toying with us from the start. We've been playing in his hands the entire time, but that does not mean it will end in his favour."

"Bastard!" Barith blurted out. The usually quiet and formal man was unable to control himself, the revelation of the situation striking a nerve.

"I agree that this must end! I am sick of being treated like this is a game! We must gather what forces we have and kill that man! Without him, the Ratlings would be lost!" Tervu added on. Tensions were rising inside the tent, everyone flustered from the adrenaline of battle, mixed with the guilt of failure for having their safety boxes reached.

"Our soldiers are not yet ready for a large-scale battle! We couldn't even stop them all when they had no weapons, and now we have to march our people into the enemy's territory because he asked us to? We cannot!" Barith retorted, unable to lower his voice.

"Please, we must remain calm. We cannot make rational decisions if we are being controlled by the anger and hurt that Artruis has brought onto us," Thedan spoke in his calming tone, attempting to calm the situation. Davun was thankful to have the man here, as well as Serena's presence. Their presence brought an aura that made it easier to cool down from heated emotions. Thedan instructed everyone to take a moment to simply breathe to alleviate everyone's built up tensions as best he could.

"We must go to him, Demoria," Arkarn spoke after Thedan's instructions for silence had ended.

"I know. I hate it, but I know. He has someone we want back, and he will want to trade Davun for him. We will play right into his hands, but we will have to make that his downfall. He expects ordinary citizens with little knowledge on how to fight and standard tactics. We will have to show him that the pain he brought onto us will be his defeat instead," Demoria was feeling the energy kick back in, this time in the form of resolution. The march towards Artruis' domain was inevitable now that he had invited them.

It was time to finally end this and rescue Jethro.

Davun was eager to get his brother back to safety, but his nerves were slowly building as the thoughts of having to face Artruis came into realisation. He knew that facing a man who had the powers of a Basilisk would be dangerous no matter the situation, but he would have to be extra careful with the man who held his brother as well. He recalled the conversation he had with Arkarn about agreeing to trading places with Jethro, which he will gladly do if it meant having Jethro safe. Once he was traded over, he would survive as long as he had to until either Arkarn was killed, or he was rescued in turn.

"It would be best if we all got some rest now. Tomorrow, we'll begin preparations for kicking down Artruis' door," Demoria ordered, dismissing everyone from the tent.

They began to leave the tent in silence, the pressure of the situation on everyone's mind, when Arkarn placed a hand on Davun's shoulder.

"Please remain behind, Davun. There is something we must speak about."

Davun sat back down and waited for the tent to empty. To his surprise, Demoria remained behind, apparently also a part of this conversation. Once the last of the officers had left, Arkarn seated himself across from Davun, with Demoria also taking a seat where she usually stood.

"Davun...this will not be easy to confess, nor will it be easy to hear..." Arkarn began, clearly hesitant in choosing each of his words. His eyes found trouble focusing on Davun, fearing the reaction he might have. Demoria lowered her gaze, awaiting the confession.

"Davun..." Arkarn took a deep breath as if preparing himself, his eyes finally landing on Davun, locking onto them.

"You are not the next Balkyeros."

CHAPTER THIRTY

"Locked in with no escape, the Wendigo traps people within its home. They stay there, stuck, draining their hope of being rescued.
Forced to eat their rations to completion.
Forced to eat whatever crawls their way.

Eventually, it forces them to eat each other."

Jethro stared out through his window. It did not face the majority of the camp, but if he leant out far enough, he could see most of it. The Ratlings had finished setting up their wooden log barricade, leaving only a gap at the front without a gate, as if inviting invaders to enter through there.

He stared out of the hole in the front barricade, leaning out as far as he could without fearing of falling out. He was wondering if the large portion of Ratlings Artruis had sent would return. He had not spoken to Artruis since, their daily walk was completed in silence. Jethro feared asking about the Ratlings because he was frightened that his suspicions would be correct.

Their walks no longer provided the proper opportunities it once had for him to obtain any kind of weapon. They skirted around the outside of the barricade, still keeping to their path of circling near the trees. Artruis attempted no prompts at conversation, either not interested in talking or allowing Jethro to initiate when he was ready. Jethro no longer wished to speak with the man, instead focusing on ways that he could save Davun.

Escaping was still not an option. The utter amount of Ratlings would leave no place for him to hide, and even if Artruis weren't faster than he, he could easily send his beast of a pet to chase him down. It was either wait around to be rescued and allow Davun to trade himself over or find another way out.

The door to his room slid open, Artruis stood in the doorway. Jethro glanced to see who it was, and then returned to staring out the window.

"I have matters to attend to. You know the Ratlings will provide food at request," he spoke in his monotoned voice, closing the door and exiting the building. Jethro watched from his window as he wove through the camp with his pet in tow and exiting out of the gap at the front. Jethro did find himself hungry and had already decided to no longer starve himself. He slid the door of his room open to request food.

There was no Ratling station inside.

He had never requested food or attempted to even open his door. He had always thought that a Ratling was placed just outside to keep an eye on him or hear his requests. He glanced into the short hallway that led to the other rooms of the small building. Both were closed with the same makeshift door as his was.

But there were no Ratlings to guard them.

He stood for a moment, debating on taking the opportunity to snoop around. If he were caught, Artruis would be told and there might be dire consequences. If he wasn't found, however, he might be able to find something that could help him.

He crept forward, hoping that the floorboards would not creak under his weight, and made his way to the room opposite his, knowing that it led to the room Artruis slept in. He slowly slid the door open, attempting to muffle any sounds that it might cause.

He crept into the room and slid the door closed. The window had been left open to allow him to see into the well-lit room. It had the basic bed and drawer that contained his clothes, but nothing else appeared to be in the room. He searched under the bed to discover it void of anything, then decided to carefully search through the drawers, attempting to not disturb the clothes in a manner that made it obvious someone had rifled through them.

As he dug through the few clothes that Artruis kept, he opened one of the drawers to discover a pile of letters in place of clothing. Flicking through them, it seemed to be the same letter repeated again and again.

I will save you.
I love you.
Your beloved,
A.V.

The letters were not addressed to anyone, and no single piece of paper appeared any different from the others. All were handwritten by the same hand, that much was obvious. It served no immediate purpose to Jethro, however curious as it may be, so he returned them to their place and left the room with nothing else of interest to look at.

He quietly crept out of the room after peering into the hallway to see if a Ratling had entered. He slowly made his way to the middle door, sliding it open. The room's windows were shut, not allowing light to enter naturally. The table immediately to his left conveniently held various candles and a pinchlighter device, so he lit a single candle to shed what light he could into the room. He saw that the windows had been barricaded, no intention of ever opening them, but lamps hung around the room to provide more light. He opted to not light them, fearing it would result in being caught looking around.

The room had two chairs sitting opposite sides of a low table. The table displayed a map with various wooden figures placed about. Upon inspecting closer, Jethro determined that the map was a layout of the survivor's camp, right down to where each tent was located. Beneath that was a map of a forest, which he could only guess was the forest they resided in.

That was all this barren room had, however. He had no idea why Artruis would have barricaded the windows to protect a couple of maps and wooden figurines, so he thought there should be more to the room than he could see. He observed the room once more, finding nothing of interest. He feared being caught, so he left the room, convincing himself another opportunity would arise to look again.

He snuffed the candle, placing it back where he had found it, and closed the door to the room. He then decided it would be best to loudly open his own door and stomp his feet, should anyone be right outside to hear him.

He opened the door to the campgrounds, seeing no Ratlings stationed outside either. He stood in the doorway looking out into the camp, when a Ratling noticed him and cautiously approached, stopping before it got too close.

"I would like food," Jethro called out to it. It nodded, returning back to what it had been doing. Jethro figured that another Ratling received the message, so he awaited the food in his room.

It didn't take long for it to appear, a Ratling scurrying in and placing the usual food on the table before disappearing as fast as it had arrived. Jethro ate his food, wondering where he should look the next time, he found the opportunity to investigate the room.

It was a few hours before Artruis returned, but Jethro had decided not to risk inspecting the room again. With little else to do, he instead chose to peer out the window again just to watch the Ratlings move about. It had quickly become tiresome, but there was naught else to do for the young boy to entertain himself. He watched Artruis enter through the opening of the barrier, weaving his way through the camp as if there had been a set path. His pet walked off on its own to rest in the sun, away from the Ratlings. Artruis did not come to speak with Jethro, instead retreating to his own room. Jethro wondered what he spent his time doing in there, knowing now how desolate the room was.

He spent the remainder of the day fighting his boredom by moving between leaning out the window and laying in his bed. Jethro felt helpless waiting there until either Artruis would take him to be traded, or his brother would arrive to save him. He knew that his brother Davun wouldn't hesitate in trading his own life to save him. He was beginning to feel wracked with guilt again, the past week had taught him nothing other than he was a gullible fool and had only been trouble for Davun his entire life. He tossed and turned in his bed, not tired enough to sleep, but hoping it would come to ease his pain and boredom. Sleep was the only thing he had to do in his isolation. He dared not attempting to contact Artruis, and the Ratlings either would not hold conversation or simply wouldn't speak to him. He knew being a prisoner meant these kinds of restrictions, but that didn't make the days go by any quicker.

The next couple of days were the slowest it had been for Jethro. He wasn't aware how much the walks had helped him until he stopped taking them. Artruis did not contact him, nor did it appear he left the building at all, leaving no time for Jethro to leave his room once more. He wondered if he had insulted his captor somehow, it was unlike Artruis to not take his walks. Jethro assumed it was something the man had done daily, and he was just there to tag along with him. The Ratlings continued to be of no help, their shift in behaviour proved to be just as boring, but it at least indicated that something had happened. Jethro began feeling uneasy about the situation, wondering why everyone – or everything – at the camp had suddenly changed. He felt that something was coming, and he began to dread at what it might be. It appeared the Ratlings were preparing for something, but Jethro couldn't quite tell if it was to attack the survivors, or to defend against an invasion. With Artruis' sudden self-isolation, there was no one to ask what was happening. All he could do was sit and observe while situations arose around him until it decided to include him.

The group of Ratlings Artruis had sent out returned a day later, noticeably smaller in number. They merged back into the camp, heading directly for the food that the Ratlings appeared to keep underground. Artruis must have already known the result of their mission as he did not come out to speak with any, nor did they attempt to contact him. Jethro noticed that none of the Ratlings had weapons on them, confusing him further as to where they had gone and why they had returned with less. He knew Artruis would not come to offer his daily walk, but that did not stop him from hoping he was wrong. It had been days without talking to anyone, which only made him miss his brother who was always by his side even further. He longed to see him once more. Just to apologise for the difficulties that he had caused from his capture. He wanted to speak to his brother at least one more time.

One more time before it was too late.

Jethro had given up on his personal missions to acquire a weapon or to investigate the building, all opportunities and hopes dying when Artruis had decided to no longer leave the building. All he wanted now was to see his brother. To feel his loving embrace. It suddenly dawned on Jethro that he would be alone once his brother traded himself over. Even if Jethro were to survive through this war between Artruis and the survivors, there was a very real possibility that Davun would not and leave Jethro alone in life. He knew that he had Averly, and even now the friends he made at camp might stick around with him, but Davun was the last family he had left. Without Davun, Jethro would truly feel alone, even more so than he did being isolated within the enemy's camp.

Two more days went by, each slower than the last. Jethro began to feel numb, void of any situational awareness and simply trying to exist while he waited. Eating had become an effort once more, but he tried to welcome the mundane activity as it had become his only reason to move. He would eat, taking his time in doing so, and return to simply waiting. Motivation for anything had drained itself from his mind and body days ago. He accepted that he was a tool waiting to be used when needed, remaining undisturbed for days at a time. He slunk further into his blankets, covering his head to hide himself from the world.

Then the door to his room slid open.

His first instinct was that the Ratlings had brought more food, losing track of time once again and not feeling hungry enough to eat. The footsteps that followed indicated that it was most certainly not a Ratling.

"Let us take a walk," Artruis spoke to the child covered in blankets. Jethro had no willpower to feel the need to walk, but something about Artruis' tone indicated that today there would be no choice. It sounded more like a command than an offer as the other days had been, so Jethro slowly rose from his bed, his muscles weakened from scarcely moving, and followed the man outside.

Artruis was much more talkative than usual today. He seemed excited, but still managed to contain himself with the way he spoke and acted. He talked freely, not caring if Jethro would respond or not.

"This battle between myself and the survivors has gone on for some time now. Dancing with one another as a fisherman would his catch. My years of hard work is close to its end," Artruis sounded relieved. Jethro felt his nerves beginning to stir, wondering what was happening – or had happened – for Artruis to speak like this. It was clear that he planned to achieve his still mysterious goal and obtain the powers of the Phoenix.

Which could mean only one thing.

"I do apologise for needing to use you as a bargaining device, but I assure you that if there were an easier way, I would take it. My Ratlings have a very high chance of success in defeating the survivors, but it is not the guarantee that I needed. You, however, will be my guarantee. You are the symbol to the end of my long journey to reunite me with my loved one. I thank you, though I know most of what I speak is meaningless to you."

Jethro felt sick. Artruis stopped when they rounded to the opening of the barrier, facing into the forest as if they had finished their walk. Jethro peered into the forest, wondering what the man stared at beneath his cloth. Jethro immediately saw the reasoning as it approached the camp.

The survivor army had arrived.

CHAPTER THIRTY-ONE

"Though that terrible fate did not befall any of us, we did find ourselves in a position that resulted being face-to-face with the Wendigo.
What followed was both the most terrifying fight of my life, and one of the hardest things I have ever had to endure."

"**W**hat…what are you saying?" Davun felt the panic slowly seep in after Arkarn's confession. The entire time he had known the man, he had been told that he was the heir to the Balkyeros, the key that unlocked the power that remained in the orb.

But now he was being told it was all a lie.

"I…I am sorry. It was something I thought was necessary. I know that you will feel anger and hatred towards me, and that is fine. I will suffer from all that I have done when this is over. But it is important that you know this before we march on Artruis' doorstep," Arkarn spoke quietly, holding back the pain of his guilt as best he could. Davun couldn't believe what he was hearing, but Demoria's sad expression as she stared into the table confirmed what Arkarn was saying.

"What…what? Why? Why would you lie to me like this? Because of you, my little brother is being held hostage so that Artruis can get to me! What happens when he finds out I'm not who he thinks I am?!" the frustration and hurt expressing itself through the volume and coarseness of his voice as he shouted. He couldn't believe he had been deceived all along.

Just another piece in Arkarn's game.

"I know your brother has been captured, but there is a reason I have lied to you. I know it is going to be a lot to ask of you that I do not deserve, but I must ask that you hear my reasoning and do what you will with me once this is over," Arkarn continued to speak in his soft tone, as if begging. Davun didn't want to hear the man anymore, anything that came from his mouth could simply be more lies. There was no way for him to tell anymore. He finally came around to trust the man, and now he is being told his entire reasoning and role in the camp was a lie.

Demoria placed her hand on Davun's clenched fist. Davun wanted to yell, scream until his throat was sore and bleeding, but he knew Demoria was trying to plead with him to listen. He waited, internally suffocating his anger as long as he could to allow Arkarn to speak.

"Davun. Your little brother is the true heir to the Balkyeros," Arkarn spoke, locking onto Davun's eyes to convey his sincerity.

Davun felt his body stop for a moment, unable to process anything.

"I know what I have done. But please know that it was all to protect Jethro. I had to deceive my own friends, the people who trust me and all who I care deeply about. I chose to deceive them, so that I could deceive Artruis. Artruis believes in his entirety that you are the next Balkyeros, which means that your little brother will be safe as long as we are willing to listen to Artruis. I am sorry that I had to do this. I have had to lie to nearly everyone in my life, but it was all to stop Artruis. I still do not know what he wants, but I fear that he has learned the secret to the orb."

More untold truths behind the lies. Of course there was more to the orb that Davun had not been told, but why would he if he were not the true heir to the Balkyeros? Demoria squeezed Davun's hand, non-verbally trying to connect with Davun to help him through this difficult situation.

"Tell me the secret," Davun demanded through seethed teeth, his eyes screaming what he could not.

"Of course. Your little brother will learn it himself once he places his hand on the orb. There are many people who have studied the power of the Phoenix before, and some have gotten close to the truth. The books they wrote were destroyed or hidden from the commonfolk to hide the most powerful thing that the orb can provide. Many people believe that the Phoenix is a symbol for rebirth. They believe that the Phoenix is reborn when it dies. In a way, it is truth because the powers will transfer to another, but it goes deeper than that."

Arkarn shifted in his chair, leaning forward a little as if to let Davun know how serious it was that no one else should hear what he said.

"When the rightful hand is placed upon the orb, the heir is given a decision. They are offered the chance to fix something that has gone drastically wrong in their life. They are given the offer to be sent backwards in time to right a wrong. They are sent as they are, with all the knowledge they have obtained, to a place and location in time that will set them on their path to change the course of the future that was once their present. If the heir accepts this offer, however, they will be stripped of their Phoenix powers once their mission is fulfilled."

Davun stared at the man in disbelief. Such an unrealistic claim from a man who spouted only lies could not possibly be the truth. Demoria did not raise her head or acknowledge Arkarn's words in any way, but her silence was enough to tell Davun that she believed in it. It didn't seem possible that such a power existed.

But neither did any of these powers until Davun heard about them.

He was conflicted with wanting to believe Arkarn, but his mind was doing its best to convince him that his instincts were wrong, that the man could no longer be trusted. Davun took a deep breath.

And then another.

And another.

"Arkarnryus. I will accept to deal with all of this once our fight with Artruis is over, on one condition."

"Anything."

"Are you truly going to rescue my brother?"

"Even if it kills me, I will return him to safety."

"We all will," Demoria added, her words meaning more than Arkarn's to Davun. He still couldn't properly process all the information, but he knew that his brother needed to be rescued no matter the situation.

"Fine. You and I will speak once this fight is over, Arkarn. If my brother is harmed because of you, then I will see to it that you suffer the same fate."

"I vow in names of the lost gods to place myself at your mercy when the ordeal has come to its completion."

Davun stared at the man, who stared back at him. Arkarn seemed sincere, his eyes begging to be believed, but Davun could no longer put his trust completely in the man.

"Jethro will be easy to return. I will trade my life willingly to Artruis, and once Jethro is in the safety of our people, we will fight Artruis and recover the orb. I don't care what happens to me, just keep Jethro safe."

"He will be my top priority," Arkarn promised.

"Then the matter is settled. I don't want to speak with you until it is over."

Arkarn nodded, not willing to debate with the boy he had hurt so much. Demoria looked towards Davun, silently pleading to calm down and to talk things out. Davun had no intent on speaking with Arkarn further, his head felt like it was boiling with rage, causing his mind to be addled. He couldn't collect his thoughts, anger now in control, muffling any sense of understanding.

No longer wanting to stay in the presence of Arkarn, Davun stood and stormed out of the tent, not looking back.

He marched towards his tent, the few who were awake to watch the camp at night keeping out of his way. He entered his tent with the urge to break something to vent some built up tension but grew annoyed when the only thing in his tent was the single small table that held the candles. He fought himself against breaking it, convincing himself it was not worth the damage, and paced angrily in the darkness.

He had no idea how to deal with this sense of betrayal. It felt like Jethro himself had just cut into him with a monumental lie that he had been hiding his entire life.

He thought he wouldn't feel this kind of pain again when he had finally accepted that his parents would never be coming back for him. He had long ago accepted that he was alone with Jethro and didn't need anyone else.

Finally allowing himself to connect to someone else only ended up hurting him all the same.

***

The camp was busy with planning their attack on Artruis' camp. Demoria had kept calling meetings throughout the day to plan their attack strategies and evacuation plans. When not in those meetings, the officers were set about ordering the soldiers to prepare. They announced their plans to attack Artruis, sending out an energy into the camp that boosted moral and kept them all driven towards a goal as they ran through preparations.

Thedan and Serena were in put in charge of arranging an escort party to guide those who weren't joining the fight to safety, finding a nearby village or town to reside in. Arkarn stated that they were most likely safe to travel through the forest, Artruis' would have no intentions of stopping them now that he had invited them to his camp.

Davun remained silent as he sat through the meetings. Somehow pushing through his poor night's rest, he managed to pay enough attention to listen to the plans being made. Arkarn spoke only when necessary, seemingly still wracked with guilt after the previous nights' confession. It was obvious that Davun and Arkarn had something troubling them, but no officer would point it out during the meetings. Wayne and Kalavud attempted to get Davun involved to distract him from what was disturbing him, but to no avail. As soon as the meetings would end, Davun returned to residing in his tent alone. Davun was having trouble processing his emotions. The anger and betrayal from Arkarn still fresh, combatting with nervousness and eagerness as the time was finally approaching that he would once again see his brother. He could only hope that Artruis would truly trade Jethro for him, and that his brother was unharmed. He no longer cared what might happen to him once the swap was completed, but it seemed it no longer mattered as long as Jethro was returned safely.

As much as he hated Arkarn at that moment, he had to give him credit for convincing Artruis that Jethro was not the heir. In the end, it would be what truly saved his little brother.

The day went by slowly for Davun. He had become too distracted with the revelation that he failed to respond to Rekura when she called out to him. The few people who tried to interact with him quickly learned to leave him alone.

The camp continued to pack supplies, inspect their equipment, and were given speeches about the upcoming battle to both prepare and encourage them. Surprisingly, no one backed down from the battle to seek safety other than those who were already deemed as non-fighters. It seemed as though everyone were still resolved to seek out vengeance against Artruis as the day they had joined. Captain Demoria was too preoccupied with planning to feel proud for the people she would lead into battle. The time to relax and relish in her people's bravery would come after tomorrow's victory.

Night fell quickly for most who spent the day preparing. Thedan and Serena had left in the morning once they had organised where the non-fighters would reside while the fight would take place. They attempted to say their goodbye's to Davun, who had been too distracted to give a proper farewell. He felt regret as soon as he had half-heartedly waved his goodbye, but his childish ways kept him from chasing after them to correct his mistake.

Shayarv gave Davun no chance to avoid her, marching right up to him when she saw his reluctant mood.

"I am to be going, too. My place is not in this fight, and my reason here is done," Shayarv spoke directly to Davun who was trying to avoid eye contact. "You will see him again soon. You must keep your eyes up and allow the Gods to watch over you. Keep smiling, my friend," she placed a hopeful hand on his shoulder, before departing without a word from Davun. He felt guilty for not having responded, but he wasn't sure what he would say if he did.

He wanted to believe her words, but his doubts were not so easily persuaded.

Night came once more, signalling the last night at camp before they set march, Demoria instructing everyone to prepare for an early morning. Davun could not rest once again, the previous nights' lack of sleep doing little to aid him. He decided to take a walk, knowing the camp would be quiet save for those who kept night watch.

He exited his tent, surprised to see Rekura and Vincent were no longer in their watchful position in front of his tent. He admitted to himself that he simply would have ignored them, but still felt disappointed when he did not see them.

He slowly wandered through the camp, few torches placed about to provide dim light. He looked up into the cloudless sky, staring at the stars. He recalled the nights he had seen them during his rests in the forest, but never really gave them much time. He had seen them plenty of times in his hometown, but it somehow felt different tonight.

The sound of metal objects clinking with each other brought his attention to the tent he had been standing next to. It was one of the medical tents, specifically the one he was sent to when Feyra had to take care of him.

A curse followed the sound a moment later. Davun entered the tent to see Feyra standing over odd medical equipment that he didn't recognise. She sighed as she stared at the mess, the empty wooden box by her feet. She kneeled down to begin picking the equipment up and placing it in the box, so Davun knelt beside her to assist.

"I wouldn't have thought that an elderly woman in need would be the cure to your attitude," she spoke quietly, not looking at him as she wiped a piece clean from the dirt.

"You're not that old, Feyra," Davun gave a half-hearted smile.

"You know, I was tempted to send for you so that I could administer a different treatment to cure what ails you."

Davun looked at her, confused and curious. "What would that have been?"

"A good talking to."

Davun felt slightly ashamed as he picked up the last of the equipment and placed it in the box after wiping it down. Feyra placed the box with its lid onto a nearby table that contained similar boxes.

"Word is, you and Arkarn had a bit of an argument."

"And who gave out those words?"

"You know Kalavud. Doesn't know when to keep his mouth shut."

Davun guessed that Kalavud must have been near the tent when he left that night, possibly curious as to what Arkarn had to speak with him about. He had no idea why he would have told Feyra, but at least it seemed like she didn't know any specifics.

"Look, kid, I don't care what you two argued about, but you need to suck it up for tomorrow. You have to do all you can to save your brother, but you can't do that if you're too distracted moping about. Your brother needs you. We all do."

Davun hadn't expected anyone's words to be able to get through to him, but perhaps Feyra knew the right time to be able to scold him.

"I know, Feyra. I'm sorry. I've just been a little distracted with some things."

"Don't apologise to me, kid. You need to just get off your arse and do what needs to be done. You can't have any of those things distracting you tomorrow. And one other thing…" she leaned towards Davun, staring him down, "Why haven't you returned to get your wound checked out?" she lightly slapped him on the side of the head as one would a child. Davun smiled slightly, but it felt more genuine this time. She lifted his shirt to inspect his arrow wound. She prodded the area, but Davun felt very little pain when she did.

"It's healing nicely. Nothing more needs to be added, just don't get hit there again."

"I won't if I can help it," Davun joked with her.

"If you come back to me and you've made that worse, you better hope it kills you."

Davun's smile grew a little bigger, lowering his shirt.

"Thanks, Feyra."

"If you stop sulking that'll be thanks enough."

Davun smiled at her once more before speaking his goodbye. He wandered around a little more, watching the guards move the platforms into place to observe over the barricade, before returning to his tent where sleep had been awaiting him.

***

They stuck to their schedule, the entire camp beginning the march in the early hours of the morning. It was a tense march, nerves beginning to build as they approached ever closer to Artruis and his Ratlings. Even Wayne and Kalavud didn't resume their usual mocking of each other as they marched along, steeling themselves for the anticipated battle. Arkarn kept to his solitude, not speaking to anyone unless spoken to. Davun wondered if his demeanour would affect the moral of the army, so he did his best to not look worried, keeping his head up and eyes focused ahead. He did his best to not let his nerves get the better of him, knowing full well he needed to remain in control if he truly wanted to save Jethro and recover the orb. He noticed Shayarv clumsily riding beside Arkarn. He had thought she would have returned to her refuge in the mountains, but it appeared that she intended on joining in the fight, or at least observing it. The girl didn't appear to have a weapon, and he doubted that her staff that held the orb was designed for fighting.

Davun continued to walk amongst the idle chatter of the people wanting to get their minds off of the dangerous situation ahead. He listened to them retell tales of mythical beasts and debating on if they were real or not. It was an interesting topic to listen to, knowing the truth made them wonder how far the truth spread. It was an exciting prospect to find out, should Davun still feel like it without the powers he had been promised.

The army marched until nightfall, where Demoria had instructed for them to try get a good night's rest before they fell upon Artruis' camp the next day. The suspense did not make it easy for any to sleep. The next battle would be the largest they have faced, and in the enemy's territory. It was clear that the soldiers were becoming nervous, but still none dared to abandon their mutual goal of seeing Artruis' downfall.

The army awoke early, eager to see this fight through. Demoria called for them to continue their march once they had packed their supplies, and so they walked together to face a threat without any assistance.

Despite the surrounding Lords and Kings denial that the threat exists, they march on to save the unknowing innocents from a threat that would likely reveal itself if it accomplished its mission.

They marched, and once the enemy's barricade was in view, the chatter grew. The sight of the enemy's camp dealt a blow to their nerves they had not been expecting. The army grew restless, some fidgeted with their weapons, becoming on edge, while others felt their adrenaline rise as they were eager to avenge their loved ones.

They drew closer to the camp, before Demoria called them to a halt. She ordered them to set up small stations to treat the wounded. Davun stared at the camp, wondering why there was a gap in the middle where a gate should have been.

As he stared, he saw to figures appear in the entryway. It was too far to gather any details, but it was obvious they were human, and there was no mistaking the smaller figure.

Davun felt a whole new force of motivation after finally laying eyes on his little brother.

CHAPTER THIRTY-TWO

"Those who know of the Wendigo's existence believe it has a connection to death. The creature is either fascinated by it or is the embodiment of death itself. It slays any creature that is unfortunate enough to not outrun it, feeding on its flesh. In this particular case, I believe that the powers of the Wendigo overwhelm the mind of the holder, no longer themselves, but more accurate to the creature described in books.

Unless the holder's mind is powerful enough to detain the Wendigo's instincts."

The survivor army cautiously marched closer to the barricade. Inside, the Ratlings could be seen massing around Artruis and Jethro, who stood in the only entryway, waiting. As they neared, they were called to a halt when Ratlings began to line outside of their own defences. A small portion had been sent outside, as if to warn the advancing army that they were prepared.

Artruis stepped forward, Jethro close behind him.

"Let us negotiate a trade, Demoria," he called out, not sounding enticing nor threatening, simply stating the business he wished conducted.

Demoria glanced to Arkarn, who nodded in return.

They dismounted off their horses, gesturing for Davun to approach. Demoria also called Wayne and Kalavud, along with a small group of soldiers as an escort. They turned to face the man they had been fighting against, who showed no emotion.

They walked forward, suppressing their nerves and walking with confidence. They already knew that Artruis would be in control of the trade, but they still put on a show for their people.

"That is far enough," Artruis called out when they were close enough so they wouldn't have to yell to communicate, simply talking loudly would do. They stopped as requested, Demoria giving the signal to be on guard but to not raise weapons. Their uneasiness of being in close proximity to Artruis would have to be contained until the moment came.

"We already know what it is you seek, Artruis. Is the boy unharmed?" Arkarn called out, beginning the negotiations on his own terms.

"He has been untouched and fed during his time here."

Arkarn glanced down at Jethro, inspecting him from where he stood. It was apparent that the boy was happy to see them but fighting the stress of the situation. After being satisfied with the answer, Arkarn nodded.

"Have yours reveal his arm to me," Artruis requested in return. Davun didn't wait for permission, knowing precisely what Artruis was after. He rolled up the sleeve of his numbed arm, revealing the distorted black and green arm that had resulted from the Lakkerfel bite. Artruis did not smile, nor did he acknowledge it in any physical way.

"You know what the trade is. He will approach me, and I will release mine into your custody."

"That's no-" Demoria began to retort but was quickly quelled by Arkarn's raised hand. He gave Davun a nod, his face full of worry.

Davun confidently walked towards Artruis, not caring what happened to him as a result, no step required hesitation or a second thought. Once he was over the halfway point, Artruis allowed Jethro to sprint forward, immediately running into Davun's welcoming arms. Davun held back his tears of joy, knowing that the moment wouldn't last. Jethro had no such self-control, bawling his eyes out into Davun's shoulder. Davun simply embraced his brother while he was attempting to sputter out words between his rapid breaths.

"D..D..Davun…"

"It's okay, Jeth."

"N…No, Davun…H…He's…"

"Jethro. I know it's going to be hard, but I need you to do something."

Jethro looked up at his brother, eyes filled with tears as they streamed down his face, still trying to get words out.

"Jeth, I need you to be brave now. You need to go to Arkarn and stay with him. Listen to everything he says, and you'll be alright."

"But, Davun…He…he's going to kill…"

"Jeth. I know. It's okay," Davun spoke with as much confidence as he could muster to emphasise to his brother that this was no time to worry about him. Davun stood and looked around. He debated making a run for it with his brother in tow, hoping that they could reach their army in time to be protected. The line of Ratlings dissuaded him from attempting, knowing that they would most likely be faster than he, and the rest of them were just on the other side of the barricades. He turned back to Artruis, prepared to accept his fate.

An arrow flew past him, aimed for Artruis' heart. Artruis stepped to the side and the arrow flew into a Ratling behind him. Davun turned, instinctively grabbing Jethro and running. He saw Wayne charging towards them, behind him was Kalavud preparing another arrow. Behind him, the Ratlings had begun their attack, racing towards Davun in an effort to beat Wayne.

Davun didn't notice Arkarn had already reached them. He prepared to hand Jethro over, expecting Arkarn to have grabbed him to protect him.

Instead, Arkarn ran straight past him, sword raised. Davun turned, momentarily shocked that Arkarn had abandoned his plans to protect Jethro.

Arkarn yelled, sprouting wings of fire and taking flight. He hovered not too high above them, flames shooting from his hands to create a line that the Ratlings dared not cross. The reveal stunned everyone. They all paused, staring at Arkarn as his fiery wings flapped to keep him elevated.

Jethro and Davun could not believe what they were seeing.

Wayne shook off the stunning display and grabbed Davun by the shoulder.

"Move!"

Davun took another step before he heard another yell.

"Wayne!" Arkarn screamed in warning from above. Through the flames, the Lakkerfel leapt, unaffected by the blazing heat. He landed on Davun, pinning him to the ground, face first. Davun's shield was still placed on his back, the metal blocking the powerful claws of the beast as it stood on him.

Wayne reacted, grabbing the large beast with both of his hands and swung his body with all his might. He managed to lift the beast, throwing it to the side where it quickly recovered. Davun stood, seeing Jethro had run further, but stopped to see what was happening.

"Run, Jethro!" he screamed, taking his shield off his back and unsheathing his sword.

Demoria wrapped an arm around Jethro, pulling him back. The soldiers had sprung into action already, approaching them rapidly.

Unfortunately, the Ratlings were closer to them than their allies.

Arkarn continued to shoot his flames from the sky, burning many Ratlings as they screamed in pain. There were simply too many for him to take care of, and they began circumventing the flames as others were trying to kick dirt onto the fires in attempt to extinguish them.

Wayne swung his greatsword at the Lakkerfel, keeping it at bay while Davun prepared himself. Kalavud shot an arrow at the distracted creature, unsuccessfully penetrating its hide. Davun could see the Ratlings appear behind the Lakkerfel but were not running towards them. They instead met the army head on, slowing them down enough for the rest of the Ratling army to join.

The beast lunged after dodging a swing from Wayne and tackled him to the ground attempting to bite through his breastplate. Davun heard the metal crinkle within the beasts' jaw and charged to Wayne's aid. He swung his sword onto the beasts back, but it merely bounced off with no effect. He was simply not strong enough to get through the thick mutated hide. He started battering the beast with his shield, distracting it long enough for Wayne to throw it off of him.

"I'll take care of this, help Arkarn retrieve the orb!" Wayne called out, staring the beast down as it growled at him menacingly. Davun knew that Wayne would likely not be able to defeat the beast, but Wayne would have also known that. He looked up to see Arkarn flying towards where Artruis had been, but Davun could barely see through the flickering flames. They had begun to die down through the efforts of the Ratlings, but he was unable to spot Artruis. Davun continued to see the Ratlings swam in great numbers towards the survivors. The colour of the Ratlings quickly drowning out the survivors.

Davun eyed Demoria, fending off Ratlings as they were trying to enclose the gap between the army and her, with Jethro by her side. He wanted to run to their aid, but saw the horsemen charging through the Ratlings to assist them. He decided to trust them, turning to face the flames. He raised his shield and leapt through them. The flames burned for only a second, seemingly doing no real damage to him. He took a quick look around to see the Ratlings still attempting to subdue the flames, pouring out of the barricade, but Artruis was nowhere in sight. He prepared for the Ratlings to notice him, but it seemed they didn't care for his existence. He made eye contact with one, who quickly dismissed him and ran around the flames. He approached them cautiously, but they made no move when he drew close. He decided to try his luck and head through the gap of the barricade where few Ratlings were still running through. He walked between them, undisturbed.

"Well, I guess Artruis still wants me alive then."

Jethro moved out of the way of the outstretched Ratling hands that were desperately trying to reach him, only for Demoria to cut them down. She was quickly tiring having to fend off the surrounding Ratlings, but she would not give in. She continued to swing, hoping to intimidate the Ratlings into backing off.

The Ratlings surged forward at once, the front few being cut down, the ones behind simply climbing over their corpses to reach Demoria and Jethro. They managed to grab hold of her weapon arm, and few grabbed Jethro by the legs. Jethro's feet were pulled from underneath him, landing on his back with a thud. He looked up to see the Ratlings quickly scurrying away as horse hooves replaced where they stood, barring them from Jethro. The rider looked down to inspect him, and then turned his attention back to the rats. More horsemen joined him, slaying the Ratlings that had grabbed hold of Demoria and encircled the two. They made no attempts to push the Ratlings back, only creating a wall that would allow none to pass.

The Ratlings seemed to be waiting for an opportunity to attack, keeping their distance as more continued to appear, adding to their ranks. Jethro knew that it was too many to defend against from reaching him and waited for the moment they would strike. Suddenly, hands gripped his shoulders, startling him. He was pulled to his feet, facing to see a young woman and man. Each held a spear and wore little armour but bore the symbol of the survivor's army.

"You okay, Jethro?" the woman with pink hair spoke. Jethro nodded, as he saw more soldiers had made their way to him.

"Damned vermin! How are we supposed to retrieve the orb now?!" Demoria cursed beside him. Jethro looked towards the barricade, which seemed meaningless as the Ratlings had all rushed outside. He stared at where he knew the building would be, but unable to see much beyond the Ratlings that were surrounding them.

"I think I know where it is!" he called out to Demoria. She looked down at the young boy, as if weighing the truth to his words. She stared into his eyes for a moment.

"Where?"

"I think it's in a room in the building at the other end of their camp."

Demoria looked towards the camp, as if trying to spot what he was looking for.

"Soldiers! Give me a horse and an escort!"

***

Wayne sidestepped the Lakkerfel's lunge, its mouth wide open in an attempt to clamp down on his arm. Wayne was having great difficulty taking down the beast, unable to get an opportunity to swing down on it with all his might. Something was off about the beast, aside from its already obvious forced mutation. Green liquid oozed around its fangs, but the mysterious substance didn't appear to affect the beast. Lakkerfel's were not venomous, but it appeared that somehow Artruis altered that fact. Wayne wasn't sure what the poison would do, only knowing that he had to avoid it at all costs.

The beast lunged again, going for his arm in an attempt to disable it. He quickly sidestepped once more and followed it with a quick slash of his greatsword. It landed against the beast, but scarcely made more than a mark on its durable exterior.

The Ratlings had begun to quell the flames further, near the point of extinguishment. Behind him, Kalavud was fending off as many Ratlings as he could while Wayne attempted to take down the beast.

The problem was he had no plan to take it down. The beast was strong, fast, and resisted most of his attacks. He needed the beast to stand still to allow him a well-placed strike with all of his force. Right now, he was doing little more than simply scratching the Lakkerfel. He at least had it distracted enough not to give chase to Davun, who he assumed was its target.

He swung again at the beast, who backed away from the attack, hunched down and ready to pounce. Wayne had little knowledge on Lakkerfel's, but that didn't stop him from trying to find its weakness.

He feinted with his weapon at the beast. He swung, making it appear is if he would strike, but not throwing all his force behind it so that he could stop his swing short. He did this several times, baiting the beast.

His feints worked as it lunged after Wayne swung again. He quickly crouched to the side, swinging his sword upwards as fast as he could. The weapon impacted against the underbelly of the beast, sending it sprawling towards the little flames that were left.

Wayne suppressed a curse at his plan not working for a new plan to replace it. He had tried to see if the beasts' underbelly was softer, allowing him to slice the beast, but it appeared it was just as durable. His new plan, however, was to see how heat resistant its hide would be.

He charged the beast, not allowing it time to move forward. The beast rose to its feet to meet the oncoming attack. Wayne placed his sword behind him, as if to swing, but instead dropped his sword to grab at the beasts' head.

He placed his large arms around the beasts' mouth, clamping it shut with all the might he could muster. The Lakkerfel struggled to break free, flailing wildly and growling. Wayne pushed against the Lakkerfel, slowly managing to push it towards the flames. The beast tried to resist, its powerful legs pushing back against Wayne.

Wayne gave a yell as he gave one more large push against the Lakkerfel, moving the back half of the beast into the flames. For a moment, the beast seemed unaffected as it continued to wriggle violently, but as the flames danced around it, it began to whine from pain.

Wayne held it for as long as he could, the heat of the flames reaching him, but he would not give in. He let the beast suffer, trying to let the flames do their damage for as long as possible.

The beast broke free from the large man's grip, quickly jumping out of the flames, limping with its hind legs as it whined. Wayne quickly grabbed his weapon, cursing to himself.

All he could do was stall the beast further. He couldn't pierce its hide, nor could he hold the beast long enough for the flames to take care of it. It was obvious that the flames had done something, but the Lakkerfel's hide protected it from most of the damage. Wayne panted, trying to draw in as much breath as he could while the beast, no longer bothered by the heat, snarled and prepared itself to lunge.

Kalavud appeared by Wayne's side, sword drawn and staring down at the beast.

"I thought you were taking care of the Ratlings," Wayne spoke between heavy breaths.

"Yeah, but it seemed like you were having a spot of trouble, so I came up with an idea for you."

"Thanks."

"It's what friends are for, Wayne!"

"What's your plan? Clearly your skinny arms won't get through it if mine can't."

"You think you could open its mouth for me?" Kalavud smiled, patting the belt that held the Daritian darts at his waist.

***

Davun walked through the now empty campsite. Artruis was nowhere in sight, but if he had fled within the barricade, the only place to hide would be the solitary building located at the back. He marched towards it, wary of his surroundings. No Ratling had followed him, but that didn't mean they wouldn't change their minds.

He continued walking straight to the building, little else of any interest. There were a few raggedy tents that had been poorly set up, and not much else.

As he took another step forward, the ground below gave way and he fell. His legs gave way as he landed, falling to his side. He ignored the bruises that were forming and forced himself to his feet.

The light shone through where he had fallen, exposing the dug-out hole he stood in. It appeared to be a small room with only one tunnel where light was also shining in from. He noticed other patches in the dirt ceiling that had been weakened to allow others to fall in should they step there.

When no Ratling came to slay him, he decided to take the tunnel, leading back to the surface. He looked around to see various other holes similar to the one he had climbed out of and came to the conclusion that the camp was riddled with these traps. It would be dangerous for the survivor army to push the enemy back into their own boundaries. The fight could quickly turn should their soldiers continuously fall into the traps.

He looked up at the sky, trying to spot Arkarn. He wanted to send Demoria the message but could not see the man anywhere. He debated returning the way he came, hoping that his temporary immunity to the Ratlings would hold long enough. He decided against it, realising that if the Ratlings had changed their mind, he was now on the opposite side of Demoria and the survivors. He would not be able to reach her alone. He turned towards the building, cautious in his steps as he advanced. He prodded the ground with his sword before each step, collapsing a few holes that would have caught him otherwise.

The house door exploded as flames shot out. It appeared Arkarn had already made his way inside and was dealing with Artruis.

Davun hastened, prodding the ground frantically as he gave himself little time to react should a hole appear. He had to reach the house to recover the orb before the Ratlings were called to Artruis' aid.

***

Jethro clung onto Demoria as they rode around the outside of the barricade. Few others rode alongside them, including the two people that helped him to his feet earlier. A large portion of Ratlings gave chase, but they could not catch them as the horses increased the distance between them.

They skirted a round until they had reached the building, located on the opposite side of the wall.

"Rope!" Demoria yelled, throwing her tied rope around the tip of the spiked logs.

"It looks like the Ratlings don't know how to properly construct their own defence. Pull it down with the horses!"

The other riders followed suit, quickly tying their ropes and looping them around various wooden logs. The Ratlings were closing the distance quickly. Demoria held tightly to her horse, one arm around its neck while the other held tightly to the rope.

"Pull!" she yelled, giving her horse the command to run. The wooden wall was quickly torn out of the ground, having not been planted deep enough to give it proper stability. Demoria dismounted, followed by a few other soldiers. The others remained on horseback, spears at the ready to meet the oncoming wave of Ratlings.

Jethro turned towards the building, staring at the barricaded windows to the room he wanted access to.

"Archers!" Demoria called out, as arrows flew towards them. Jethro turned to see an arrow heading straight towards him. The male who had helped him stand jumped in front of him, the arrow piercing his side.

"Vincent!" the pink haired girl yelled, ducking in an attempt to avoid the arrows. The young soldier stood his ground, not allowing himself to collapse from the wound. He snapped the end of the arrow and threw it to the ground.

"I'm fine! More are coming!" he pointed towards the enemy, as several Ratlings prepared their arrows.

"Defend behind their own barricade! We'll hold them at the hole we made!" Demoria yelled, pulling Jethro with her behind the enemy's wall. The others followed suit, the riders dismounting off their horses and sending them away from the fight.

An arrow found its mark into one man as he failed to reach safety in time. He fell to the ground, lifeless.

"Jethro! Where is it?" Demoria yelled. Jethro was flustered for a moment but pointed to the barricaded room with the windows.

"Curse these damned…Is there another way in?"

Jethro thought for a moment, then went wide eyed with realisation.

"Yeah, we can go thro-" he was cut off at the sound of the Ratlings charging towards them. They defended themselves against the attack, slaying the Ratlings as they came within distance. They fought as hard as they could against the large wave of Ratlings, who were now scaling their own wall in an attempt to get to the other side.

"We're not gonna hold them! Jethro, go! Find it and touch it!" Demoria yelled behind her, keeping her eye on the enemy.

"But-"

"NOW!" she turned towards him, fury and desperation in her eyes. Jethro nodded, and turned to run. Vincent collapsed in front of him, laying on the ground unmoving.

"Go Jethro!" the girl yelled as she replaced where the fallen soldier had been standing, fending off the Ratlings as they desperately tried to reach him. He run, being protected by the soldiers whose names he didn't even know. He corned the building, reaching the window to the room he had been imprisoned in. He climbed through the open window, running towards the doorway to reach the other room.

He stopped as a thick stream of flames burst through the doorway to the room, breaking down the front door.

***

Wayne and Kalavud struggled side by side, failing to stop the beast from attacking. The beast was wary of Wayne's attempts to grapple it again and wouldn't allow itself to be caught. It dodged Wayne's weapon as he swung it, and seemingly ignored Kalavud's attack entirely as his weapon slid across the surface of its skin. It chose not to pounce on either of them, cautious now that there were two of them.

"Damned beast!" Wayne cursed after it dodged his outstretched hand.

"Looks like you scared it, Wayne."

"I did kind of force it into the fire."

"I saw that! Very impressive."

"Now the damned thing won't come near me unless I let it attack me...hmm..."

"Wayne, as your best friend, I must tell you that idea you just got, is probably your stupidest one so far. Classic Southerner logic"

"I wasn't going to do it."

"Sure, laddy."

Kalavud swung, knowing his weapon wouldn't affect the beast at all, but trying to create an opening for Wayne. The beast didn't react as Kalavud's weapon had no effect on it whatsoever. It snapped its powerful teeth towards his arm, but Kalavud was able to react fast enough to draw it back in time.

Wayne swung his sword, landing it onto the beast and pushing it back slightly.

"I think it's dulling my blade."

"Then just bludgeon it to death."

"That would probably be more effective," Wayne bent down, picking up a loose rock and throwing it at the beast. It bounced off, doing little more than annoying the Lakkerfel.

"I just need a bigger rock."

"You Southerner's, I swear..."

"Oh really? Then tell me, oh great and wise Northerner, what is your plan?"

"I already told you," Kalavud threw down his sword and grabbed all three of the darts from his belt, "You grab it, I put it to sleep."

"Kal, no!" Wayne shouted, but his friend did not listen.

Kalavud swung at the beast with his empty hand. The beast saw its moment to attack, and clamped its jaw shut around the man's exposed arm. Kalavud screamed in pain, the green ooze entering his body. Wayne quickly reacted, throwing his weapon down, and running towards the beast. He placed his hands around the beasts' jaw and summoned all the strength left in his body. The beast was attempting to tear Kalavud's arm off, now twisting and flailing harder with Wayne around its head. Kalavud screamed in pain, but continued to try and bear it, waiting for his opportunity.

Wayne yelled, trying to pry the beast off of his friend, his hands turning red as he refused to let go of the beast.

The beasts jaw' began to slowly open. Wayne yelled once more, forcing the beast to widen its mouth further. He pried it open far enough for Kalavud to free his arm.

"Just a second more, Wayne!" Kalavud yelled, ignoring the damage done to his arm, and shakily breaking the darts open, pouring the contents into the beasts open mouth. Kalavud scrambled away, but Wayne held onto the beast. He held on until the toxin began to take its effect, noticeable slowing the Lakkerfel down. Wayne let go of the beast, who clumsily snapped towards him. It became shaky on its feet, unable to properly maintain its own standing.

Wayne grabbed his sword off the ground.

"Let's see how much you dulled my blade, cursed beast," Wayne took a moment to draw his strength back. The Lakkerfel stumbled to the side, fighting the urge to sleep.

Wayne shifted his stance.

Raised his sword above his head.

And swung it down with a mighty yell, cleaving through the beasts' neck.

The head and body toppled to the ground separately. Wayne sat down beside his friend, who was clutching his arm in pain.

"I thought my plan was stupid?"

"Well, it was, wasn't it?"

"Yeah, it was, Kal. But it worked."

"It sure did, Wayne."

They sat side by side, watching the Ratlings form a circle around them.

They began to accept their fates, when arrows rained down onto the Ratlings.

***

Davun sprinted towards the building when he drew close, hoping that no more holes would appear beneath him. He walked through the singed doorway, following the trail left behind by the flames to the open room in front of him.

Arkarn was standing to one side, sword laid down in front of him. Artruis stood opposite him.

Clutched beneath one of his arms was Jethro, sword pointed towards him.

"Finally, the boy arrives," Artruis spoke, barely able to control the anger his tone. "Drop your sword."

Davun tossed his sword down. The fear in his brothers' eyes as the sword was placed against his neck told Davun to not hesitate in doing anything the man asked.

"Good. I have reached the limit of my patience now. I have waited and prepared so long for this, and you had to complicate it by pulling a stunt like that."

"It is not their fault, Artruis," Arkarn spoke, trying to calm the man.

"I wasn't speaking to him, Arkarnryus. You really surprised me with your revelation. I wouldn't have thought another living Balkyeros was still in existence."

Jethro looked towards Arkarn, his eyes filled with hope.

"Arkarn, are you…our father?" he asked, afraid of the sword against his neck, but not wanting to miss out on the answer he needed if anything happened.

Artruis smiled. It was creepy, almost deranged.

"No, he isn't your father, Jethro. I know that for certain," Artruis answered, staring at Arkarn beneath his face cloth. "Your father is most certainly dead, I'm afraid. He and your mother foiled my attempts the first time, and his children will not foil my attempts at the second."

Artruis pulled the cloth off from his face, revealing his eyes. They had been prepared for it, averting their eyes. Artruis bared his teeth, now protruding to long fangs, dripping with a green liquid. Venom.

"Now that is something that is curious to me. I kept my eyes a secret from the world, so how is it that you all knew what was coming?"

"Because you are doing the wrong thing, Artruis. I do not know what has happened to Seraferan, but I know that if you undo what she has sacrificed herself for, then you are sending others into suffering."

"I do not care for their suffering! I care only for Sera's! She regrets her mistake, I know it! She doesn't want to live her life as a monster! She only wants to return to me! We must be reunited once again! Garthin knows nothing of how she feels!"

"Neither do you, Artruis. If she is still around, has she expressed to you her regret?"

"She doesn't have to. I know her better than anyone, she does not have to speak to me for me to know how she feels!"

"Then why hasn't she spoken to you, Artruis? Why is it that she is not here aiding you?"

"Because she cannot control herself anymore! She is no longer the woman I fell in love with, and she longs to return to that person!

"Bu-"

"No more! You, Davun," Artruis yelled, dragging Jethro forward with him towards Davun.

"No!" Arkarn yelled, but Artruis emphasised his threat against Jethro. He momentarily let go of the boy, holding his weapon by his neck, and reached down to his belt. He untied an object wrapped in cloth, holding it by an extended piece of the cloth.

"Davun! Look into my eyes!"

"No, Davun! You mustn't touch it!" Arkarn pleaded, unable to move in fear of Jethro suffering the consequence.

Davun stared at his little brother, watching the tears swell into the young boys' face.

"Look!" Artruis yelled once more.

Davun smiled weakly at his brother.

"I love you, Jeth," he spoke with confidence, not wanting to scare his little brother any further.

Davun looked into Artruis' eyes. In an instant, Davun's surroundings disappeared. The only thing he could see were Artruis' eyes.

He couldn't turn away from them. They were too captivating, like a moth to a flame. He stared, studying all the fine details as the eyes were all he could see.

Words echoed in the darkness.

"You will take the orb."

"Yes."

"You will designate me to be your heir."

"Yes."

Artruis' full form appeared in the darkness. He held the orb aloft, still wrapped in its cloth.

Davun held his hand out.

Artruis tugged at the piece of cloth he held, and the orb slowly unfurled.

It was such a pretty orb. A vibrant sky blue mixed with swirling white and red clouds. The clouds twisted and turned, the red dancing with the white.

"No!" Arkarn screamed in desperation.

The orb landed in Davun's extended hand.

Davun wasn't sure if it was the numbness of his arm, or that he still felt mesmerised by the enthralling eyes he had just seen, but he felt nothing as he watched his arm disintegrate into ash.

"Davun! No!" Jethro called out, choking on his own words as tears filled his eyes. He didn't care as they dripped into his open mouth as he screamed for Davun.

The orb fell through the scattering ash that was Davun's arm and landed on the back of Jethro's outstretched hand as he clawed for his brother.

Then everything that Jethro could see turned white. He closed his eyes to shield against the brightness as it took over his vision.

When he opened his eyes, he was standing on a white floor. Standing across from him was a man with similar resemblance to Arkarn, including the red robe he wore. The man smiled as Jethro saw him.

"Hello, son."

CHAPTER THIRTY-THREE

"The Wendigo slaughters many. It takes lives that should not have ended so early, not caring for age, race, or sex. We were fortunate enough to slay the beast, ending its rampages and killing sprees.
But what would happen to the next unfortunate soul who becomes trapped with the Wendigo's power?
What would happen to the innocent lives of men, women, and children who never deserved the death that the Wendigo seeks as though it itself would die if it does not claim them?
The power needed a strong mind to contain it. And so, she gave it one."

"**S**on…?" Jethro looked at the man, confused. Despite sharing similar features to Arkarn, he had never seen the man before. He had brown hair that was showing signs of age, tied into a neat bun, except for the front part of his sides that dangled down. His brown eyes confirmed that he was a Southerner, his clothes plain aside from his robe.

He looked around his environment, wondering where he was. The floor was a flat sea of white, no other objects could be seen. Then he realised that he could still see Davun and Artruis, except they were gigantic and standing well above where he stood, as if they were the walls and sky itself.

"Am I…"

"In the orb? Yes and no. Your mind is, but you aren't physically within the orb itself. Time will not move until you decide to leave."

Jethro returned his attention to the man who had called him son. The man was still smiling at him, as if he had just seen a loved one that he had been missing for years.

"How do you...You're my...Father?" Jethro was trying to piece it together. His emotions were still blaring within him from seeing his brother's arm disintegrate, and the sudden change of scenery didn't help to calm him.

"Yes. Take a moment, you seem a bit riled up. Just take some breaths, no rush. We have all the time you need," the man didn't move from his spot, keeping his distance from Jethro to allow him to process everything on his own. Jethro tried to take breaths but found it difficult as his mind raced ahead of him.

Jethro was uncertain of how long it had been trying to calm himself down, when the man moved over to place a hand on his head.

"It's alright, take your time. I'm here if you need it."

Despite being a stranger, the gesture helped Jethro a bit. He began to calm a little, his breathing becoming easier.

"Are you really my father?" he looked up at the man, sceptical and hopeful. The man smiled back at him and nodded. Jethro's instincts were to believe him, but he couldn't just accept the man's word.

"Then where have you been?!" Jethro surprised himself in the way he lashed out. He hadn't expected it, but he was having trouble trying to figure out what was happening. The man didn't drop his smile, not caring for Jethro's outburst.

"To be honest, I am dead," the man stated it so casually as if it didn't bother him. Jethro looked at him confused. He could see the man, so how could he be dead?

The man chuckled at Jethro's expression.

"Remember how I said your mind was in the orb? Well, so is mine. As the Balkyeros, your mind is transferred inside of the orb until the time comes that the heir you designated touches it. It is to give them some guidance and advice before they accept the power."

Rightful heir?

Jethro became even more so confused. Nothing so far had been making much sense. He failed to take deep breaths again as he looked up at Davun.

"But I'm not the heir. Davun is."

"Davun?"

Jethro was startled. How could the man know his name, but not his other son?

"My brother, your oldest son. He is the heir to the orb."

The man's smile finally dropped. He looked down at Jethro, eyes filled with sorrow. Jethro knew the expression all too well. Bad news.

"Jethro…You don't have a brother."

Jethro was bewildered. How could the man say such a thing when Davun was literally standing above them as if he were a statue to prove his statement wrong. He couldn't find the right words straight away and ended up pointing towards Davun far above them.

"But he's right there! How could you say that?"

"I see. So that is his name," the man stared up at Davun for a moment, inspecting him, before returning his gaze towards Jethro. "I know it will be difficult to hear, Jethro, but he is not your brother. Not by blood, at least. You are an only child, and I chose you as my heir."

Reality came crashing down around Jethro. The boy who had taken care of him his whole life, his only living relative, was not his real brother. It was a heavy truth to hear, and completely unfeasible. Why would someone not related to him have taken on such a responsibility for his entire life.

Unless he hadn't known himself.

The man sat near Jethro as he let the boy deal with the words in his own manner, seemingly unable to choose between crying and asking questions.

"He is still your brother, Jethro. That hasn't changed. He is simply not your brother by blood. It hasn't changed everything that boy has done for you," the man spoke calmly, trying to convince Jethro to calm down. Eventually, the words helped. They may not share the same parents, but Davun was still his older brother.

"You have a choice to make, son," the man announced when Jethro had settled. He stood to his feet, placing his hands behind his back in a respectful manner. Jethro stared at his father, preparing himself for what was going to be said.

"I assume you haven't been told the truth behind the orb?"

"It gives you the power of fire?"

"Yes, but that is not the truth I am referring to. You have a large decision to make, and it will not be an easy one, so you must not make it hastily. The truth behind the orb is that it allows you the power of rebirth. When you first touch the orb, as you already have, you are given a choice that will never arise for you again. You may either accept the powers, and use them responsibly and without evil intent, free to use them for your life. Or, if there is something in your life you wish would have ended differently, I can send you back to change it. You will have your powers up until that moment is changed."

Jethro looked at him, lost in thought about what he could possibly mean. There was nothing he'd want to change, except one thing.

"Is he going to...be okay?" Jethro asked, afraid of the answer, looking up at his older brother. The man followed his gaze, taking a moment before answering.

"I am sorry, Jethro. I do not know. There was something different about his body when he touched the orb, but that did not exclude him from the punishment. The orb draws energy from my powers so it may rid anyone who dares to touch it. Davun is no exception."

Jethro held back tears, firm in his decision.

"Then I want to go back."

The man stared at him for a moment, contemplating the words.

"Before you commit yourself to the answer, I should tell you something. You already have gone back once," the man's eyes shifted towards Arkarn. Jethro hadn't noticed before, but Arkarn had flames emitting from his hands, shooting towards Artruis. He followed the path until he came across another sight he had missed.

Artruis had his sword thrusting towards Davun.

The image was frozen before Jethro, as if it were a nightmare that would not end.

"I..already went back?"

"Yes…You wished to go back, to change your own outcome. You needed something that you didn't have, and you went to great lengths to ensure it was there when the time came."

Jethro turned towards the man, who had been staring at him.

"What didn't I have the first time?" Jethro asked, curious as to what he had now that he couldn't have possibly had before. His whole life it was just him and his brother, he had no materials or devices that were precious to him, or that could change anything that happened.

"Him," the man pointed towards Davun.

Jethro was stunned. How could he have not had his brother the first time? What had happened to him? He could not imagine a life without Davun, the possibility just wasn't there. He looked up at his brother, watching as if the picture could play at any moment and his brother would be pierced by Artruis.

"What do you mean? He's always been with me."

"Yes, he has always been with you because you already went back to change that fact. You were once sent back to me, before your mother ever gave birth to you. You explained to me everything that had happened, and together we came up with a plan. You needed a protector, and so you chose him."

"So…if I go back…"

"Things may end differently. You might be able to save him, however, you might let Artruis win in doing so. This is why it is a difficult decision. You have already gone back to change the outcome once, and you appeared to have succeeded. You have placed your hand on the orb, and Artruis does not suspect it right now. Once you leave the orb, he will discover the truth, but he will be taken down. Arkarn will see to that. So, accepting your world as it is, Artruis will be defeated, but you will most likely lose your brother. Should you go back to save your brother, well…Artruis may succeed if things end differently."

Jethro stared up at his brother. His brother who had sacrificed everything to save him. His brother who had taken care of him his whole life.

His brother who knew what he was accepting when agreeing to listen to Artruis' demands.

Jethro cried. The pain of losing his brother hurting before it even happened. It was already too late for Davun, he knew that, but he couldn't accept it. He struggled with himself, knowing what the right thing to do was, but finding it hard to take the necessary step.

His father embraced him, knowing how much pain his son was going through. He wished that such a young child would not have to face such decisions, but it was inescapable.

"Jethro, I think it is time for you to decide. You cannot avoid it forever. You must face your fears, no matter how much it may hurt you. I have the utmost respect for Davun. Anyone who has taken care of my son his entire life will also be a son of mine. If Arkarn stuck to the plan, then Davun would have known by now that he was not the real heir. He would have known that you were, and yet he stayed. Do not undermine his decisions."

Jethro took his time in calming himself down and came to a decision. He turned to face his father.

"I…won't go back," the words felt like he had just sentenced his own brother to death.

His father smiled. "You are going to grow into a fine man, Jethro. Your mother and I are very proud of you."

Jethro couldn't find the strength to smile, but the words had reached his aching heart. His father took off his red robe and handed it to Jethro.

"I love you, son."

Jethro put on the robe, and white filled his vision once more.

CHAPTER THIRTY-FOUR

"It is for these reasons I do not know if I shall ever reveal the truth to the world. My greatest accomplishment may never reach the eyes and ears of the people who are hungry for the truth that history hides. Those people must starve for now, until I can decide if I can trust humanity and their behavioural instincts that make them yearn for power.
My friends have already suffered from knowing the truth.
Is it something the world can handle?"
- Garthin Maldimon, Truths And Questions, Unpublished

The orb dropped to the floor, its sky blue now a dull grey, the clouds seemingly vanished. Arkarn's flames stopped streaming from his hands, the power no longer within him. The flames he had already sent found their mark and landed in Artruis' face, causing the man to shout in pain as they scorched his vision. Artruis became temporarily blind, but his sword kept its momentum.

Davun was pierced through the stomach. He stared down as Artruis let go of the sword that was now embedded through him. He showed no reaction, his arm continuing to convert to ashes. As he stared at the sword, he noticed Jethro, wearing a robe he had not noticed before.

"Nice robe, Jeth," Davun muttered. His arm stopped disintegrating at the shoulder, and he fell over backwards, eyes closed.

"Davun!" Jethro cried, racing towards his brother. Artruis cursed once more, but quickly recovered from the scorching of the fire. He turned to see Arkarn racing towards the sword he had given up earlier and panicked as he was unarmed himself. He turned to see Davun lying on the ground, sword protruding from his stomach, and the little boy wearing a red robe.

"What?! How could this be?!" he seethed with anger, darting towards Jethro. Before he could reach the boy, a fist appeared, knocking him down with a single blow. He was dazed from the force behind it, the room span, and his eyes couldn't focus. When he was finally able to recover, he saw Arkarn standing over him, sword pointed, and a large bald man staring angrily at him.

"I...failed..."

"Yes, you did, Artruis."

"It is over then."

"Yes"

Artruis slumped where he lay. Defeat overwhelmed him, sapping the strength and motivation to continue.

"Then send me to my wife, please," the man pleaded.

"What? No!" Wayne yelled, furious that the man was making demands.

"As much as I do not think you deserve it, I think it is best if you confront her," Arkarn spoke, staring into Artruis eyes, who made no attempts to use his powers. Arkarn plunged his sword into Artruis' heart, killing the man in an instant.

Wayne made no comments as he watched the ordeal unfold.

"Wayne, carry the body and show the Ratlings. They will scatter once they see their master is dead," Arkarn requested, and the large man began to lift the body.

"You only need to show one," Jethro called out between his cries. He sat with the unmoving body of his brother, red robe draping across the ground, twice his size.

"What?" Arkarn asked, curious as to what the boy had meant.

"The Ratlings all share one mind. He told me. If you show just one Ratling, then they all know."

"Go, quickly!" Arkarn pleaded to Wayne, who carried the body out of the building.

Arkarn walked over to Jethro, taking a seat beside him.

"Why him?" Jethro cried. Arkarn removed the sword from Davun, blood seeping out of the wound. He applied a bandage around the young boy, knowing it would unlikely change the boy's outcome. He placed the shield on top of Davun and stared at the symbol.

"He saved you in so many ways, Jethro. He saved us both. In my time, I did not have him. I had my parents, and I watched them both die before me. A small band of survivors had formed from Artruis' attempts to lure out my father. Within the band was a young boy, forcing his way through the Ratlings to reach me, and he had no idea who I was. I stared at him as his shield was almost like the sun itself. A beacon of light within the world of darkness. Miraculously, he reached me, but Artruis slew him before me too. The boy spoke little words before the life left his body. He recalled his home and his will to avenge it. That's when I knew that if he had been with me earlier, things would have been different."

Arkarn embraced Jethro as they both shed tears.

***

"The Daritian's actually left their mountain?" Arkarn was surprised to see them as they integrated with the survivor's army. The Ratlings had all indeed scattered once Wayne displayed Artruis' body, running off in all directions to safety.

"We did not have much of a choice. The heir was in trouble, and we as a people must ensure the line of the Balkyeros remains uninterrupted," Shardian responded to him.

"That, and the wretched girl took my stick!" Takas angrily added, gesturing to the staff Shayarv had brought with her.

"I had to convince you somehow. Our people had grown scared of the world we seek to help," Shayarv added, no regret for her actions.

"Regardless of why, I am glad that you came. We needed the assistance" Arkarn smiled, happy to see his Daritian friends.

"On behalf of the army, we thank you for your aid in the fight. We could not have survived without you," Demoria saluted them, covered in bandages from her wounds. Many survivors had fallen in the fight. Vincent did not survive his wounds, and Rekura suffered a terrible wound to the chest, but would recover. Tervu was slain protecting the archers from the Ratlings flanking them, and Barith was severely injured from fighting on the front lines.

"I would like to have a chat with you after I conduct some business, Nyamyt. It appears that I must attend to an ally's wounds before it worsens. Notherner's apparently like to jam their arms down venomous animals for some reason," Arkarn joked, but Shardian only looked confused. Arkarn did not clarify, letting the woman ponder about Northerner's intelligence. He walked off to make a concoction for Kalavud before the poison spreads too far.

"So, shall we escort Jethro back when we travel to our home?" Shardian asked Demoria, spying the boy not far behind her. Demoria shrugged.

"That's up for him to decide. He'll probably want to stay with Davun for a little while. Give him some time to think about everything that's happened and let him clear his mind."

Shardian nodded in understanding. She noticed Davun lying beside Jethro, arm missing.

"Arkarn had only recently told me about the boy. It is not something I would agree to do, which is probably why he kept it a secret."

Demoria felt the guilt build up inside her. She had been told about it too but had chosen to go along with the ruse. In the end, it had succeeded, but Davun had paid the price.

"He's a good kid. Jethro is lucky to have him."

Shardian nodded again, staring at the boy who had protected the Balkyeros to the very end.

A crowd began to gather near the medical stations. Curious as to what was happening, Demoria headed over. People allowed her passage as she reached the front, hearing Wayne's voice before she saw him. He was standing near Kalavud who was patiently waiting for Arkarn to create his concoction. Wayne laughed as he slapped his friend on the shoulder.

"You guys want to hear about how Kalavud shoved his arm down a Lakkerfel's throat because he thought the beast had eaten his ring?"

***

Jethro followed the Daritian's back to the mountain he had met them. They had stayed at camp celebrating their victory before accepting to travel alongside the Daritian's to their home. He was to be guided by them, learning how he should use his powers responsibly, and how to control them. The Daritian's were experts in the powers of the Phoenix and had been so for nearly as long as the powers had been known. He was reluctant to be taken away for a long period of time, but knew it was a necessity.

Arkarn did not travel with them, having a personal matter to attend to. He promised to visit should he find himself free of a crime he had committed. Jethro took it as a metaphor, Arkarn had a knack for dancing around the truth, so he assumed that Arkarn had lied to someone else and went to apologise.

Kalavud and Wayne travelled with them, deciding to spend some time with the Daritian's before deciding where to go from there.

He felt the sun warming his back, finally feeling happy for the first time in a while. The stress and nerves of having to learn about his powers and responsibility were still there, piling with each step he took that drew him closer to the mountain.

He looked up at Davun who walked beside him, missing arm a symbol of all that has happened and still remaining by his side, knowing that none of it mattered while he was with him.

EPILOGUE

The forest proved quiet now that the ordeal was over. It's calming nature returning to what it had been before it was disturbed by the secret war. The animals would slowly return to their nesting grounds and homes, with the freedom to explore the forest, fearing only the hunters that would soon come in search for dinner.

Arkarn stared up at the rustling leaves, basking in the sound as they danced. He let the pressure he had carried for so long continue to melt away.

Though, an obligation still remained.

He took a deep breath, filling his nostrils with the sweet smell of not fearing an ambush, and continued on his journey alone. He had stayed for most of the celebration before the guilt had crept its way to the front of his mind.

He embarked on his own path, promising to meet with the Daritians should he ever be released from his shame. It was difficult to say goodbye to those who he fought alongside with, building an army and saving lives. The tension in the relationships he had made died along with Artruis. He felt better now that all the secrets he had kept were out in the open, no longer having to try outwit Artruis or deceive his friends. Thankfully, he managed to slip away without any questions about his former abilities. It seemed that anyone close to him understood the situation, or simply waited for Arkarn to explain. He did decide to hide from the rest of the army, knowing they would likely not hold back.

Demoria had been the most difficult to say goodbye to. She was one of the first who listened to him and believed in his plans to form an army. She had been the driving force he needed to bring people together. She was a natural leader, taking on all the burdens to ease the situation for others. Arkarn knew she would have been a great mother and hoped that she was able to continue living her life. She deserved to be happy once more.

Arkarn's trek was now his alone to take. A burden he carried prior to the formation of the army, prior to having even met any of his companions that fought alongside him, had to be faced. Arkarn had made many necessary decisions that resulted in his allies feeling betrayed, and in some cases, resulted in deaths. He carried the guilt of having to make those decisions but knew that they were necessary in order to stop Artruis from succeeding.

However, there was one decision he could never forgive himself for, no matter how essential it had been.

The path that he took scared him, deeper than Artruis ever could have. Each step required a mental push to force himself to finally face the consequences he deserved. His stomach began to toil a little, fearing what was awaiting him at his destination.

He left the edge of the forest, feeling no attachment or obligations to return. The feeling of freedom was suppressed by his commitment to a new location. As much as leaving the forest provided relief, he knew that he was not yet allowed to be his own person. He was still chained down by his actions, the key to the lock that held it in place held only by the people he sought.

He walked North, stopping by villages to resupply. The folk were mostly friendly, happy to see a traveller visit their town. The sword he carried at his belt resulted in many suspicious looks, but he made certain to never give them reason to believe he would place his hand on it. He could not summon the courage to separate from his weapon. He had carried the sword for nearly as long as he had been working towards preventing Artruis from stealing the Balkyeros title. It was sentimental to him, being handed down to him by his father before his untimely death. The sword was well made, the metal of the blade still standing after prolonged use. He had made sure to take care of it, but he was no expert in smithing, and could not precisely tell its condition. He had already decided to have the sword inspected by a professional if he was ever released by his past.

Days went by, but he finally laid eyes on the village he sought. The moment it came into view, he froze, the realisation of the situation settling in. He took a deep breath, urging himself to continue. There was no other choice.

He felt as if he was dragging his feet, his body reluctant to face what was coming. His mind began racing, attempting to piece together the words that he would have to say. His robe began to feel heavy, his body giving him all the signs to turn around and leave.

But he knew that it was time to confront something he long feared.

He reached the village, the smiling Northerners greeting him as they saw him. He could not force himself to smile back, only absent-mindedly nodding in their direction.

He began to sweat. He knew the people he sought were in this village, but he was not entirely certain where. His eyes darted around, his brain panicking at each person, knowing that whoever his eyes landed on could be them. He searched around the village, looking like a scared and lost child.

His body stiffened as his eyes landed on a loving couple. They were about his age, the wife's blond hair flowing down past her shoulders, neatly woven into a common Northern hairstyle, while the husband's darker brown hair was kept at medium length and messy.

Arkarn's forced his numb body to edge closer. The sweat continuing to drip from his forehead, his mind racing. His mouth felt thick and pasty as he tried to summon the words to call out to them, his tongue feeling like it had swollen to fill the entirety of his mouth. He drew close enough to grab their attention, their bright green eyes piercing through him like daggers.

The husband took a step forward, sensing that Arkarn was a little off.

"Hello there, laddy. Not common seeing a Southerner come to visit our little town. Can I help you with anything?" the man's words struck Arkarn deep inside, the guilt rising in an uproar of emotions and heat, as he felt the blood rush inside him. He stuttered, unable to take his eyes away from the man's as if pleading to be punished without having to speak his confession.

"Are you okay, friend?" The wife stepped forward, concerned at Arkarn's complexion.

Arkarn quickly unhooked his sword from his belt, letting it fall beside him. He dropped to the ground, unable to face them any longer, bowing before them in a submissive position, ready to receive whatever consequences they deemed fitting.

"Fifteen years ago, I was the one who took your child from you. I left a note, promising he would be unharmed. I have broken that promise," Arkarn let the tears flow, unable to control his own body. His body began to shake at his own confession, images of Davun without an arm flashing before him, reminding him of his failure and what he had done to these poor people.

He remained fixated in his position, facing the ground crying, waiting for what a man like him truly deserved.

"You...You're the one who took him?" The wife looked at him as if trying to remember who he was, but she had not seen him on that night. Her face slowly turned into a mixture of confusion and anger, unable to comprehend the feelings that Arkarn's presence stirred inside her.

The husband stepped forward, grabbing Arkarn's should and helping him rise. "You took our child fifteen years ago?"

Arkarn nodded, unable to speak, though his eyes met the man's.

The man took a moment to think before asking, "Why?"

Arkarn took a deep breath, attempting to refrain his lips from quivering as he spoke, "He was destined to do something great. And he did just that. He protected a young boy for ten years, and not once did he falter. Even at the face of great danger, he did not waver and stood firm in order to protect this young boy, who he saw as his own brother. Your son saved more lives than you could ever know."

The man's thoughtful expression to did change. "You said that he was harmed? Is he dead?"

Arkarn was taken aback at how straight forward the man was but looking into his eyes told him the man had been waiting fifteen years for an answer, and he wouldn't delay any longer than he had to.

"No, he is alive. However, he has lost his right arm entirely. I am sorry," Arkarn dove to the ground again, begging. He wasn't sure if he was begging for his life or understanding from the family. It was the only thing he could think to do as he awaited their decision.

The man grabbed him once more by the shoulder, forcing him to rise to his feet again.

"Tell us everything."

So, Arkarn did. They entered their home where Arkarn proceeded to detail all of the events after he had taken their child fifteen years ago. He highlighted all of Davun's sacrifices and achievements, told them of the boy he cared for, told them of Artruis and the Ratlings. Everything.

Including his lies to Davun.

It took a while to recount fifteen years' worth of events, but the couple listened patiently. They did not argue against him, nor question any validity to his words. They simply sat, listened, and judged. Once Arkarn had finished, they sat in silence, weighing everything that had been said.

The man met Arkarn's gaze. "I want to see him."

Arkarn had expected this response. He was already willing to retrieve Davun and Jethro before the consequences of his actions caught up to him.

"Me too," the mother added, also locking eyes with Arkarn, "He is fifteen years of age now. He is old enough to decide for himself. We will hear what he has to say before we decide what to do with you."

Arkarn had not considered Davun would have a hand in this decision. He knew that the parents would likely want to meet him, but he thought they would have made up their mind about him regardless of what Davun' said.

Perhaps they already had and only wish Davun returned before they spoke it aloud.

"I can retrieve him. And Jethro. Immediately, if you desire."

The couple looked at each other and agreed.

Arkarn returned to the village a couple of weeks later, with Davun and Jethro in tow. He had explained to them where they were headed, and they had agreed to it, but he did not tell Davun about his role in the matter. He did not wish to feel like he influenced any decisions that would be made along the way.

The reunion was awkward but emotional. Fifteen years without seeing each other made it difficult to form an immediate connection, but once Davun let down his inner walls, he embraced his parents that he had longed for.

To their surprise, the parents also welcomed Jethro as one of their own.

It only made Arkarn feel worse, seeing what great parents they would have been.

Arkarn remained silent, letting them talk and bond while he patiently waited for them to decide his fate.

He sat alone in the corner of their house, not wanting to be an obstacle for them. After a few hours, the father approached him.

"I talked with Davun and my wife, and even Jethro gave his opinion too."

Arkarn straightened himself, ready for his sentencing.

The man crossed his arms and straightened his back in turn.

"You promised to take care of him, right?"

Arkarn nodded, "Yes."

"And did you also promise to take care of Jethro?"

Arkarn nodded again, "Yes."

"Well, it seems to me like your work isn't done. If you truly wish to repent for you crime, then you will accept our decision for you. You will watch over the both of them, as you promised. They are still destined for great things, and listening to the way they talk, we cannot convince them to stay. So you will act as their guardian until we declare it otherwise."

Arkarn was not sure how to react. He was thrilled, of course, to be given his life, but he had been taken of guard by it. He had expected to be turned over to the guards where he would confess his crimes and be executed.

"If that is what you truly wish, then I will protect them with my life. It is the least I can do."

The man did not smile, simply nodding in agreement before returning to the others, joining in on the conversation. Arkarn sat in his corner chair, collecting his emotions.

With his request fulfilled, he no longer had the powers of the phoenix, making it difficult to protect the boys from any other mythical dangers, but he had been sentenced to it.

And he would dedicate his life to guiding and protecting the brothers.

ABOUT THE AUTHOR

Andrew Maes lives in Melbourne, Victoria. He discovered his love of storytelling through roleplaying games, enjoying creating stories for friends and family.

In his spare time, he enjoys video games, painting miniatures, board games, and the occasional voice acting.